David Baldacci's remarkable detective Amos Decker—the man who can forget nothing—was first introduced in the sensational #1 *New York Times* bestseller *Memory Man*. Now Decker returns in a stunning new novel...

THE FIX

Amos Decker witnesses a murder just outside FBI headquarters. A man shoots a woman execution-style on a crowded sidewalk, then turns the gun on himself.

Even with Decker's extraordinary powers of observation and deduction, the killing is baffling. Decker and his team can find absolutely no connection between the shooter—a family man with a successful consulting business—and his victim, a schoolteacher. Nor is there a hint of any possible motive for the attack.

Enter Harper Brown. An agent of the Defense Intelligence Agency, she orders Decker to back off the case. The murder is part of an open DIA investigation, one so classified that Decker and his team aren't cleared for it.

But they learn that the DIA believes solving the murder is now a matter of urgent national security. Critical information may have been leaked to a hostile government—or worse, an international terrorist group—and an attack may be imminent.

Decker's never been one to follow the rules, especially with the stakes so high. Forced into an uneasy alliance with Agent Brown, Decker remains laser focused on only one goal: solving the case before it's too late.

ACCLAIM FOR DAVID BALDACCI'S THRILLERS

THE FIX

"A compelling puzzler...Baldacci is a truly gifted storyteller, and this novel is a perfect 'fix' for the thriller aficionado."
—*Associated Press*

"The set-up for THE FIX is one of the best this master of the thriller has ever come up with, and there is no letdown as Amos and his associates dig into an increasingly bizarre case...[Baldacci's] plotting is more masterful than ever, and THE FIX is nothing less than terrific from start to finish."
—*Connecticut News*

"Crackling with tension...Reads at a breakneck pace...Bestselling author David Baldacci delivers a thrill ride, as always. Big time. Pick up THE FIX, and you won't put it down until you reach the end. Guaranteed."
—*BookReporter.com*

"Cleverly perverse, full of surprises and touched throughout by the curious sense of congeniality."
—*Toronto Star*

"[Baldacci] continues to show why he is a master of the mystery."
—*Florida Times-Union*

NO MAN'S LAND

"Be prepared for an action-packed ride...Baldacci once again partners [John Puller] with Veronica Knox, making for a lethal and legendary combination. Anticipation intensifies on each page."   —*RT Book Reviews*

"This thriller, featuring U.S. Army criminal investigator John Puller, has a very plausible theme with a compelling and action-packed plot....[A] riveting and heart-wrenching story...NO MAN'S LAND is an edge-of-your-seat thriller. Readers will be hooked from page one."   —*Military Press*

"David Baldacci is one of America's favorite mystery writers, and he has earned that adulation fair and square. He is constantly turning out one readable and enjoyable adventure after another. His latest novel, NO MAN'S LAND, is his fourth John Puller story and it is a good one. It is fast reading from the start as the pages grab the readers' interest and off they go."
          —*Huffington Post*

"[A novel of] dramatic depth and intensity...an unforgettable read...Action-packed and thought-provoking."
          —*Associated Press*

"Bestseller Baldacci makes the implausible plausible in his riveting fourth thriller featuring U.S. Army criminal investigator John Puller...Baldacci maintains tension throughout and imbues his characters with enough humanity to make readers care what happens to them."

THE LAST MILE

"Entertaining and enlightening, *The Last Mile* is a rich novel that has much to offer…In the best Baldacci tradition, the action is fast and furious. But *The Last Mile* is more than a good action thriller. It sheds light on racism, a father-son relationship and capital punishment. Both Mars and Decker are substantive, solid characters.…Utterly absorbing."

—Associated Press

"[Amos Decker is] one of the most unique protagonists seen in thriller fiction.…David Baldacci has always been a top-notch thriller writer…[his] fertile imagination and intricate plotting abilities make each of his books a treat for thriller readers. *The Last Mile* is no exception."

—BookReporter.com

"The intricate details in Baldacci's explosive new novel engage until the final word. He's hit the pinnacle traveling the Deep South and exploring its traditions. Decker and his compatriots are characters to remember long after reading this impressive undertaking."

—*RT Book Reviews* (4 ½ stars / Top Pick!)

"A compelling mystery with emotional resonance. Just when the story line heads to what seems an obvious conclusion, Baldacci veers off course with a surprising twist. The end result is another exciting read from a thriller master." —*Library Journal* (Starred Review)

"Baldacci excels at developing interesting, three-dimensional protagonists...Baldacci fans will not be disappointed, and *The Last Mile* gives good reason to look forward to the next Amos Decker thriller."
—*New York Journal of Books*

THE GUILTY

"The story sings...Baldacci is a gifted storyteller, and he knows how to keep the pages turning."
—Associated Press

"Baldacci fans will not be disappointed. The action is slam-bang with his trademarked twist. Once past the climax, you'll find yourself flipping back and rereading to find the clues the author has sprinkled throughout."
—*Florida Times-Union*

"A fast-moving thriller that will force readers into that 'zone,' where you don't want to put the book down... Whether you are a diehard fan or a newcomer to his work, you will not be disappointed in *The Guilty*."
—BookReporter

"A first-class thriller... David Baldacci's four bestselling novels about government assassin Will Robie have straddled that line of edgy, high-concept suspense, augmented with a bit of the political thriller, and deep character studies. In *The Guilty*, Baldacci takes a different tack with a more personal but just as thrilling tale about Will's past, giving compelling insight about how he became a man so willing to kill for his country."

—*Sun-Sentinel* (FL)

"David Baldacci has never been better than in *The Guilty*. His latest to feature conflicted assassin extraordinaire Will Robie takes the character—and series—to new heights... A stunning success from one of America's great literary talents." —*Providence Sunday Journal*

"It's indisputable that Baldacci's handling of action just gets better and better... the action in small-town Texas will end up rivaling anything Robie has encountered in his long years of serving his government."

—NJ.com

"Another tremendous entry in the best-selling thrillermaster's increasingly impressive resume... A multilayered conspiracy tale that, despite the Grisham-esque backdrop of a legal mystery set in small-town Mississippi, quickly explodes into full-Baldacci thriller territory... It is the relationships that truly stand out. Among the most noteworthy is the rapport between Robie and Reel, with the professional and personal trust and respect that the two share for one another—having risked it all for each other several times before—feeling believable and compelling, not to mention being the source of a fair amount of witty banter. The tense dynamic between Robie and his father is palpable as well, and their shifting relationship—and how they both deal with the wounds of the past—is one of the book's highlights...A labyrinthine journey full of dead ends and surprising turns, with new reveals doled out at regular intervals as the story builds to its shocking conclusion, a spectacular double-twist climax that will leave even the most jaded thriller readers impressed."

—*The Strand Magazine*

MEMORY MAN

"It's big, bold and almost impossible to put down... Decker is one of the most unusual detectives any novelist has dreamed up...I call this novel a master class on the bestseller because of its fast-moving narrative, the originality of its hero and its irresistible plot....Highly entertaining."
—*Washington Post*

"David Baldacci has written another thriller that will have readers engaged from the first page....Baldacci is a master storyteller...*Memory Man* works because Amos Decker is an amazing character. Reading how Decker journeys from hitting rock bottom to finding ultimate redemption is nothing short of rewarding."
—Associated Press

THE ESCAPE

"One of the most compelling characters in David Baldacci's thrillers is John Puller, a crackerjack investigator of military crimes...Twists and turns come fast and furious in the best Baldacci tradition. *The Escape* is much more than a thriller. It's a moving tale of two military brothers and their father, a retired Army general and fighting legend now suffering from dementia. Emotionally intense, *The Escape* is Baldacci's best to date."

—Associated Press

"A heck of an opening chapter, guaranteed to jettison readers into hours of addictive reading...Baldacci's last few books have been among the best in his long, busy career, and *The Escape* stands near the top for sheer adrenaline-fueled entertainment. It's alarmingly topical, too, taking us into the intelligence community and raising questions about privacy rights in the age of government surveillance and other buzz-worthy issues (no spoilers here). Indeed, the crime at the center of *The Escape* could have been pulled from recent newspaper headlines. Who says thrillers have to be the stuff of escapist fantasies?" —*Richmond Times-Dispatch*

"Highly entertaining...*The Escape* is a terrific read."

—*CT News*

"A phenomenal read, as usual, from David Baldacci—don't miss it!" —BookLoons.com

THE TARGET

"Brilliant use of language...vivid supporting characters, and numerous sudden and unexpected plot twists...[Baldacci] doesn't let the action sag at any point...In [Chung-Cha], Mr. Baldacci has created one of his most memorable characters."

—*Pittsburgh Post-Gazette*

"[A] no-holds-barred tale of perfidy and murder at the highest level...Baldacci's prose crackles with urgency...Robie and Reel fans will thrill to see their favorite spies back in action."

—*Kirkus Reviews*

"Robie and Reel are complex characters, and anything they do is a pleasure to follow...Baldacci knows how to get readers to turn the pages, and he's in top form here."

—Associated Press

"A heck of a ride...Baldacci has been on a hot streak for the past few years, and *The Target* continues the trend. This isn't a garden-variety thriller or even a garden-variety Baldacci. It's among his most exhilarating books yet."

—*Richmond Times-Dispatch*

"Baldacci deftly plots *The Target* so that readers can never get a firm grasp on what is going to happen next."

—BookReporter.com

THE FIX

DAVID
BALDACCI

THE FIX

GRAND CENTRAL
PUBLISHING

NEW YORK   BOSTON

Copyright © 2017 by Columbus Rose, Ltd
Cover copyright © 2017 by Hachette Book Group, Inc.

Grand Central Publishing
Hachette Book Group
1290 Avenue of the Americas, New York, NY 10104
grandcentralpublishing.com
twitter.com/grandcentralpub

Originally published in hardcover and ebook by Grand Central Publishing in April 2017
First International Mass Market Edition: September 2017

Grand Central Publishing is a division of Hachette Book Group, Inc. The Grand Central Publishing name and logo is a trademark of Hachette Book Group, Inc.

The publisher is not responsible for websites (or their content) that are not owned by the publisher.

The Hachette Speakers Bureau provides a wide range of authors for speaking events. To find out more, go to www.hachettespeakersbureau.com or call (866) 376-6591.

ISBNs: 978-1-5387-2899-4 (international mass market), 978-1-4555-8655-4 (ebook)

Printed in the United States of America

OPM

10 9 8 7 6 5 4 3 2 1

To Jamie Raab,
a great publisher and a wonderful friend,
may your future endeavors be filled with both fun and success!
Thank you for all your support the past twenty years.
I will always be your biggest fan.

THE FIX

CHAPTER

I

IT WAS NORMALLY one of the safest places on earth.

But not today.

The J. Edgar Hoover Building was the world headquarters of the FBI. It opened in 1975 and had not aged well— a blocks-long chunk of badly dilapidated concrete with honeycomb windows, and fire alarms and toilets that didn't work. There was even safety netting strung around the top of the building to catch chunks of crumbling concrete before they could fall to the street below and kill someone.

The Bureau was trying to build a new facility to house eleven thousand employees, but a new location hadn't even been chosen. So the opening of a new headquarters was about two billion dollars and seven years away.

For now, this was home.

The tall man striding down the tree-lined sidewalk was Walter Dabney. He had taken an Uber to a coffee shop down the street, ordered some food, and was now walking the rest of the way. He was in his sixties, with thinning salt-and-pepper hair parted on the side. It looked recently cut, with a bit of cowlick in the back. His suit was expensive and fit his portly frame with the touch of a tailored hand. A colorful pocket square adorned the front of his dark suit. He wore a lanyard around his neck loaded with clearances sufficient to allow him access into the inner sanctums of the Hoover Building with an escort along for the ride. His green eyes were alert. He walked with a determined swagger, his briefcase making pendulum arcs in the air.

A woman was coming from the opposite direction. Anne Berkshire had taken the Metro here. She was in her late fifties, petite, with gray hair cut in parentheses around her long, oval face. As she approached the Hoover Building she seemed to hesitate. There was no lanyard around her neck. The only ID she possessed was the driver's license in her purse.

It was late morning and the streets were not as crowded as they would have been earlier. Still, there were a great many pedestrians and the street hummed with activity as cars passed up and down with some vehicles making their way into an underground parking garage at the Hoover Building.

Dabney picked up his pace a bit, his Allen Edmonds wingtips striking the stained pavement with purpose. He started to whistle a cheery tune. The man seemed not to have a care in the world.

Berkshire was now walking faster too. Her gaze went to the left and then swung right. She seemed to take in everything with that one sweeping glance.

About twenty yards behind Dabney, Amos Decker trudged along alone. He was six-five and built like the football player he had once been. He'd been on a diet for several months now and had dropped a chunk of weight, but he could stand to lose quite a bit more. He was dressed in khaki pants stained at the cuff and a long, rumpled Ohio State Buckeyes pullover that concealed both his belly and the Glock 41 Gen4 pistol riding in a belt holster on his waist-band. Fully loaded with its standard thirteen-round mag, it weighed thirty-six ounces. His size fourteen shoes hit the pavement with noisy splats. His hair was, to put it kindly, disheveled. Decker worked at the FBI on a joint task force. He was on his way to a meeting at the Hoover Building.

He was not looking forward to it. He sensed that a change was coming, and Decker did not like change. He'd experienced enough of it in the last two years to last him a lifetime. He had just settled into a new routine with the FBI and he wanted to keep it that way. Yet apparently that was out of his control.

He stepped around a barricade that had been set up on the sidewalk and that stretched partway into the street. A manhole cover surrounded by an orange web barrier had been opened and workers were congregated around the area. One man in a hard hat emerged at the opening of the manhole and was passed a tool by another man. Most of the other workers stood around, some drinking coffee and others chatting.

Nice work if you can get it, thought Decker.

He saw Dabney up ahead but didn't focus on him. Decker didn't see Berkshire because he wasn't looking that far up the street. He passed by the garage entrance and nodded at the uniformed FBI security officer in a small windowed guard shack situated on the sidewalk. The ramrod-straight man nodded back, his eyes covered by sunglasses as his gaze dutifully swept the street. His right hand was perched on top of his holstered service weapon. It was a nine mil chambered with Speer Gold Dot G2 rounds that the FBI used because of their penetration capability. "One shot, one down" could have been the ammo's motto. Then again, most ammo would do that so long as it hit the intended target in the right place.

A bird zipped across in front of Decker, perched on a lamppost, and looked down curiously at the passersby. The air was chilly and Decker shivered a bit even in his thick pullover. The sun was hidden behind cloud cover that had materialized on the horizon about an hour before, passed over the Potomac, and settled upon Washington like a gray dome.

Up ahead, Dabney was nearing the end of the block, where he would turn left. The FBI's "business appointments" entrance was located down there. Years ago public tours were freely given and people could view the famed FBI lab and watch special agents practicing their aim on the shooting range.

In the modern era of terrorism that was no more. After 9/11 the tours were canceled but then restarted in 2008. The FBI had even put in an education center for visitors. But a request for a visit had to be filed at least a month ahead of time to allow the FBI to do a thorough background check. Most federal buildings were now simply fortresses, hard to get into and maybe harder to get out of.

Dabney slowed as he approached the corner.

Berkshire, by contrast, quickened her pace.

Decker continued to lope along, his long strides eating up ground until he was only about ten yards behind Dabney.

Berkshire was about five yards on the other side of Dabney. Moments later that distance was halved. A few clicks after that, they were barely three feet apart.

Decker now saw Berkshire because she had drawn so close to Dabney. He was about ten feet behind the pair when he started to make the turn too.

Berkshire glanced over at Dabney, seemingly noticing him for the first time. Dabney didn't look back at her, at least not initially.

A few seconds later he saw her gazing at him. He smiled, and if he'd been wearing a hat, he might have even doffed it to her in a show of courtesy.

Berkshire didn't smile back. Her hand went to her purse clasp.

Dabney slowed a bit more.

Across the street Decker spotted a vendor selling breakfast burritos from a food truck and wondered if he had time to buy one before his meeting. When he decided he didn't and his waistline would be worse off for it he looked back; Berkshire and Dabney were now beside each other.

Decker didn't think anything of it; he just assumed they knew each other and were perhaps rendezvousing here.

He looked at his watch to check the time. He didn't want to be late. If his life was going to change, he wanted to be on time for it.

When he looked back up, he froze.

Dabney had fallen two steps behind the woman. Unknown to Berkshire, he was aiming a compact Beretta at the back of her head.

Decker reached for his weapon, and was about to call out, when Dabney pulled the trigger.

Berkshire jerked forward as the round slammed into the back of her head at an upward angle. It blew out her medulla, pierced her brainpan, banged like a pinball off her skull, and exited through her nose, leaving a wound three times the size of the entry due to the bullet's built-up wall of kinetic energy. She fell forward onto the pavement, her face mostly obliterated, the concrete tatted with her blood.

His pistol out, Decker ran forward as others on the street screamed and ran away. Dabney was still wielding his weapon.

His heart pounding, Decker aimed his Glock at Dabney and shouted, "FBI, put your gun down. Now!"

Dabney turned to him. He did not put down his gun.

Decker could hear the running footsteps behind him. The guard from the shack was sprinting toward them, his gun also out.

Decker glanced quickly over his shoulder, saw this, and held up his creds with his free hand. "I'm with the FBI. He just shot the woman."

He let his lanyard go and assumed a two-handed shooting stance, his muzzle aimed at Dabney's chest. The FBI uniform ran up to stand next to him, his gun pointed at Dabney. "Put the gun down, now!" the guard shouted. "Last chance, or we *will* shoot."

It was two guns versus one. The response should have been obvious. Lie down and you won't fall down.

Dabney looked first at the guard and then at Decker.

And smiled.

"Don't!" shouted Decker.

Walter Dabney pressed the gun's muzzle to the bottom of his chin and pulled the trigger for a second and final time.

CHAPTER

2

Darkness. It awaited us all, individually, in our final moments. Amos Decker was thinking that as he sat in the chair and studied the body.

Anne Berkshire lay on a metal table in the FBI's morgue. All her clothes had been removed and placed in evidence bags to be later analyzed. Her naked body was under a sheet; her destroyed face was covered as well, although the fabric was stained with her blood and destroyed tissue.

A postmortem was legally required even though there was no doubt whatsoever as to what had caused the woman's death.

Walter Dabney, by an extraordinary twist, was not dead. Not *yet*, anyway. The doctors at the hospital to which he'd been rushed held no hope that he would recover, or even regain consciousness. The bullet had tunneled right through his brain; it was a miracle he had not died instantly.

Alex Jamison and Ross Bogart, two of Decker's colleagues on a joint task force composed of civilians and FBI agents, were with Dabney at the hospital right now. If he regained consciousness they would want to capture anything he might utter that would explain why he had murdered Anne Berkshire on a public street and then attempted to take his own life. Dabney's recovering to the point of being questioned was simply not going to happen, the doctors had told them.

So for now, Decker simply sat in the darkness and stared at the covered body.

Although the room was not actually dark for him.

For Decker it was an ethereally bright blue. A near-fatal hit he'd received on the football field had commingled his sensory pathways, a condition known as synesthesia. For him, death was represented by the color blue. He had seen it on the street when Dabney had killed Berkshire.

And he was seeing it now.

Decker had given statements to the D.C. police and the FBI, as had the security guard who had joined him at the scene. There hadn't been much to say. Dabney had pulled a gun and shot Berkshire and then himself. That was crystal clear. What wasn't clear was *why* he had done it.

The overhead lights came on and a woman in a white lab coat walked in. The medical examiner introduced herself as Lynne Wainwright. She was in her forties, with the compressed, slightly haunted features of a person who had seen every sort of violence one human could wreak on another. Decker rose, showed her his ID, and said he was with an FBI task force. And also that he had witnessed the murder.

Decker glanced over as Todd Milligan, the fourth member of the joint task force, entered the room. A fifth member, Lisa Davenport, a psychologist by training, had not returned to the group, opting instead to go back to private practice in Chicago.

Milligan was in his midthirties, six feet tall, with close-cropped hair and a physique that appeared chiseled out of granite. He and Decker had initially butted heads, but now the two men got along as well as Decker could with anyone.

Decker had trouble relating to people. That had not always been the case, because he was not the same person he had once been.

In addition to the synesthesia, Decker also had hyperthymesia, or perfect recall, after suffering a brain trauma on the same vicious hit in his very short career in the NFL. It had altered his personality, changing him from gregarious and fun-loving to aloof and lacking the ability to recognize social cues—a skill most people took for granted. People first meeting him would assume he was somewhere on the autism spectrum.

And they might not be far off in that assumption.

"How you doing, Decker?" said Milligan. He was dressed, like always, in a dark suit with a spotless crisp white shirt and striped tie. Next to him, the shabbily attired Decker looked borderline homeless.

"Better than she is," said Decker, indicating Berkshire's body. "What do we know about her so far?"

Milligan took out a small electronic notebook from his inside coat pocket and scrolled down the screen. While he was doing that Decker watched as Wainwright removed the sheet from Berkshire's body and prepared the instruments necessary to perform the autopsy.

"Anne Meredith Berkshire, fifty-nine, unmarried, substitute schoolteacher at a Catholic school in Fairfax County. She lives, or rather lived, in Reston. No relatives have come forward, but we're still checking."

"Why was she down at the Hoover Building?"

"We don't know. We don't know if she was even going there. And she wasn't scheduled to teach at the school today."

"Walter Dabney?"

"Sixty-one, married, with four grown daughters. Has a

successful government contracting business. Does work with the Bureau and other agencies. Before that he worked at NSA for ten years. Lives in McLean in a big house. He's done very well for himself."

"*Did* very well for himself," corrected Decker. "His wife and kids?"

"We spoke with his wife. She's hysterical. The kids are spread all over the place. One lives in France. They're all coming here."

"Any of them have any idea why he would do this?"

"We haven't spoken to them all, but nothing pops so far. They're apparently still in shock."

Decker next asked the most obvious question. "Any connection between Berkshire and Dabney?"

"We're just starting out, but nothing as yet. You think he was just looking to shoot someone before he killed himself and she was the closest?"

"She was definitely the closest," said Decker. "But if you're going to kill yourself why take an innocent person along? What would be the point?"

"Maybe the guy went nuts. We might find something in his background to explain his going off the deep end."

"He had a briefcase and an ID. It seems he was heading to the Hoover Building. Was he going to a meeting?"

"Yes. We confirmed that he was meeting to go over a project his firm was handling for the Bureau. All routine."

"So he goes off the 'deep end' but he could still put on a suit and come downtown for a *routine* meeting?"

Milligan nodded. "I see the inconsistency. But it's still possible."

"Anything's possible, until it's not," Decker replied.

Decker walked over to stand next to Wainwright. "Murder weapon was a Beretta nine mil. Contact wound at the base of the neck with an upward trajectory. She died on impact."

Wainwright was readying a Stryker saw that she would use to cut open Berkshire's skull. She said, "Definitely jibes with the external injuries."

"If Dabney dies will you be doing the post?"

She nodded. "The Bureau is taking the lead on this since Dabney was a contractor for them and it happened on their doorstep. So I'm your girl."

Decker turned away from her and said to Milligan, "Has the FBI assigned a team to the case yet?"

Milligan nodded.

"Who's the team? Do you know them?"

"I know them very well, because they're *us*."

Decker blinked. "Come again?"

"Bogart's team, meaning us, has been assigned to the case."

"But we do cold cases."

"Well, that's what the meeting today was about. They were changing our assignment. Cold to hot cases. And since you were on the scene of this one, it made sense to let us work it. So we're a go."

"Even though I'm a witness to the crime?"

"It's not as though there's going to be any doubt as to what happened, Decker. And there were lots of witnesses to what he did. They don't need you."

"But I came here to do *cold* cases," protested Decker.

"Well, we don't get to decide that, Decker. The higher-ups do."

"And they can just pull the rug out from under us like that? Without even asking?"

Milligan attempted a smile, but when he saw the troubled expression on Decker's face, the look faded. "It's a bureaucracy, Decker, and we have to follow orders. At least Ross and I do. I guess you and Jamison could call it quits, but my career is locked up with the Bureau." He paused. "We'll still be catching bad guys. Just for newer crimes. You'll still get to do what you do so well."

Decker nodded but hardly looked appeased by Milligan's words. He looked down at Berkshire's body. The pulse of blue assailed him from all corners. He felt slightly sick to his stomach.

Wainwright glanced over and registered on the name on Decker's ID. "Wait a minute. *Amos* Decker. Are you the guy who can't forget anything?"

When Decker didn't say anything, Milligan said quickly, "Yes, he is."

Wainwright said, "Heard you guys have solved quite a few old cases over the last several months. Principally the Melvin Mars matter."

"It was a team effort," said Milligan. "But we couldn't have done it without Decker."

Decker stirred and pointed to a purple smudge on the back of Berkshire's hand. "What's that?"

"Let's have a closer look," Wainwright said. She gripped a magnifying glass set on a rotating arm and positioned it over the mark. She turned on a light and aimed it at the dead woman's hand. Peering through the glass, she said, "Appears to be a stamp of some sort."

Decker took a look through the glass. "Dominion Hospice." He looked at Milligan, who was already tapping keys on his notebook.

Milligan read down the screen. "Okay, got it. It's over near Reston Hospital. They handle terminal cases, obviously."

Decker looked down at Berkshire. "If the mark is still on

her hand, presumably she went there today. A shower would have taken it off."

"Do you think she went to visit someone?" asked Milligan.

"Well, she wasn't exactly terminal, until Dabney killed her."

He abruptly walked out without another word.

Wainwright looked at Milligan with raised eyebrows at this sudden departure.

"He kind of just does that…a lot," said Milligan. "I've sort of gotten used to it."

"Then you're a better person than I am," replied Wainwright. She held up the Stryker saw. "Because if he kept walking out on me like that, I might just clock him with this."

3

WALTER DABNEY'S CHEST rose and fell with the spasmodic twitch of someone not long for this world. It was as though the lungs were the weary rear guard holding out as the spirit prepared to exit the body.

Alex Jamison was in her late twenties, tall, slim, and pretty with long brunette hair. She sat on the right side of the hospital bed in the CCU. Ross Bogart, an FBI special agent in his late forties, with a bit of gray the only thing marring his perfectly combed dark hair, stood ramrod-straight on the left. His fingers clutched the bed's safety rail.

Dabney lay in the bed, hooked up to a complex array of monitoring lines and tubes carrying medications. His right eye was an empty crater because the bullet he'd fired into his chin had burst from there after catapulting through parts of the brain. His facial skin was deathly gray, where it wasn't swollen and stained purple by burst capillaries. His breathing was erratic and the monitor showed his vitals to be fluctuating all over the place. He was in the critical care unit, the place designated for the sickest and most badly injured patients at the hospital.

But he wasn't just injured; Walter Dabney was dying.

The doctors who had been in and out during the day had

all confirmed that it was simply a matter of time before the brain told the heart to stop pumping. And there was nothing they could do about it. The damage was such that no medicine and no surgery could bring the man back. They were just counting down the time until death.

Mrs. Eleanor Dabney, better known as Ellie, had arrived thirty minutes after the FBI had told her what had happened. They would have to question her, but right now the woman was simply a grieving widow-to-be. She was currently in the bathroom throwing up, a nurse assisting her.

Bogart eyed Jamison. She seemed to sense his attention and glanced up.

"Any word from Decker?" he asked quietly.

She checked her phone and shook her head. "He was going to be at the morgue with Berkshire's body." She thumbed in a text to him and sent it off. "I copied Todd on it," she said.

Bogart nodded. "Good. He'll keep Decker on track."

They both knew that Decker was not always the best at communicating. In fact, he pretty much sucked at it.

Bogart looked down at Dabney again. "Nothing in the guy's record to indicate something like this happening. And no connection that we can find to Berkshire."

Jamison said, "There must be *something* unless it was completely random. And that doesn't make much sense either."

Bogart nodded in agreement and then glanced at the monitor. The dying man's heart rate and respiration danced around like bare feet on sizzling coals.

"Chances are very good he's going to die without saying anything."

"But if he does say something we'll be here," replied Jamison.

The bathroom door opened and out came the nurse and Ellie Dabney. She was tall and broad-shouldered, with long legs and a slender waist and narrow hips. Her features were quite attractive, the jaw elegantly structured, the cheekbones high and firm, the eyes large and a pleasing light blue. Her hair was long and she had let it go naturally silver. She looked like she might have been quite the athlete in her youth. Now in her early sixties, the mother of four grown children with three grandchildren and one mortally wounded husband, the stricken woman appeared about as close to death as one could get without actually being dead.

Bogart placed a chair next to the bed for her as Jamison rose and helped the nurse guide Ellie over to the chair, into which she fell rather than sat.

The nurse checked the monitor, gave Bogart an ominous look, and left, closing the door behind her. Ellie had reached through the rails and gripped her husband's hand, her forehead resting against the top of the bed rail.

Bogart stepped back and Jamison resumed her seat. They exchanged glances while listening to the woman's quiet sobs.

"Mrs. Dabney, we can arrange to have your children brought here when they get into town," he said after a few moments.

She didn't respond to this at first but finally nodded.

"Do you have that information or is there someone else we can—?"

She lifted her head and without looking at him said, "My daughter, Jules, she…she'll know that." She pulled a phone from her pocket, tapped some keys, and passed it to him. Bogart wrote the phone number down, handed Ellie her phone back, and walked out of the room.

Jamison put a hand on the older woman's shoulder and said, "I'm so very sorry, Mrs. Dabney."

"Did he...did Walt really h-hurt someone? The FBI...they...they said..."

"We don't have to talk about that now."

Ellie turned her tearstained face to Jamison. "He couldn't have. Are you sure someone didn't shoot him? You see, Walt wouldn't hurt anything. H-he..." Her voice trailed off and she placed her forehead back on the rail.

The monitor started to beep and they both glanced at it, but the device quieted down.

"We *are* sure, Mrs. Dabney. I wish I could tell you otherwise. There were a lot of witnesses."

Ellie blew her nose on a tissue and said in a firmer voice, "He's not going to recover, is he?"

"The doctors aren't hopeful, no."

"I...I didn't even know he owned a gun."

After studying the woman for a few seconds, Jamison asked, "Did you notice a change in your husband recently?"

"In what way?" Ellie said absently.

"Mood? Concerns at work? Appetite changed? Maybe he drank more than normal? Any signs of depression?"

Ellie sat back in her chair, wadded the tissue up in her hand, and stared down at her lap.

Outside the door footsteps could be heard, along with occasional running feet, the sounds of a monitor alarm, voices over a PA, and equipment and patients being rolled up and down the corridor. The air smelled like hospitals always did: antiseptic. And the air was perpetually chilly. There was also an ominous tenseness present in the CCU, as though only a monitor's sudden warning screech separated the living from the dead.

"Walt didn't talk about business at home. He didn't really drink at home either, although I know that he did at business dinners and industry events, that sort of thing. I

attended some with him. But he only drank enough to so-
cialize, to get deals done, build contacts, you know, that sort
of thing."

"I understand. Were there any financial worries?"

"Not that I knew of. But Walter handled all that. We never
had any bill collectors show up at the house, if that's what you
mean."

"Did his mood change?"

She dabbed at her eyes and shot a glance at her husband
before quickly looking away, as though she was uncomfortable conveying information about him to a stranger. "He had
a variety of moods. He worked very hard and when business was good he was happy, when it was down, he got
depressed, just like anybody would."

"So nothing out of the ordinary?"

Ellie balled up the tissue even more and then tossed it
into the trash can.

With finality.

She turned to Jamison, who waited patiently. If being
around Amos Decker had taught her anything, it was patience, for both positive and negative reasons.

"He went on a trip recently."

"Where?"

"That was the unusual thing. He didn't tell me where. He
had never done that before."

"How long was he gone?" Jamison asked.

"I think about four days. It could have been longer. He
was on another trip in New York and left from there. He
called me and said something unexpected had come up and
that he had to attend to it and wasn't sure how long he'd be
gone."

"Plane, train? Another country?"

"I don't know. He did tell me it had to do with a potential

client. He had to smooth over something. The way he described it the matter didn't seem too significant. I suppose his office would have handled the travel arrangements."

"Okay, and he mentioned nothing to you about it when he got home?"

"Nothing. I just assumed it was business. But from that day on, there was something, I don't know, off."

"And when was this?"

"About a month ago."

"And your husband has his own government contracting firm?"

Ellie nodded. "Walter Dabney and Associates. It's located in Reston. Everything they work on is pretty much classified. It started out with just my husband, but now about seventy people work there. He has partners at the firm, but Walter is president and owns a controlling interest." Her eyes widened. "Oh my God, I guess I'll own it now." She looked in alarm at Jamison. "Does that mean I'll have to run it? I don't know anything about his business. I don't even have a security clearance."

Jamison gripped her hand. "I don't think you need to worry about those details right now, Mrs. Dabney."

Ellie relaxed and looked back at her husband. "What was the person's name again? That Walter . . . ? They told me, but I can't remember. Everything is just a blur right now."

"Anne Berkshire. She was a substitute teacher at a Catholic high school in Fairfax. Do you know her?"

Ellie shook her head. "I never heard of her. And I don't know why Walt would know her either. High school teacher? Walt and I had our children fairly early. Jules, our oldest, is thirty-seven. And our oldest grandkid is only in first grade. And they don't even live in Virginia anyway. And we're not Catholic. We're Presbyterian."

"Right. Well, thank you for the information. You've been very helpful."

"Will I need to get a lawyer?" Ellie blurted out.

Jamison looked uncomfortable. "I'm really not the one to advise you about that. If you or your husband used a lawyer or know one, you should check with that person."

Ellie nodded dumbly and then reached through the rails and gripped her husband's hand once more.

A minute later Bogart came back in. "It's all taken care of, Mrs. Dabney," he said. "According to your daughter, everyone except Natalie will be in by tonight."

"Natalie lives in Paris. I tried to phone her but no one answered. And it wasn't…it wasn't something I could leave on a voicemail or tell her by email."

"Your daughter Jules reached her and told her the situation. She's trying to get a flight here as soon as possible."

"I really can't believe this is happening," said Ellie. "When Walt left this morning everything was…perfect. And now?" She looked up at them. "It's all gone. Just like that."

Just like that, thought Jamison.

CHAPTER

4

THEY HAD TRAVELED from a place filled with dead bodies to a place filled with dying people.

After making inquiries at the front desk, Decker and Milligan had been given over to the director of Dominion Hospice, Sally Palmer. The woman was shocked to hear of Anne Berkshire's death.

"She was just here this morning," she said as she faced them from across the desk in her small, cramped office.

"That's what we understand," said Decker. "And it's why we're here. We saw that her hand was stamped with the name of the hospice."

"Yes, we do that as part of our security procedure."

"Does this place need much security?" asked Milligan.

Palmer looked at him sternly. "Our patients are weak and on heavy medications. They can hardly protect themselves. It falls to us to do that, and we take that matter very seriously. All visitors are checked in through the front entrance. The hand stamp is easily seen and we change the color every day. That way at a glance our staff knows if a visitor has been properly cleared through or not."

Decker asked, "Did Berkshire have a family member who's a patient here? Is that why she was here this morning?"

"Oh, no. Anne was a volunteer. She would come and spend time with certain patients. Oftentimes the patient's family may not live in the immediate area, and visits aren't so frequent. We have volunteers, carefully vetted of course, who come in and talk to the patients, read to them, or just sit with them. It's not easy dying. And it's even harder dying alone."

"Did Berkshire talk to anyone in particular today?" asked Milligan.

"I can certainly find out. Excuse me for a minute."

Palmer rose and left.

Milligan took out his phone and checked messages. "Dabney's wife is at the hospital with her husband. Alex says he hasn't regained consciousness and probably won't."

"Did the wife tell them anything?"

"She didn't know Anne Berkshire and was pretty sure her husband didn't either. She also knew nothing about her husband's business and had no idea why he would do what he did. But Alex texted again. Mrs. Dabney said her husband had taken an unexplained trip about a month ago and that he didn't seem the same afterwards."

"Not the same how?"

"Different mood apparently. And he wouldn't tell her where he went."

"Okay."

Milligan looked around the small office. "Do you really think we're going to get a lead from this place?"

"People *are* killed by strangers, but most people know the one who kills them."

"Well, that's always comforting," said Milligan dourly.

The men lapsed into silence until Palmer returned a few minutes later.

"She met with three patients early this morning. Dorothy Vitters, Joey Scott, and Albert Drews."

"Were they people she normally would visit?" asked Decker.

"Yes."

"You said she came in early this morning. Did she usually come in at that time?"

"Well, no, come to think of it. She usually came in around noon. Our patients are generally more alert then."

"Can we speak with them?" asked Decker.

Palmer looked taken aback. "I'm not sure what they can tell you. They're very ill. And weak."

Decker rose. "I appreciate that, but Anne Berkshire was murdered this morning and it's our job to find out why. And if she came here at an unusual time shortly before she went downtown and was killed, then we have to run that possible lead down. I hope you can understand that."

Milligan added quickly, "We'll be as gentle as possible."

"Do you have to tell them that Anne was killed? That will be extremely upsetting for them."

Milligan said, "We'll do our best to avoid that."

Decker said nothing. His eyes were already on the hallway.

Dorothy Vitters was in her late eighties, frail and shrunken in the last bed she would occupy. Because of patient confidentiality, Palmer had not told them what specific illness she might have. She left them in the doorway and walked back to her office.

Decker stood in the doorway and looked around at the small, sparsely furnished space.

"You okay?" said Milligan in a low voice.

Decker was not okay, not really.

What he was seeing here wasn't the flash of electric blue he associated with death but rather *navy* blue. That was a first for him. But when he looked at the terminally ill Vitters he could understand why. Near death was apparently represented in his mind simply by another shade of blue.

Well, that is interesting. My altered mind keeps throwing me curves.

He didn't want to be here when Vitters died, because he didn't want the navy to abruptly change to electric blue.

"I'm good," he finally said.

He walked into the room, pulled up a chair, and sat next to the bed. Milligan stood next to him.

"Mrs. Vitters, I'm Amos Decker and this is Todd Milligan. We're here to talk to you about Anne Berkshire. She was in to see you this morning, we understand."

Vitters looked up at him from deeply sunken eyes. Her skin was a pale gray, her eyes watery and her breathing shallow. Decker could see the port near her clavicle where her pain meds were administered.

"Anne *was* here," she said slowly. "I was surprised because it was earlier than usual."

"Do you remember what you talked about?"

"Who are you?"

Decker was about to take out his creds when Milligan stopped him. Milligan said, "We're friends of Anne's. She asked us to stop in today because she wanted to come back and keep talking to you but then found out she couldn't make it."

The watery eyes turned to alarm. "Is she…is she all right? She's not sick, is she?"

"She's feeling no pain at all," said Decker quite truthfully. He was counting on the fact that whatever meds the woman was on would slow her mental processes somewhat, otherwise Vitters might figure out that nothing they were saying made much sense.

"Oh, well, it was just the usual things. Weather. A book she was reading and telling me about. My cat."

"Your cat?" said Milligan.

"Sunny's dead now. Oh, it's been ten years if it's been a day. But Anne liked cats."

"So nothing other than that?" asked Decker.

"No, not that I recall. She wasn't here that long."

"Did she seem okay to you? Nothing out of sorts?"

Her voice grew more strident. "Are you sure she's all right? Why are you here asking these questions? I might be dying, but I'm not stupid."

Decker saw the watery eyes turn to flint before flickering out again.

"Well, if you have to know the truth, the fact is—"

Milligan cut in. "We know you're not stupid, Mrs. Vitters. As my colleague was about to say, the fact is, Anne fell down and hit her head today. She'll be fine, but she's got short-term amnesia. And she needs to remember the passcode to her phone and her apartment's alarm system and her computer. She sent us here to find out what she was talking about to people so that we can tell her and maybe jog her memory. The doctors said that that might do it."

Vitters looked relieved. "Oh, well, I'm so sorry she fell."

Decker glanced at Milligan for an instant before gazing back at Vitters and saying, "So anything you can tell us would be appreciated."

"Well, again, we didn't talk about much. Although, it did seem that Anne was preoccupied. She usually led the conversations we had but today I had to prompt her a few times."

Milligan glanced sharply at Decker, but Decker kept his gaze on Vitters.

"Did you ask her if anything was wrong?"

"I did actually. But she said everything was fine. She just had something on her mind, but she didn't say what."

"Do you know if you were the first person that Anne visited today, or were there others before you?"

"I think I was the last. She mentioned she had to leave after seeing me. She had somewhere to go."

"She didn't mention where that was?"

"No."

Decker rose and turned to leave.

Milligan said hastily, "Thank you for your help. Is there anything we can do for you?"

Vitters smiled grimly. "Put in a good word for me with the man upstairs."

As they left, Milligan whispered, "Hey, Decker, you need to go a little easy with these folks, okay? They're dying."

He passed by Decker, who turned and looked back at Vitters lying in the bed, her eyes now closed. He walked back over to her and looked down. The navy blue image in his mind was starting to turn electric blue. Decker didn't believe he could foresee someone's death, but his mind was obviously making the logical leap with the terminally ill Vitters.

He reached down and adjusted the woman's pillow to make her head rest more comfortably. His hand grazed over the white hair and then he said in a low voice, "I'm sorry, Mrs. Vitters."

He didn't see Milligan watching him from the doorway. The FBI agent hurried off before Decker turned around.

CHAPTER

5

JOEY SCOTT WAS an even sadder case than Dorothy Vitters.

Decker and Milligan stood in the doorway with Palmer. Scott was only ten years old, but his short life was nearing its end. Eschewing patient privacy law, Palmer, who had escorted them here, had said in response to their blank looks, "Leukemia. The untreatable kind."

Milligan said, "But why would Berkshire have to visit *him*? Don't his parents come?"

Palmer bristled. "He was in the process of being adopted out of foster care. When he got sick his 'adoptive' parents pulled out. I guess they wanted a healthy model," she added in disgust. "And it's not like they couldn't afford it. Anne visited him at least twice a week. She was really all Joey had."

Then she turned and left, her face full of despair.

Decker looked down at the little body in the bed and his thoughts wandered back to the daughter he'd once had. Molly had been murdered before her tenth birthday. Decker had found her and his wife's bodies at their old home. And because of his hyperthymesia, he would always remember every detail of this tragedy like it had just occurred that second.

There could be nothing that ever happened to Decker that could be more horrible and depressing than finding his family murdered. But seeing this came close.

He sat down next to the boy, who slowly opened his eyes. IV and monitoring lines ran all over his withered frame.

With a quick glance at Milligan, Decker said, "Hello, Joey, I'm Amos. This is my friend Todd."

Joey raised a hand and made a little wave.

"I understand your friend, Anne, was in today?"

Joey nodded.

"Did you have a good talk?"

"She read to me," Joey said in a small voice.

"A book?"

He nodded. "*Harry Potter and the Prisoner of Azkaban.* It's on the shelf over there. She said she'd be back tomorrow to finish it."

Decker reached over and snagged the book, flipping through some pages until he came to the bookmark about ten pages from the end. He glanced at Milligan before looking back at Joey. "That's great. Is that all she did? Read?"

Joey shook his head. "We talked some."

"What about?"

"Are you friends with Anne?"

Decker said, "I just saw her this morning. She's the reason we came to see you. She wanted us to meet her friends here."

"Oh, okay."

Milligan said, "How long have you been here, Joey?"

Joey blinked up at him. "I don't know."

Milligan took a step back and put a hand against the wall. He looked hopelessly at Decker.

Decker said, "Do you remember what you talked about with Anne? Maybe things about the book?"

"She asked me if I saw the sun come up."

Decker looked to the large window, which faced east. He slowly looked back at Joey. "Did you?"

Joey nodded. "It was nice."

"I used to get up early and watch the sun rise when I was a kid," said Decker, drawing a surprised look from Milligan. "I grew up in Ohio so the sun got to us later than it does here."

On the nightstand next to the bed was a framed photo. Decker picked it up. It was a picture of Peyton Manning.

"You like Manning?"

Joey nodded. "I used to watch football a lot. And I played before I got sick."

"I played too."

Joey ran his gaze over Decker's huge physique. "You look like a football player. I might have grown up to be big like you."

Milligan rubbed at his eyes. Regaining his composure, he said, "Joey, Decker here played in the NFL. For the Cleveland Browns."

The little boy's eyes grew wide and a tiny smile crept across his features. "You did?"

Decker nodded. "My career was short and not necessarily sweet." He put the photo back. "Before that I was an Ohio State Buckeye. Some of the best years of my life."

"Wow," said Joey. "Do you know Peyton Manning?"

"No, but he was one of the greatest. First-ballot Hall of Famer." He sat back. "Did you talk with Anne about anything else?"

The smile faded. "Not really."

"Did she tell you where she was going after she left here?"

Joey shook his head.

Decker rose, glanced at Milligan, and said, "Thanks, Joey, you've been a big help."

"You're welcome."

Milligan looked down at him and said, "Hey, would it be okay if I came back and saw you again?"

"Sure. Maybe you can come with Anne."

Milligan said, "Well, we'll see." He took a card from his pocket and put it on the nightstand next to the Peyton Manning photo. "You need anything, have them give me a call on that number, okay?"

"Okay."

"Thanks again."

"Can I shake your hand?" asked Joey, eyeing Decker. "I never met an NFL player before."

Decker put out his hand and slowly gripped the little boy's. It was like a whale swallowing a minnow.

"It was an honor meeting you, Joey." Decker put the book back on the shelf and walked out, followed by Milligan.

"Damn," said Milligan. "I'm not sure I'll ever smile again."

"You will," said Decker. "But whenever you feel things are bad, you'll think of Joey and then things will look a lot better for you."

* * *

Albert Drews was in his forties and volunteered that he had final-stage pancreatic cancer. He was pale and thin and his skin looked brittle and jaundiced.

"By the time I had any symptoms it was too damn late," he said after they'd introduced themselves and shown him their IDs. "Chemo, radiation, kicked the shit out of me. Then

I go into remission, for about two months. Then it comes back like a hurricane, and now this is it."

He stopped talking and started breathing heavily, as though this bit of speaking had exhausted him.

When his lungs settled down he said, "You're lucky you caught me now. When my pain meds kick in, I'm out for the count. Morphine. Don't know what I'd do without it. The pain...well, it's not nice," he added resignedly.

"I'm sorry to be bothering you, Mr. Drews," said Decker.

Drews waved this off. "It's not like I've got anything else to do except lie here and wait to die."

"We understand that Anne Berkshire came to talk to you today?"

"This morning. Why?"

Decker decided to just tell the truth. "She was shot and killed this morning in D.C. Shortly after she left here."

"What?" gasped Drews, rising up on his elbows. He started to cough. Milligan poured out a glass of water from a carafe on the nightstand and helped Drews drink it. He shot Decker a stern look and then stepped back with the empty glass.

Drews finally settled down and stared helplessly up at them. He gasped, "Anne, shot? How? Why?"

"We don't know why. That's why we're here."

"But I don't know anything."

"You may know more than you think," said Decker. "What did you two talk about today?"

His brows knitted, Drews said, "She was a nice lady. Started visiting me about four weeks ago. We just talked about...things. Nothing in particular. Nothing of importance. Just things to pass the time, take my mind off...my situation."

"Did she talk about herself?"

"Sometimes. She said she was a schoolteacher. She wasn't married. No children."

"What did you do before you became sick?" asked Milligan.

"I was a software engineer with a local tech company." His eyes closed and he started breathing deeply.

"Are you okay?" asked Milligan.

Drews opened his eyes and snapped, "No, I'm not okay! I'm terminal, all right! I'm dying!"

"I'm sorry, Mr. Drews, that's not what I meant. I'm sorry," Milligan added in a contrite voice.

Decker studied Drews. "Did you ever talk with Mrs. Berkshire about the work you did?"

"No. What would have been the point?"

"Just chitchat?"

"No. And that seems like a lifetime ago. I barely remember it."

"You're not married."

"How do you know that?"

"No ring on your finger. And no mark that showed a ring used to be there."

After a moment he said resignedly, "I never met the right woman, I guess."

"Parents still alive?"

Drews shook his head. "I've got a brother, but he lives in Australia. He came up when I got sick and stayed a while. But he had to get back. He has five kids." Drews paused. "He'll come back for the funeral. He's my executor. I'm being cremated. Makes it easier all around."

Drews closed his eyes and his lips trembled. But then he reopened them and sighed. "You never think you can talk so candidly about your coming death. But when you don't have a choice, you just...do."

"What do the doctors say?" asked Decker.

Drews shrugged. "Some days, it feels like tomorrow will be it. Some days I *hope* tomorrow will be it."

"We're sorry to have bothered you, Mr. Drews. We appreciate your help."

As Decker rose, Drews put out a hand and lightly gripped Decker's fingers. The man's skin felt like ice.

"Anne was really nice. She didn't have to come here and do what she did, but she wanted to. I...I hope you find whoever did this."

"We already found him, Mr. Drews," said Decker. "Now we just have to find out *why* he did it."

CHAPTER

6

"A SUBSTITUTE SCHOOLTEACHER?" said Decker.

He was looking around at Anne Berkshire's condo on the top floor of a luxury building directly across the street from the Reston Town Center.

Milligan nodded. "That's what her file says."

"You know this area better than me, what do you think a place like this would run?"

Milligan looked around at the space. It had tall windows, high ceilings, hardwood floors, about three thousand square feet of professionally decorated space with sweeping views of the area, and a large private balcony with a hot tub.

"Two million, maybe more."

"And the building management says she has a Mercedes SL600 parked in the underground garage."

"That's well over a hundred grand," said Milligan.

"Did she inherit?"

"I don't know. We'll have to dig on that."

"How long has she been a teacher?"

"She's been substitute teaching for four years."

"Before that?"

"She lived in Atlanta for three years."

"Doing what?"

"We don't have an occupation, just an address."

"Before that?"

"Seattle."

"So no job there either?"

"Not that we could find."

"Before that?"

"We didn't find anything else on her."

"How far does her file go back?"

"When you add it all up, about ten years."

"But she was nearly sixty. So that takes us back to her late forties. What about before then?"

"We couldn't find anything. But we haven't had much time to dig yet. Something else will turn up. And it'll probably explain the money angle. She might have been injured in an accident and gotten a big settlement. Or maybe a malpractice suit. Hell, maybe she won the lottery."

Decker didn't look convinced.

"She's very neat," remarked Milligan.

"I think the term would be minimalist," said Decker, noting the spare furnishings. He walked into the master bedroom and looked through the walk-in closet.

"Four pairs of shoes, a few purses and bags. No jewelry that I can see. And no safe where they might be kept." He looked at Milligan. "We weren't rich by any stretch, but my wife had probably thirty pairs of shoes, and about that many purses and bags. And she had some jewelry."

Milligan nodded. "Mine does too. Do you think Berkshire was just unique, or is it something else?"

"I also haven't seen a single photo of anyone. Not Berkshire. Or family or friends. Nothing. In fact, the entire place looks like a model unit. I bet she bought it furnished and none of this is even hers."

"What does that tell us?"

"That maybe she was not who she appeared to be."

"You think Dabney knew her?"

"Maybe. And did we confirm that she was going to the FBI? I just assumed that because of where she was. But we need more than assumptions now."

"We've confirmed that she wasn't scheduled to meet with anyone at Hoover. And visitors just coming to tour the place need to file a request ahead of time so the Bureau can do a background check. And there's no record of such a request for her."

Decker sat on the bed and looked around the room. "She leaves here, goes to the hospice, and then heads downtown. She had a Metro card in her purse that showed she got off at the Federal Triangle stop about ten minutes before she was killed."

"And she was seen in one of the surveillance cameras leaving that station."

"And then Dabney shoots her."

Milligan stared at Decker. "If he planned to shoot her, how did he know what time she was going to be there? Or that she was going to be there at all?"

"Maybe *he* was the reason she *was* there," suggested Decker.

"What? He communicated with her and told her to meet him outside the FBI building?"

"Maybe."

"We're checking phone, email, texts, fax, all the typical communication portals, to see if we can find a connection."

"They may have done it face-to-face. If so, we may not find a record. If he didn't plan for her to come there, then only two other explanations make sense. He either knew she was going to be there from some other means—"

"—or it was a coincidence," finished Milligan. "And he could have easily killed someone other than Berkshire."

"And if so, for what reason? Why kill a stranger in such a random fashion? Other than the guy being nuts?"

Milligan shook his head. "I don't have a clue."

Decker rose off the bed and held up a set of car keys. "They're to the Mercedes. They were in a drawer in her closet. Let's go check it out."

Berkshire's Mercedes was a silver convertible and sat in a coveted slot near the elevators. Decker used the wireless key fob to open the vehicle, and Milligan began to search it. The confines of the car were too small for the bulky Decker to easily navigate. Milligan handed Decker a packet of materials from the glove box and continued his search.

Five minutes later Milligan got out and shook his head. "Nothing. Smells like it was just taken off the lot."

Decker held up the envelope Milligan had handed him. "Registration says it's only three years old. Check the mileage."

Milligan did so. "About five thousand miles."

"So she's barely driven it, really. I wonder how she got to work. Public transportation?"

"There's no Metro stop within walking distance from here and there's none where she worked as a teacher. And why would you go by bus if you could drive this baby?"

"We'll just have to file that one away as another curious question with no current answer."

Milligan shut the car door and Decker used the key fob to lock it.

Milligan checked his watch. "It's getting late. So where to now?"

"To see another dying man," said Decker.

CHAPTER

7

THE BREATHS were coming so slowly now it seemed like the next one would be the very last.

Decker stared down at Walter Dabney for a few moments, as his mind whirred back to the morning when he'd seen this man walking down the street, seemingly without a care, until he pulled out a gun and murdered Anne Berkshire in front of Decker and dozens of other people. Decker's perfect memory went step by step through that scenario. He came out at the other end, though, not as enlightened as he would have liked.

Sitting in the same chair she had been in earlier was Ellie Dabney. Milligan stood by the door. Bogart and Jamison were on the other side of the bed. Ellie still clasped her husband's hand.

Decker had learned that the critically injured man had said nothing. He had never even regained consciousness.

Decker knelt next to Ellie. "Mrs. Dabney, when your husband left the house this morning were you up?"

She nodded, the grip on her husband's hand lessening a bit. "I made him some coffee. And he had his breakfast. Eggs, bacon, roasted potatoes, and toast," she added, smiling weakly. "I could never get him to eat better."

"So his appetite was good?"

"He ate everything and had three cups of coffee."

"You never saw a gun?"

Ellie shook her head. "He had his briefcase already packed. I guess it could have been in there, but I didn't see it. As I told the other agents, I didn't even know he had a gun. As far as I knew he didn't even like them. I certainly didn't. When our kids were small we had a neighbor who had one. Our kids went over there to play one day. He left his loaded gun out and one of his children accidentally shot his sister. She died. Walter and I were stunned. All we could think was that it could have been our child."

"I understand. Now, I'm sure you've been asked this, but this morning, your husband didn't appear upset or anything to indicate something was wrong?"

"No. He had a meeting to go to. I suppose at the FBI. I know he was working on something for them. He kissed me goodbye."

"So nothing out of the ordinary, then?" Decker persisted.

Ellie stiffened a bit. "Well, come to think of it, he didn't say he'd see me for dinner." She looked at Decker. "He always would tell me he'd see me for dinner. I mean when he was in town and didn't have a previous engagement, which I knew he didn't today."

"So he didn't say he'd see you tonight, then?" said Decker.

"No." She shook her head wearily. "It's such a small thing, but it always made me feel . . . good. I don't know why I didn't think of it until now."

"You've had a lot to deal with, Mrs. Dabney."

"So he must have known he wasn't coming home," she said blankly. "And I didn't pick up on it." She suddenly jerked upright. "Oh my God, maybe if I had—" She looked like she might start sobbing.

Bogart went over, put a hand on her arm, and said, "There was absolutely nothing you could have done to prevent this."

Decker rose and looked at Bogart. The FBI agent said, "Mrs. Dabney, I know the timing couldn't be worse, but we're going to have to send a team of people to your home to do a search. We're doing the same for your husband's office too."

Ellie didn't object. She simply nodded, squeezed her husband's hand, and said, "Do you know when Jules will be here?"

"Her flight gets in in another hour. We're sending people to bring her directly here."

"Thank you," she said dully.

Decker walked over to a corner of the room and motioned for Bogart to join him there. In a low voice he said, "I'd like to be there when they go through the home and office."

Bogart nodded. "Todd can stay here with me for now. You can take Alex with you. Anything of interest with Berkshire?"

"She spent time with dying people. Everyone has nice things to say about her. She lives in a place that it doesn't seem she can afford on a substitute teacher's salary. And it looks like no one has even really lived there. And we can find nothing on her past ten years ago."

"So, odd, to say the least?"

"Different, anyway," noted Decker.

"Does that mean you think she was specifically targeted by Dabney?"

Decker shrugged. "Too early to tell. But a random victim with some weird shit in their lives? I don't know. Could be a coincidence, or it could be a clue as to why she was killed in the first place."

"Which would entail Dabney having some connection with her."

Decker shrugged again. "If her money came through

some lawsuit or inheritance, then maybe the connection lies there, though I can't see what that might be. It could be personal between the two."

"Mrs. Dabney is certain that her husband didn't know Berkshire."

"But you also told me she said she knows nothing of her husband's business. So if it was a professional relationship she might *not* know about it."

"But maybe someone at his office would," pointed out Bogart.

"We can only hope."

Decker looked at Jamison and said, "Let's go."

* * *

Walter Dabney and Associates was located off the Fairfax County Parkway in Reston, Virginia. The area was home to lots of government contractors, from massive ones like Lockheed Martin to one-person shops. Dabney's business wasn't a Fortune 500 behemoth, but as Decker and Jamison walked into the bright, open, and fashionably furnished reception area on the top floor of a modern glass-and-steel six-story building, it was apparent that Dabney had built a very successful enterprise. Though the hour was late, the news had reached the local and national pipelines and people who worked here had not gone home, as normal. They were out in the hallways looking pale, confused, and distraught.

After showing their IDs, Decker and Jamison were escorted to a small conference room by a young woman. A minute later a woman in her late thirties opened the door and stepped in. She was about five-five, with a runner's trim build, shoulder-length reddish-blonde hair, and square-rimmed glasses perched on her freckled face.

"I'm Faye Thompson. I'm a partner here. Is it…is it really true?"

Decker said, "I'm afraid so."

"Is Walter…?"

"He's still alive, but the prognosis is not good," said Jamison.

Decker said, "We'd like to ask some questions."

"Of course, please have a seat. Would you like anything? Coffee, water?"

Jamison opted for water and Decker for black coffee. Thompson ordered a hot tea.

When the drinks arrived and the door closed behind the assistant, Decker took a sip of his coffee and said, "Tell us about Walter Dabney."

Jamison took a small recorder out of her pocket and put it on the table. "Do you mind if I record this?"

Thompson shook her head and sat back. "I'm not sure where to begin. Walter is a great guy. I joined the firm a year out of college. I've been here fifteen years, made partner eight years ago. He was a wonderful mentor and friend. And also one of the nicest men I've ever met. I can't believe what happened."

"So nothing you observed to explain what he did?" asked Decker.

"That Walter would shoot and kill someone on the street? No. No way. It's unthinkable."

"We know he went downtown this morning for a meeting at the FBI. Were you aware of that?"

"Yes. We're consulting with the Bureau on some projects. We partner with some major contractors, lending our expertise to give the Bureau the best possible resources so they can do their job at optimal levels."

Decker said, "That's the official pitch anyway."

Thompson stared defiantly at him. "And it's also the truth. We're very highly ranked in our space. Our reputation is stellar."

"So he didn't come into the office today?" asked Decker.

"Not that I'm aware of. We officially open at eight-thirty. But those with a key card can come and go when they want."

"But if he did come here the security system would have a record of that?"

"Yes. I can check."

"Thanks. Was he in the office yesterday?" asked Decker.

"Yes. I met with him. I had just come back from overseas and was filling him in on what had taken place. I'm still jet-lagged. And now this."

"Where overseas?"

Her lips pursed. "What does that have to do with what happened?"

"Maybe nothing. But I like to get a full picture."

Thompson kept looking at him as she took a sip of tea. "The Middle East. That's about as specific as I can be."

"Any projects that he was working on that might explain what happened this morning?"

"I highly doubt it. And I can't really get into that. Most of the projects we work on are classified. And most of the people who work here and all of the partners have the highest security clearances. What security clearances do you have?"

"I don't even have a security *system* where I live."

Thompson's eyebrows hiked and she glanced at Jamison. "So what else would you like to know?"

Jamison said, "How did he appear yesterday? Normal? Worried?"

"Normal."

"Nothing that would have raised your suspicions?"

"Like what?"

Decker said, "Unusual phrases. Agitation. Lack of focus."

"No, nothing like that."

"Might he have been on drugs?"

Her complexion changed. "Walter! Most assuredly not. I've only seen him drink the occasional glass of wine."

"Was he the only one from your firm attending the meeting today?" asked Decker.

"Yes. Walter knew the technical side of our business as well as anyone. But the meeting today was high-level strategic. Walter often did those solo, particularly when he was meeting with the top people at a client."

"Anything in his behavior out of the ordinary in the last month or so?" asked Jamison.

"Not really. I mean nothing that jumped out."

"His wife said that Dabney took an unexplained trip about a month ago. And that when he got back he didn't tell her where he'd been. And to her he seemed different ever since that point."

Thompson looked surprised by this. "A month ago? I don't know where he went. If our travel people handled it they would have a record of that."

"We'd appreciate if you would check," said Jamison.

"Of course." She took out her phone and tapped in a message. "Done. As soon as they get back to me, I'll let you know."

Decker rose and walked around the room while Thompson watched him.

"The firm is obviously very successful," noted Decker.

"We work hard, and yes, it has paid off, very handsomely. We just landed two large contracts that alone will nearly double our revenue from the previous year."

He looked at her. "And with Dabney not around, what happens to the firm?"

Thompson looked uncertain. "We're a limited partnership, but Walter is the general partner and he holds the majority of partnership interest. I'm sure there's language in the documents that addresses his...his passing, but I don't know it off the top of my head. Our in-house counsel would know."

"We'd like those documents," said Decker.

"Are they relevant to why he would do what he did?" asked Thompson.

"Everything's relevant until it isn't," replied Decker.

His phone buzzed. He looked at the text and nodded at Jamison. She rose and pocketed the recorder. "Thank you, Ms. Thompson. We'll be in touch."

"And remember to check whether Dabney was here this morning," said Decker.

She said tersely, "I have an excellent memory, Agent Decker."

"So do I," replied Decker. "So I'll hold you to it."

They walked out and over to the elevator bank.

"What's up?" asked Jamison.

"Dabney just died."

"Oh my God. Well, I guess it's not unexpected."

"But he regained consciousness before he did."

"Did he say anything?" she asked excitedly.

"Yes."

"What was it?" Jamison asked eagerly.

"Apparently a string of words that made absolutely no sense to any of the people there."

"So gibberish? Because of the brain injury?"

"Well, having suffered a brain injury myself, I can tell you that one person's gibberish is another person's revelation."

CHAPTER

8

TWELVE TIMES. DECKER had listened to the recording of Dabney's last words a dozen times and still nothing had struck him. No revelations. Not even a glimmer of one.

He was sitting in an office at the Hoover Building staring at the recorder. Across from him were Jamison and Milligan.

Milligan, his tie loosened and his normally straight-backed posture drooping a bit, slumped in his chair and said, "We can listen to this thing for the next ten years and it'll still make no sense. The guy had blown out a chunk of his brain. He was incapable of rational thought, Decker. It's meaningless."

"Was Mrs. Dabney there?" he asked.

"Yes. Right up until the end."

"And it made no sense to her either? Something that only she would know? Something very personal?"

"Well, she was crying so hard when he started talking, it was difficult to tell whether she actually heard what he said. We had to filter her sobs out of the recording."

"But when she settled down?" persisted Decker. "Still nothing?"

Milligan said, "I think she thought he was going to sit up in the bed and start talking to her. And then he just stopped breathing. The machines started going crazy and a crash team came in to try to resuscitate him, but they couldn't. He was just gone."

Ross Bogart walked in and sat down across from Decker. "Anything pop?" he asked.

Decker said, "Right now the victim is more interesting than the killer. She lives in a multimillion-dollar apartment and has a car that costs over a hundred grand that she's barely driven, all on a substitute teacher's salary. And once you go back ten years, there's no record of an Anne Berkshire."

"You mentioned that before. A big coincidence, as you said, if she was a random victim."

"And she might have changed her name," suggested Jamison. "That might be why we can't find anything on her going back more than ten years."

"I think she clearly did change her name," said Decker. "The important question becomes why."

Bogart said, "You thought Melvin Mars's parents were in Witness Protection. Maybe Berkshire was."

"Well, we need to find that out. If she had another previous identity then the person she was might have had a connection to Dabney, which would explain why he targeted her."

"I'll get some people on it," said Bogart. He rose and left the room.

Jamison said to Milligan, "So I understand that the task force is officially being transferred from Quantico to the Washington Field Office in D.C."

"That's right."

Decker broke off staring at the recorder and glanced at him. "Transferred to the WFO?"

Milligan said, "Since we're no longer doing cold cases we're being shipped from Quantico to the WFO. It's actually an up-grade. The higher-ups have appreciated the work we've done."

Decker said, "Wait a minute, does that mean we can't live at Quantico anymore?"

"You don't want to make that commute every day," said Milligan. "It's a killer up Interstate 95. I was in luck because I live in Springfield. I was going against traffic every day. Now I'll be slogging along with all the traffic heading north. Ross is in D.C. So his commute will be easy."

Decker said, "I don't have another place to live."

Jamison spoke up. "Funny you mention that."

"Why is it funny?" asked Decker sharply.

"I was going to tell you about this at some point, when the timing seemed right. But then again, this might work out very fortuitously."

"What the hell are you talking about, Alex?" asked a clearly irritated Decker.

"Okay, don't get upset."

"I'm *already* upset."

"I've actually been doing what amounts to another job on the side."

Milligan cracked a smile and said, "What, working for the FBI isn't fulfilling enough for you?"

"Another job?" said Decker.

"There's a building in Anacostia."

"A *building*," exclaimed Decker.

"Yes, well, to make a clean breast of it, I've been hunting for a fixer-upper building for the last couple of months. And I found the perfect one."

"You've been looking for a building?" said Decker dully. "I don't need a building. I just need a room. A small one. And why have you been looking for a building in the first place?"

"As an investment. And a way to do some good."

"And you're just mentioning this now?"

"Well, I was going to tell you very soon. We recently closed on the place."

"*We* closed on a building? Who's 'we'?"

"Well, *he* actually closed on it."

"Who are you talking about?" asked Milligan.

"Wait a minute," said Decker. "You don't have any money to invest in a building. You keep complaining that you can't afford gas for your car."

"Well, thanks for sharing," said Jamison, glancing embarrassedly at Milligan. "And I'm just his rep."

"Whose rep?" asked Milligan.

Decker's features slackened as the truth hit him. "It's Melvin, isn't it?"

"Melvin?" said Milligan. "Melvin Mars?"

Decker stared directly at Jamison. "*He* bought the building, didn't he? With some of the money from his settlement with the government?"

Jamison nodded. "Yes, he did. But only after I found it."

"When did all this happen?" asked Milligan.

"Melvin had all this money and didn't know what to do with it. So I suggested that he could make money and also help people, which is what he really wanted to do."

"How does buying a building help people?" asked Milligan.

"The building has, well, tenants. And they pay rent."

"So what?" asked Milligan. "My wife and I pay rent too. It's not like it's a handout. It's expensive."

"This place is a little different. We got it for a great price. And while it needs a little work, we can afford to charge rent that, well, that people who don't make a lot of money can afford to pay."

"You mean like low-income housing," said Milligan.

"Sort of, but it's not like he's required by law to do it. Melvin can because he doesn't care about making a killing like pretty much all other landlords. He gets what we think is a reasonable return on his money and folks who otherwise couldn't afford a place to live, can. A win-win."

"So this place has tenants," said Decker. "But where will *I* live?"

"In the *building*. Top floor. You'll have a room. And so will I. And our own en suite bathrooms. And we'll have an office and a big kitchen. Very spacious, in fact."

Decker just stared at her.

She hastily added, "I didn't know we were going to be moving from Quantico to D.C., but I always thought we could live there regardless. We'd be going against traffic if we were still working at Quantico. Now it's even closer."

"Do you mean we'll be living *together*?" said Decker slowly, apparently not having heard what she'd just said.

"Well, not *living* together. We'll be roommates. Like in college."

"My college roommate was an offensive lineman who made me look small," said Decker. "He was messy and disgusting, but he was a guy."

"Well, I'm sorry I'm a *girl*, but I can cook, so how about that?" retorted Jamison.

"You can?" said Decker in a dubious tone.

"Well, a little."

His gaze continued to bore into her.

"I *can* microwave pretty much anything," she snapped.

Decker closed his eyes and said nothing.

Jamison focused on Milligan. "And best of all, Melvin's going to let Amos and me stay there rent-free in exchange for looking after things." She added, "In addition to our jobs with the FBI."

Decker opened his eyes and said firmly, "I am *not* looking after a building. I don't even know if I want to be roommates. This is a lot of change being thrown at me," he added in an offended tone.

"But I already said we would look after the place, Decker. I promised Melvin."

"Then *you* can," said Decker. "One job is plenty for me."

She looked at him appraisingly. "Okay, if you want to find a place on your own, feel free. Keep in mind that D.C. is one of the most expensive real estate markets in the country. And you don't have a car, so it's not like you can live way out and commute in that way. So you'll probably need to take out a loan to pay your rent. Just saying."

Decker continued to stare at her.

Jamison said, "Look, I can deal with the tenants, all right? And everything else. You won't really have to do much, if anything."

Milligan said, "Sounds like a deal you can't refuse, Decker."

Decker didn't say anything for a few moments. "Can I at least see the place first before I decide?"

"Absolutely. We can go right now. But you're going to love it. It's very charming."

"Is that a code word for needing a lot of fixing up?" he asked.

"It does need a bit of TLC," she conceded. "But Melvin said I can hire professionals to do that."

Decker stared at Jamison. "Is there anything *else* you haven't told me?"

"Not that I know of," said Jamison, refusing to meet his eye.

"That is not a response that inspires confidence," he said grumpily.

CHAPTER

9

DECKER STARED AT the moonlit building.

Jamison stood next to him, watching her friend closely.

When Decker finally turned to her she looked away. "See, it's everything I told you it would be," she said, smiling at the asphalt.

"And then some," replied Decker tersely.

The building had once been an old brick warehouse with huge windows; Jamison had informed him that it had been divided up into apartments. Decker took a deep breath and the smells from the nearby Anacostia River filled his lungs. On one side of the warehouse was an abandoned building. On the other side was a demolished structure. Across the street was a string of homes that looked to be about a hundred years old. They were actually leaning into one another and looked uninhabited.

The parking lot of the former warehouse had seemingly more cracks than asphalt, and weeds were growing up through them. An old chain-link fence that surrounded the building was torn down in places and the gate was gone, leaving rusted hinges behind. A few cars were parked in the lot. The newest of them was about twenty years old. Two had plastic trash bags duct-taped over broken-out windows.

"Has Melvin seen the place?" he asked.

"He's seen pictures. He asked me to look around and I did. And I found this."

He glanced at her. "So how much 'looking around' did you do?"

"Melvin didn't want to buy a place in a ritzy area, Decker, even though he could afford it. He wanted a place where he could make a difference. The rent on these places is well under the going rate. Everyone living here has a job. Most have multiple jobs. They work hard and they're trying to better their lives and the lives of their families. It's really a neat place. And within walking distance are a bunch of restaurants that just started up, all mom-and-pop shops. And there are churches and a park and..." Her voice trailed off as Decker gave no reaction to any of this.

Jamison added, "So, you don't like it? I know it's not the Taj Mahal."

"I used to live in a cardboard box in a Walmart parking lot, and after that in one room at a Residence Inn. So if it has its own toilet this is actually a move up for me."

"Okay?" she said tentatively. "So you're good with it?"

"How many tenants?"

"Fifteen units are rented. Two residents are single. The rest have families."

"So you've met them?"

"Yes. I wasn't going to give Melvin a recommendation without doing proper due diligence. He wants to do good things with his money, but I would never put him in a situation where he would lose his investment. And it's got good bones. Once the rest of the improvements are done, it'll be great. And the area around here, while I know it doesn't look like much, is really starting to come around. Like I said, the restaurants are coming in, and buildings like this one are being renovated. All good stuff."

"And then the rents rise and the taxes go up and the people you're trying to help can't afford it anymore."

"Well, our rents *aren't* going up. And we did a deal with the local government. They've given Melvin some tax abatements and other incentives so he can afford to keep helping those who need it."

"Abatements and incentives? When exactly did you do all this?"

"In my spare time. I know I was a journalist when we first met, Decker. But my heart has always been about doing stuff like this."

Decker nodded and looked back at the building. "And where will we be living?"

"Like I said, on the top floor. It's got great views. And it's all built out."

"Is it furnished, or do we have to go shopping?"

"I took the liberty of getting some things. If you don't like it we can always do a redo."

"Does it have a place to sit and a place to sleep?"

"Yes."

"Then I'm sure it'll be fine."

"Do you want to go inside?"

He motioned for her to lead the way.

Jamison punched in a code on a box next to the entry door and pushed it open. Decker followed her in to where they were confronted by a set of stairs.

"It's a true walk-up," she explained. "No elevator."

Six flights up they reached a door that Jamison unlocked while Decker leaned against the wall and caught his breath. She looked back at him.

"I thought you'd been working out," she said.

"I just did."

He followed her in and stopped. The ceilings were

twenty feet high with exposed metal beams and concrete columns constituting the support structure of the building. They all had been painted black. The space was wide open, with a large seating area near the twelve-foot-tall windows, and a modern kitchen with stainless steel appliances and granite counters. There were two large bedrooms with en suite baths. Down another hall was a large office with a desk and shelves and a window with wooden shutters. A laptop sat on top of the desk.

"That's your office. I have a space next door. There's also a Jacuzzi in there," she added, pointing to a door on the left. "And a sauna. But I haven't used either one. I'm not even sure if they work."

"Holy shit, Jamison," said Decker. "When you were describing the place as needing TLC, I sure wasn't expecting this!"

She looked at him a bit guiltily. "This was the former building owner's apartment. He put all the money into this space and went cheap everywhere else. The other apartments do not look like this."

"What happened to him?"

She looked nervous. "I'd rather not say."

"And why would that be?"

"I just wouldn't."

"Alex!"

"Okay, he got shot in the parking lot by some drug dealer he stiffed."

"Shot as in dead?"

"Well, yeah. I thought that was sort of implied."

Decker looked around. "And did he use the money he was supposed to pay to the dealer to build this out?"

"It's not clear. But I wouldn't worry about it. I mean, it's not like *we* owe the drug dealer anything."

"So he was never caught?"

"Well, the police had a suspect, but since there were no witnesses willing to come forward they had to let him go. The building went into bankruptcy and Melvin bought it. He got a really good deal, actually. Apparently there were no other bidders."

"Shocking," said Decker.

"But you like it, right?"

"Yeah, I like it. It's a palace compared to what I'm used to."

"I already brought my stuff up. You can move in anytime."

"All my possessions fit inside one bag, so it won't be a huge undertaking."

She held out her hand. "Welcome to our new home, roomie."

Before shaking her hand Decker said, "Let's get a few more locks on the door."

CHAPTER

10

THE NEXT MORNING Decker blinked himself awake and looked around at the unfamiliar surroundings.

But they weren't unfamiliar. They were the new digs. Big place, not a cardboard box. But with tenants. And maybe a pissed-off drug dealer lurking. The FBI had delivered his few personal belongings from his place in Quantico late last night. It had taken Decker about five minutes to put away all of his worldly possessions.

He sat up and got out of bed. He walked over to the window and peered out. It was still dark outside, but the sun would soon begin to rise.

As he continued to peer out, Decker saw a short, wiry man and a little boy walk outside and get into the car with the plastic bags taped over the rear side windows. The man was dressed in jeans, work boots, and a sweatshirt. He carried a yellow hard hat. The little boy had a large bag slung over his shoulder. They drove off, the car's tailpipe peppering the air with dark fumes.

Down the road paralleling the building, Decker saw two people, a man and a woman, staggering along under the glow of a streetlight. They didn't look homeless, but to Decker's experienced eye, they weren't too far removed from it. The man cuffed the woman on the side of the head and she fell. He kept going. Finally, the woman struggled up and followed. She pulled something from her pocket, raised her hand to her mouth, and swallowed whatever it was.

Decker watched them go, then used the bathroom, showered, and dressed. It was not yet seven o'clock. He walked down the hall to the kitchen and made himself coffee and a bowl of cereal. He had passed Jamison's room and heard her soft snores through the partially open doorway.

He sat and drank his coffee and ate his cereal, but mostly stared out the window into the gathering light.

He had come a far distance from his former life in Burlington, Ohio.

He had lost his family, his job, and his home.

He had avenged the murders of his wife, daughter, and brother-in-law. But that did nothing to take away the loss, the pain. Nothing ever could. Time did not heal wounds for Decker. The passage of time was irrelevant to his unique mind. Everything he had ever experienced in life was as freshly minted in his brain as the moment it was created.

That was the vast downside of having a perfect memory. He had so much he wanted to forget. And couldn't.

But that wasn't all.

He was no longer who he used to be. He knew that he did things that irritated others. Leaving rooms too abruptly. Zoning out and becoming unresponsive. Not having as much empathy as others would have liked.

As *he* would have liked.

He rubbed his head. What was up there had changed. Meaning he had changed along with it. There was no separating the two: his brain and the rest of Amos Decker. That was just the way things worked.

That's the way I work now.

He put the dirty dishes in the dishwasher, sat back down, and thought about the case.

Berkshire the victim. Dabney the killer.

Berkshire's hazy past. Did the answer lie there?

Or would the truth come from Dabney's end?

Or a combination of the two?

He thought back to the shooting. He went through each frame in his head, looking for anything that would lead him in the right direction.

They had tracked Dabney's movements that day. He had taken an Uber from his home in McLean to a coffee shop near the Hoover Building. Decker knew he had walked from there toward the FBI building, where he had murdered Berkshire.

As the frames whirred through his head an inconsistency popped up.

Decker loved inconsistencies. They tended to point him in the direction of the truth, or at least to a lead.

And right now he would dearly love a lead.

Ellie Dabney had told Decker that she had made her husband breakfast. Eggs, bacon, toast, and roasted potatoes. Dabney had eaten it all, she had told them. Plus three cups of coffee.

So why would he stop at a coffee shop on the way to his destination?

It could be nothing. He might have been killing time before his meeting. Or else he had a quick cup of coffee while going over some notes.

Although why do that if he knew he was never going to have that meeting? The man assuredly couldn't have expected to murder someone in broad daylight with lots of witnesses around and then attend his meeting with the FBI as though nothing had happened. And it couldn't have been a spur-of-the-moment thing commencing after he left the coffee shop. He had the gun in his briefcase. They had found traces of gun oil and other forensic fragments in there that proved this was so.

Decker made a mental note to go to the coffee shop and find someone who had seen Dabney. Maybe he met with someone there. They had checked his phone records. He had made no calls that morning and sent no texts and no emails.

Was that because he was about to commit murder? And he was steeling himself to do the deed? But if he did know Berkshire, how would he know she would be there that morning? The FBI had determined that she hadn't called or scheduled a meeting with anyone. But then again, she might have been going there unannounced for some reason. Maybe she had something she wanted to tell the FBI.

And Dabney stopped her from doing that. That was an interesting theory.

Although it was just possible that she wasn't going to the Hoover Building at all. She might have been turning that way to go somewhere else.

Lots of possibilities and nothing conclusive. But then most cases started out that way. The truth was always hidden on the inside, the core, Decker thought. And you had to peel away every single layer of the outside to get to that core.

He looked up to find a sleepy-eyed Jamison dressed in gym shorts and a U2 T-shirt, staring at him.

"You're up early," she said hoarsely.

"I'm always up early. You'll find that out now that we *live* together. *Roomie.*"

She padded over to the coffee machine, put in a coffee pod, and slid a cup under the dispensing slot. As it did its thing she leaned against the counter and said groggily, "Any brilliant revelations in the night?"

"Apparently Dabney had two breakfasts. I'd like to know why."

"Okay."

The coffee machine dinged and Jamison doctored her coffee with raw sugar and cream and took a sip.

"We're scheduled to search Dabney's house this morning."

Decker drummed his fingers on the table and didn't answer.

"I understand some of their kids will be there," she added.

"A little boy and his dad."

"What?" she said in confusion. "Dabney had four grown *daughters*."

"The car with the plastic bag windows in the parking lot here. The gray Sentra."

"Oh, what about them?"

"Who are they?"

"Tomas Amaya and his eleven-year-old son, Danny."

"He goes to school nearby?"

"Yes. Did you see them?"

"They left before six."

"Tomas drops him off at the school. They have a before-school program for parents who have to go to work early. Tomas works construction and has to be at work by six-thirty."

"And the mother?"

"As far as I know it's just Tomas and Danny."

"How do you know all this?"

"I told you that I met with all the tenants. I wanted to introduce myself to everyone after Melvin bought the building. I just wanted to assure them that everything would be okay. That they weren't being evicted or anything. And I spent time with Tomas and Danny. Tomas is devoted to his son. And Danny is very bright. He draws. I've seen some of his sketches. The kid has talent."

"And all the tenants are *nice*?"

"Well, that's a relative term."

"Give me a relative answer."

"Some are nicer than others. And I get where some of them are coming from. They're all people of color. And I'm not sure all of them are here legally. And I'm this white woman knocking on their door and telling them that an unknown investor has bought the building and I'll be their landlord? I'd be suspicious too."

Decker sighed. "It's 2017, but it doesn't feel like it. When I was a kid they had those TV shows on about what the future would look like. Robots cleaning houses and people flying their cars to work. And instead we've got...this."

"Preaching to the choir, Decker. Hey, Melvin said he would come in soon to meet the people here and look over the property."

Decker perked up. "It'll be good to see him again."

"I know you two really hit it off."

"He's my best friend."

Jamison frowned slightly at this comment but didn't respond.

Decker's phone buzzed. It was Bogart. Decker listened for a few moments and then clicked off.

"Change of plan. Bogart wants us at the morgue."

"Why?"

"They just completed the autopsy on Dabney."

"Okay, but we know what he died of. A self-inflicted gunshot wound."

"Yeah, but there's something else."

"What?"

"The man was apparently already dead when he shot himself."

CHAPTER

11

THE SAME MEDICAL EXAMINER, Lynne Wainwright, looked at Decker as he stared at the cut-up body of Walter Dabney, the standard V-incision stapled shut over his torso.

Bogart stood next to him and Jamison behind them, her eyes averted from the butchered body.

Not too long ago the man was a successful businessman with a loving family. Now he was a lifeless and violated sack of flesh and bone on a metal table.

"And you're sure?" said Bogart.

Wainwright picked up an X-ray and slapped it against a light box on one wall. She pointed to a dark area.

"A massive brain tumor, inoperable because of where it's located and how far it had invaded vital regions. I had already taken X-rays and knew something was there. But when I pulled the brain out I couldn't believe how bad it was."

"How long would he have had to live?" asked Decker.

The ME considered this. "You'll want to get a second opinion, but my rough estimate would be six months or less. Probably less. Because he also had a ready-to-burst aneurysm right there," she added, pointing at another spot on the X-ray. "I'm surprised he was able to still fully function, actually."

"Maybe he had something left to live for," said Decker. "Like killing Anne Berkshire."

Bogart said sharply, "You really believe that?"

"I don't disbelieve it."

"Do you think his wife knew?" asked Jamison. "About the tumor?"

"Doubtful," answered Bogart. "I mean, you would think she would have mentioned it."

"Maybe that was the unexpected trip he took a month ago," said Decker. "To get the diagnosis." He turned to the ME. "Was it possible he didn't know about the tumor?"

"Anything's possible," Wainwright said cautiously. "But there would have been outward symptoms. Some slightly impaired motor functions. Disruption in thought processes. I think a person in his position, educated, well-off, good health insurance presumably, he would have seen a doctor. A simple MRI would have confirmed the tumor's presence. Other tests would have confirmed its true malignancy."

Bogart said, "I wonder why none of his business associates noticed anything amiss. They would have been with him a great deal."

"For that matter, why wouldn't his wife?" noted Jamison.

The ME said, "With this sort of cancer the end comes very swiftly. But he might have been able to work at a fairly normal level up to a certain point, until the cancer just became too widespread. By the looks of his brain, I think that time was rapidly approaching."

"So he might have been able to disguise his illness from his family, friends, and coworkers?" asked Decker.

"Again, anything's possible. He also could have been taking some medications that would help him."

"And the blood work will show any present in his system?" asked Bogart.

"I've already sent the samples out for processing," said Wainwright.

Decker looked back down at the body. "Since he was already dying, taking his own life makes more sense. He saved himself and his family months of suffering. But it doesn't explain Berkshire's murder."

"Well, to put it bluntly, I think his family would have taken months of their father suffering his final illness over what's happened now," countered Jamison.

"Which means he must have had a really compelling reason," retorted Decker. "And we have to find out what that was."

He headed out.

"Where are you going, Decker?" Jamison called after him.

"To get a cup of coffee."

* * *

The coffee shop that Dabney had visited before killing Berkshire was just down the street from the FBI building. It was part of a chain and the interior was open, light-filled, and furnished with comfy chairs and tables where people could work. Power-charging stations were dotted along the walls.

Decker and Jamison walked up to the counter—Bogart had stayed behind to talk to the medical examiner and to make some phone calls—and Decker flashed his FBI creds to the young woman working there. She was in her early twenties, with brown hair tied back with an elastic band. She had on white pants and a black polo with the store's logo. Round glasses fronted her face.

After ordering coffee Decker said, "Did you work yesterday?"

The woman nodded.

Decker held up a photo of Walter Dabney. "Street cameras confirm that he entered here at ten o'clock and left about fifty minutes later."

"Is he the guy who shot the woman? I saw it on the news."

"He is. Did you see him here? Did you take his order?"

"Both."

"What did he have?"

The woman thought a moment. "Hot tea and a black-berry scone. At least I think. I serve a lot of food and drinks during the course of a day."

"How did he appear to you? Nervous?"

"Not particularly, no. He seemed, well, normal."

"Where did he sit?"

She pointed at a table over by the front window.

Decker looked around the space and memorized the lo-cation of all the tables. "Was the place full when he came in?"

"No, the morning rush was over by then. There were maybe two tables occupied."

"Which ones?"

She pointed them out. They were near the counter.

Decker said, "Did you notice whether anyone came over to him? Spoke with him?"

"I was fairly busy with some inventory work, so I can't say for sure. I remember I looked over once and he was just sitting there alone staring out the window."

"Anyone else who works here who might have seen any-thing?"

"Billy was on duty yesterday too, but he's not in today. He might have seen something. He was delivering orders and bussing tables."

Jamison handed her a couple of cards. "Tell Billy to give us a call. And if you remember anything else, give us a ring."

While she'd been speaking, Decker sat down at the table that Dabney had occupied. "This chair?" he asked.

The woman looked over. "No, the one to the left of you."

Decker changed chairs and looked around as Jamison walked over to him and sat down in the chair he'd vacated.

"What are you thinking?"

Decker gazed out the window. From here he could see the FBI building. And the guard shack. There was someone inside, but he couldn't tell if it was the same guard as before.

He said, "This place was empty, so he had his pick of tables. He walked past a bunch of empty ones to get to this one. It gives the clearest field of view toward the FBI building. So did he come here to observe something? Or to meet with someone? Or was there another reason?"

"How will we find out which one?"

"We keep asking questions."

Decker's phone buzzed. He listened for a few moments and then said, "We'll be there as soon as we can." He clicked off and said to Jamison, "That was Bogart. Dabney's daughter Jules has something to tell us."

"What?"

"Something her father told her a week ago."

12

WALTER DABNEY *HAD* done well for himself.

Decker was standing right in the middle of it all.

The house in McLean was easily worth four or five million bucks. The grounds were extensive and professionally landscaped and maintained. A crew was outside right then trimming bushes, cutting the broad, plush lawns, and generally sprucing up the outdoor space. Another crew was working on the Olympic-size heated pool. And there was a poolhouse that was about the size of a normal home. The cost of merely maintaining this place each year was probably far more than Decker was paid by the FBI.

He turned from the window to stare over at Jules Dabney. She was an interesting mixture of her parents. Tall and athletically built like her mother, she had her father's jawline, long forehead, and pale green eyes. Her blonde hair hung straight down and skimmed the tops of her shoulders.

Her manner was brisk, businesslike even, and she hadn't shed a tear since Decker and the others arrived. Her mother, she told them, was in her bedroom, heavily sedated.

Translation: She's not talking to you.

Jules instantly struck Decker as a micromanager and

able handler of adverse situations. He wondered if that was going to help or hinder their investigation.

They were in the library, three walls of books clearly proclaiming the purpose of the room. Bogart sat in a comfy leather recliner, Jamison in an upholstered settee, and Jules in what looked like an antique wing chair. Decker stood in the center of the room.

Bogart said, "I can appreciate how difficult this is for you, Ms. Dabney."

Jules waved this off. "It's not difficult, it's *impossible*. But we have to get through it, and so we will."

"Where did you come in from?" Decker asked her.

She looked at him as though bewildered why this held any relevance.

"Palm Beach, why?"

"What do you do there?"

She frowned. "Is that important? Or pertinent?"

"It's hard to say since you haven't told us yet."

Her lips pursed, she said, "I have my own company. Health care consulting."

Jamison said, "I would imagine Florida is a good place for that. What with the large retired population."

"Most of them are on Medicare, of course, but there's a great deal of wealth down there and people have supplemental insurance. Health care is complicated. It's hard for people to navigate it. And we advise businesses too. In fact, that's where most of our revenue comes from. We have twenty employees and are growing double digits every year."

"That's very impressive," said Decker. "When I was your age, I could barely take care of myself."

She said curtly, "My father instilled an excellent work ethic in all his children. Along with ambition."

She suddenly looked away, and for a moment Decker

thought she might burst into tears. She rubbed her mouth and turned back to them.

"My father is . . . was a huge influence on me."

Decker said, "I'm sure. And you wanted to meet with us because your father told you something?"

"*Things*," she said. "I wrote them down on the flight in."

She handed the paper to Decker. He looked down at it.

Bogart said, "Can you read them out loud, Decker?"

Decker appeared not to have heard him.

Jules stared impatiently at the silent Decker for a few moments and then said sharply, as though she were giving a business presentation, "One, he told me to take care of my mother. Two, he said for me to get married and have a family. Because life was too short. Three, he told me that above all I was to remember that he loved me."

Bogart said, "And was this unusual?"

"My father was attentive and caring, but, yes, these particular statements were unusual because he had never spoken to me about these things before. At least not like that."

Jamison said, "So were you concerned?"

"I point-blank asked him if something was wrong. He said no. Just that he'd been thinking about life in general and wanted me to know these things. He joked that he must be getting old, but it still struck me as odd."

"Did you talk to anyone else about it?" asked Bogart.

"No. I was going to phone my siblings to see if he'd a similar conversation with them, but then I got busy. By the time I got around to thinking about doing it I got the call about Dad."

Decker held up the list. "You have a number four marked here but nothing beside it."

Jules reached in her pocket and pulled out a key. "He sent me this the next day."

Decker took the key and looked it over. "Appears to be a safe deposit box key," he said, handing it across to Bogart.

"It is," said Jules. "He has a box at a bank in downtown McLean. He's had it for years."

"Do you know what's in it?"

"I assumed it was just things one puts in a safe deposit box. I've never seen inside it."

"Why would he send you the key?"

"I don't know. I was going to call him, but then, like I said, I got distracted with business. I assumed I would have plenty of time to talk to him about it. I just thought it might have something to do with his estate planning. It would make sense that he would involve me. He'd named me executrix a couple of years ago." She added in an explanatory note, "I'm the oldest. That stuff sort of fell to me by virtue of birth order."

"But your father obviously had confidence in you too," said Jamison.

"I hoped he did."

Decker looked at Bogart. "Can we look inside it?"

Bogart glanced at Jules. "If your mother is a signatory on the box we'll need her permission. Otherwise, we'll have to get a warrant."

"Get the warrant, because I'm not disturbing my mom right now. She needs to rest, not worry about signing papers."

Bogart pulled out his phone and stepped from the room.

Jules looked around the space and her expression changed from flint to despair. "I grew up in this house. I love every nook and cranny of it."

Jamison said, "I can see why. It's beautiful. So warm and inviting. Did your mother do the decorating?"

Jules nodded. "She had an eye for that. Dad was great

at his business. But Mom did everything else. She was the perfect partner. Wonderful hostess, a great sounding board when he needed it. And she raised four kids, mostly on her own because Dad was always traveling back then."

Jamison said, "Wealth like this doesn't come easy. A lot of hard work went into it."

"Yeah," said Jules absently.

"So his words to you, given what happened, make sense," said Decker. "Sort of parting advice?"

She looked up at him, her face reddening. "So you're suggesting he told me to get married and have kids before he goes and murders someone and then blows his own head off? How screwed up is that?" she added shrilly.

Decker said imperturbably, "But he might not have thought he had a choice."

"What does that mean?"

"Did you know your father was sick?"

"What do you mean, *sick*?"

"He had an inoperable malignant brain tumor. He was terminal."

Jamison gave a little gasp at Decker's blunt words, but he kept his gaze squarely on Jules.

Tears appeared in Jules's eyes. "W-what?" she stammered.

Decker sat down across from her. "The autopsy revealed the tumor *and* an aneurysm. He had maybe a few months left to live. You're saying you didn't know?"

She shook her head as the tears suddenly spilled down her cheeks.

Jamison pulled some clean tissues from a pack in her purse and handed them to Decker, who passed them to Jules. She wiped her eyes.

"Do you think your mother knew?" asked Decker.

She shook her head. "Impossible. If Mom knew we all would have known."

"Even if he didn't want the children to know?" asked Jamison.

She took a few moments to compose herself. "Wouldn't have mattered. My mother is incapable of keeping something like that secret."

Decker nodded. "Understood. Is there any reason you can think of for your father having done something like this?"

She barked, "You might as well ask me why the sun won't be coming up tomorrow. This is... this can't be happening." The next instant, she bent over and started to sob uncontrollably.

Decker looked at Jamison with an awkward expression. Jamison rose and knelt down next to Jules, wrapping an arm around her shoulders and offering more tissues. "Decker, go get her some water," she hissed.

Decker left the room and found the kitchen, a large, airy space that looked like it should be in the pages of an architectural design magazine. He opened some cupboards. In one he saw some medicine bottles. He quickly looked at the labels. One was for increasing bone density; another was Zoloft. He found the glasses in another cupboard, filled one at the tap, and walked back to the library. He handed it to Jamison, who helped Jules to drink it.

They heard a car drive up to the front door. Decker left the room again and walked down the hall in time to see the front door fly open. A woman stormed in and threw her coat and bag down on the hardwood floor. Behind her Decker could see an airport taxi gliding back down the paved driveway.

The woman was in her early thirties, with brown hair cut short, glasses, and the same tall, lean build as Jules.

"Who the hell are you?" she demanded.

Decker held out his FBI credential. "I take it you're one of the daughters."

"Samantha. Where's my mother?"

"Sedated. Your sister Jules is in the library."

Samantha Dabney brushed past Decker and hurried down the hall. Decker followed. He got there in time to see her kneel down and hug her still-weeping sibling. Jamison rose and backed off, giving the women space.

When Jules finally composed herself, she sat up.

Samantha said, "What the hell is going on? Why is the FBI here?"

Jules said, "I told you what happened, Sam. Did you think they wouldn't be investigating? Dad mur... Dad shot someone. Right outside of the FBI building."

Samantha collapsed into the chair that Jamison had been sitting in. "I know that's what you told me. But it... it can't be, Jules. You know that. Why would he do this? He had so much to live for."

"Daddy was terminal. He had a brain tumor."

The blood drained from Samantha's face. She jumped up from the chair and glared down at her sister. "What? And you didn't tell me?"

Decker interjected, "I just told *her*. His autopsy revealed it." He paused. "Did your dad phone you recently?"

"No. About three weeks ago he sent me an email. Nothing special. Just checking in."

She shot Jules a glance. "First Dad shoots someone. And now a brain tumor. What is going on? Wait, do you think the tumor affected his mind? Is that why he did it?"

Decker said, "Anything's possible. But if there's another reason, we need to find it. Have either of you ever heard your father mention the name Anne Berkshire?"

They both shook their heads.

Samantha said, "Is that the woman he shot?"

Decker nodded.

Samantha looked at her sister. "Jules? You kept in touch with Dad more than me. You sure it doesn't ring a bell?"

"No. I never heard of the woman."

Jamison said, "It might have been random. There might be no connection. Maybe he *was* affected by his illness. Maybe Berkshire was in the wrong place at the wrong time."

Decker said, "I found some medicine bottles in the cupboard. One was for increasing bone density, the other was Zoloft. Who were they for? Part of the labels were removed."

Samantha looked at her sister and then back at Decker. "For Mom. She's had a problem with brittle bones. The Zoloft was for her depression."

"How long has she suffered from that?" asked Decker.

"At least since we were kids," said Samantha.

"She also has kidney issues," added Jules.

"But she looks so healthy," said Jamison. "Tall and athletic and robust."

"Looks can be deceiving," said Jules curtly. "Anyway, Dad took good care of her. Now, I don't know. I might have her come and live with me."

Bogart returned a moment later. He said, "The warrant is coming in now. Let's head to the bank."

Samantha said, "What bank?"

"Daddy sent me the key to his safe deposit box," said Jules.

"Why, what's in it?"

Bogart held up the key. "That's what we're going to find out."

CHAPTER

13

Eᴍᴘᴛʏ.

They were staring at an empty safe deposit box.

Decker gave a disappointed grunt. Bogart glanced up at him. Jamison mimicked this move.

Decker said, "He cleaned it out."

"We're just assuming he had anything in it," said Bogart.

"He sent his daughter a key to access it. Why do that if there was nothing in it?"

"True," conceded Bogart.

Jamison said, "They must have a record of him coming in."

Soon they were sitting across from the bank manager, who tapped some keys on her computer. She nodded. "Five days ago Mr. Dabney came in and accessed his box."

"And took things from it?" asked Bogart.

"We wouldn't know about that," said the manager. "What's in our clients' boxes is private."

Decker said, "Then we'll need to look at your video footage."

Ten minutes later they were staring at a computer screen in a small room off the bank lobby.

"There he is," said Jamison, pointing at Dabney walking into the bank on the day he'd emptied his safe deposit box.

"And he's not alone," said Decker.

There was a woman with Dabney. It wasn't his wife. She was shorter and stout, with dark hair. They couldn't get a good look at her face because she had on glasses and kept her gaze pointed down.

"The hair looks like a wig," noted Bogart.

A minute later she entered the room next to the vault with Dabney and his safe deposit box. After a few minutes they came out.

The woman was carrying a small bag that clearly had something in it. From the bulge in the side of the bag that they could see when the manager magnified it, it looked to be rectangular in shape, about six inches long and half that wide.

Decker said, "Is there any other angle on this video we can look at?"

"That's it, I'm afraid," said the bank manager.

"We'll need a copy of it," said Bogart.

* * *

They left the bank with a copy of the video, dozens of questions, and not a single answer to any of them. They returned to the Dabneys' house.

Another daughter, Amanda Riley, had arrived just a few minutes earlier. She was shorter than her sisters and rounder, lacking their athletic build. And she had a physical disability, her left arm ending at her elbow. Riley told them she was married with two young children.

They were surprised to see Ellie Dabney sitting with her daughters in the light-filled kitchen. She was dressed, her hair and makeup done, but the haunted look in her eyes made it clear that the normalcy of her appearance was only skin deep. They showed the video to her and her daughters. None of them recognized the woman.

"Why was she even there?" asked Jules. "I mean, it was Daddy's safe deposit box."

Decker answered, "She was there to make sure he emptied it."

Jules and Samantha stared at him.

"What exactly does that mean?" asked Jules.

"That exactly means that your father was involved with some people who sweat the details very seriously."

"This is cloak-and-dagger stuff," said Samantha. "I mean, it's like a TV show."

Bogart said, "Your father dealt with highly classified matters, so it could very well be that he was involved with some folks in that world."

Decker added, "And the fact that they sent someone with him to the bank shows that they didn't trust him to do it alone. You'll note on the video that the woman was carrying the bag, not your father."

"So they were *making* him do this," Jules said accusingly.

"Then maybe they made him kill that woman," added Samantha.

Amanda spoke up. "You can't *make* anyone kill someone else, Sam. Not really. Dad was the one who pulled the trigger."

Amanda's features were calm and her eyes intelligent. After she spoke she looked at her mother, whose gaze was pointed at her lap.

"Amanda!" snapped Jules, who glanced quickly at her mother.

Samantha said, "That is so out of line."

"No," said Ellie Dabney. "Your sister's right. Your father *did* pull the trigger. He made that choice. No one else."

Jules and Samantha stared at their mother as though they didn't recognize her.

Ellie looked over at Decker. "I don't know that woman. And I don't know what Walt had in that safe deposit box."

To Decker the woman's demeanor had changed dramatically from the day before. Maybe it was the sight of another woman accompanying her husband to access a safe deposit box, the contents of which were unknown to her. She now seemed resigned, confused, and angry. Perhaps even betrayed.

Decker said, "Could that woman be someone your husband works with? Does she resemble anyone from his office?" He looked at all the Dabney women.

"Not anyone that I recognize," volunteered Jules. "But I'm not really that familiar with the people that work there."

Samantha and Amanda simply shook their heads.

Decker next looked at Ellie. She cleared her throat and spoke in the slow, halting manner of someone coming off powerful sedatives. "I would only see some of his colleagues at the holidays. I rarely went to his office. And not in the last five years." She added wistfully, "I...I guess I had really lost touch with that part of his life." She glanced around at the opulent interior of her home.

Decker could read the thought in her mind.

I just enjoyed the fruits of his labors.

Samantha said, "Could the woman in the video be this Anne Berkshire?"

Decker shook his head. "Not even close."

"So this video didn't help at all," said Jules. "You're back at square one."

"No, it did help," said Decker.

"How?" Jules demanded.

"It shows us a possible reason for why your father did what he did."

"But you don't even know if what's shown in the video is even connected to the shooting," said Jules.

"We actually do know that it is," said Decker. "Your father sent you the key to the box *before* this bank video was taken. I think he wanted you to know what was in it. But this woman, and/or whoever else is connected to this, didn't want that to happen. So they made him empty the box before you ever had the chance to access it. And that means they knew about the box somehow. And they knew or perhaps suspected that he had sent a key to someone." He paused. "And there's something else."

He clicked some keys on the laptop they had used to show the video. He moved it forward until they could see Walter Dabney looking directly at the camera.

Ellie glanced away, apparently unable to take her late husband staring at her.

"Okay, why is that important?" asked Jules.

"Because I was there when your dad killed Berkshire. And when I ordered him to put the gun down he turned around and looked at me." He pointed at the screen. "And he had the exact same look on his face."

All four Dabney women now glanced back at the screen.

"And what does that look show?" asked Ellie breathlessly.

"Not to be overly dramatic, but it shows that he was resigned to his fate," replied Decker.

CHAPTER

14

"SHE WAS VERY good. Quiet, but everyone respected her. And she was an excellent teacher."

Decker and Jamison were sitting across from Virginia Cole, the principal of the Catholic school where Berkshire had been a substitute teacher. It was in Fairfax County, in an old brick building. But Decker had noted the new-looking surveillance cameras as they pulled into the parking lot.

They had signed in at the front office, gotten visitor badges, and been escorted to the principal's office.

Cole was in her fifties, with glasses on a chain and bleached blonde hair. She sat back and looked out the window of her office. "I really can't believe she's dead."

"And Berkshire had worked here four years?" asked Jamison.

"Yes, that's right," replied Cole.

"I assume she needed to have a background check and possess a teacher's certificate," said Decker.

"Of course. The Diocese is very strict on that. We ran a background check. That's standard. And she had a teacher's certificate. Her résumé was all in order. She had excellent credentials. We were lucky to have her."

"So her résumé went back farther than ten years?" asked Decker.

Cole looked at him confusedly. "What? Well, of course, we needed to see that she had graduated from college. And had the requisite teaching experience."

Decker glanced at Jamison. "We'll need to see all that," he said.

"I'll get you a copy of the file."

"Did you know Berkshire well?"

"I wouldn't say well. I never saw her outside of school. But I've talked to her a number of times within these walls."

"Did you know that she was rich?" asked Decker.

"Rich?" Cole once more looked confused.

"She lived in a penthouse in Reston worth two million dollars."

Cole looked stunned. "No, I never knew that. I've never been to her home. I saw her drive into work one day. I think it was a rather beat-up Honda."

"Did she ever talk about her past? Where she came from? What she did?"

"No. But as I said, her background checked out fine. Nothing of interest, no red flags."

"Did she have any friends here? Someone she might have confided in?"

"I'm not sure. I can check. She might have socialized with some of the other teachers."

Jamison said, "That would be great. Here's a number you can reach us at." She handed across a card.

Cole took it and glanced at Decker. "If you had asked me before all this happened, I would have said that Anne Berkshire was the last person on earth to be involved in something like this."

"Well, maybe that was intentional on her part," said Decker.

"You mean it was all a façade?" asked Cole.

"I mean if she had a secret past, she would have every

incentive to keep it secret. But then again, she might have simply been in the wrong place at the wrong time. Unfortunately, that happens far too often."

They were given a copy of Berkshire's employment file before they left. Decker tucked it under his arm. On their way back to their car his phone buzzed. It was Faye Thompson, Walter Dabney's partner.

"Our travel department did not schedule that trip for him," said Thompson. "And he didn't use the corporate card for any travel. He might have used his personal card."

"We'll check that," said Decker. "And did you find out what happens to the firm now that Dabney is dead?"

"Yes. I spoke with our in-house counsel. Walter's partnership interest goes half to Mrs. Dabney and half to the four children, in equal amounts."

"So together they control the company?"

"Yes."

"We have a video of a woman with Dabney at his bank. I'll send it to you. I want you and the people at your office to look at it and tell us if you recognize her."

"At Walter's bank?"

"Yes."

"Okay. Does this have to do with what happened?"

"I can't tell you. I'm just in collecting-stuff mode."

"Agent Decker, do you know if a memorial service has been planned for Walter?"

"No, I don't know. You might want to check with his wife for that."

"It's just that I wasn't sure if they would want to do one, what with the circumstances of his... You know, the papers are going to have a field day as it is. We've already gotten calls from the *Post*, CNN, the *Wall Street Journal*, and a slew of others. I don't know what to tell them."

"Then don't return their calls."

"But then they'll write the story anyway, and without our input it might be pretty bad. We have tons of government contracts. With Walter doing what he did, there's the possibility the Feds might terminate some or all of them."

"Sorry, that's not my department." He clicked off and looked at Jamison.

"Anything?" she asked.

"Other than her worrying far more about the firm's ass than her *really good* friend shooting someone and then killing himself, not really. Dabney booked this mysterious trip on his own. And his wife and kids share his partnership interest. So they control the company."

"That would be a good motive to kill him, if he hadn't killed himself," said Jamison.

"What would drive a seemingly rock-solid guy like Dabney to murder someone and then shoot himself? I get that he was terminal, but that's a little much."

"Someone must have been holding a sword over his head. The woman on the video probably indicates that."

"Maybe," said Decker, though he didn't look convinced.

"What are we going to do now?"

He held up the file. "You're going to drive to someplace we can get some food, and I'm going to read."

* * *

Decker wedged himself into the front seat of Jamison's subcompact; he had to push the seat as far back as it would go, but his knees were still uncomfortably close to the dash.

As she drove off, he opened the file and started to read. Every word he took in was permanently imprinted onto his memory. The file wasn't long, but it was instructive.

"She had passed a background check, which meant there was no criminal history for the woman." He shuffled through some pages. "Okay, we couldn't find anything for her from over ten years ago, but the file says she has her teacher's certificate. And it also showed that she held undergraduate and master's degrees from Virginia Tech."

"So we know she has a past, then."

"Well, yeah. But why couldn't Bogart find it when he did his search? I have to believe the FBI has a few more resources than a Catholic high scho—Wait a minute."

"What?"

He held up a page. "The file lists her name as Ann Berkshire."

"Okay."

"Her driver's license, which was used to run her background check, lists her as Anne with an *e* on the end."

"Wouldn't someone have noticed that?"

"Apparently they didn't. Lots of people wouldn't, in fact. Her Social Security number is on here. We'll have to check it with the one that Bogart came up with. Since he couldn't find her educational history on his search I have to assume that something's off. Driver's licenses in Virginia don't use the Social Security number as the ID number anymore. Probably no state does. Yet it should have brought up all the stuff in this file from some database. But it didn't."

"So is the background in that file even hers, then? Or someone else's?"

"I don't know, but the degrees listed are in engineering. Computer engineering."

"Is that important?"

"I have no idea. It also says she worked for twelve years at Ravens Consulting." He got on his phone and did a quick search. "Okay, Ravens is now defunct. Ten years back."

"Lots of companies go belly up."

"And why do I think if we try to check on that we'll find no one from Ravens Consulting who will confirm that she worked there?"

"This is so weird."

"So her past is an enigma. And maybe a fake one. But she's apparently fifty-nine, obviously rich, and also a part-time volunteer for hospice patients and a substitute teacher at a Catholic school even though she doesn't need the money." He glanced at Jamison. "What does that suggest to you?"

"That she lucked out somewhere, maybe in her business career, and is now giving back?"

"Close, but not quite how I see it," said Decker thoughtfully.

"Well then, how do you see it?"

But Decker had gone back to reading and didn't answer her.

They pulled into the parking lot of a restaurant. Decker kept reading the file as he and Jamison walked into the place. They sat at a table near a window. While Jamison gazed out, Decker closed his eyes and began whirring through frames in his memory vault. When he opened them, Jamison was tapping keys on her phone.

"Something from Bogart?" asked Decker, glancing at her phone.

She shook her head. "The apartment building."

"What apartment building?"

"The one we live in, Decker. I *do* manage it."

"Do you really think you can do that *and* work at the FBI too?"

"Yes, I can. And I want to very much, so I'm going to make it work. I don't want to spend my entire life chasing a paycheck. I like working at the FBI because we're helping people who need it. But most, if not all, of them are already dead. I'm trying to be a little more proactive with what I'm doing with the building. You try to help people so they never need the FBI in the first place."

He picked up the menu, looked longingly at all the fat-laden pages of food, and then glanced up to see Jamison staring at him.

"You're looking so much healthier, Decker."

"Yeah, so you keep telling me."

She gave him an impish grin.

When the waitress came he ordered unsweetened iced tea, a Greek salad with oil and vinegar dressing on the side, and a bowl of vegetable soup.

"Good boy," said Jamison with a smirk.

When the food came, Decker said suddenly, "Honda."

"What?"

"The principal at the school said Berkshire had a beat-up Honda."

Jamison lowered her fork. "That's right. She did."

"Berkshire has a Mercedes convertible sitting in the underground parking garage of her condo building. She's barely driven it."

"So she must have another car, this Honda."

"No. It wasn't listed in her information at the condo building, just the Benz. She was only assigned one parking space because she only had one car. With the size of her condo she could have had two spaces, but she required only the one."

"That's odd."

"Apparently, everything about the woman is odd."

"So maybe it wasn't a random shooting. Maybe Dabney *did* kill her for a specific reason."

"Oh, I believe he did. But I have a hunch it's for a reason none of us are thinking of right now."

"It would have made things so much easier if Berkshire had been the woman on the video with Dabney at the bank," she said wistfully.

Decker gave her a dubious look. "If you want easy, Alex, I think you picked the wrong profession."

CHAPTER

15

Six in the morning. The capital city was blessed by a crisp breeze. The sky was cloudy and the promise of rain was in every air molecule.

Decker was sitting on the front steps of his apartment building drinking his first cup of morning coffee. He had risen especially early, showered, and dressed in faded jeans and his Ohio State pullover. His scraggly hair was still damp. He sipped his coffee and occasionally closed his eyes, letting his perfect memory roll back over the last few days, looking for something that would give him traction on this case.

But each time, he opened his eyes with the firm conclusion that his memory was actually perfectly imperfect, because nothing had occurred to him.

The door opened behind him and two people stepped out.

Tomas Amaya had on his work clothes: corduroy pants, heavy work boots, and a denim shirt with a white T-shirt underneath. A San Diego Chargers football cap was on his head, his curly brown hair poking out from under it. His hard hat was in his right hand.

Danny had on jeans and a navy blue sweater. His school bag was over his shoulder. He looked sleepy and his chin drooped against his slender chest. As Decker moved aside to let them pass, Danny yawned deeply.

Tomas nodded at Decker and then glanced quickly away. Decker watched as the pair headed to the old car with the garbage bag windows. Danny put his bag in the backseat as Tomas opened the driver's side door.

Decker heard a car coming fast and turned his attention to the right.

Tomas evidently heard it too, because he called out to Danny in Spanish. The little boy jumped into the passenger seat while his father pulled out his keys and slid into the driver's seat. He hadn't even managed to close his door before a Camaro slid to a stop in front of the beat-up car. Two men climbed out, one large and one small. Pistols were in their waistbands. The large man was white, the small one Hispanic. The small man had on a suit with a vest but no tie. His dress shirt was buttoned all the way to the top. The large man had on cammie pants, a long-sleeved compression shirt outlining an impressive physique, and what looked like combat boots.

The small man walked over to the driver's side while his partner stood in front of the car, his hand on top of his pistol.

A string of spoken Spanish made Tomas Amaya get out of the car. He stood there staring at his feet.

The small man coolly appraised him, cocking his head from side to side and then smiling. Then he called the other man over.

The white guy took two long strides to reach them. Then, without warning, he clocked Tomas so hard that he flew backward and landed on the hood of the car. The guy stepped forward and cocked his fist back to deliver another blow.

"Hold it right there!"

The two men looked over at an advancing Decker. His pistol was out and aimed at them, and his FBI creds were held up in his other hand.

"FBI. Guns down, on the pavement, hands interlocked behind your heads. Now!"

Instead the two men ran for their car, jumped in, and tattooed rubber on the pavement as their smoking tires gained traction and they hurtled backwards out of the parking lot, hit a sharp J-turn, and then the driver floored it. Within a few seconds they were out of sight.

Decker raced over to Tomas, who was still slumped on the hood.

"Dad!" called out Danny as he jumped out of the car and ran to his father.

Decker holstered his weapon and helped Tomas to sit up. "You okay?" he asked.

Tomas nodded and rubbed the blood off his mouth. When he looked up at Decker, his features hardened. "I'm fine."

"You sure? He hit you pretty hard. You might have a concussion."

"I'm fine!"

Tomas pushed off the hood, staggered momentarily, and then regained his balance. He barked at his son, "*Entrar en el coche*."

"Wait a minute," said Decker. "Who were those guys?"

Tomas glanced at him. "It is nothing to do with you. I will deal with it."

"But I can help you. I'm with the—"

"*No necesito ayuda!*"

Tomas got in the car and started it up. Decker had to jump back as he slammed the car into gear and screeched out of the parking lot, leaving Decker to stare after them.

He caught a glimpse of Danny looking back at him, and then the car turned the corner and, like the Camaro, disappeared.

Decker walked back over to the front steps, picked up his cup of coffee, and walked back inside. "So much for a relaxing morning," he muttered.

As he stepped inside his apartment, Jamison was leaning against the kitchen sink yawning and rubbing her hair. She was still in her sleepwear—shorts and a T-shirt. Decker could hear the Keurig machine doing its thing.

Jamison yawned again. "Did you hear like a car racing by or something?"

"Or something," said Decker as he rinsed his cup and put it in the dishwasher.

"So you know anything else about Tomas and Danny?" he asked.

"Like what?"

"Like is he in a gang or something?"

She shot him a startled look. "What, why do you ask that?"

"Because two guys with guns just tried to shake him down. One of them nearly knocked his head off."

"What! Is that what I heard?"

Decker nodded. "I intervened with my gun and creds, but the assholes didn't stick around to get read their rights. When I tried to help Tomas he told me to mind my own business."

"Did you get the license plate of the car?"

"Gee, why didn't I think of that?" Decker said dryly.

"Well, we can run it and find out who those guys are."

"They seemed to have a problem with Tomas. And the fact that he wants no help might mean he doesn't have clean hands."

"That's a big leap of logic, Decker."

"Not that big," he retorted. "The fact that two guys he obviously knows showed up with guns and tried to beat his brains out might suggest there is an issue there."

Jamison made her coffee before answering. She took a sip and said, "I'm not awake enough to intelligently discuss this."

"Okay, when you are, let's talk about it. And you might want to let Melvin know."

"Why Melvin? I'm the manager."

"And it's his money and building."

She sighed. "I'll call him. Are you going to run the plate?"

"I will. But I'm not sure what else I can do. It's not my case. We can pass it on to the local cops?"

"But if Tomas *is* involved in something bad...?"

"What do you want me to do, Alex? I don't have a magic wand to make the world all perfect."

"Why don't you run the plate but don't tell the local cops. Maybe we'll have time to run something down. And I can talk to Tomas and see if he'll open up to me."

"From the look on the guy's face this morning you'd have a better shot at flying out that window."

"I can try."

"Alex, these guys are dangerous. You don't want to get mixed up in this."

"Oh, because my day job is so full of peace and quiet?" she shot back.

He sighed and leaned against the counter. "You don't want to bring trouble to where you live. I know that better than most."

Her features softened. "I know what happened to your family, Amos. But you can't blame yourself for that."

"All I'm saying is tread lightly. And don't do anything dangerous. And if you're even thinking of treading close to that line, make sure I'm with you, okay?"

"Okay."

He gave her a long look and then said, "I'll always have your back, Alex."

Before she could answer he turned and walked away.

CHAPTER

16

HARPER BROWN.

That's what the visitor's nametag said.

Decker and Jamison had walked into a small conference room at the Hoover Building and found Brown sitting next to Bogart and across from Milligan.

Brown was about five-seven, lean and fit, with blonde hair down to her shoulders. She wore a black pleated skirt, a white blouse, and high heels. Decker put her age at late thirties. The face was mostly unlined except for a trio of creases in the middle of her forehead, which made Decker think that she either frowned a lot or thought deeply a great deal, or frowned when she thought deeply.

She smiled when she saw Decker, rose, and held out her hand.

"Amos Decker, your reputation precedes you."

There was a southern twang to her words that Decker placed somewhere between Tennessee and Mississippi.

Decker shook her hand and glanced questioningly at Bogart.

"Agent Brown is with a sister agency. She called last night and asked for this meeting."

Decker and Jamison sat down after Brown shook hands with her too.

"What sister agency?" asked Decker.

"DIA."

"Defense Intelligence Agency," replied Decker.

"That's right," said Brown.

Decker said, "You're like the military's CIA, only your global reach is arguably bigger."

"And how did you come by that knowledge?" asked Brown, her smile not quite reaching her eyes.

"I like to Google as much as the next person. Are you with the Clandestine Service, the Attaché Systems, or the Cover Office?"

"I doubt you have the security clearances to hear the answer."

"There's no doubt about it. I *don't* have the security clearances to hear it."

"Amazing what's on the Internet these days," interjected Milligan, glancing nervously between the two as they stared stonily across the table at each other.

Bogart cleared his throat and said, "Agent Brown has some things to share on the Dabney-Berkshire matter. Things that we apparently *are* cleared for."

Decker sat back and looked expectantly at her. "That would be helpful. All we have right now are lots of unanswered questions."

Brown said, "I can't promise to answer all of them, but I think I can give some clarity to certain pieces."

She put her elbows on the table and assumed a more businesslike look. "Walter Dabney has been involved in a lot of high-level government contracting work."

"We know that," said Milligan.

"But you don't know of the work I'm going to tell you about."

She pursed her lips, took a few moments to marshal her

thoughts, and plunged ahead. "Walter Dabney was apparently not the patriotic citizen that people believed he was."

"What does that mean?" asked Bogart.

"That means that he was selling secrets to our enemies."

Jamison glanced at Decker, whose gaze held steadfastly on Brown.

She continued, "We don't believe that he was a true spy in the sense that he wanted to bring America down."

"Then what was his motivation?" asked Milligan.

"Gambling debts. They were enormous."

"We don't have any record of him being a gambler," said Bogart. "Trips to Vegas, or—"

Brown cut in, "There are many ways to gamble, Agent Bogart. Nowadays you don't have to get on a plane and fly to Vegas or go out to the racetrack. All you need is an Internet connection. And the losses can be staggering. And he had to pay them off."

"By selling secrets," said Jamison.

"Yes."

"What sorts of secrets?" asked Decker.

She looked at him. "*Classified* secrets. But I can tell you that they involve multiple contracts that his firm was working on across a half dozen DOD and civilian agency platforms."

"So serious matters," said Bogart.

"Very serious."

"Did anyone else at his firm know about this?" asked Bogart.

"We don't believe so, but we're still looking into it."

"So why kill himself?" asked Jamison.

"We were closing in," she replied. "He saw it coming."

"You took a while to come forward on this," said Decker.

"This has been a very sensitive and long-running investigation. But after assessing the situation, the decision was made to send me here to convey certain information. We didn't want you to be spinning your wheels unnecessarily."

"And why kill Anne Berkshire?" asked Decker.

She scrutinized him. "I understand that you have hyperthymesia. And synesthesia. From a football injury."

"And does that somehow explain why he killed Anne Berkshire?" Decker said impassively.

"No, just making an observation. As to Berkshire, we believe that she was in the wrong place at the wrong time."

"And so why kill her if he was going to kill himself?" asked Decker. "What was she in the wrong place for? Him going nuts?"

"It's difficult to fully understand what's going through the mind of a person who's about to lose everything. Dabney was under enormous pressure. It's highly possible that he just snapped. Or he thought she might be with the FBI, since they were right outside the Hoover Building. He may have been paranoid at that point."

"And it's also possible that you're wrong," said Decker.

"He *was* stealing secrets and he *did* it because of gambling debts," retorted Brown.

"Granted, that might be the case. But you could still be wrong about why he killed Berkshire."

"Do you have a theory?"

"No. But when I do you can be pretty certain it'll be the correct one."

"You seem very sure of yourself, Mr. Decker."

"Well, if I can't be, who can?"

"Right," said Bogart suddenly. "We appreciate the information, Agent Brown. Where do we go from here?"

She slowly turned to him. "I think, for you, nowhere. This is an active DIA case. We're pursuing all possible leads. This is a national security matter and thus anyone investigating it must have the proper security clearances." She glanced at Decker. "Which, unfortunately, leaves you out."

Decker ignored this and said, "What do you know about Berkshire?"

"What?"

"You must have investigated her. We found some curious elements about her past. You must have done the same."

"What we have found or not is an internal DIA matter. I only came here today as a courtesy to a sister agency."

"And to tell us we're off the case," added Decker.

She looked directly at him. "Without getting into too much detail, I can tell you that the secrets that Dabney stole compromise strategic assets of this country. If certain of our enemies gain access to this information it could be 9/11 again, only far worse."

"That's a big statement," said Bogart, staring at her in amazement. "If things are that dire, our agencies cooperating may be the best strategy."

Brown rose. "Thank you for your time. I would appreciate any files you have collected be sent over to my office, Agent Bogart. You can use the contact information I've already provided."

She had turned to leave when Decker spoke.

"I saw Walter Dabney shoot Berkshire. And I saw him try to blow his head off."

She turned back to look at him. "And your point?"

"I'm not sure you're cleared for it."

She gave him a tight smile, pivoted on her heels, and walked out.

Bogart looked over at him. "We might need to give you a refresher course in interagency etiquette."

Decker said, "Then make sure Agent Brown attends it too. So what's our next step?"

"Next step in what?"

"The Dabney case."

"Decker, didn't you just hear the woman? We're off the case."

"I heard someone from DIA come here and tell the FBI that they're off the case. I haven't heard anyone from the FBI tell us that."

Bogart started to say something but remained silent.

Milligan said, "I think Decker has a point, Ross. And far worse than 9/11? Our mission is to protect the United States. If the Bureau's not going to be involved in something potentially this big, then what the hell are we doing?"

Jamison added, "I think so too. And can I just say that I do not like that woman one teeny little bit."

Bogart stirred. "I can't say I much like her or getting thrown off a case that happened right on Bureau territory. If the stakes are this big we can keep going, but we have to do so cautiously. Any misstep and we could get in trouble. And that won't help anything."

Decker rose.

Bogart said, "Where are you going?"

"To find a beat-up Honda."

17

"I'LL ALWAYS HAVE your back too, Amos."

He and Jamison were in her car.

His knees jammed against the dashboard, he turned to look at her. "I know you will. Have you talked to Melvin yet?"

"I left a message. I haven't heard back yet. What did you think of this Harper Brown?"

"She's apparently good at what she does."

"Which is what exactly?"

"Bullshitting."

"So you don't believe what she said?"

"She works in the intelligence field. They're trained to lie and sell it like the truth. They obviously undergo the same indoctrination as politicians."

"So if she's lying, that complicates an already complicated situation."

"Yes, it does."

"But why would she lie?"

"She may not be entirely lying. Dabney might have been

selling secrets. Maybe he had a gambling habit. But the reason for killing Berkshire doesn't make sense."

"But he was terminal. Maybe he was on meds. Maybe the cancer messed with his brain."

"And *maybe*, Alex, the truth lies in another direction."

A frustrated Jamison refocused on the road. "How are we going to find her Honda?" she said tersely.

"We've only heard one person mention the Honda. So that means we're going back to school."

"You mean Virginia Cole, the principal."

"Yes."

"But she basically just saw her drive in one day, she said. Do you really think she got the license plate number?"

"I doubt she did."

"Okay, then what's your idea?"

"I plan to consult an eyewitness."

Jamison continued to pepper him with questions. What eyewitness? What was he thinking? But Decker only closed his eyes and said nothing.

* * *

When they got to the school Decker pointed at the doors to the office, where surveillance cameras were aimed at the parking lot.

"Crap," said Jamison. "I didn't notice them before."

"Most schools have them now," said Decker. "Some schools have metal detectors and armed guards and armed teachers and armed students. Welcome to education in the twenty-first century."

They spoke with Cole and she led them back to the office where her technical support staff worked. One of the techs pulled the recorded feeds from the surveillance cameras and put them up on a computer screen.

Decker asked Cole, "Do you remember the date when you saw her drive the Honda in? Just ballpark?"

Cole thought for a few moments. "Within the last two weeks. It would have been in the morning, around seven-thirty."

The tech hit some keys and said, "I put those time parameters in. You can use these keys to move through the frames."

"Thanks," said Jamison as Decker settled himself in front of the computer.

Cole asked, "Do you know if there have been any funeral arrangements made for Anne?"

Decker didn't answer.

Jamison said quickly, "I'm afraid we don't know that information. The thing is we haven't been able to locate any family members. Do you know of any?"

"No, she never talked about her family. On our employment form we have a section for a point of contact in case of emergency. She left it blank. She never really talked about her past, actually. At least not to me. I do have the name of one teacher who might be able to tell you more. She's not in today, but I can have her contact you."

"Great. Thank you."

"Absolutely. Anything that will help us get to the bottom of all this."

Cole and the tech then left them alone.

Jamison pulled up a chair and sat next to Decker as he used the keys to fast-forward through the frames of video. She eyed him curiously. "Is that how your memory works, Decker? Flashing frames like that?"

"Pretty much," he said absently. "Only mine are in color."

He stopped advancing the video and pointed at the screen.

"There she is."

It was indeed Anne Berkshire in her dark Honda Accord. As Cole had earlier told them, it *was* beat-up. A front fender was knocked in, the passenger door had a long scrape, and there were some rust spots on the hood.

"And there's the license plate number," said Decker, who memorized it on the spot even as Jamison wrote it down.

Berkshire pulled into an empty space, got out, and opened the rear door to retrieve her small briefcase and purse. She walked toward the door and thus toward the cameras.

"God," said Jamison with a shiver. "Knowing she's dead, this is creeping me out."

Decker looked at the time stamp on the film. "Ten days ago."

"She looks…normal enough. Not like anything's weighing on her mind," observed Jamison.

"You mean like a spy ring about to be cratered," said Decker. "And she arrested for espionage?"

Jamison snapped her fingers. "Maybe that's where she got the money."

"Maybe. But Agent Brown didn't tell us how long this had been going on. And we still can't find a connection between Berkshire and Dabney."

"Well, Dabney obviously had another life that was invisible to those who knew him. Maybe Berkshire was also a gambler and they met that way."

"Right, pick someone with a gambling addiction like yourself to convey secrets to. I'm sure nothing could go wrong there."

"It's still possible," persisted Jamison.

"But why would he need her, Alex? What skill set or advantage does a substitute teacher offer to a connected guy like Dabney who's selling government secrets?"

"Maybe teaching is a cover. Maybe she's an *actual* spy. That's why we can't find anything on her going back past ten years."

"That might be," said Decker, though his tone evidenced he was not convinced of this. "We need to run the plate."

"You think it's registered to someone else?"

"No, I don't. I think it's registered to Anne Berkshire, just under another address. And maybe another name."

"So you *do* think she's a spy or something."

"Or something," replied Decker.

When she looked at him he added, "Brown said that critical secrets were stolen by Dabney. He had to pass them along to someone. If they were working together, you're right, Berkshire had to be part of some spy ring. If she didn't pass the secrets on yet, we might be able to stop the apocalypse that Brown was describing."

"But if she was a spy why wouldn't she have passed on the secrets by now?"

"There could be any number of reasons."

Jamison added, "And pray that our enemies don't have them already. Or else we're in deep shit." She paused. "You don't think Brown was talking nukes, do you?"

Decker looked at her. "Keep saying prayers, because I don't know if she was or not. But the lady didn't strike me as someone who overstates the case. So her worst-case scenario is probably Armageddon."

"Wonderful."

"DAMN!"

Todd Milligan stood shoulder to shoulder with Decker as they surveyed the house the next morning.

The rundown on the Honda's license plate had led them here. A ramshackle farm cottage down a rural road in the middle of Loudoun County, Virginia.

Decker nodded at Milligan's exclamation. "From multimillion-dollar condo smack in the middle of upscale suburbia to this."

"But why would she even have this place, Decker?"

Decker started walking toward the house. "That's what we're here to find out. But Berkshire's starting to strike me as someone who had a purpose behind every act. So let's start with that notion and see where it takes us."

There was a small outbuilding behind the cottage, more a lean-to than anything else. But inside it was the Honda.

"We might need a warrant to search the house and car," Milligan pointed out.

"The only person able to object is dead," replied Decker.

He tried the car door but it was locked. "The keys might be in the house," he said.

They trooped to the front door. It was also locked.

Decker leaned his heavy shoulder against it and it was no longer locked.

They stepped inside and the old wooden plank floors creaked ominously under their weight. The air was musty and the room was chilly.

Milligan pointed to a fireplace in the front room. "That might be the only source of heat."

"No, there was an aboveground oil tank at the rear, and there's a radiator against the wall over there, though none of that may be working."

They walked through the three rooms. The kitchen had an ancient, empty fridge, a small stove, and a sink with stains. Decker turned on the water and a small blob of brown gunk came out.

He poked his head into the sole bathroom. There was a toilet, a cracked mirror, a roll of toilet paper on the wall, and that was about it. The bathtub/shower had no curtain and there were rust stains on the linoleum, which was curled up in innumerable places. Decker flushed the toilet. Nothing happened. He tried a light switch. Again, nothing.

"Okay, I doubt she was actually living here," he said. "No water and no working bathroom and no juice."

Milligan gazed around. "I wonder if she even owned this place. It looks abandoned. Maybe she just used it as sort of a hideout."

"Which raises the question of who she was hiding from. And if she was hiding, why buy a multimillion-dollar condo and expensive car, work at a school, and volunteer at a hospice? All that puts you out in the public eye."

"My wife's a schoolteacher. And while I know she loves working with the kids, if she had millions in the bank, she might be doing something else."

"What grade does she teach?"

"Eighth. Where kids make the jump from nice, innocent kids to something a lot more complicated and emotional drama runs deep and hormones are out of control. Some days she comes home looking like she got hit by a bus."

"In my book, all teachers are underpaid," said Decker.

There were wooden steps leading down to a dank cellar. The floor down there was dirt. Milligan had pulled out his flashlight and shone it around.

Behind massive cobwebs there were wooden planks set on top of cinderblocks, forming crude shelving. Stacked on the planks were rotting cardboard boxes. Decker opened each of them and Milligan pointed his light inside.

"Junk," said Milligan, after examining old lamps and ragged magazines and broken bric-a-brac. "I bet all this belonged to the former owners," he added.

Decker nodded absently. He looked around the small space, his gaze, with the aid of Milligan's powerful light, reaching into each corner.

"I bet she's never even been down here," noted Milligan.

"No, she has."

"How do you know that?"

"Point your light at the steps coming down."

Milligan did so and saw the new wood that had replaced boards that had obviously rotted away.

"The cellar door also had a new hinge on it." Decker took the flashlight from Milligan and aimed it at a patch of dirt in a far corner.

Milligan drew closer and said, "Footprints. Small. A woman's."

"Berkshire's."

"Good eye, Decker," said Milligan.

Decker didn't seem to hear him. He leaned against the stone wall of the cellar and cast the light beam around. The illumination flitted over the walls and rough ceiling like a horde of fireflies.

"So why would she come down here?" asked Milligan.

"To hide something. We just have to find the place."

Milligan glanced toward the door. "Wait a minute. If the Honda is here, how did she come and go from this place?"

"There's a small clearing on the right side when you enter the road this house is on. There were tire marks on it. My hunch is she'd drive the Mercedes here, park, and then walk. She might not have come that often, only when she taught class and needed the Honda, so that would jibe with the low mileage on the Mercedes. Then she'd reverse that path, leave the Honda here, and drive off in the Mercedes."

"But why do that at all?"

"A substitute teacher arriving in a six-figure luxury car would no doubt invite gossip among the teachers, staff, and students. And I don't think Berkshire liked to encourage attention. It's why she kept to herself."

Milligan nodded. "I guess you're right. But she *did* have the car and the condo."

"Which means the woman didn't dislike living in the lap of luxury. And maybe she enjoyed the secret double life she was leading. It might have been quite a kick for her."

Decker kept gazing around. He looked at the spot in the dirt where the footprints were. Then he looked at the new planks on the crude shelving. Then he gazed upward at the cellar door with new hinges.

A moment later he pushed his bulk off the wall and rushed up the stairs.

"Decker!" Milligan called out. He hurried after him.

By the time Milligan reached the doorway Decker had disappeared down the hall. Milligan found him in the bathroom.

"What is it?" Milligan asked.

"Why have a roll of toilet paper if the toilet doesn't even work?"

Decker reached down and popped the roll off the holder. He set it down on the sink. The tube the toilet paper had been mounted on was the usual kind, with a spring keeping the two ends together inside the wall holder.

Decker separated the two ends and the car keys dropped into the palm of his hand.

"The Honda," he said. He looked inside the tube. "And that's not all." He dug inside the hollow piece and slid out a flash drive.

"Damn, Decker, you might have just hit the jackpot."

"Well, let's get to a computer and see."

"Sounds like a plan."

They went back outside. Decker took out the Honda keys and said, "I'll drive her car back. We didn't find anything of interest at her condo, so maybe something will be in the car that'll help." He held up the flash drive. "And this might answer all our questions."

They separated and Milligan climbed into the Bureau car.

Decker went to the Honda and had to put the car seat all the way back to accommodate his long legs. The car's interior was battered. Before Decker had climbed inside he had calculated that the vehicle was probably over fifteen years old. Then he had checked the glove box and found the original owner's manual that confirmed that the model was actually seventeen years old.

Milligan led the way down the dirt road to the asphalt one they had originally turned off from. Thick trees on either side of the road and the cloud cover overhead dissipated the light, turning things gloomy.

When Decker looked up, Milligan had already turned onto the asphalt road and had sped up. Decker pulled out onto the road.

"Shit."

The car was wobbling along.

He put it in park, got out, and looked down at the front tire. It was flat.

He glanced down the road. Milligan was already out of sight.

Decker pulled out his phone to call him and tell him what had happened.

The call did not go through because there was no service in this area.

"Shit again."

He popped the trunk, figuring that Milligan would finally notice he was not behind him and would circle back.

He got out the jack, lug wrench, and the spare.

When he knelt down in front of the tire, he saw it.

He had started to pull his gun when the blow hit him. He slumped forward, hit the front fender of the Honda with his face, and toppled sideways to the asphalt.

CHAPTER

19

"YOU NEED TO stop waking up in hospital beds."

Decker rapidly blinked his eyes and Alex Jamison's face came into tighter focus. The room was very dark.

He rubbed his head.

"Concussion," said Bogart, who was standing next to Jamison.

"Not my first one," said Decker, wincing as he sat up and moved around a bit.

Bogart added, "It's why the lights have been turned off. Doctors said your brain needs to rest and you need to avoid light."

Milligan was on the other side of the bed. "I'm sorry, Amos. I should have noticed sooner that you weren't behind me. But I was trying to make a call and it wouldn't go through."

Decker slowly nodded. "Someone shot the tire out," he said. "I noticed the entry hole on the tire's sidewall when I got down to change it."

"We saw that too," said Bogart.

"So they must have been watching us," said Milligan.

Decker said, "They took it, didn't they?"

Milligan said, "We searched your pockets. And we didn't find the flash drive, so yeah, they took it."

"How did they even know you found it?" asked Jamison.

"They either had the place bugged or they had some sort of long-range surveillance pointed at us," said Milligan. "Or they may have just searched you as a matter of course and found it."

Decker sat up more. "I held the flash drive up when we got out of the house. If they were watching they'd know that I had it, and not you." He paused. "When can I get out of here?"

Milligan said, "The doctors said you're good to go, you just have to take it easy for a few days. You have quite a knot on the back of your head. And you have some bruises on your face where you hit the car fender. But they did X-rays and other tests. There was no significant damage."

Jamison added with a smile, "The attending physician said you had a very hard head."

"That makes me feel so much better," growled Decker.

"So you saw nothing?" asked Bogart.

"No. They attacked from behind. I was down for the count. Whoever it was, they were good and fast."

"If they shot out the tire, I guess you're lucky they decided not to shoot you as well," said Bogart.

"That thought had occurred to me too."

"It was a long-range rifle round," added Milligan. "I don't know how far away the shot came from, but I didn't see anyone around when I drove down that road. If they fired from the woods it was a hell of a shot. If they fired from the road it was still a tough target."

"I didn't hear the shot," said Decker.

"Suppressed round, in all likelihood," said Milligan knowledgably. "With the noise that old Honda was making it would have been a miracle for you to hear the shot. I'm guessing the shooter was hundreds of yards away."

"So that means a professional," said Jamison.

Bogart added, "And it also means there was more than one person. A shooter that far away couldn't have reached you that quickly, and knocked you out, not without making noise."

Decker climbed out of the bed and stood a bit shakily, holding on to the bedside rail for support.

Bogart said, "I want you to go home and rest, Amos, and stay in a dark room."

"I can't sit out days on this, Ross! Worse than 9/11? Remember?"

"Okay, so long as you have no other complications, you can hit the trail again tomorrow. But for today, we're shutting you down."

Decker started to protest, but Jamison gripped his arm. "Let's go," she said in a voice that brooked no opposition.

* * *

An hour later Decker was lying on a sofa in their apartment with a cup of tea next to him on a table and dark glasses over his eyes.

Jamison looked down at him. "I know you're not happy about this."

"*That* is an understatement."

She sat in a chair next to him. "Hey, we need that big brain of yours, so you have to take care of it."

"Since it's the only one I have, I have an incentive to want to keep it too."

"What do you think was on the flash drive?"

"I have no idea. She took great pains to hide it, so whatever it was, it was important to Berkshire."

"If that is her real name."

"It is definitely not her real name."

"So you think her past is the reason for all that happened?"

"If it's not, it's a coincidence the size of Russia."

"And you don't believe in even small coincidences, I know."

He looked at the cup of tea, picked it up, and took a sip. "Todd ran the plate on the Camaro."

Jamison stiffened. "And?"

"And it was stolen from a couple who live in Woodbridge."

"Are you sure they're telling the truth?"

"Well, they're in their sixties. He's retired from the Forest Service and she's a Sunday school teacher. He bought the car as a retirement present to himself. Four days later it was gone from in front of his house. It was found trashed behind a strip mall in Annandale. The husband is understandably pissed, according to the local police."

"So a dead end, then? I mean the two guys in the car."

"It's not a dead end if Tomas will tell us who they are. Because he knows them, that's for certain."

"But you said he seemed to have no interest in doing that?"

"Well, it was a stressful time. He'd just gotten the crap kicked out of him. And I came on a little heavy with him. With the badge, gun, and all. He might just think I made matters worse. Like poking a hornets' nest. You might have better luck. *If* you want to try."

She looked at him strangely. "Is this a test to gauge my sincerity in helping our fellow tenants?"

"No, this is a test in how well you multitask. And you said you wanted to try to speak with him."

She nodded and sat back. "I know. You're right. How's your head? Really? Tell me the truth."

"I've been hit a lot harder, Alex. Don't worry about me.

But the thing is, Bogart was right. They could have easily shot and killed me. But they didn't."

"What does that tell you?"

"That they made a choice not to commit murder."

"Unlike Walter Dabney, who chose to do that very thing."

"Yes, he did. And I wish I knew why."

"We have clues. We have some leads."

"The clues keep eluding us. The leads keep falling away. That flash drive would have told us a lot. But now we'll never know."

"What I don't get is how did they even know you and Todd were going to be out there?"

"I don't think they did. The roads out there were pretty lonely and rural. We would have noticed someone following us."

"How, then?"

"I think they were already there. I think they found Berkshire's hiding place before we did and then set up surveillance on it. They apparently had already searched the place but didn't find anything. We came along and found what they were looking for. And then they took it. So we probably did them a big favor."

"We're talking manpower and resources."

Decker nodded. "And which also means it will be difficult to trace them. But it tells us for certain that Berkshire was involved with something pretty serious."

"But from her past?"

"Yes."

"So maybe these people have been looking for her?"

"They might have been, for years, perhaps. When she was killed her photo was all over the media. They might have recognized her."

"But how did they find her hiding place so fast? They seemed to beat you to it."

"Good question, to which I have no answer."

They sat in silence for a few moments before Decker looked at his watch. It was after four o'clock.

"The Amayas will be home soon."

"I know. When I found out Danny draws, I picked up a sketchpad and some charcoal pencils. Maybe I can use that as an excuse to visit."

"Works for me."

"And if he tells me who these guys are?"

"Then we'll see what we can do."

"He may be afraid to talk. They might try to harm him and Danny."

"They already *harmed* him. And I have to think they're just the muscle. Some of these local gangs are super-violent."

"Well, they know who you are too, Decker."

"I'm pretty hard to miss. But they know I'm with the FBI, so I doubt they'll come after us."

"That's not guaranteed."

"What in life is?"

She looked away. "I'll go and talk to them this evening."

"I'll go with you."

"But your concussion."

"My brain will have had plenty of time to rest by then."

"But I thought you wanted me to handle it."

"I'll let you do the talking. But like you said, I'm already involved after what happened. So I might as well follow it through."

She grinned weakly. "So this will be a test to see how well *you* multitask too."

"Let's hope we both pass," he answered.

20

Tomas Amaya did not look happy to see them standing in his doorway.

"Yes?" he said stiffly, staring at them. He had positioned himself so he was blocking their path into his apartment.

"Mr. Amaya, we met before. I'm Alex Jamison. I manage the building."

Behind him Decker could see Danny Amaya poke his head around the corner.

"Yes?" said Amaya again, still blocking the doorway.

"We understand that you had an issue with two men in the parking lot yesterday morning?"

"Is-shew? *No entiendo*," he added sharply.

"She means the guys who attacked you, Dad."

Amaya turned to see his son standing behind him, holding a sketchbook in his right hand and a pen in the other.

Amaya started speaking rapidly in Spanish to his son, who paled, turned, and raced back into the shallow depths of the small apartment.

Amaya turned back to Jamison and Decker. "I have no is-shew with nobody."

Before Jamison could respond, Decker said, "They attacked you, like your son said. The car they were in was stolen. They had guns. They're bad guys, obviously. We can help."

Amaya looked up at Decker. "I don't need nobody's help."

"You needed my help yesterday," replied Decker. "If I hadn't intervened, they might have killed you."

At this Amaya began to shut the door.

Decker wedged his big foot into the opening before it could fully close.

"What about your son, Mr. Amaya? What about Danny? What if they attack *him* next? You going to wait and let that happen?"

Amaya screamed, "*Vete ahora. Ahora!*"

Decker removed his foot and the door slammed shut.

Jamison scowled up at Decker. "Thanks for letting *me* do the talking."

"He's one scared and angry man," said Decker as they walked back up to their apartment.

They turned when they heard footsteps behind them. At first Decker thought it was Tomas Amaya, but it was Danny. He had on faded jeans, a white T-shirt that accentuated how thin he was, and ripped and dirty sneakers that were too large for his feet.

"Danny, are you okay?" asked Jamison.

He nodded. "I'm sorry for how my dad was."

"No need to be. He's obviously in a difficult situation."

"Do you know who those men were?" asked Decker.

Danny shook his head. "But I know my dad knows them. I've seen him talking to the shorter one in the parking lot. The big guy has been around too a few times. But my dad never lets me get near them."

"Until this morning," said Decker.

Danny nodded. "I was so scared. I . . . I didn't know what to do." He looked down. "I should have tried to help my dad, but I didn't." He looked up at them. "I'm not very brave, I guess."

"You're a kid," said Decker. "I'm a big guy and even I was scared. And I had a gun."

"Did your dad say anything to you about what those men wanted?" Jamison asked.

Danny shook his head. "One day my dad picked me up from school, but he had to go back to work for a bit. So he drove me there and I did my homework in the car. It's at a building he's working on near the waterfront. I saw the short man there. He passed in front of our car, but didn't see me. He had on a suit and a hard hat like my dad wears when he's working."

"He was wearing a suit yesterday morning. You think he works at the building?"

"Or maybe is one of the owners?" added Jamison.

"I don't know. He went up in one of the construction elevators."

"Where exactly is the building?" asked Decker.

Danny told him and then said, "I've got to get back."

"Wait a minute, Danny, I got this for you." She pulled the sketchpad and charcoal pencils out of her handbag.

He took them with a look of surprise. "Why?" he asked.

"I know you're an aspiring artist and I thought you could use them."

"Thanks."

Decker was studying the boy closely. "Where's your mother?"

Danny slid the pencils into his jeans pocket before answering. "She's dead."

"What happened to her?"

"She was killed. Before we came here."

"Killed? In an accident?"

"It wasn't an accident."

Before Decker could say anything else, Danny turned and rushed back down the stairs.

Decker and Jamison stood there for a few moments before turning and heading to their apartment. When they got there they sat in the living room area looking out the window. The sun had begun its descent, blistering the sky with red and gold.

"How's the multitasking going?" asked Jamison.

"I'm hungry. Let's go *multitask* dinner."

* * *

Walking, they reached a hole-in-the-wall place about a half mile from their apartment. It was a seat-yourself establishment and they took a table near a window facing the street. The place was only a quarter full. The menu was written on a chalkboard.

When the waitress came over, Decker said, "Cheeseburger medium, with the works, steak fries, and onion rings. And a Budweiser, full strength."

He looked almost defiantly at Jamison.

"Make it two," said Jamison, staring right back at him.

When their beers came, they each took a long drink before settling back in their chairs.

"No salad tonight?" asked Decker.

"There's lettuce and tomato on the burger, Decker. So what about the Amayas?"

He shrugged. "If the guy in the suit works at the construction site we can have him checked out."

"I wonder what his beef is with Tomas?"

"It could be lots of things."

"So we're going to try to help them, right?"

"I think the answer to that is pretty obvious, don't you? But we also can't let that distract us from our day job, Alex."

"I know, I know. And I can run some of the stuff down on the Amayas. But I won't do anything dangerous," she quickly added. She took another drink of her beer and set the bottle down on a coaster. "What do you really think was on that flash drive?" she asked.

"Answers to a lot of our questions about Anne Berkshire. Answers that now we don't have," he added grimly.

"We can find them another way, hopefully."

Decker did not look encouraged by that comment.

When their food came they ate in silence. As Jamison finished her last French fry she moaned and said, "I'm going to need to work out all week to compensate."

Decker eyed her. "Anne Berkshire had a stock and bond portfolio worth north of twenty million," he said. "Todd checked."

"Damn," said Jamison, licking salt off her fingers.

"The thing with financial accounts is you need Social Security numbers and valid personal information. And all of hers seemingly checked out, at least well enough for her to open an account with a management firm."

"Did she ever meet with anyone there?"

"Todd looked into that too. Because of the size of her portfolio she was assigned a person, a financial account manager, but he said he only met with her once. The office she opened it with is on the West Coast. And the interest and dividends from her portfolio poured directly into her checking account. And she'd pay her bills from that. She paid cash for the condo and the car, so her monthly bills weren't that much. The cash flow from the portfolio easily covered everything, with a lot left over."

"Must be nice," said Jamison ruefully. "Like I told you

before, when I look at my account at the end of the month, all I see are zeros. I don't know where my money goes, I really don't."

"Well, we know where Berkshire's went. She opened her current portfolio about eight years ago with ten million dollars. There were no other cash infusions by her. So it's more than doubled over that time, even with the outlays for the condo and car. Todd said that's entirely possible because the stock market's been on a tear the last seven or eight years. Apparently she put her money in companies like Amazon and Apple and Google and more recently Facebook. They're all up huge during that time period."

"Well, lucky her," said Jamison.

"Not so lucky since she's dead. The point is, her initial wealth seemed to come in a lump sum. I know there are laws in place that you have to show where money came from. If someone walked into, say, Merrill Lynch, with ten million and wanted to open an account, there would have to be questions answered and a record of where the money came from."

"You mean because of the possibility of money laundering?"

Decker nodded. "So she presumably passed the smell test with her current management firm. At least according to Todd. All of her records seemed to be in order. But when he checked into the background of those records—her old address, for instance—it didn't pan out."

"And the financial management firm didn't discover that?"

"I don't think they looked as hard as the FBI did. I mean, come on, it's not like they were going to work very hard to turn down a ten-million-dollar account."

"Right. But did they say where she told them the money came from?"

"Yes. Savings, investments, and a small inheritance."

"Okay."

"She bought the condo in Reston four years ago. The car was purchased a year after that. She lived in Atlanta previously and Seattle before that. At least we think she did. But we only have her past going back ten years. Before that, nothing. It's like she didn't exist. But then she has a résumé stretching back to college that passed the muster of the school's background check."

The dinner bill came and Decker paid it, refusing Jamison's offer to chip in.

"I corrupted you tonight," he said. "Let me pay for the privilege."

She smiled, a smile that faded as someone approached their table.

Harper Brown looked directly at Decker. She was dressed in jeans, a leather jacket, and a white blouse. Narrow-toed boots raised her height a few inches.

"Mr. Decker, I wonder if I could speak with you." She glanced at Jamison for an instant before staring back at Decker. "Alone."

"I can wait outside," said Jamison, not looking very happy.

"You can head on, Ms. Jamison. I can drive your friend home."

"I don't mind—"

Decker said, "I'm sure that'll be fine. And I probably won't even have to give directions, since I'm pretty sure you know exactly where I live."

Brown took a step back, smiled, and gestured to the door. "Shall we, then?" She glanced at Jamison. "Don't worry. I'll take exceptional care of your colleague."

"You better," said Jamison grimly.

21

THEY DROVE IN silence for five minutes.

She glanced at him. "You don't talk much, do you?"

"You said you wanted to talk to *me*. I'm waiting."

She smiled and looked ahead.

Brown's ride was a late-model BMW 7 Series sedan. He looked at the car's interior. "Nice car. This would be like almost two years' salary for me."

"I lease. It's a lot less financially onerous."

"I guess."

"And I tend to get tired of things after a few years."

"Then never get married."

"Are you still working the Dabney/Berkshire case?"

"You mean you haven't cracked it yet? What's taking DIA so long?"

She pulled to the curb and put the car in park. She turned to look at him.

"One of my assignments was to liaison with the Bureau. I'm trying my best to do that."

"I was under the impression that being a liaison involved more than kicking a 'sister' agency off a case."

"Is that what Agent Bogart thinks?"

"I don't know because I haven't asked him. I'm just telling you what *I* think."

"These are very delicate matters, Decker. We all must tread extremely carefully."

"Well, according to you, we can't tread any longer."

"I was speaking generally."

"Then let me speak specifically. Does DIA use guys who can shoot long-distance?"

She looked puzzled. "Out of all the possible questions I thought I might get from you, that was not one of them. Why in the world would you want to know that?"

"Let's chalk it up to my being a very curious guy. So does it?"

"We're a military support organization."

"So I'll take that as a yes."

She gazed at him curiously for a few moments. "I've read your file."

"I didn't know I had one."

"The moment you step on the federal playing field, you have a file. You have a fascinating background, what with the hyperthymesia and synesthesia."

"Some might call it fascinating, I wouldn't."

"What would you call it?"

"Different. *Painfully* different."

Brown's features lost some of their cocksure manner. "I know about your family. I'm very sorry. I've never been married or had children, so I could only imagine how devastating that had to have been for you."

Decker looked out the window. "All of this is pretty far afield from the matter at hand."

"Granted. But you still haven't answered my question about working on the case or not."

"And if I refuse to answer? Which I guess I'm entitled to do."

"Then I may take that as an answer in the affirmative."

"I wasn't aware that the DIA could tell the FBI to stop work on a case. Maybe I'm wrong."

"No, I doubt that you are wrong. At least technically. But other channels can be employed to make the directive more authoritative."

"You're speaking a different language. What the hell does that mean?"

"SecDef is cabinet-level. He makes a call to someone, and that party leans hard on the FBI director."

"So that's how it works in D.C.?"

"Pretty much. You're from Ohio."

"I know I am. The flyover land between the coasts."

"The land of deep mistrust in government."

"Well, can you blame us, when you pull shit like you're pulling now?"

"Don't think that we don't want to get to the truth, Decker. We do."

"So in order to do that you kick out an agency when they're trying to solve a murder right on their doorstep? And you're the one who said the outcome could be far worse than 9/11. What did you expect us to do with that? Sit on our hands and play nice?"

"I see your argument, I really do."

"But that's as far as you'll go?"

"Orders are orders. Don't you have to follow orders?"

"No," Decker said bluntly. "Not if it goes against my instincts or my ethics."

"Then I don't see you having a long career in the federal space."

"Then I'll take that as a good thing."

"Are you always so cavalier about things?"

"I do my job and let the chips fall."

"So you're not into CYA?"

"My butt is way too big to cover," Decker replied.

"You just want to get to the truth?"

"Yeah. How about you?"

"I already told you that we do."

"So what progress have you made?"

She seemed surprised by the question. "It's an ongoing investigation."

"It sure as shit is, which is why I'm asking."

"I mean I can't discuss it with you."

"Okay, then I'll *discuss* it from my end. Berkshire has a secret past. A past where she came into a great deal of money. She bought a fancy-ass condo and car but she drove an old Honda to work. She used an old farmhouse as a switching spot for the cars. And maybe for other things too."

"I'm finding this highly interesting."

"So we have mystery behind Berkshire, or whoever she really is. And on the Dabney end we have a woman helping him clean out his safe deposit box after he sent a key to his daughter, presumably so she would open it after his death and the contents would provide answers. And you told us that Dabney allegedly sold secrets to pay for an alleged gambling habit. So we have mystery at that end. And a few mornings ago those twin mysteries met in the middle of Washington, D.C. with the result that two people died. So the question becomes why?"

"Neatly summed up."

"Summaries are for idiots. Anybody can do them."

"You said 'allegedly' just now in referring to Dabney's espionage and gambling habit."

"Yeah?"

"There's nothing alleged about it."

"Maybe to you, but not to me. All I have is your word for it. Not good enough."

She put the car back into drive and they pulled off. "You always this cooperative with a sister agency?"

"Ironic, since I've seen *zero* cooperation from yours."

"Look, you've actually given me some valuable information. How can I return the favor?"

"By making no objection to our working on the case."

She kept driving, turning down one road and then another. "How exactly would that work?" she asked.

"That would *exactly* work with us investigating the case and finding the truth."

"You mean a joint investigation?"

"If that's what you want to call it."

"I'll have to think about it, talk to my superiors."

"Great. You can give me your answer tomorrow morning."

"You have no authority to give me directives."

"I see you *do* know where I live," said Decker, as they pulled into the parking lot of the apartment building. "I can't say that's comforting."

"Friends close, enemies closer."

"I wouldn't imagine I was either. *Yet*."

"You like this area? It's still a little dicey."

"It's growing on—"

Brown had pulled her pistol and killed the engine. It was then that Decker saw what she already had seen. Two men were stuffing another man into the trunk of a car.

Brown was out and sprinting toward them before Decker even got his car door open.

"Federal agent, hands in the air!" she barked, her pistol pointed at the men.

One ducked down behind the car. The other pulled a gun. Before he could turn and fire, Brown had dropped him with two bursts of her pistol.

The next instant she was bowled over and pinned to the pavement by a huge weight.

"What the—" she gasped.

The rounds ripped through the air right above her.

The man who had ducked down was firing from behind the car with an AK-47 assault rifle.

Decker, who'd knocked Brown down when he saw the AK pointing her way, rolled off her, sprawled on his belly, took aim, and fired at various spots under the car. The scream told him that at least one of his rounds had hit the shooter in the ankle or foot.

As the man fell beside the car grabbing his leg and screaming, Decker emptied his mag at the same narrow space separating the bottom of the car from the asphalt.

The screams stopped.

Brown and Decker leapt up. When they raced over and peered around the rear of the car, the man was no longer moving. There was blood all around him and the AK was lying next to him. As Decker knelt down next to him, the man remained still.

Brown pointed to the entry wound on the side of the man's head. "You got him in the leg, but this was the kill shot. Good aim," she added coolly.

"I wasn't aiming, I was just trying to hit something on him," said a pale Decker.

"Well, better to be lucky than dead."

Decker rose and hurried to the open trunk of the car, where a bound Tomas Amaya was struggling to free himself. There was a gag over his mouth. Decker untied him and helped him out of the trunk.

Amaya, breathing hard, swayed on his feet. Decker observed the purplish knot on the man's forehead and said, "Sit down before you pass out."

At first Amaya seemed about to protest, but then he followed Decker's instruction and sat down on the asphalt.

Then something occurred to Decker. "Danny! Where's Danny?"

"He's at a friend's *casa*," murmured Amaya. "He is...my *hijo* is okay."

"Who's Danny?" asked Brown.

"His eleven-year-old son."

Brown nodded and said, "You want to call this in?"

Decker pulled out his phone and called Bogart. In one efficient minute he conveyed what had happened. "Can you call the locals in?"

Bogart said, "Doing it right now. I'll see you in thirty minutes. You sure you're okay?"

"We're fine."

"We? You mean Jamison?"

"No. Agent Brown is here with me."

"Right," said a clearly puzzled Bogart. "Well, you can explain that all to me later."

Decker clicked off and looked at Brown. "Thanks for the assist."

"Jesus, Decker, you saved my life. I never saw the AK coming my way. If you hadn't pushed me down, *I'd* be heading to the morgue too."

Decker looked down at Amaya. "Mr. Amaya, the police are on their way. You're going to have to be prepared to tell them what's going on."

Amaya said nothing, and he would not look at Decker.

Frustrated, Decker glanced at Brown. "He's not been very cooperative. Seems to be my lot in life," he added.

Before Brown could respond, Jamison, who had walked back from the restaurant, turned into the parking lot. When she saw what was going on, she raced forward and said, "Decker, what the hell is going on?"

"Just another day in the neighborhood," he said, becoming even paler. Then he abruptly started off toward the building.

"Wait a minute, where are you going?" said Brown.

Without turning around he said, "To throw up a cheeseburger."

AMAYA REFUSED TO say anything to the police. "*No entiendo, no entiendo*," he kept saying over and over. When they brought in an officer who spoke Spanish he just shut up altogether.

The two dead men had no ID, but one of the cops thought he recognized the AK shooter.

"Hired gun," he said. "Rents out to lots of different gangs. Don't think we'll be able to run anything down there. Those guys do all cash and never face-to-face. Sometimes it's just a phone call and the name of the target and a wad of bills or pills in a paper bag when the job's done."

Bogart had arrived and was dealing with the locals. Decker, minus a burger in his gut, and Brown had given their statements.

Bogart came over to where Brown was standing and said, "Surprised to see you here."

"Not as surprised as I was," said Brown.

"You going to be put on admin leave by DIA after this?" asked Bogart.

"Hardly. Not how we operate. And besides, it was clear what happened. Any investigation would back up what we did." She eyed Decker. "How about him? He discharged his weapon. Will this get him stuck behind a desk?"

"Normally, yes. But he's not a special agent. He was re-instated as a homicide detective in Burlington, Ohio, so he's a sworn officer with arresting authority on loan, as it were, to the Bureau. So we'll have to see."

"Right. Good old bureaucracies."

"I understand you wanted to talk to Decker about something. Anything that you can share with me?"

Brown glanced at Decker as he walked over to them. "I don't know, is there?"

Decker said, "We talked about a joint effort to get to the truth."

"And I made no promises," said Brown. "In fact, I said certain phone calls might be made that would draw a mandate from within the FBI for you to stand down."

Bogart raised his eyebrows as he glanced at Decker. "So we don't seem to have made much progress."

Brown said, "I'll think on all this, Agent Bogart. Decker saved my life tonight. I owe him. And I don't like owing people."

And with that she walked to her car and drove off.

Jamison, who had been standing in the background, hurried over and whirled on Decker. "So what the hell was all that about?"

Decker took a step back. "What was what about?"

"Why did she show up at the diner and want to talk to you? She's obviously been following you."

"I know that."

Bogart said, "What did she say?"

"She wanted to know if I was still working on the Berkshire case."

"And what did you tell her?"

"Nothing that could be taken as a definitive answer to that question."

"So maybe she was on a fishing expedition?"

"She seems to be a person who likes more rather than less intelligence," Decker said slowly. "And I can't fault her for that."

Jamison looked at him in disbelief. "That's all you can come up with? If I had pulled something like that you would have cut me off at the knees. Why does she get special treatment?"

Decker started to say something, but he stopped and said instead, "We need to get Danny."

Jamison's features softened and she looked down. "Right." She let out a rush of breath and with it her hostility seemed to fade. "Did Tomas tell you where he was?"

"At a friend's."

"I'll go and ask him where. Then I'll go get Danny."

After Jamison hurried off, Bogart said in a low voice to Decker, "We can't go down that road. This is a local police problem."

Decker looked over at Jamison, who was heading into the building. "But it's also Alex's problem." Decker paused and sighed. "Which means it's my problem too."

Bogart gazed at him, apparently taken aback. "You going soft on me, Decker?"

Decker put his hands in his pockets and didn't answer.

"What do you think this is about, anyway? Easy answer would be drugs. Smells like it."

"Could be. Amaya may not want to talk because he's in deep."

"You mean dealing?" asked Bogart.

"Somewhere along the supply chain. I know that world a lot better than the one I'm in right now. Dealers and street punks versus cabinet secretaries leaning on agency directors. It's like a different planet."

"Not to worry. I've been in this world my entire working life, and sometimes it makes no sense to me either." He paused. "So you think Amaya screwed up? Skimming maybe?"

"Well, they didn't come here tonight to give him a performance bonus."

"If he won't cooperate there's not a lot the cops can do."

"Then I'll just have to make him cooperate."

"You think you have a way to do that?"

"I think I have eleven of them," replied Decker.

"You mean the kid, Danny," said Bogart. "Eleven years old."

"If I were the guys after Tomas, that would be my next target."

"You want me to ask the cops to put them in protection?"

"We live in the building. We can keep an eye out."

"Look, I don't need you and Jamison getting killed over this."

"I'm not looking to get killed over this either. But it sort of comes with the territory."

"You mean wearing the badge?"

"No, being a fucking landlord, apparently."

* * *

Decker ended up driving with Jamison to pick up Danny. The boy had paled when they showed up at the door of the friend's house, but they quickly explained that his father was okay. Since the car was only a two-seater, Danny had to ride in Decker's lap with the seat belt around both of them. Luckily, it wasn't far to drive.

"They came back," said Danny nervously as they drove back. "Didn't they? Those guys."

"Actually, it was two new guys, but we think it's all connected."

"Did you catch them?" he asked.

"They won't be bothering your dad anymore, that I can guarantee," said Decker. "But they might send some other guys."

"So what do we do?" asked Danny helplessly.

Jamison said, "We need your dad to talk to the police. Without that, there's not much that can be done."

"I've tried to get him to do that. But he won't. He just keeps telling me not to worry. But that's all I do, worry."

"Well, we're going to have to be more convincing," said Decker.

* * *

When they reached the apartment building, the crime scene was still being processed but the bodies had been taken away. They escorted Danny up to his apartment. His father was sitting on the couch holding an ice pack against one side of his face and a beer in his other hand.

Danny ran to him and hugged his father. They spoke in low voices. All the while Tomas kept a wary eye on Decker and Jamison.

"Mr. Amaya, it won't stop here," said Jamison. "They'll just send other people."

Amaya looked away even as his son clutched at him more tightly.

Decker added, "And next time it won't be just you. It'll be your son."

A trembling Danny looked back at Decker. Amaya turned his head to stare at Decker.

Decker approached Amaya and sat on the couch next to him. The furniture groaned under his bulk.

"You know that's the way it's going to play out, right? That's your Achilles' heel. Whatever you're involved in, that's where they'll come at you next. And we can't be here all the time to protect Danny. So what are you going to do? Wait until they come and take him?"

Amaya abruptly rose and threw the beer and the ice pack across the room. Danny sprang back and Decker gazed steadily up at the man.

Amaya shouted, "Get out of *mi casa. Ahora!*"

Decker held his gaze for a few more moments and then rose. He glanced at Danny. "You see anyone suspicious around here, call us." He handed Danny a card with his cell phone number on it. "But call 911 first." Then he looked back at Amaya, who stood there, his hands balled into fists and his chest heaving.

"I hope you know what you're doing, Mr. Amaya. Because you only have one *hijo.*"

CHAPTER

23

THE NEXT MORNING, Decker, gun in holster, watched Danny and his father drive off. Then Decker went back to his apartment, changed into his workout gear, tramped back downstairs, and started to jog.

His run took him along the waterfront where seagulls swooped and soared and the stiff surface current collected trash along the riverbanks. The sweat pouring, his breaths coming faster, Decker kept going until he could go no farther. He felt onion rings and French fries marching up his throat.

He stopped and took a couple minutes to cool down, letting his blood pressure and breathing settle slowly, and stretching out tired muscles. And then he started to walk. The sun had risen and he could see people emerging from their homes and climbing into their cars or walking down the streets.

He had put aside the issue of the Amayas and come back to the Dabney/Berkshire investigation. He sat down on a bench, looked out over the river, and closed his eyes.

There were far too many questions, and, as of now, basically no answers.

Harper Brown had told them that Dabney was selling secrets to cover gambling debts. That may or may not have been true.

But what DIA couldn't tell them was why he had targeted and killed Berkshire.

Berkshire's history was full of holes and shadows and contradictions. A murder victim with that sort of past? They *had* to be connected. Whatever had led Dabney to kill her had to have something to do with the woman's past. And if that was the case, then Dabney had to have some connection to that past. Now they just had to find out what Berkshire's past really was.

Decker stood, his tired legs quivering a bit. He fast-walked back to the apartment and found Jamison sitting at the kitchen table drinking a cup of coffee and peering out the window. He grabbed a bottle of water from the fridge and sat down across from her.

"Good workout?" she asked, without looking at him.

"Any workout I have that doesn't involve a coronary is a good workout for me."

She smiled weakly and then looked down at her cup.

"Something on your mind?" asked Decker.

"I don't think you'd understand."

"Thanks for giving me the benefit of the doubt."

She gazed up at him. "I'm *always* giving you the benefit of the doubt."

He studied her. "And coming away disappointed with the results, you mean?"

She shrugged. "I know it's the way you're wired. You can't help..." Her voice trailed off.

"I can't help being oblivious to most things?"

"If that's how you want to describe it."

He sat back and fingered his bottle. "Last night I remembered something I had forgotten."

"I thought you never forgot anything."

"I'm not a computer, Alex!"

A long moment of silence passed before she said, "I know you're not. I'm sorry. I didn't mean it that way."

Decker rubbed his head and didn't respond.

"What did you remember?" she prompted.

"That my daughter loved orange popsicles."

Jamison looked taken aback. "I thought you were referring to something about the case."

He eyed her steadily. "I'm not a computer *and* I don't only think about cases, Alex."

She looked stricken by his comment and then sighed. "I just keep putting my foot in it, don't I?" She paused. "I'm sorry, Amos," she added earnestly. "I loved popsicles when I was a kid too. Tell me more about Molly?"

He looked away. "When I came home from work she'd be out on the front steps with one. And then she'd take one from behind her back and hand it to me. She had obviously been waiting for me to come home."

"Why do you think you forgot that?" asked Jamison, looking quite interested in his story.

He took a sip of water before answering. "Maybe because I'm so focused on figuring out why people want to kill each other. My brain doesn't have the bandwidth for personal stuff."

Jamison reached out and gripped his hand. "It also might mean that a little bit of who you were is coming back."

"I'm not sure that's possible."

"But you don't know that it's impossible." She paused. "Todd told me about the hospice."

"You mean how I made a mess of things?"

"No, how you went back to Dorothy Vitters and adjusted her pillow. And told her you were sorry."

"I didn't know he saw or heard that."

"Well, he did."

"It didn't matter to her. She was asleep."

"It does matter, Decker. It should matter to *you*."

"I checked back with the hospice yesterday. Dorothy Vitters died an hour after we left her."

Jamison withdrew her hand. "I guess it was only a matter of time."

"The thing is, I saw her as navy blue when I first went in. But when I was leaving..." He stopped.

"What?" asked Jamison.

"When I was leaving I saw her changing to electric blue, which I associate with death. And an hour later she *was* dead."

"She was dying, Decker. Your mind knew that and responded accordingly. It's not like you can predict death."

"I know. But it was still...weird."

"I can understand that," she said sympathetically.

He glanced at her. "I know I'm not...normal, Alex."

"Not that any of us are," she said.

"Right, but I'm more not normal than most."

"But because of that you're great at what you do."

"Yeah, but is that a fair trade-off?"

"Some would think it is."

They sat there in silence for a few moments. Finally, he said, "I sometimes remember who I used to be, Alex. Only I can't be that person again. I know that." Before she could reply, he rose. "I'm going to shower and change."

She looked up at him. "Okay. I'll do the same."

"Did Virginia Cole contact you yet about the teacher who was friends with Berkshire?"

"Not yet. I can ping her today about it."

"We've been trying the Berkshire angle for a while and we've come up empty. So let's go back to Walter Dabney. We need to find out where he went on that trip."

"You think it's important?"

"He went somewhere and came back *changed*. I'd like to know why."

* * *

Ellie Dabney was sitting in her kitchen staring out the window when Decker and Jamison were shown in by the housekeeper.

"Are your kids still here?" asked Decker.

"Yes, but they're out finalizing the funeral arrangements. I just can't seem to..."

"Did your daughter from France get in?" asked Jamison.

"Natalie arrived yesterday. She didn't go with the others. She's upstairs asleep. Jet lag. And..." Her voice trailed off once more.

"Right," said Decker, sitting down across from her.

Ellie Dabney looked like she had aged twenty years. Her face sagged, her hair was unkempt, and her tall, athletic body had collapsed in on itself. Decker wondered if she'd been taking her depression meds.

Jamison sat down next to her. "I know how incredibly hard this has been on you."

"Do you?" demanded Ellie. "Do *you* have a husband who murdered someone and then shot himself?"

"No, I don't. I was just—"

"I understand what you were trying to do. I'm sorry. I just can't..." She simply shook her head.

"Has anyone else been by to see you?" asked Decker.

"Like who?"

"Other federal agents?"

Ellie shook her head. "No, do you expect them to?"

"It's possible." Decker leaned toward her across the table. "Were you aware that your husband might have had a gambling problem?"

"Gambling problem?" scoffed Ellie. "Walt wouldn't have known a craps table from a roulette wheel."

"And you base this on what?"

"Did someone say he had a gambling problem? Someone at work?"

"Not at work, no."

"Who then?"

"I'm not at liberty to disclose that. But you don't think that's possible, I take it?"

"I never knew Walt to even buy a lottery ticket. He thought it was stupid. Like flushing your money down the toilet."

"Have you checked with your bank recently? To see if there might be any funds missing? Or maybe you have a financial manager?"

"We do. And he actually called yesterday to check in and see if I needed anything. And though we didn't talk business, I've known him a long time, and if there were any issues with our money, I'm sure he would have told me."

Decker glanced at Jamison. "Okay, that's good to know."

"Why would someone think Walt was a gambler?"

"They thought he might need the money."

"Why? Look around. It's not like we're destitute." As soon as she finished speaking, Ellie's face flushed and she looked ready to burst into fresh tears.

Decker was about to say something else, but Jamison snagged his arm and said, "You're absolutely right. Thank you. We'll be leaving now."

As they walked to the front door, Decker glanced up the stairs to see a young woman standing at the top in a long T-shirt. Her face was red, presumably from crying. She was tottering on her bare feet and staring down at Decker with a hopeless look.

Decker raced up the stairs with Jamison right behind.

He caught the woman before she fell. He lifted her up in his arms.

Jamison said, "This must be Natalie. That door is open. Maybe it's her bedroom. Is she okay?"

"She's drunk," said Decker, sniffing her breath.

Jamison held open the door and Decker passed through and laid Natalie on the unmade bed. He looked around and saw the suitcase by the wall. He fingered the airline tag still on it.

"Charles de Gaulle Airport. Okay, that confirms this is Natalie, the one who lives in France."

He glanced over at Natalie. It was then he noticed that she had two toes missing on her right foot.

"Are you sure she's okay?" asked Jamison.

"Until the hangover kicks in."

They turned to see Ellie standing in the doorway. "I'll take it from here." She ushered them out and closed the bedroom door after them. "This really has destroyed our family," she said.

"I guess so," said Decker.

As they walked outside, Jamison said, "So maybe Miss high-and-mighty Harper Brown lied to us. Maybe Walter Dabney *didn't* have a gambling problem."

Decker went over to Jamison's car and stood next to it, surveying the property but not really seeing it.

"What is it?" she asked.

Decker didn't answer, because the frames were whizzing by in his head. He went from first to last and last to first. Then he turned to Jamison.

He said, "Brown told us that Dabney was selling secrets."

"Right. To pay for his gambling debts."

"She never said they were *his* gambling debts."

CHAPTER

24

HARPER BROWN HAD just sat down across from Decker at the café where Walter Dabney had gone right before killing Berkshire. She was dressed in a black two-piece suit with a seafoam-green blouse. The slight bulge at her waist showed where she kept her pistol.

Decker had on faded jeans, a rumpled flannel shirt, and a windbreaker.

Brown eyed his clothing and said, "I take it the Bureau has suspended its dress code for you?"

"Bogart already told you, I'm not a real agent."

"Your phone call was interesting," she continued.

"As I'm hoping your answers will be. So whose gambling debts were they?"

"As I already told you, I haven't decided whether you're on or off this investigation, so I can't possibly answer that."

"As I've already told *you*, I don't think that's within your power to decide."

"Did you forget the phone call the SecDef can make?"

"I checked on that," said Decker. "That won't be happening. That was bullshit on your part and you know it."

She sat back. "Can you at least buy a girl a cup of coffee while you accuse her of dishonest things?"

Decker rose, bought a black coffee, and carried it over to her.

"Thank you," she said sweetly. She took a sip and smiled. "Good and hot and just coffee. I could never understand all the crap people put in their cup."

Decker studied her and took a drink of his own coffee. "When I was a cop back in Ohio, I ran into someone who reminded me of you."

"Another cop?"

"No, she was a criminal. Con artist. Really good at what she did."

"You flatter me, Decker."

"Then I must have said it wrong."

"I was raised in Alabama by God-fearing parents. They instilled a sense of honor and integrity in me."

"Alabama?"

"Yes."

"So they're fans of *To Kill a Mockingbird*."

"You got that from my name?"

"Harper Lee, yeah." He leaned his bulk in toward her. "So last night didn't you say you owed me? If you don't want to pay the debt, enjoy your coffee and I'll get on with my day."

When she said nothing he started to rise.

"Just hold your horses," she finally said, motioning for him to sit back down. She looked around the nearly empty café as Decker dropped back into his chair. "This is not the ideal place."

"Then let's take a walk." He eyed her cup. "As you can see, I got your coffee to *go*. Just in case you came over from the dark side."

Out on the sidewalk a breeze swirled Brown's hair around her shoulders. The wind also caught her jacket and revealed her sidearm. Decker saw this and said, "A Beretta. That's what Dabney used to kill Berkshire."

Brown buttoned her jacket closed. "So this is the route he took?"

"You *know* it was. We were talking gambling debts."

"How do you know they weren't Walter Dabney's?"

"Because you never said they were. And I've decided to take you quite literally."

"I actually always try to be as vague as possible."

"So much for honor and integrity. So was it Natalie?"

She shot him a glance. "What makes you say that? Have you met her?"

"You could say that, although we never actually spoke, principally because she was in an alcoholic stupor."

"But what makes you think it was her with the gambling problem?"

"Her three sisters were distraught about their father, but none of them got so drunk they passed out. And she had farther to come, and was the last to arrive, which means she had more time to process the news. But she was shit-faced in the morning while her sisters were out making funeral arrangements and her mother was downstairs all by herself. I understand everyone is different, but, other things being equal, it struck me as odd. And the other sisters were angry about what happened. They were in disbelief. But Natalie didn't look angry or surprised. And even though she was drunk, there was something in her expression, in the eyes, really, that made her look…guilty."

"And you can tell when someone looks 'guilty'?"

"I was a cop for twenty years, so I had a lot of practice," he shot back.

They walked along for another minute in silence. They passed by the guard shack and Decker nodded at the uniformed man inside. He was the same security officer from the morning Dabney had shot Berkshire.

Across the street, workers were hauling construction materials through the open doorway of a building that was being renovated. Taped to the front window was a building permit. D.C., like New York, was constantly being stripped down and rebuilt. Decker had traveled to New York once, where a cab driver had told him that there were only two seasons in the Big Apple: winter and construction.

Brown said, "We don't think it was Natalie. We believe it was her husband, Corbett."

"He had the gambling debts?"

She nodded. "And they were enormous. Apparently, some very bad people loaned him the money, and they wanted to get paid back. We're talking Russian mobsters."

"So they were threatened?"

"It was more than a threat. If the debt wasn't paid, Corbett, Natalie, and their four-year-old daughter were dead."

"So she called her dad?"

"Last hope. He had money, but not nearly enough in liquid assets, apparently."

"So he sold secrets to raise the money?"

"That's the way we see it."

"So Natalie blames herself?"

"Looks like it."

"But that doesn't explain why he killed Berkshire."

"No. We haven't gotten there yet."

"How did you find all this out?"

"Legwork. Asking questions, doing follow-up. We got a tip on Corbett's end and ran it down from there. We got on to Dabney after we found out about his son-in-law's gambling debts. Dabney's firm is well known to DIA. Any connection to him that would lead to possible national security issues raises a red flag for us. It was connect-the-dots fieldwork."

"So Natalie knew what her father was doing?"

"Unsure. We traced some of the calls after the fact with an assist from another agency."

Decker looked at her curiously.

She explained, "Natalie used a couple of words that triggered an NSA algorithm so it got recorded and dumped in a data box that we accessed later on."

"I didn't think NSA eavesdropped on U.S. citizens."

"Yeah, and I'd like to sell you the deed to the White House. Anyway, one end of the call was from overseas, so there you are. Loophole of all loopholes. Dabney pretty much told Natalie he'd take care of the problem. There was a tight timeline. But he didn't say how he'd do it. We learned about this after the fact, of course, or else we would have stopped it."

"But he got the money and paid the debt?"

"Natalie and her family wouldn't be here if he hadn't. They'd be in little pieces at the bottom of a river somewhere in Europe."

"When did the payment go through?"

"The electronic trail wasn't totally clear. Rough guess, six weeks ago. Maybe longer."

"Have you talked to Natalie?"

"I haven't, no. We're actually not that interested in her. The gambling and the Russian mob connection is not our jurisdiction. We turned that over to international authorities."

"What secrets were sold? You said they were critical enough to trigger something worse than 9/11."

"I was not exaggerating when I made that comparison with 9/11."

"So if the stakes are that high, why wouldn't you want the FBI helping?"

"Need to know is not some bullshit line you hear in the movies, Decker. It does have real purpose."

"Meaning what?"

"If you want it straight, it means we don't really know who to trust on this. The fewer people looped in the better."

"And in doing so you might cut out the very people who could help you solve this and save us from another 9/11," he shot back.

She looked uncomfortable at this, but didn't argue the point.

"Do you know who the buyers are?"

"We're working on it."

"Are you sure it wasn't the Russian mob? Maybe he just gave them the secrets in exchange for forgiving the debts."

She shook her head. "The fact is, these mobsters wouldn't know how to monetize stuff like that, nor would they even want to try. You don't want to bring the U.S. military down on your head if you don't have to. No, they got their cash from Dabney, and Dabney got that cash by selling secrets to someone else."

"Another government?"

"Very likely."

"Why?"

"Couple of reasons. Only another government would be willing to take this sort of risky operation. It takes resources and deep pockets. And only another government would be so wired in to the intelligence world that they would know what secrets they wanted Dabney to get them."

"So he didn't pick what he stole? They did?"

"Almost certainly. You're not going to run an op like this and not get what you want as the prize. The people behind this, I'm certain, told Dabney exactly what they wanted and to which they knew he had access. This was very well planned out. Which makes me believe they had some inside help. Which is why we want to keep as many people out of the loop as possible. If we've been compromised, we could be doubly screwed if we read in the wrong people on this."

"Did you trace the money?"

"On the back end. Ten million."

Decker's jaw went slack. "Ten million dollars! Did this Corbett guy gamble twenty-four/seven?"

"He played for high stakes, and when your creditor is charging a thousand percent interest a day, it adds up pretty quickly."

"But if the buyer has the secrets isn't it already too late?"

"Not how the game is played, Decker. If we find out who did it, and it *is* a foreign government, that's a chit we can play later. Perfectly accepted diplomatic blackmail played out every day among allies and enemies."

"But what if it's a terrorist organization?"

"To execute on the information that Dabney sold takes infrastructure and lots of capital. Dabney worked on large-scale military projects: ships, tanks, and planes. That's why we think it might be another government. ISIL is not shelling out billions to build a *Zumwalt*-class destroyer."

"So you're going to keep looking for the buyer."

"Of course. That's my job."

"And we're going to keep looking for why Dabney killed Berkshire."

She stopped walking and looked at him. "And if there's overlap?" she asked.

"Then we have a joint investigation. And we'd welcome the cooperation."

"How sweet. Tell me, is that your best chess move?"

"No, I always hold something back."

"You can keep doing what you're doing, and so will I. How's that sound?"

"Great, if you actually mean it."

"You're a smart guy. I'll let you figure that one out on your own," she said, and walked off down the street. "Thanks for the coffee," she called back over her shoulder.

25

"WE FOUND WHERE Dabney went on the mysterious trip."

Todd Milligan was studying the computer screen in front of him. He, Decker, Jamison, and Bogart were sitting in a small conference room at the WFO, the Bureau's Washington field office on Fourth Street. Decker had filled them all in on his conversation with Brown.

"Where?" asked Bogart.

"Houston. His name popped up on a passenger manifest. He went there exactly once five weeks ago today."

"I wonder why Houston?" asked Jamison.

"Something to do with the sale of secrets?" ventured Milligan.

Decker shook his head. "According to Brown, the payment happened about six weeks ago, or maybe longer. So why take a mysterious trip to Houston *after* the deal was done and his daughter was safe?"

"Maybe there was some snafu or other issue?" suggested Bogart.

"Or maybe it's because the MD Anderson Cancer Center is in Houston," said Jamison.

They all looked at her.

She said, "Dabney might have suspected something was

wrong with his health and wanted to get an expert opinion. MD Anderson is one of the best places for that."

Milligan said, "How do you know that?"

"When I was a journalist, I did a local interest story about a woman who went there when she was diagnosed with a rare cancer. They were able to get her into remission."

Milligan smiled and said, "I forgot you had a life prior to joining the FBI."

Bogart said, "That's a good idea, Alex. You might be right."

"We can certainly check," said Milligan. "Even with patient confidentiality, we can get his wife to contact them and see if Dabney was there."

Bogart said, "Todd, get going on that. If he knew he was terminal over a month ago, it might provide some motivation to do what he did, meaning kill Berkshire."

Milligan rose and hurried from the room.

"Meaning he would never be tried for the crime," Jamison said to Bogart.

"Right."

"But it still won't explain *why* he killed Berkshire," Decker pointed out.

"No, but it'll fill in one more piece of the puzzle. And it may help us answer that question at some point. And the ME got back to us on the blood screens. Dabney *was* taking painkillers, which reinforces the notion that he knew he was sick."

Decker rose.

"Where are you going?" asked Bogart.

"For a walk."

* * *

He started at the café. After a full breakfast at home, Dabney had stopped here, sat at a table overlooking the street, then got up, walked out and down the street, and shot Berkshire in the head before putting a round in his own brain.

As Decker was sitting there the same female employee he had spoken to earlier came over.

"I saw you in here earlier with that woman. You guys still looking into what happened?"

"Still looking," said Decker absently.

"I guess it doesn't matter much."

He shot her a look. "What doesn't matter much?"

"Billy's in today. I gave him the card you left, but I don't know if he ever called you guys. He was working when that man was here. If you want to talk to him, he's not busy right now."

"I *do* want to talk to him."

She left and came back with a tall middle-aged man with graying hair worn in a ponytail. He had on a black shirt like the woman wore, and faded jeans. A green apron was tied around his waist.

"Hey," said Billy, as the woman went back to the counter. "I hear you're with the FBI. You want to ask me some stuff?"

"Yeah, you want to take a seat?"

Billy sat across from him.

"You work here long?" asked Decker.

Billy laughed. "Back in 2008, I was an investment banker, if you can believe it. Then came financial Armageddon and I got tossed out on my ass. Lost everything. So I said to hell with it and never looked back. I've been working here four years. I can barely rub two dimes together, but I'm happier than I've ever been."

"Good for you. You remember Dabney?"

"Yeah. He came in that morning."

"Had he ever come in before?"

"No. Least not that I saw. Now that I've seen his picture

in the paper and on the TV I think I would've remembered."

"He sat at this table?"

"Yeah. I passed by a couple times with some orders. Funny thing is, he didn't eat a bite of his scone. I actually asked him if something was wrong with it."

Decker tensed. "Wait a minute, you talked to him?"

"Well, yeah. The dude wasn't drinking his tea and the scone thing caught my eye. They're really good and they're not cheap. And the guy hadn't touched it."

"What did you say to him?"

"Asked him if the scone was cold or something. Told him I could heat it up for him if he wanted. Get him some butter."

"What did he say?"

"He said he didn't have much of an appetite. Weird, huh, since he had just ordered it."

"Yeah," said Decker. "But apparently he was a weird guy."

Billy chuckled. "Right, the whole murder thing. That is *weird*!"

"Right," said Decker dryly.

"Anyway, he got really focused on something outside the window."

Decker tensed once more. "What do you mean, *focused*?"

"I mean he straightened up so fast he almost knocked his tea off the table. He was looking right past me. Next thing he was on his feet and out the door. Almost forgot his briefcase. In fact I called out to him about it, otherwise he would have left it behind."

And if he had, Anne Berkshire would be alive right now, thought Decker.

"So I cleaned the table off. Thought about putting the scone back behind the counter, but we have rules about that. So I just threw it away."

"Anything else?"

"No. I guess I should have called you guys. Amy gave me the card. But I've been off and just chilling." When Decker said nothing, he added, "You want anything to eat or drink? I can warm a scone up for you."

"I'm good, thanks."

"You sure?"

Decker didn't answer. He was staring out the window.

Billy finally got up and left.

From this vantage point Decker could see pretty far down the street. He closed his eyes and clicked through mental frames until he got to the series he wanted. He traced every footstep that he had seen Dabney and Berkshire take. The timing here was critical, but he didn't have all the information he needed to make an accurate analysis. But still, he had to try.

Step by step.

Decker wasn't focused on the end of their respective walks, which had led to Berkshire's death and Dabney's mortal wound.

He opened his eyes and peered down the street.

He was fairly certain of one thing. The catalyst that had prompted Dabney to tense and stare out the window, as Billy had described, could not have been his seeing Berkshire. It just wasn't possible from this vantage point. She would have been much farther down the street at that time and out of sight from this spot.

So what had the catalyst been?

And then it occurred to Decker.

He got up and went outside and stood on the other side of the window.

No phone had been found on Dabney, so it wasn't an electronic communication. Since this had been planned out and Dabney was not supposed to survive, they could not use the phone. It would leave a trail, even if he tried to erase it. And perhaps whoever he was working with could not completely trust him to do that.

But there was one signaling device that left no trail.

There had been someone out on the street that Dabney had seen, and that person's presence had been the signal. Perhaps it was the clothing the person wore, a gesture made, but something had triggered his abrupt departure from the café. And that also explained the untouched tea and uneaten scone. The café was simply the place for him to wait for the signal.

And it was clear what the person would be signaling.

That Anne Berkshire was on her way.

Decker crossed the street and walked down the pavement. He was tracing the route he had taken, and also the one Dabney had navigated. He turned his head from side to side, taking everything in and comparing it to what he had seen on the day of the shooting.

The construction barrier that had been there earlier around the open manhole cover was gone, but everything else looked the same.

He passed the guard shack and kept going. Up ahead would have been Dabney. In his mind's eye Decker placed the dead man on the street walking.

Then there was Berkshire coming from the other way. Decker had had no reason to focus on her, but he pulled up the memory frames he did have of her to see what he could make of it.

He had been too far away to really see her face, so he couldn't tell her expression. He did remember that she was not walking like Dabney had been, with long confident strides.

The man walking the last mile to his death.

The pair had moved closer. They had eventually turned, Dabney to the left and Berkshire to the right. Then, like two passenger trains aligned on parallel tracks, they had drawn nearly shoulder to shoulder.

That's when Decker had looked away to the food truck to decide whether or not to buy a breakfast burrito. He had checked his watch, opted not to, and turned back.

By then the gun was out and pointed at the base of Berkshire's neck.

Then the shot rang out.

She dropped to the pavement, dead.

The guard came running up. They confronted Dabney.

He shot himself.

Memory frames over.

Decker stood there in the middle of the sidewalk as people walked past on either side of him. He stared down where there were still minute traces of blood from the two dead people.

Then he looked up and wondered what had happened to the person who had possibly signaled to Dabney.

"So that's where you went."

He turned to see Jamison standing there.

"Milligan called Mrs. Dabney, and she in turn called MD Anderson. I was right. Walter Dabney did go there, where his brain cancer was diagnosed. He had told the hospital he was not going to seek treatment."

When Decker didn't react to any of this she said, "What is it? You got something? You usually do after wandering around alone."

"We need to get the camera feeds from this area for that day."

"But we know what happened here, Decker."

"No, we really don't."

26

IT WASN'T THE cliché of the lady in red.

It wasn't even a lady. At least it didn't appear to be, but it was impossible to tell.

Decker sat there and stared at the person holding a giant lollipop while wearing a clown suit.

"You really think that's it, the signal?" asked Bogart.

"We looked at six days' worth of film," said Decker. "Did you ever see a clown in any of the others at that location at that time of day? And we made inquiries and no one could account for why the clown was there. No circus or other show in town. The clown had no sign advertising an upcoming event. I think the probabilities are the clown *was* the signal."

Bogart glanced at Milligan. They were once more at the WFO, in a small room where an enormous TV screen dominated one wall.

"You're probably right," Bogart admitted.

Jamison said, "And the clown disappeared around the building only *after* he had a clear sight line of Dabney—in other words, after it was confirmed that Dabney had gotten the signal and was on his way to kill Berkshire."

Bogart sighed. "And the clown was wearing makeup and a floppy hat and bulky clothes and gloves. I couldn't even tell if he was black or white. I couldn't say for sure whether he was actually a male."

Milligan said, "And we've checked other cameras from the areas where the clown was headed. He or she is on some of them, but then there's a gap and the person's gone."

"The clown obviously knew where the cameras and the gaps were," opined Bogart. "A well-thought-out plan."

"So there's a conspiracy going on here," said Jamison. "These people got Dabney to kill Berkshire. And since he was already dying he killed himself."

Bogart said, "But how did they get him to do that? According to Agent Brown, the gambling debts were paid off. The Russians or whoever it was had no incentive to do this. And Brown also said that she didn't think the mob would be involved in this. They just wanted the money. And having worked on some of those cases, I agree with her."

Milligan said, "So, again, how did whoever it was get him to do it?"

Jamison looked at Decker. "Do you know?"

Decker didn't say anything right away. His mind was whirring and facts and suspicions were crowding in on one another, threatening to cancel each other out.

He said, "Dabney stole secrets from military projects he was working on. DIA found that out." He paused. "If they found it out, others could have too."

Bogart said, "And you mean blackmailed him with evidence of his treason? To kill Berkshire?"

"It would help explain the fact that we have as yet been unable to establish a link between Dabney and Berkshire. They may have *no* connection."

"It's sort of like *Strangers on a Train*," said Milligan. "But just one way. They blackmail Dabney to kill someone they want done away with for their own reasons."

"But why would he do it?" asked Jamison. "The guy was dying. Why would he care if what he did came out?"

"He might've been dying, but his family wasn't," replied Decker. "And from the interactions we've had with his wife and daughters, it's quite clear that they thought the man walked on water. The fact that he was dying might've made it easier for him. He knew he'd never go to trial on this. And he might've hoped that his actions would be blamed on his illness."

"But if he were unmasked as a spy?" said Bogart.

"Then he would have no way around that," said Decker. "His career would end in disgrace. And he might take his daughter down with him. If he kills Berkshire and then himself, maybe he hoped everyone would focus on that. He might not have known the DIA was on to him. But if someone was blackmailing him, they would have him dead to rights. That might have been enough for him to take the deal."

"But how could Dabney be sure if he carried out the killing that they'd live up to their part of the bargain and not reveal the espionage part?" asked Milligan.

"I'm not sure he had much of a choice. But if they did try to reveal that information, it might somehow draw focus on them. And why would they care if the espionage ever came to light? Dabney was already dead. And people who blackmail other people to murder aren't necessarily altruistic. For all we know they're actually enemies of this country. No, they would have every incentive to keep mum so that our side wouldn't even know the theft had occurred. Dabney probably figured the same thing."

Milligan said, "So he kills Berkshire and himself. That means the blackmailer is out there still."

Jamison said, "Other things being equal it might be

someone Dabney was working with. Otherwise, how would they know he was stealing secrets?"

"Could be," said Bogart. "But there are also lots of ways someone he wasn't working with might have gained access to that knowledge."

Decker said, "Which leads us to the question of why this 'third party' would want Anne Berkshire dead in the first place."

"So now instead of a connection between Dabney and Berkshire, we need to try to find one between Dabney and this unknown blackmailing third party?" said Milligan, frowning. "But the third party must have some connection to Berkshire too, since they wanted her dead."

Decker nodded. "That's exactly right."

Bogart said, "Where do we start?"

"Well, as Alex and Todd suggested, the blackmailer had to have some connection to Dabney and Berkshire, however extenuated, even if Dabney and Berkshire didn't know each other. The 'third party' would be the conduit between them. They had to know about the theft of secrets and they had to communicate with Dabney. They hopefully left enough of a trail for us to follow."

"So we have to go back to square one," said Milligan wearily.

"There are a couple of ways to attack this," said Decker. "One is the Berkshire angle. If someone wanted her dead, there's a good reason. That reason may lie in her exceptionally sketchy past. So we may be able to track down the blackmailer by digging more deeply into Berkshire's history."

"And the other way?" asked Jamison.

"Dabney. You're not going to agree to kill someone without persuasion. And that sort of persuasion isn't going to come in a tweet, text, or email, because I doubt anyone would write something like that down. So there had to be meetings with Dabney. We just have to find who they were with."

Bogart said, "Why don't Todd and I run that angle down. You and Jamison can hit it from the Berkshire end."

Jamison nodded. "And we can compare notes along the way to see where we stand. Sound like a good plan, Decker?"

Decker sat there staring off.

"Amos, I said does that sound like a good plan?"

Decker finally stirred and looked at her as though he had just realized she was in the room. He said slowly, "I don't know, Alex. I don't know if anything sounds like a good plan right now."

27

WHEN DECKER AND JAMISON got home that night, someone was waiting for them. Danny Amaya looked pale and nervous.

said, "Danny, what's wrong?"

"It's my dad. He didn't pick me up from school today."

"How did you get home?"

"A friend's mom drove me here."

"Have you called the police?"

"No, I was . . . I didn't know what to do. I was scared."

"It'll be okay, Danny. We'll come up with something."

Jamison took his hand and led him up to their apartment. "Are you hungry?" she said.

He nodded, glancing anxiously at Decker.

"I'll make you something to eat. Now, Danny, tell us anything you can that might help us find out where your dad is." Jamison got busy in the kitchen and Danny sat at the bar watching her while Decker stood beside him.

"He dropped me at school today, like always."

"Did he say anything to you then that might explain why he didn't show up to get you later?" asked Decker.

"No, not that I can think of. I go to aftercare. And Dad is always there by six. But when he didn't show up, I didn't know what to do."

"Do you have a phone?" asked Jamison.

Danny shook his head. "My dad has one, but it's too expensive for me to have one too."

"But couldn't you use a friend's phone to call your dad?"

"I did. I borrowed a phone and called, but no one answered."

Jamison said, "Okay, for now, we're going to call the police and they can start looking for your father."

Decker said, "I can go over to the construction site where he works. You told us where it is. Near the waterfront."

Danny nodded.

Jamison stopped slicing up a tomato for a salad she was making and said, "Decker, you shouldn't go alone."

"I'm not going to do anything dangerous. I'm just going to take a look at the place, that's all. If I see anything suspicious, I'll call the cops." He held out his hand. "I'll have to take your car, Alex."

She drew the keys from her jacket pocket but hesitated handing them over. "You promise nothing dangerous?"

"Promise."

Decker looked at Danny. "What exactly does your father do, Danny, at the construction site?"

"Lots of things. He's a bricklayer mostly. He's really good at it."

"I'll be back shortly."

* * *

A minute later Decker wedged himself into Jamison's car and drove off. It only took about fifteen minutes to reach the construction site. It was well dark now and Decker couldn't see anyone around. The buildings on either side of his destination looked to be in the process of being torn down. This whole area was undergoing a vast renovation.

A chilly wind whistled in between buildings. Decker parked on the street across from the site and drew up the collar of his jacket. He took a minute to look all around. He still didn't see anyone. And he also didn't see Amaya's Sentra parked anywhere.

He jogged across the street and stood in front of the unfinished building. The exterior walls were up and concrete floors had been poured. Decker counted twelve floors. Construction elevators were grafted to the concrete skeleton like tendons on bone.

He maneuvered through some barriers, stepped through an opening, and stared around at the empty first floor. He was very surprised there were no security guards on site here. He put one hand on his pistol and pulled a flashlight from his other pocket. He shone it around but saw nothing except stacks of construction material.

He glimpsed a set of steps leading down to the floors belowground. He debated whether to do this, but decided he had to. For all he knew Amaya might be down there hurt or even dead.

He walked down the steps and reached the lower floor. He pointed his light around and saw that the space here was partially completed. There was a hole in the floor in the far corner, and stacks of bricks set against one wall. When he looked down, he saw that the floor was mortared brick laid over a concrete slab.

The next moment he heard a noise and killed his light. He moved to a corner and listened. He thought he heard voices, but he couldn't make out any words.

Then came footsteps.

Then came a light.

Decker moved back farther into the shadows.

Four men appeared on the stairs. They were carrying something.

When Decker saw what it was, his hand went to his phone.

It was clearly a body.

They carried it over next to the hole and set it down. Then a light one of the men was holding flicked around the space.

That's when Decker saw a very nervous-looking Tomas Amaya. His face was bruised and bloody.

Two of the men had guns out. They pointed them at Amaya and he and the fourth man lifted the body and placed it into the hole.

"*Preparar el hormigón.*"

Decker's Spanish wasn't that good, but he didn't need it to be.

Amaya lifted up a bag of cement mix, cut it open, and poured it into a portable mixer. He added water and turned the machine on. Meanwhile, the other man had taken the body and dumped it into the hole.

It was now clear what was going to happen.

And why they needed Amaya.

He was going to put the concrete in the hole and then brick it over, seamlessly matching, no doubt, the work he had already done here.

That was why they wanted him.

To hide the body. And Decker didn't think the bricklayer was going to live to work on another job after this one.

Decker took out his phone and saw with dismay that down here he had no service.

Shit.

And then he realized there was another person down here with him.

Because that person had just stuck a gun muzzle in his back.

28

Dᴇᴄᴋᴇʀ ᴡᴀs sʜᴏᴠᴇᴅ forward, stumbled, nearly lost his balance, and then regained his footing. A light hit him in the face.

"Traerlo aqui."

Decker was shoved in the back again.

"Move!"

He reached the hole and stared down, saw the body, and then looked over at his captors.

There were five of them, plus Amaya. They were young, tough-looking, and all of them were armed.

Decker did not like these odds at all.

He wondered for a moment about Jamison's reaction to his being dead.

Told you so, Amos.

But he actually knew it would not be that. She would be devastated. And right now that made him feel worse than the imminent danger he was in.

The little man he had seen at the apartment building was not among the five. Danny had said he had seen the man in a suit with a hard hat. Apparently the actual murder and hiding-the-body part was not within his job description.

And that was probably why no security guards were posted

here tonight. They didn't want anyone around for this little extra task.

But the other men here seemed more than prepared to do the burial honors.

One of the men looked at Amaya and said, "*Espacio para dos.*"

Decker didn't need to be fluent in Spanish to understand that order either. The *dos* part was all he required. He was the spare and they were going to bury him along with the other guy.

He had something going for him, however long the odds would still be against him. They hadn't searched him for a weapon. That was a mistake.

Yet there was a guy behind him with a gun. And the guy holding the light had a gun in his other hand. Both were pointed right at Decker.

And there were three others there, all with weapons. He could maybe take out one or two, but after that one of the others would be able to kill him. It was simple math, and he came up short in every scenario that flashed through his mind.

"*Él es un federale,*" said Amaya suddenly, pointing at Decker.

The men turned to stare at him.

"*Es un federale,*" Amaya said again. "FBI!" He pointed feverishly at Decker.

The man holding the flashlight took a step toward Decker. "*Federale?*"

Decker nodded.

The man smiled. "I don't give a shit. You're dead."

Decker had no choice now. He didn't care if the odds were not in his favor. If he was going to die, he was going to take at least one of the pricks with him.

He lowered his shoulder, dropped into a squat, and exploded out of it. He drilled the guy right in the sternum, maxing out the thrust from his legs. He hit the man so hard he was lifted off his feet, flew backward, and with a scream fell into the hole.

Now Decker's problem was obvious: There were four other guys to deal with.

The good thing was the only light had just disappeared into the hole.

Darkness was his best friend right now.

Gunfire erupted all around. Fortunately, Decker had dropped to the floor an instant before, pulled his gun, and was about to fire when he saw something flash past him so fast, he couldn't even tell what it was.

But he did hear the impact as body met body and one of them gave. He next heard the clunk of something hitting the brick floor hard.

He rolled to his right, aimed his gun, and fired.

The man who had jammed his gun into Decker's back caught the round in his belly. He doubled over screaming, and a few moments later, blood came out of his mouth. He dropped to the floor and out of the fight. Belly wounds were a bitch, Decker knew. The guy would probably bleed out right there, and he could not have cared less.

Shots hit the floor near him. He could sense chips of concrete and brick whizzing through the air. And then he felt something cut into his arm. Either a slug or a chip. Either way it hurt like hell.

He kept rolling along the floor as more shots were fired. He ran into something, realized it was a wall, rose, pivoted, and went into a crouch. He focused on the situation.

By his count three down, two to go.

As he spun around trying to gauge where the remaining

two were, he sensed another flash of something, resulting in another collision. He heard a muffled scream and a gun hit the brick, followed by a body doing the same thing.

Okay, there was only one man left.

He liked these odds a lot better.

He crept forward, his gun ready, when he saw Tomas Amaya struggling with the last man. The guy had a gun. He was bigger and stronger than Amaya. He threw the smaller man off, took aim, and started to squeeze the trigger.

Decker was about to fire when the other man was hit so hard he was lifted off his feet. Whoever hit him was holding on, and when the guy slammed into the brick, the gun fell from his hand.

Okay, fifth and final man down for the count.

It was pretty much unbelievable.

Decker moved forward, panting slightly, his pistol held out in front of him. He swung it around, looking for movement, looking for additional threats. Someone was still out there. And though he had attacked the other guys, he hadn't done anything to identify himself to Decker either.

So he could still be a problem.

The next moment, Decker saw a pop of light. Then he saw a hand grip the side of the hole and looked over as a head emerged.

It was the guy he had knocked into the hole.

He had the flashlight clamped in his mouth.

His other hand came up and it held a gun pointed right at Decker.

There was no way Decker could react in time. He started to bring his gun around, but he instinctively braced for the impact of the shot.

Then a work boot came down hard on the man's free hand. He screamed. Then the same boot kicked the gun out of his hand. The man let go and fell back into the hole, while the gun dropped harmlessly to the floor.

Decker eyed Amaya, who stood next to the hole, breathing hard.

"Thanks," said Decker.

A pale Amaya nodded, obviously too shaken to even attempt a response. He staggered away from the hole and sat down on the floor.

"Damn, man. Can you never stay out of trouble?"

Decker whirled around and stared over at the source of the query.

A light came on. It was pointed away from Decker and toward the person holding it.

Melvin Mars, bent over and breathing hard, smiled and said, "See, Decker, sometimes Hail Marys do work!"

29

"NICE PLACE."

Melvin Mars, nearly six foot three and two hundred and thirty muscled pounds, stood in the middle of Jamison's and Decker's kitchen looking around. He was a former All-American running back from Texas, a sure lock for the NFL, who had been falsely imprisoned for murdering his parents and sentenced to death. After twenty years in jail and on the eve of his execution date, someone else had confessed to the crime. That had led to Decker and his FBI team's involvement and the truth eventually coming out. The state of Texas and the federal government had chipped in on an enormous payday for Mars, allowing him financial independence for the rest of his life.

Jamison smiled up at Mars. "Hey, it was your wallet that provided it."

The local police had been called to the construction site and taken over the investigation. Or mess, rather.

The guy Decker had shot was dead, and the other three, handled by Mars, were still unconscious but alive. The fifth man, the one in the hole, was identified as Roger Baker, a low-level enforcer for a local gang. The other men there were part of his crew.

The body in the hole was identified as Mateo Rodriguez, an accountant who, they had been told, was working with law enforcement to bring down the local roots of a Central American cartel that had muscled its way into the D.C. area.

They were still looking for Luis Alvarez, the man in the suit and hard hat. He had been one of the construction supervisors, but allegedly had criminal ties. He had disappeared, but the police were hopeful they could track him down.

Danny and his father had been reunited and taken to live somewhere else. Tomas Amaya would need to testify at the trial of Roger Baker. They were hoping that Baker, in turn, would rat on others farther up the line. Jamison and Decker had told the Amayas that they would help them every step of the way.

"I'll be by to check on you both," Jamison had told Danny before they were taken away by the police. "And don't worry, everything is going to be okay now."

The police had kept them for hours, so it was now around six in the morning. Mars had driven Decker home. Decker was sitting at the kitchen table, still looking a little pale.

Mars eyed him. "Man, it was hairy in there. I can hold my own in pretty much any fight, but those dudes had some serious firepower. Good thing Alex told me where you were. I got in from the airport about ten minutes after you left. I drove my rental car right over to the place. Looked around and then heard all the noise from the basement. When I got down there it wasn't looking too good."

"You saved my life, Melvin," said Decker. "I'd be under a slab of concrete now but for you."

"Payback, man. How many times did you save my butt? Besides, I just treated it like running plays. Blow through the line and deliver some hurt."

He looked at Jamison. "You're doing good work with

him, Alex. He's even skinnier than when I saw him last time."

Jamison did not appear to be listening. "Amos, you told me you weren't going to do anything dangerous. You almost got yourself and Melvin killed!"

"Look, I'm sorry. But something was obviously going down in there."

"Then you should have called the police. Like you told me you were going to."

"Well, *you* shouldn't have given Melvin the address, then he wouldn't have come."

"Hey, man, don't get mad at her. I made her do it. Had to make sure you were okay."

Decker looked at Jamison, who was still scowling at him.

"Because he's your friend, Amos. Friends don't put other friends' lives in jeopardy."

"Okay, Alex, message delivered loud and clear."

"Has it been really? What, until next time you ignore it?"

No one said anything for a long moment.

Finally, Decker turned to Mars and said, "How are things in Alabama?"

Mars sat down on one of the barstools and Jamison poured him out a cup of coffee, though it was easy to see that she was still upset at Decker.

"Not bad. I did my thing with the high school football team and then decided to take some time off."

"Are you living down there?" Jamison asked tersely.

"Had a short-term rental. I'm looking around now to find a permanent place. Maybe somewhere up here." He glanced at Decker. "How about that, Decker? Me living up here?"

"You can live wherever you want, Melvin," Decker answered. "You can buy a mansion if you want."

Grinning, Mars said, "I spent twenty years in a little box, what would I do with a mansion? I'd get lost."

"There are a lot of nice places around here," said Jamison. "And it's a fun area. Lots to do."

Mars sipped his coffee. "So you guys working on something? I mean, besides what happened last night?"

"If Decker doesn't go off and get killed, yeah, we are working on something," said Jamison with one more glare at Decker. "And it's pretty complicated. We haven't made a lot of headway."

Mars motioned to Decker. "That dude's middle name is 'complicated.' What he can't figure out can't be figured out."

"Well, this might be the one," said Decker, heaving himself to his feet and plopping down on a stool next to Mars.

"Want to tell me about it?" asked Mars.

"You heard about the guy who shot the woman outside the FBI headquarters?" asked Jamison.

"Yeah. Saw the story a few days ago on CNN when I was having lunch. Saw some more stuff when I was waiting at the airport."

"Well, that's the case."

"We know part of what happened," said Decker. "But we don't know why Walter Dabney shot Anne Berkshire."

"We think he was blackmailed by someone to do it."

"Blackmailed? How?"

"This is confidential, Melvin," said Jamison.

He chuckled. "Hey, who do you think I'm going to tell? Hell, I don't know anybody *to* tell."

Decker said, "Apparently, Dabney was stealing secrets from a military project he was working on. He sold those secrets to raise money to help his daughter. Her husband was in to some bad guys for gambling debts. Russians. It was either pay or get slaughtered."

"Damn, so this Dabney guy was caught between a rock and a hard place?"

"He committed treason, Melvin," said Jamison.

"Yeah, but it was his family, Alex. Tough to turn your back on that."

"So that part we know," said Decker. "What we don't know is the Berkshire piece. We can't find a connection between them. But there may not be one if he was black-mailed to do it. Which means we have to try to get there from Berkshire's side and the people who wanted her dead."

"Bogart and Milligan are tackling it from Dabney's end," interjected Jamison.

"And Dabney shot himself, right?"

"Yes, but he had terminal brain cancer," said Jamison. "He'd be dead in six months or less. So maybe he didn't care."

Mars frowned and slowly shook his head. "Wow. Black-mail, gambling debts, brain tumor. This Dabney guy had a dark cloud over him."

"It *is* pretty sad," said Jamison. "You think you're hav-ing a bad day, think about what happened to him. His family is devastated."

"What about the daughter whose husband got him into this mess?" said Mars.

"What about her?" asked Jamison.

"Well, she must feel pretty bad."

"She does. We've seen that firsthand."

"Yeah, I get that. But what about something her old man might have told her?"

"Told her about what?"

"Well, I take it this whole gambling thing was a secret between them?"

"It was," said Decker. "His wife didn't know anything about it. Neither did the sisters. At least so they claimed."

"So maybe he had a closer relationship with this daughter. Parents do, you know, have that special thing with certain kids. And if he did something illegal to help her and then he gets blackmailed to do something else bad, he might have talked to her about it."

"Why?" asked Jamison.

"Because he'd want her to know why he did what he did. He wouldn't want her to think he was some kind of crazy murderer. If they were blackmailing him for stealing secrets that he stole and sold to help *her*, I think he'd want her to know."

Mars looked between Decker and Jamison. "Hey, just my two cents."

Jamison stared at Decker. "But didn't Agent Brown say that Natalie knew nothing about what her dad was planning in the way of stealing secrets to pay for the gambling debts?"

"She did. But there's no way she could know that for sure. I'm not sure she even talked to her."

"But if Natalie and her dad communicated via phone or email or text, there'd be a record of it."

"But what about face-to-face? We checked on Dabney's travel schedule. We never looked at Natalie's."

"So you mean she could have come here, or met up with him somewhere?"

Decker looked at her. "If you were sick and suspected what was wrong, would you go to MD Anderson, or any hospital, alone? Or would you want a family member with you?"

"I'd want someone with me," replied Jamison. "But why not his wife?"

"Maybe he didn't want to freak her out. She seems the

nervous type. And if he was closer to Natalie, like Melvin suggested, she might have gone with him. I mean, she owed him big for saving her husband's butt."

Jamison said, "We never asked the hospital if someone was with him. But do you really think Natalie might know who was blackmailing her father?"

"If there's even a remote possibility that she does, or has information that could lead us to whoever it is, we have to follow it up."

"But Decker, Agent Brown told us that Natalie—"

He snapped, "I know what Agent Brown *told* us. That doesn't make it true."

"But we're working the Berkshire angle. Ross and Todd are doing the Dabney side of the equation."

"I don't care who's doing what, Alex. I go wherever a case takes me."

Decker rose.

Jamison looked at her watch. "What, you mean go now? It's not even six-thirty yet."

The next moment, Decker was out the door without responding.

With twinkling eyes, Mars looked at Jamison and said, "Dude doesn't change, does he?"

"*That's* the problem, Melvin," retorted Jamison.

CHAPTER

30

It was nearly seven o'clock when they arrived at the Dabney home. A couple of cars were in the circular driveway. They were probably rentals being used by the daughters while they were here. The house looked dark, with only the front porch light on.

Mars had come with them. They had driven over in his car because Jamison's would barely fit her and Decker. But he waited in the car while they walked up to the house.

Decker knocked on the front door. No one came.

"Do you think the housekeeper's here yet?" asked Jamison.

"I don't know anything about housekeepers," said Decker.

They turned toward the door when they heard footsteps.

Jules Dabney opened the door. She was dressed in sweatpants and a GW sweatshirt. Her hair was tied back in a ponytail, and she was barefoot.

She looked at them and said crossly, "Jesus, it's a little early, you know."

"Is your sister Natalie here?" asked Decker.

"Yes, but she's asleep."

"We need to talk to her."

"Can't this wait?"

"If it could we wouldn't be here this early."

"Look, I'm going to have to insist—"

Decker held out his creds and said, "We *need* to talk to her."

Jamison stepped in front of him. "Just tell your sister that we want to talk to her about Corbett."

"Corbett? Is he okay?"

"Just tell her. If she still doesn't want to talk to us, we'll leave and come back later."

Jules hesitated and then closed the door. They heard her walking away.

As they were standing there waiting, a small Kia SUV pulled up and parked off the main drive. The housekeeper, an older black woman whom Decker and Jamison had seen on a previous visit, got out of the car and walked past them, nodding and smiling. She opened the front door with a key and went in.

Jamison looked at her watch. "Okay, now we know. Housekeepers to the rich get in at seven sharp."

Another few minutes passed, and when the door opened again, it was Natalie. She had on an ankle-length robe. Her hair was stringy and matted on one side. Her eyes were bloodshot.

"Jules said you wanted to talk about Corbett?"

"Maybe we can come inside?" suggested Jamison.

"I guess," she said sullenly. She stepped back and they walked past her.

She led them to the library and closed the door behind them. They sat on the couch and she sat across from them. Natalie wouldn't look at them. Her gaze remained directed at the floor.

"My mom's not up yet."

"That's okay, we don't need to bother her," said Jamison. She glanced at Decker.

He said, "We know about the gambling debts. And we know how your father got the money to pay them off."

"Oh, God!" Natalie put her face in her hands and started sobbing.

Jamison rose, crossed the room, and sat down next to her, wrapping an arm around her quaking body. She gave Decker a scowl.

Natalie started to gasp for air.

"Are you okay?" asked Jamison.

Natalie reached into her pocket and pulled out an inhaler. She took two quick puffs and her breathing rapidly settled down.

"I'm okay now. Asthma," she added, holding up the inhaler. "We all have it, except Dad. We got it from Mom." She leaned back against her chair and closed her eyes, breathing deeply.

Jamison sat back next to Decker and whispered, "I think you need to go a little easy."

Decker waited for Natalie to regain her composure. She slowly sat up, rubbed her eyes dry with the cord of her robe, and looked at him.

"I didn't know who else to turn to," she said, her voice scratchy and raw. "They were going to kill him. They were going to kill all of us."

"Did you know about the gambling?" asked Decker.

"I didn't know the extent of it. And I didn't know he was mixed up with the sort of people who would murder you."

"Are you sure he's not going to do it again?" asked Jamison.

"This scared the shit out of Corbett. But at this point, I don't really care. I'm divorcing him. He cost me my father. I hate him. I hate everything about him. I'm coming back to the States with my daughter. I just have to find a place to live."

"Do you know where your father got the money?"

She shook her head. "I know he and Mom are well-off. But the amount was so huge."

"Ten million, we heard," said Decker.

She nodded. "I didn't think they had that kind of money in cash. But maybe if they sold the house and some other stuff."

Decker said, "And you were expecting your father to do that? Sell everything they had. Everything they'd worked for?"

"I...I don't know. I don't know what I was expecting him to do, I guess." She paused. "When I was a kid and got into trouble my father always fixed things. Always. He made things right. I guess...I guess I got used to that."

Decker said firmly, "That works with falling off your bike and getting your feelings hurt when someone calls you a name. But you're not a kid anymore, Natalie."

She gazed fixedly at him. "I know that. I don't need a lecture from the FBI, okay?"

"So he said nothing to you about where he was going to get the money?"

"No. He just told me he'd take care of it."

"How was the money sent?" asked Jamison.

"I think he had it wired. But I'm not sure. I just know that it was received. Corbett told me. He was so relieved."

"I'm sure," said Decker harshly. "So when you heard about your father, what did you think had happened?"

"I didn't know what to think. I thought, I thought maybe he had snapped or something. When Jules called she was so calm and professional. Just like she always is," she added derisively. "But all I could make out was that Dad was dead and he had shot himself. I didn't even know about the woman he killed until I got here, although Jules said she told me. I guess I didn't process that part. I'm not as coldly efficient as my big sister."

"Did you think what he did was connected to how he had gotten the money?" asked Jamison.

Natalie nodded, looking miserable as the tears rolled down her cheeks. "I thought it *had* to be connected. And so I believed it was my fault. I drank on the flight from France. Then when I got here I kept drinking. I don't remember much before or after."

"I'm sure that was a big help to your family," said Decker sternly.

"Hey," she snapped, "I'm not proud of what I did, okay? So you can leave the high-and-mighty attitude for someone else. And if you keep it up I won't do anything to help you."

Decker leaned forward. "Let me lay this out so that you see clearly what's at stake here, lady. I'm not here begging for favors. Your father committed *treason* to get the money to pay *Corbett's* damn gambling debts."

Natalie went white and her mouth hung open. She looked like she might throw up.

Decker ignored her expression and continued, "So that makes you, at minimum, an accessory to treason. And you didn't come forward with any of this information that might have explained, in part, why your father did what he did. That's obstruction of justice. You combine the two with assorted other felonies, which any competent U.S. Attorney would be able to come up with, and you won't have to worry about finding a place to live after you divorce *Corbett*. Your housing will be provided by the federal prison system for the rest of your life."

"Omigod!"

Before she became hysterical Decker said, "But if you cooperate, maybe that doesn't happen."

"What do you want me to do?" she blurted out.

"Someone I greatly respect thinks your father may have told you something that might help us."

"Like what?"

Decker said, "I'm guessing you're the youngest."

"I am. How did you know?"

"You said your dad took care of everything for you. And you said Jules was all professional-like. She's the oldest. The take-charge one."

Natalie nodded.

"So you and your dad had a special relationship."

"We did."

"You flew over here and went with him to the doctors, didn't you?"

Natalie said, "He…he called me and told me he thought he was sick. I mean really sick. He said he hadn't told anyone else. He wanted me." She broke off and fought back a sob. "He wanted me to go with him to get a definitive diagnosis. He sent the money for the plane ticket."

"So you went?" said Jamison.

She rubbed her eyes, took a tissue from her robe pocket, and blew her nose. "Yes. And they confirmed that he had stage four inoperable brain cancer. They said that before long he wouldn't be able to function normally."

"And what did your dad say about that?"

"That he wasn't going to do any treatments. They would give him an extra couple of weeks or maybe a month, but he didn't want that. He was planning to tell Mom, and we talked about how he was going to break the news."

"And did he talk to you about anything else he was planning to do?" asked Decker.

Natalie looked at each of them before settling her gaze on Decker. "If you're asking did he tell me that he was planning on shooting someone a month or so later and then taking his own life, that would be a no. I would never have kept quiet about *that*."

"But did he say anything that might have hinted at what he was planning to do? It might have made no sense to you, but it could still be important."

Natalie thought for a few moments. She rubbed at her eyes and said, "We were talking one night. He had called me in France out of the blue."

"When was this?"

"About a week ago."

"Go on," said Decker.

"Well, he said he hadn't told Mom or the others yet, but he was still planning to. And then he said, 'You think you know someone for a long time, and then it turns out you don't know them at all. And then, before you know it, it's too late.'"

"Did you ask him what he meant by that?" asked Jamison.

"I did, at least I tried to. I thought he might be on some pain meds and was a little incoherent. But then before I could say anything he told me he loved me. And then he hung up. That was the last time I ever heard from him." She bowed her head and began to quietly sob. After a few moments she lifted her head and said, "Will all this have to come out? Will my mom and sisters have to know?"

"Right now, I don't see any way to keep this secret," said Decker.

As they walked out Jamison looked at Decker. "What do you make of that?"

"I think Walter Dabney was being quite literal."

CHAPTER

31

THEY LEFT THE STRICKEN HOUSE and Mars drove them to the WFO.

On the way Jamison said, "What did you mean that Dabney was being literal?"

"That someone he trusted had screwed him. I just don't know who that is."

Mars shot him a glance. "You mean like my old man? Or who I thought was my old man."

"Yeah, like him."

"You were sort of hard on Natalie, Decker," said Jamison.

Decker looked at her. "How?"

"She just lost her dad and you were busting her chops."

"If she was feeling guilty, she should have been. *She* was the reason her father stole secrets."

"But her husband—" began Jamison.

"You make choices," interrupted Decker. "Walter Dabney would never have done what he did but for Corbett not being able to control his gambling. So the result is the guy who should have had consequences gets off without a scratch. And the guy who should have been left to deal with his terminal cancer and die with dignity is lying on a slab at the morgue. After decades of busting his ass to give his family a great life, he'll be remembered as a traitor and a murderer."

"Well, he made choices too," countered Jamison.

"I don't see it the same way," said Decker. "Natalie was his baby girl. What was he supposed to do?"

"He could have said no," answered Mars. "But he didn't. I'm not saying it was an easy choice, because it wasn't. Maybe he should have called in the police or helped Natalie and her family go into hiding. Dabney obviously had connections. He could have maybe helped another way."

Decker shook his head and said, "Neither one of you have had a kid. I did. You'd do anything to help them. Anything."

And that was all Decker would say on the drive back.

Once they got to the WFO they needed a temporary visitor's badge for Mars, but they had called ahead to Bogart and he had taken care of it, meeting them at the front entrance.

"Damn, Melvin, you look good," said Bogart. Then he glared at Decker. "And Alex phoned me to let me know what happened last night. Decker, you took a big risk. A stupid risk. What the hell were you thinking? Oh, excuse me, it was obvious that you *weren't* thinking. You're lucky Melvin was there to save your butt."

"I always count on a little help from my friends," said Decker.

"You and the Beatles," retorted Bogart. "But lightning usually doesn't strike twice."

"Alex already gave me hell for it."

"No reason not to pile on," said Jamison tightly. "Then the message might actually sink in."

Bogart escorted them back to his office. When they were settled, Decker said, "Based on a hunch from Melvin, we spoke with Natalie, Dabney's youngest daughter." He went on to tell Bogart what had happened.

Bogart said thoughtfully, "So you think Dabney knew who was blackmailing him?"

Decker said, "But there's another piece to it. *You think you know someone?* The problem is, that could mean different things depending on the situation. Who was Dabney referring to?"

"Could be lots of possible people," interjected Jamison.

Decker nodded. "That's the problem."

Bogart said, "But at least it gives us a new lead to follow up."

Jamison said, "It might be someone he worked with over the years."

Decker said, "Well, it would be someone in a position to blackmail him *now*. We'll have to dig into Dabney's background more."

"Where do we start?" asked Jamison.

Decker answered, "At the obvious source. Walter Dabney and Associates."

* * *

"Have you found out anything else?" asked Faye Thompson, Dabney's partner they had spoken with previously. He and Jamison were in her office. Mars had gone back to the apartment.

Before he could answer she said, "By the way, I sent the photo of the woman in the video with Walter around the office. No one recognized her."

Decker said, "Okay, thanks. We were hoping you could help us on a line of inquiry."

"Me? How?"

"We'll need a list of all your employees and partners, with particular focus on ones who have been here long-term. And we'll need the same for your clients. Same focus. Long-term."

Thompson sat back looking both flustered and suspicious. "Where is all this leading?"

"Hopefully, to the truth."

"Sounds more like a scattergun approach."

"Investigations like this have to look at everything," said Decker. "And we can't discount the possibility that whatever drove Walter Dabney to do what he did originated here."

"I think that's extremely unlikely."

"Nevertheless."

"Do you have a warrant?"

"Do we need one?" He cocked his head. "I would have thought you'd want us to find out the truth behind all this."

"Of course I do. But I'm also running a business. And this sort of thing can be very disruptive. And you very well know that most of what we do is classified. We can't just start breaching confidences."

"Well, we apologize for the inconvenience, but two people are dead."

"I get that, but—"

Decker interrupted her. "And there's something else."

"What?"

"Walter Dabney needed an enormous amount of money very quickly. I won't get into why. But he stole secrets from a project he was working on here and sold them to enemies of this country."

Thompson slowly rose, wide-eyed, and stared down at him. "Bullshit!"

"DIA has been investigating this for a while. If you don't believe me, talk to them."

Thompson put a hand against the wall to steady herself. "DIA?"

Decker nodded.

"What secrets?"

"Serious, classified stuff."

"We'll have to do an immediate internal review."

"Might be a little late for that."

"This could ruin us," groaned Thompson.

"The sooner we solve this thing the better it'll be for you," Jamison pointed out.

"I have to talk to some people," said Thompson.

"Okay, but if you don't want to cooperate we can easily get a warrant," said Decker.

She said quickly, "I didn't say I wouldn't cooperate. Look, I have to check with some other partners and our lawyers. Can I at least do that?"

"Absolutely. And we can wait here while you do."

She stared hard at him, but Decker's features were unflinching.

She rose and picked up her phone. "Then please excuse me while I go and do that," she said coldly. She left the room and slammed the door behind her.

"Do you think she's hiding something?" asked Jamison.

Decker shrugged. "Other things being equal, I think she's just pissed because this is going to hit her right in the wallet."

"Do you think it was wise to tell her about the stolen secrets?"

"I'm tired of spinning wheels. We need to interject some urgency into the equation. And I didn't tell her exactly what they were, because Agent Brown never told me."

Thompson came back a half hour later with a flash drive. She handed it to Decker. "Please understand that we want you to treat this information with the highest level of confidentiality."

"We understand that," said Jamison. "And we will."

Thompson kept her gaze on Decker. "Yeah, I'm sure *you* do, but I was talking about *him*."

Decker rose and left the room.

Thompson eyed Jamison. "How do you stand that guy?"

"He's excellent at what he does," she said defensively.

Thompson snorted. "Well, he would have to be, wouldn't he? To put up with the rest of the prick."

Jamison scurried after Decker, who was striding down the hall to the exit. She caught up to him midway and fell in step beside him.

She eyed the flash drive. "Probably a lot to sort through."

"Probably."

"Hey, maybe we can have dinner with Melvin tonight. We can go out."

He didn't respond.

"Decker, I said—"

"I heard you, Alex. That sounds fine."

"Great. Say seven-thirty at Cotton's? It's on Fourteenth Street. I'll make a reservation."

"Yep. Got it."

She hesitated. "I'm sure you're glad to see Melvin."

"I am."

"I mean, after all, he is your *best* friend."

"Yes, he is."

Jamison stuffed her hands into her pockets and marched along, her features rigid.

32

THEY PRINTED OFF the files from the flash drive and spent the rest of the day going through them at the WFO. Bogart and Milligan had joined them.

"They have a lot of clients, big and small," observed Milligan.

Bogart added, "And most of them have been with Dabney for decades, which doesn't make it easy to separate the wheat from the chaff."

"Maybe it's one of the partners," suggested Jamison, as she went over some pages. "A number of them have been with Dabney since nearly the beginning. He told his daughter you think you know someone but really don't. That might apply more to a fellow partner you see every day rather than a client."

Decker said nothing. He kept going over the files, imprinting all of the information onto his memory.

Bogart said, "If we interview each of these people and companies, it could take months, maybe a year. And by then whatever intel was stolen could be used to attack us."

Decker still said nothing. He was hearing everything that was being said, but his focus was on the files. Bogart was right. They had to cut this list down somehow. The answer might not even lie in these pages. Dabney might have been referring to someone outside his business. And while Decker believed that the comment Dabney had made to his daughter was connected to all this, he couldn't be absolutely certain of that either.

Milligan dropped a file, sat back, and said, "I hope we're not whistling in the wind here."

Decker glanced over at him, then abruptly rose and left the room. The others didn't notice right away.

A few moments later Bogart said, "Wait a minute, where did he go?"

Jamison just looked toward the doorway and shook her head.

* * *

"You know I can't really come running every time you call me."

Harper Brown was staring at Decker across the front seat of her BMW.

"You tend to show up when you want to show up," said Decker, who was in the passenger seat.

She ran her fingers over the steering wheel. "Your call was intriguing, I have to admit."

Decker just stared at her, making no move to speak.

"You have quite the gift of patience, waiting for the other person to speak, and maybe slip up."

Decker put his hands over his belly. "Do you *want* to slip up?"

"Why in the world would you say that?"

"You seem to have been skirting around the edges ever since you showed up in the middle of this investigation."

"It's dinner time. You hungry?"

"Look at me. I'm always hungry."

"I know a burger place," she said.

"You don't strike me as a burger sort of person."

"You don't really know me yet."

They drove to the place, parked, and walked in. It was a dive, and Decker could smell the lard coming from the kitchen before he passed the first table in the small dining area.

They found a semi-private spot near the hall to the bathrooms. When the waitress came, Brown said, "Number Twelves for the table. And two Especials. Just the bottles, save the dishwashers some work."

The woman nodded and walked off. A moment later they could hear her calling out the order to the cooks in the back.

"Number Twelve?" said Decker.

"Trust me, you'll love it." She leaned back in her chair, stretched out her long, jean-clad legs, and looked at him. "Slip-ups?"

"You open the tap and then turn it off. You tease. You play bad, then good. You sort of agree to help, but pull back. You threaten to kick us off the case, but won't or can't make good on it."

She shrugged. "Just trying to do my job."

"Bogart checked on you with a buddy of his at DIA."

"Good for him."

"He didn't know you. Never heard of you."

"Where is this 'buddy' assigned at DIA? We operate in over one hundred and forty locations overseas in addition to a big footprint here."

"DISC in Reston."

"Defense Intelligence Support Center. He's probably a civvie and a paper pusher. I'm neither. And are you somehow implying that I don't work at DIA?"

"Your badge and creds look real."

"That's because they *are*."

"I'm not saying you're a phony. They never would have allowed you inside Hoover if your creds were fake."

"So what exactly are you saying?" snapped Brown.

"That you're interesting, and I still don't know what you're actually after."

"I thought I made that perfectly clear. Whoever Dabney sold the secrets to. *That's* who I'm after."

"Made any progress?" asked Decker.

"What, you're here to try to ride my coattails?"

"Just interagency cooperation."

She smiled and said demurely, "I'm sorry, and I know *you've* been dancing around this issue, but I don't remember saying that I needed your help."

"Everybody needs help once in a while."

Their beers came and they each took a long sip.

"So you're here to help me?" she asked, setting her bottle down. "How generous of you."

"I don't really care how I get to the truth, so long as I get there. I figured if we combined resources we might get there faster, instead of running on parallel tracks. Hell, you're the one saying this could lead to an apocalypse. Excuse me for taking you at your word."

She took another sip of her beer and then rubbed her mouth with a napkin. "Okay, I get the point. But I did try to explain why I was reluctant to bring others into the loop."

"I'm not a damn spy, Brown! I just got to this town a few months ago. Your world is stranger to me than living on Mars would be, but I just want to get to the truth. That's all."

She considered this and said, "Okay, where do things stand with your investigation?"

"We have two angles to exploit: Dabney's end and Berkshire's background."

"I told you I'm only interested in Dabney."

"But you might be interested in Berkshire. Or at least you *should* be."

She looked intrigued. "And why is that?"

"If someone blackmailed Dabney to kill Berkshire, they could be the same people he sold the secrets to, or someone who knew about it and used it to manipulate Dabney. If that's correct, then *that* party is looped into this whole espionage circle and could be a national security threat. That's right up your alley."

They didn't say another word until their food arrived a couple minutes later. Decker stared down at a double-stacked burger with thick bacon strips, two fried onion rings, and a fried egg topping it all, with a large steak knife drilled right through the middle of it. A giant mound of fries was delivered along with the burger.

He looked up from the meal to Brown. "You're really going to eat this? You weigh, what, one-twenty? And you look like fat wouldn't dare attach itself to you."

She plucked a fry from the stack and bit half off. "Genetic gift, a fabulous metabolism. Plus, I work out, a little."

"Right, a little."

They began to eat. She poured ketchup onto a small plate in the middle of the table and said, "Hypothetically speaking, let's say you're right. How would you attack the problem?"

"Dig on both ends. We met today and discussed going at it from the two angles like I said. Maybe we get lucky and end up meeting in the middle."

She took a bite of her burger, while Decker chewed on an onion ring.

She said, "Dabney's end has a lot of potential suspects. Guy's had a long career in the industry."

"It was suggested that it might be somewhat like *Strangers on a Train.* The third party who has a beef against Berkshire gets Dabney to kill their enemy in exchange for their not revealing what he's done. Dabney may have no connection to Berkshire at all."

"He obviously had no idea we were already on to him," said Brown thoughtfully. "Or he would have known that the game was over."

"If he had known that, he might not have bothered to kill Berkshire."

"Or you could be totally wrong and he did have a connection with Berkshire, only you haven't found it yet."

"Perfectly true," said Decker, taking a huge bite of his burger. He dipped a fry into the ketchup, ate it, and then wiped his fingers on his paper napkin. "But we have to start somewhere. And if that is the case, we should turn that up when we look into their backgrounds, especially Berkshire's."

"But you have no leads right now," she said.

"We have a clown," said Decker.

She had taken a sip of beer and almost spit it out. "Come again?"

He told her about the possibility of the clown being the signal for Dabney.

"Let's finish up here and go some place we can talk in private," she said.

"Like where?"

"Like my place."

* * *

After they finished their meals and she paid, Harper drove them to a street full of old high-dollar row houses that looked newly renovated. It was a couple blocks off Capitol Hill. She pulled into a space and cut the engine.

Decker looked out the car window. "Nice area."

"Yeah, it is."

She got out and led him to the front steps of a three-story house with a façade of white-painted brick with another wing fronted by stone. The door was solid wood and looked about a century old. There was a gas lamppost in the small front yard, which was enclosed by a three-foot-high wrought iron fence. She opened the door and turned off the alarm. Decker followed her inside.

The interior was warm and inviting, the furnishings tastefully selected, the rugs thick and subtly patterned and colorful. The walls were brick in some places, stone in others, and solid plaster in still others. What looked like original oil paintings hung on several walls.

Brown led Decker into a small study off a kitchen that was outfitted with stainless steel appliances, granite counters, a pot filler over the Viking range, and cabinets that looked straight out of a Tuscan villa. She poured herself a scotch from a small bar set against one wall and asked Decker if he wanted one.

"Scotch isn't really my thing."

She sat down across from him in a leather wing chair. She picked up a remote on a side table, pressed a button, and a fire burst forth in the stone fireplace situated in the center of one wall.

She took off her holster and set her gun down on the table next to her. She slipped off her shoes, curled her legs up under her, and cradled her drink.

"You must be wondering how a federal agent can afford a place like this," she said. "And the BMW."

"Never crossed my mind."

She smiled. "Ever heard of Hewlett-Packard?"

"Me and a few billion other people."

"My great-grandfather was one of the earliest investors in HP and about six other now–Fortune 500 companies. He set up a trust fund. I also inherited money from him. When my parents died, I inherited still more. This house actually belonged to my grandfather."

"Must be nice."

"It *is* nice. I feel very fortunate."

He eyed the Beretta. "But you obviously didn't take the path of living off your money and doing nothing else with your life."

"I came by that naturally. My father was military. Maxed out as a full colonel. He was in Vietnam, two Purples and a Bronze. He was a helluva soldier."

"That's impressive, Agent Brown."

"Just make it Harper. We're off duty, *Amos*. My father was the reason I joined up. He could have sat back and lived off money he didn't earn too. But he decided to put on the uniform and serve."

"So you were in the military?"

"Technically, I still am. Army. Did two tours in Iraq and Afghanistan."

"What was your job?"

"EOD specialist."

"I don't know what that is."

"Sorry, we tend to talk in acronyms. Explosive ordnance disposal specialist. I defused unexploded bombs and IEDs."

"That sounds dangerous."

"Everything over there was dangerous. It was dangerous waking up and it was dangerous going to sleep. And it was dangerous for everything in between."

"I can see that. Is that what your dad did in the military?"

"No. He thought I was a nut job for joining the EOD. But I was really good at it." She took a sip of her drink. "So, back to the case. You proposed an arrangement of some type?"

"I think working together makes sense. But you obviously wanted to talk in private, which is why we're here." He sat back and eyed her expectantly.

She rubbed her bare foot and took a few moments to marshal her thoughts.

"The secrets that Dabney sold were critical to the security of this country. Without going into too much detail, he may have divulged a back door into some of our most important cyber-security platforms."

"Wait a minute! You told me before that these stolen secrets had to do with tanks and planes and stuff terrorists couldn't afford to build."

She sipped her scotch. "That was before I knew you better."

"So you lied."

"I used a standard tactic to allow me sufficient opportunity to calculate your trustworthiness."

"So you lied," Decker said again.

"But now I'm telling you how it really is. We have unauthorized back doors into our intelligence platforms."

"Which means they're hackable?"

"Which means they've probably already been hacked."

"But now that you know about the theft, can you take steps to prevent further damage?"

"Easier said than done. The thing is, we don't know precisely when Dabney conveyed the secrets. Thus whoever he sold them to could have already installed malware or spyware on the systems. We can't shut everything down. And secrets may already have been stolen and national security compromised."

Decker nodded. "I can see the problem."

"No, I don't think you do. I *wish* they had simply stolen stuff on tanks and planes. That takes a long time to build. This...this can be used against us immediately. In fact, it may already have been used against us. We could be sitting on a time bomb right now and have no idea where it is or when it's going to go off." She added coolly, "What do you think about that?"

"I think I'll take that scotch now."

She rose and poured it out for him before settling back down in her chair. Decker took a small sip of the drink and let it burn down his throat.

"How do you know exactly what Dabney stole?" he asked.

She drank some scotch before answering. "I have a DIA top secret clearance with an SCI, or Sensitive Compartmented Information, access kicker. Anyone at CIA or NSA with those security clearances from their agencies would not be allowed to know that information, because that's just how our world works. There's no reciprocity on that score."

"Which is your polite way of telling me you can't answer my question."

She held up her glass in affirmation of his statement. "But what I can tell you is that we are satisfied that we're correct in what was stolen. We just don't know who has it, or how long they've had it. Or what they've done with it."

"So how do we work this together?"

"Can you really remember everything?"

"More or less. Emphasis on the more."

"How many people were in the restaurant tonight?"

Decker clicked through his frames. "Fourteen, not counting us or the staff."

"There was a guy sitting at the right side of the bar. What was he wearing?"

Decker told her, down to his sock color. Then he added, "Your odometer reading on the BMW is 24137. Do you want to know your VIN? I saw it the first time you gave me a ride, so I've got that too." He recited it for her. She grabbed her purse, took out her wallet, slipped out her insurance card, and read out the VIN. Her expression said it all—Decker had been perfect.

She sat back. "That's remarkable."

"So, again, how do we work this? Together?"

"As I said before, Dabney interests me more than Berkshire. Do you agree?"

Decker shook his head.

"Whoever got Dabney to kill Berkshire blackmailed him to do it. That means they know about the secrets he sold. And I'm betting that they know who he sold them to. It actually might have been one and the same party. We figure out the Berkshire end, then we solve *your* problem too."

She put down her scotch. "That actually makes a lot of sense."

"So you'll work with us on Berkshire?"

She nodded. "Yes, I will."

"Good, I might have some information that will help."

"Like what?"

"Like maybe *what* Anne Berkshire used to be."

33

Brown's features froze for an instant. "*What* she used to be? You care to explain that statement?"

"It's the reason I called you tonight. She has no past further back than ten years. But she had a résumé showing she graduated from Virginia Tech, only her first name was spelled differently. And she's rich, and we don't know how she came by the money."

"Okay, what does that tell you?"

"I was speculating that she might be a spy. Maybe the one that Dabney passed the secrets to. But then why kill her? And we can find no connection between them. So we considered the Witness Protection angle, but I don't think any of the people in that program are rich. And she volunteered and worked as a schoolteacher. That really put her out there in the public eye some. I don't think the U.S. Marshals encourage that. They have their protectees keep low profiles."

"Which leaves what?"

"She did something on her own that caused her to put together a new identity. And whatever she did in the *recent* past gave her great wealth."

"Don't keep me in suspense, Decker."

"It stands to reason that the people who blackmailed

Dabney might be in the military arena. Defense contracting more specifically. That allowed Dabney to have the access to get the secrets and them to buy the secrets or at least know he committed treason."

"And that is all speculation on your part," pointed out Brown.

"Without facts, that's all we can do at this point. But I'm trying to deal in probabilities."

"Okay, go on."

"I think she could have been a *whistleblower*."

Brown put her feet on the floor and stared at him. "Keep going."

"If she was the whistleblower on some defense contract that went sideways, she might have gotten a reward. Sometimes they're tied to a percentage of the amounts saved by the government because of the person's actions. That would explain Berkshire's wealth. She might have gotten some of the people she informed on sent to prison. That would explain why she adopted a new identity. To hide from them."

"And those people might be out now," said Brown.

"They might be, yes. And maybe some of them didn't go to prison, but her whistleblowing might have ruined their business, caused them to go bankrupt, shut them out of the government feeding trough. That could be a motive to have someone kill her."

"Yes, it could. How did you come up with this angle?"

"Something Todd Milligan said earlier about whistling in the wind."

"So what do we do with this information?"

"We follow it up. We have to look at whistleblower cases."

"There are a lot of them."

"That's where you come in. I believe this is tied to the defense sector."

She nodded and took another sip of her scotch. "You'll need to be read into some things. And you don't have a security clearance, which makes things difficult."

"I've applied for one through the FBI. I've taken and passed the polygraph, but they haven't finished the background check on me yet." He added, "My past is a little complicated."

She gazed keenly at him. "I would imagine it is." She set her glass down. "I might be able to work something out. I'll call you tomorrow."

* * *

Brown dropped Decker off at his apartment and drove away. For a moment Decker stood there in the darkness staring up at the windows of the apartment where Danny and his father had lived.

Danny Amaya was a year older than Decker's daughter was when she'd been killed. She'd never actually reached her tenth birthday. Her murderer had gotten to her before that could happen.

Molly Decker would have turned twelve this year. His wife, Cassie, would have turned forty-two.

They were dead and buried back in Ohio.

He was five hundred miles from them, farther than he ever thought he would be.

Five hundred miles farther than he thought he ever *could* be.

He sat down on the front steps of the building and stared down at his feet.

Though his memory was near perfect, there were many emotional tethers that Decker struggled to recall or even reform in his head.

He had once been someone very different. And that was difficult if not impossible for most people to come close to understanding. There were many days when even Decker didn't understand it.

He knew that he irritated people with his behavior. He knew that he drove Alex Jamison and the others to distraction sometimes. There was a part of him that wanted to do something about this. To let her and others see the person he used to be. But a larger part of him seemed to crush any attempt to enable himself to do this.

If it was frustrating for others, it was maddening for Amos Decker.

What they failed to fully comprehend was that the hit on the football field had done far more than give him perfect recall and the ability to see things in color. It had forced him into being a different person, as though a stranger's personality and attendant quirks had been superimposed over his own.

But now the stranger's footprint *was* Decker.

I am now the stranger. I'm a stranger in my own body.

He would sometimes wake up in the middle of the night and wonder not where he was—as many people, confused and muddled by weariness, did—but rather *who* he was.

And sometimes the answer was not all that easy.

He stood, turned, and headed inside. It was after eleven now and he expected that Jamison would be asleep. So when he opened the door to their apartment he was surprised to see her sitting at the kitchen table fully dressed. He closed the door behind him.

"Where have you been, Decker?" she said quietly.

"I'm sorry, Alex. I was with Agent Brown. I came up with a theory and we're going to work together to run it down."

"That's great, Decker, really wonderful."

Decker did not appear to catch the edge to her voice. "It had to do with—"

"The man who forgets nothing," she said.

He looked at her strangely. "What?"

She stood. "But that's not entirely right."

"What's not entirely right?" he said in a perplexed tone.

"That you don't forget anything."

He drew closer. "I'm not following where this is going."

"Well, then let me enlighten you." She paused, drew a long breath that seemed to swell her body, and said in a strident tone, "You *forgot* that we were supposed to have dinner with Melvin tonight. Cottons on Fourteenth Street, seven-thirty?"

The color drained from Decker's face. "Oh, shit, Alex, I'm—"

She pushed on, her voice starting to crack now. "We waited at the restaurant for two hours for you. *Two fucking hours*, Decker. I called Bogart. I called 911. I called everybody I could think of."

"But why didn't you call me?"

"I did! Twelve times."

He reached into his pocket and pulled out his phone. He turned even paler.

"I forgot I turned it to silent."

"*Forgot* something else, huh? Wow, that perfect memory of yours is just going to hell in a handbasket."

"Alex, I'm—"

Tears crept into her eyes. "You can listen to my frantic voicemails later. You'll probably get a real chuckle out of them. You asshole!"

Before he could say anything else she had turned and stormed down the hall to her room. He heard the door slam behind her.

Decker looked down at his phone and saw all the missed

calls. He sat down at the kitchen table and listened to the increasingly panicked voicemails. Jamison sounded like she was going out of her mind with worry. And with the fact that he had been nearly killed twice recently and had enemies still out there, he could hardly blame her.

The old Decker would have gone to her door, knocked, and profusely apologized.

The new Decker just sat there staring out the window at the darkness that was not so nearly as opaque as the one currently residing squarely in his head.

CHAPTER

34

BLEARY-EYED, JAMISON got up the next morning, washed her face, and walked down the hall to the kitchen to make coffee.

She stopped dead when she got to the kitchen.

"Have you been sitting there all night?"

Decker looked up from his chair.

She said, "Decker, it's seven in the morning. Have you even been to bed?"

In answer he held up his phone. "I listened to the messages. All of them."

She frowned and leaned against the wall, wrapping the folds of her robe around her because the apartment was chilly. "Okay," she said slowly.

"I screwed up, Alex. I'm sorry. I'm sorry you were so worried. And I'm sorry I missed dinner."

She came and sat down next to him. She rubbed her eyes and looked at him. "Knowing you, I probably shouldn't have overreacted when you didn't show up. I mean, it's not like it's the first time you've stood me up." She played with the cord on her robe and added, "But with all that's taken place recently, with the Amayas and everything, I just thought something terrible had happened to you."

"If you ever call again I will answer it. And if I don't then you probably *will* need to call 911."

She gave him a grudging smile, squeezed his arm, and rose to go make coffee. "I called Melvin last night and told him you were okay."

Decker flinched because it had never occurred to him to do this.

What the hell is wrong with me?

"Thanks for doing that."

"Maybe we can grab dinner tonight?" she said cautiously.

"Yes, we can."

"Don't be too quick to agree. You might live to regret it."

She brought two cups of coffee over and set one down in front of him before retaking her seat. "Now, talk to me about this theory you came up with."

Decker went through it step by step.

Jamison looked impressed. "A whistleblower, huh? That would explain a lot of the questions we've got."

"The problem will be finding out which whistleblowing case. There have been a lot of them over the years."

"But it shouldn't be *that* hard. We can circulate Berkshire's picture all over. Someone will have to recognize her."

"The thing is, Alex, her picture *has* been all over the place. After the murder it was on all the news cycles and still is in some places."

She took a sip of coffee and looked perplexed. "That's true. I wonder why no one has come forward, then?"

"She changed her name, obviously. She could have changed her appearance too."

"You mean plastic surgery?"

"There are lots of ways to change your appearance other than going under the knife. She could have lost weight, changed her hairstyle and color, started wearing glasses, or used tinted contacts to change her eye color. It all adds up."

"We could ask the ME if Berkshire had had surgery. The autopsy would have shown that."

"I emailed her last night. She must be an early riser. She emailed me a half hour ago and said there were no signs of plastic surgery."

"Speaking of early risers, don't you think you should get some sleep?"

"I'm not tired."

"Well, at some point you're going to need to rest or else you're going to wear out. You want some breakfast?"

"I'll get it."

"Okay, I'm going to grab a shower."

As she walked off, Decker's thoughts trended back to Berkshire. Specifically, to the old house in the woods. The flash drive, he knew, would have been a treasure trove of information. It might have detailed Berkshire's past, answering so many questions. But someone had followed them there, shot out Decker's tire, assaulted him, and taken it. So someone was watching them. Or else they had been watching the old house.

He heard a buzzing sound and looked down. It was Jamison's phone. He didn't recognize the number and the caller ID came up as unknown, so it wasn't on Jamison's contact list.

He heard the shower running. He could have just let it go to voicemail, but decided to answer it.

"Hello?"

"Hello, this is Nancy Billings. I was calling for Alex Jamison or Amos Decker with the FBI?"

"I'm Amos Decker."

"Oh, hi. I'm a teacher at the school where Anne Berkshire worked as a substitute. I understand you might have some questions for me. I'm sorry to be calling so early, but I have to leave for work soon."

"No, that's no problem. Could we meet after school?"

"Yes. I have to go home and let out the dog, but there's a Starbucks near where I live." She gave him the address and they set a time.

He called Bogart and filled him in on what had happened with Agent Brown. Next he told him about Billings and the meeting later that day.

Bogart said, "I'll start following up on the military whistleblower angle. I know that's Brown's bailiwick, but I have some contacts there too. And the FBI investigated and the DOJ prosecuted a great many whistleblower cases over the years."

Decker clicked off and put his phone in his pocket. He went to the bathroom, splashed water on his face, and brushed his teeth. He came out at the same time Jamison did. She was wrapping a scarf around her neck.

"Did you eat?" she said.

"No. Slipped my mind."

"Wow, the old memory is just crapping out on you," she said dryly. "That's okay. We can get something on the way in to Hoover."

"Nancy Billings called. She worked with Berkshire at the school. I've arranged for us to meet her after she finishes at school today."

"Hopefully, she can tell us something helpful."

When they opened the exterior door to their building, Harper Brown was standing there. She wore jeans, boots, a black turtleneck, and a brown leather jacket. She held up a bag.

"Bagels. And I've got coffee in the car." She glanced at Jamison. "But not enough for you."

Jamison said, "We were about to head out to run down a lead."

Brown looked at Decker. "DIA HQ. Whistleblower files. You in or out? There won't be a second offer."

"Can't Alex come with us?"

Brown shook her head. "I had a hard enough time getting permission for you to come out. We can't have a tagalong."

Jamison bristled at this comment but said, "Okay, Amos, I'll let Bogart know about this when I get in to the office."

"I'll fill you all in on everything when I'm done at DIA."

"Well, to the extent they're cleared to hear it," said Brown, staring at Jamison.

Staring directly at Brown, Jamison said, "And I'm sure I'll do the same, so long as *you're* cleared for it."

They drove off, leaving Jamison standing in the parking lot. She shook her head, apparently trying to clear her thoughts.

"Maybe I should just go back to being a journalist," she said to herself.

CHAPTER

35

DIA'S SPRAWLING HEADQUARTERS was at Joint Base Anacostia-Bolling. It was located on the east side of the Potomac River, and across that body of water from National Airport. The Potomac cut a path northwest, with the far shorter Anacostia River snaking northeast.

At the entrance Decker received a visitor's badge and went through the security protocol. On one wall was the seal of the agency, a flaming torch of gold on a background of black with a pair of red atomic ellipses encircling a globe.

Brown pointed to it and said, "Flame and gold represents knowledge, or intelligence, as we like to call it. The black equals the unknown."

"And the red?" asked Decker.

"Scientific aspects of intelligence."

"Is it that scientific when you're dealing with people?"

"Maybe more than you know."

They passed a wall with names on it. Decker stopped and stared at it. Brown, who had been walking down the hall, came back to stand next to him.

"Torch Bearers Wall," she said. "The people on here have been awarded the highest honor for service to DIA and the country. We also have a memorial wall in the courtyard with the names of the seven DIA personnel killed on 9/11 during the attack on the Pentagon."

Decker pointed to one name on the list. "Colonel Rex Brown. Any relation?"

"My father," said Brown, before heading off again.

Decker fell in step behind her.

"Think you'll end up on the Torch Bearers Wall?" he said.

"I'd rather that than the memorial wall."

"What'd your father do to be on the wall?"

"Classified."

She opened a door and motioned Decker inside. He stepped through and gazed around at three walls of computer screens all alive with pictures but no sound. Brown closed the door behind her.

"We have around-the-clock watch centers everywhere literally taking in everything of significance going on all over the world. This is just a bit of feed from some of those operations."

"Impressive," said Decker as he sat down in a chair set around an oval conference table. "And how does this help us?"

The door opened and a man came in. He was about six feet tall with burly shoulders, massive arms and thighs, and close-cropped graying hair. His military cammies seemed unable to fully contain his muscular physique. And he wore a scowl.

"Agent Brown," he said gruffly.

"Colonel Carter," she said pleasantly. "This is Amos Decker with the FBI."

"Highly irregular. Couldn't believe it when I got the email. Man hasn't even passed his FBI security clearance, much less DIA protocols."

"The whole case is a bit *irregular*," said Brown. "But we feel Decker is vital to getting to the bottom of this."

"It's your professional funeral."

"Just working a case," retorted Brown. "And I'll use any asset I have to get to the truth. And Decker is a hell of an asset."

For the first time, Carter looked at Decker, who was wearing the same clothes as yesterday: wrinkled jeans, a stained sweatshirt, and a rumpled windbreaker. His hair was uncombed and jutted out every which way. And he hadn't shaved, so his five o'clock shadow was prominent.

Carter looked at Brown in disbelief. "What the hell! Does he work undercover at the FBI?"

Decker stirred and said, "No, but I did brush my teeth for the meeting."

Carter stared at him for a few seconds and then slammed his electronic notebook down on the table and sat. Brown slipped into a seat on the other side of Decker and took out a notebook and pen.

Carter started tapping keys on his notebook and the screens on the wall all went dead except for one. "Whistle-blowers," he said. "Starting from A and going to Z." He looked at Decker. "There's a lot, so try to keep up."

"Do my best," mumbled Decker, staring at the live screen.

On the screen there appeared a photo of a man.

"Karl Listner," said Carter. "From 1986. Military contract with a company we won't be disclosing to Mr. Decker. Listner was the liaison. He found out about certain irregularities and came forward."

"Our person's name is *Anne*," interjected Decker. "So do you have any non-males doing the whistleblowing?"

Carter looked sharply at Brown. "I wasn't given those parameters."

"Sorry, Colonel, this was all done in a rush."

"Of course it was, which is why this guy is sitting here.

And when you rush you screw up, but that's not my problem. It's *yours*."

He hit some more keys. "Okay, we have fifteen possibilities." He glanced at Decker. "Aren't you going to write any of this down?"

"I'm good," said Decker.

Carter visibly rolled his eyes, gave Brown a seething look, and turned back to the screen.

* * *

Hours later they had run through all of the whistleblower files. Brown turned to Decker and said, "I didn't see anything helpful. Not even any of the peripheral players could be Berkshire."

Decker nodded. He turned to Carter. "There's a mistake in your files."

"Impossible," barked Carter.

"Frame sixty-four and frame two hundred and seventeen. Sixty-four says Denise Turner was stationed in Islamabad in July 2003. Frame two hundred and seventeen says it was Faisalabad. You might want to pick one."

Decker got up and walked out.

Carter hit some keys and brought up the frames in question.

"He was right," said Brown thoughtfully as she looked at the screen.

"Sonofabitch got lucky," Carter shot back.

"Don't believe that for a minute."

She rose.

Carter said, "Who the hell is that guy?"

Brown stared after Decker. "Still trying to figure that out myself, Colonel."

CHAPTER

36

DECKER WAS WAITING for her outside the room. He leaned against the wall, his hands shoved into his pants pockets.

She said, "I think you shook up the good colonel."

"Yeah, look, could there be any other whistleblower cases out there? Maybe that no one knows about?"

"I don't see how. The whole point of being a whistleblower is that you blow the whistle and come forward. So we would have a record of it."

Decker sighed and closed his eyes.

Brown said, "By the way, did you spot any *other* mistakes in there?"

"Nine. Nothing substantive, so I decided to let the 'good colonel' find them."

"You're a real piece of work. But Carter is also an asshole, so it's no skin off my nose."

"So not a whistleblower, then," said Decker, opening his eyes.

"Apparently not, unless she did something unrelated to the defense sector or DIA. That's possible."

"Bogart is looking into that."

"So where do we go from here?"

Decker looked around. "How about you talk to me about your world."

"Why?"

"Why not?"

She considered this and said, "Okay, follow me."

She led him down the hall and into her office. It was small, utilitarian, and had no windows. And there wasn't a scrap of paper on the desk. Just a small laptop.

By way of explanation she said, "We don't like paper much. And we don't like windows. Surveillance issues, you know."

She pointed to a chair, which Decker took. She sat behind her desk.

"What do you want to know?"

"What can you tell me?"

"How about the very beginning? Robert McNamara created DIA when he was SecDef under the Kennedy administration."

"McNamara. Right, and later he did such a great job managing Vietnam."

"I'm just giving you the facts, I'm not providing commentary."

"What's your principal role here?"

"Intelligence gathering. We use HUMINT to get there, unlike some other agencies."

"Human intelligence, you mean?"

She nodded.

"Do you operate only internationally?"

"Why would that make sense when so much of what's going on now happens domestically?"

"So you operate in this country?"

"It's no secret."

"Have there been changes in how you do things?"

"Where is this going, Decker?"

"In the direction of the truth, one would hope."

"Whose truth?"

"Any truth works for me right now."

"You saying you don't think I'm telling the truth?"

In answer he pointed to a small poster tacked to the wall behind her. It was a DIA recruitment poster.

Decker read off the words printed on it: "You speak the language and live the culture. You could be anybody, anywhere."

He dropped his gaze to look at her. "Are you anybody anywhere?"

"I could just say it comes with the territory."

"Yeah, you could. Or you could go farther than that. Maybe with something more recent than freaking Robert McNamara."

"I'm not sure I want to."

"Well, since I'm a cop, let me tell you what comes from the territory I occupy. People commit crimes and the cops track them down and arrest them. It's a pretty linear philosophy. A to B to C."

"Not how my world works."

"Right. So you want the criminals to blow up the world while you're working some sort of backdoor convoluted spy bullshit maneuver that you can use in your *next* life?"

She put her feet up on her desk and leaned back in her chair. "Okay, I see your point." She gathered her thoughts. "Over a decade ago, DIA requested the ability to recruit U.S. citizens to spy and be informants."

"Is that so unusual?"

"No. But DIA also wanted to do it without having to reveal to said citizens that we were a government agency."

"How does that make sense?"

"It apparently didn't. That language was removed from the bill authorizing the recruitment provision."

"So does that mean DIA doesn't do it?"

"I don't. I can't speak for others."

"What else?"

"In 2008 we got approval to conduct offensive counter-intelligence clandestine ops both domestically and abroad."

"How would you do that?"

"Pretty basic stuff. Planting moles, disseminating disinformation, negatively impacting a country's information systems. You might be interested to know that we coordinate with the Bureau on that last one. Then in 2012 we expanded our clandestine collection efforts. We took over the Defense Department's HUMINT efforts and beefed up our espionage ops overseas, obviously focusing on the military component."

"What's your focus these days?"

"Nothing too surprising. Islamic terrorists including ISIL and Al Qaeda, North Korea, Iran, particularly weapon and nuclear technology transfers, and the Chinese and Russians beefing up their military capabilities."

"How about the Russians hacking us to try to influence our politics?"

"That would be a yes, Decker. Strikes right at the fundamentals of our democracy."

"So a lot of ground to cover."

"Which is why we have about seventeen thousand people working on it."

"You talked about planting moles. You guys ever have spies in your ranks?"

She nodded and her features turned grim. "All intelligence agencies have. The worst for us was probably Ana Belén Montes. Very high-ranking analyst here and very well respected. It was before my time. Turned out she'd been spying for Cuba for over twenty years. Did a lot of damage and probably cost some people their lives."

"Never heard of her."

"Not surprising. She was arrested right when 9/11 was going down. That pretty much trumped every other story out there for months."

"How'd they nail her?"

"Good old-fashioned detective legwork. And our cause was helped by the fact that spies stick to basic protocols. Shortwave radio transmissions, encryption software, standard drops in crowded places, zigzags on foreign travel. They were able to piece the puzzle together because of that."

"You'd think spies would wise up and try something new or vary their routines."

She shook her head. "It's like bomb makers, Decker. I learned a lot about them as an EOD. Once they learn a way to do something they don't like to deviate from it. It's called a bomb *signature*. That way they work out all the kinks and they don't get blown up, but it also helps us identify a particular—"

Decker got up from his chair and walked out.

Brown jumped up. "Decker? Decker!"

She raced after him.

CHAPTER

37

"Wow!" exclaimed Brown.

She and Decker had just entered Berkshire's luxurious condo.

Brown looked around in amazement. "You were right about her having money."

Decker didn't respond. He made a beeline down the hall and Brown quickly followed. He went into the master bathroom and then into the separate toilet closet. He snatched the toilet paper off the wall, slid off the roll, and opened the tube.

"Damn."

There was nothing there.

"What did you expect to find?" asked Brown.

He pushed past her, left the bathroom, and moved down the hall. He entered the second bedroom and pushed open the door to the en suite bathroom. He stared down at the toilet paper roll.

He took it off the wall, slid open the tube, and there it was.

"A key," said Brown.

"Like you said, spies don't like to learn new techniques, like bomb makers."

"So she used this device before?"

"At the cottage in the woods, yeah."

"What's it a key to?"

Decker looked at it more closely. "Could be lots of different things. A padlock, maybe."

They left the bathroom and he perched on a chair in the guest bedroom. He closed his eyes and let the frames roll back and forth.

Brown watched him curiously. "Checking the old memory?"

He said nothing.

A minute later he opened his eyes and stood. He went out into the hall and over to the broad set of windows that looked out onto the street below.

"If you had something important that you didn't want to keep here, but you wanted it close, what would you do?" he asked.

"Put it at a storage place."

"There aren't any around here," said Decker, looking out the window. "This is too high-rent a district for it to make economic sense."

"But, like you said, she'd want it reasonably accessible."

"Yes, she would. Let's go."

* * *

Twenty minutes later they passed the Catholic school where Berkshire had worked. Decker pointed across the street.

Brown looked where he was pointing.

"A to Z Storage?"

"And hopefully everything in between."

They drove into the parking lot and climbed out of the car. Inside, they showed the woman behind the counter their official creds. She looked up Berkshire's name on the database. "She paid for one year in advance. Still has a few months to go."

"Don't count on her renewing," said Decker. He held up the key. "Which unit?"

"I'm not sure I can allow that without a warrant."

Brown said, "We have reason to believe that Ms. Berkshire has been storing explosives in that unit."

"Oh my holy Lord," exclaimed the woman.

"So before we call the bomb squad we need to check it out. Or we can wait for the warrant and just hope you and this business don't get blown into the sky."

"It's Unit 2213," blurted the woman. "Out that door and to the right. Do you think I should leave the premises? I don't want to die for minimum wage."

"I think now would be a great time for you to take a break, yeah," said Brown.

The woman fled out the door, got into her car, and drove off with a screeching of tires.

Decker glanced at Brown. "I'm beginning to see you in a whole new light."

She smiled but said nothing as they walked to Unit 2213. It was a single unit with a roll-up door. Decker used the key to unlock the thick padlock, then bent down, gripped the door's handle, and pulled the door up.

Inside was a single shelf with a solitary box on it.

"Looks promising," said Brown.

They walked over and examined the box. It was plain cardboard with no writing on the sides or top. Decker pulled out his pocketknife and slit the tape, unsealing the box.

He opened the flaps and looked inside. He started pulling objects out and placing them on the shelf next to the box.

What looked like a security badge.

A typewritten paper in Cyrillic.

An old floppy disk.

And a doll.

While Brown looked at the paper, Decker examined the doll.

Brown said, "This is dated May 1985. It looks to be some sort of official communication from Moscow. The KGB."

"You can read Russian?"

"Along with Chinese and Arabic. And I can hold my own with Korean."

"Impressive."

"It's part of my job, Decker."

He had been probing the doll with his fingers until something gave and a compartment popped open. Decker looked inside, but it was empty. "You can see that there's where the batteries would go."

"Okay."

He used the blade of his pocketknife to probe around inside the battery compartment. There was a tiny pop and the whole battery compartment slid out, revealing a space just behind it.

She said, "I'm betting that was not put there by the toy manufacturer."

Decker nodded. "And it's big enough for a roll of microfiche or a microdot or whatever else they used back then."

"How do you know about microdots?"

"I watched enough old James Bond films."

He looked at the floppy disk. "Old technology like this." He picked up the security badge. The name that had once been on it had been clipped out. But Decker held it up to Brown.

The golden torch with the black background and red atomic ellipses hugging the globe.

"DIA seal," Decker said. "She wasn't a whistleblower."

"She was a spy," finished Brown.

38

DECKER, BROWN, BOGART, Jamison, and Milligan were sitting around a conference table at the WFO staring at the middle of the table.

Sitting there were the items Decker and Brown had found at the storage unit and then placed in evidence bags. All the items had been checked for prints and other forensics, but the tests had come back negative.

Bogart picked up the doll and examined the secret compartment.

Milligan slid the ID badge over and looked at it. "You said you checked and Berkshire, or whatever her name really is, never worked at DIA?"

"That's right," said Brown. "She would have been thoroughly vetted, undergone a background check, and her prints would have been taken and kept on our database. She's not there."

Bogart put the doll down, cleared his throat, and said, "We've checked all of our databases and can find no record of her. If she worked either in a government agency or as a contractor requiring a security clearance her prints would have been on file. They weren't."

Decker sat staring down at his hands.

Jamison glanced at him. "What do you think, Amos?"

"I think the part of the badge clipped out had someone else's name."

"If it were an RFID badge," said Milligan, referring to radio frequency identification devices, "it would be full of the holder's data unless it had been electronically wiped clean."

"But it isn't," said Decker. "It was obviously issued before that technology was used, at least by DIA."

Brown said, "Berkshire could have been the mole's handler. She wouldn't need to be on a database or have a badge to do that. The person on the inside would, of course. But Berkshire could have just managed the asset and collected the intel."

"*That* is far more likely," said Decker. "We just have to find out who that person on the inside was."

"But do you think Berkshire was *still* acting as a handler?" said Milligan. "I mean the old badge, the floppy disk, the 1980s KGB communication, it all dates from another era."

Bogart said, "That's a good point. She might have retired and decided to do something else with her life."

"Good works, you mean," said Jamison. "Maybe to atone for what she'd done in the past."

"But where does the money come in?" asked Brown. "Handlers are not known to make fortunes. And if she was working for the Russians, why not just go back there when she retired?"

"Maybe she couldn't," said Decker.

They all looked at him.

"Why wouldn't she be able to?" asked Brown.

"Why would a Russian operative be unwelcome back in Russia?" said Decker.

"Because they turned against their country," answered Brown.

"Are you saying Berkshire was a double agent?" said Bogart.

"I'm saying it's possible she was a spy and then was turned."

"But if she was wouldn't there be some evidence of that?" asked Milligan. "Some record?"

"Well, since we just discovered this possibility now, we have to pose that question to the right people."

"If it was over thirty years ago it might be hard to find the right people to ask," noted Bogart.

Decker looked at Brown. "You know this world better than we do. Where would you look?"

"There are lots of intelligence agencies, Decker, with overlap. Hundreds of thousands of human assets spread over two hundred countries."

"So needle in a haystack," commented Jamison.

"Compounded by the fact that the clandestine community doesn't like to answer questions about anything," added Brown.

"And if we ask they may not tell us the truth anyway," said Milligan.

"I wouldn't bet the farm on it," opined Brown.

Bogart said, "If she was managing an asset within DIA or another of the intelligence agencies, that asset may still be around. Berkshire might have retired, but that doesn't mean the asset did."

"That's true," said Brown.

"But where do you think the money came from?" asked Jamison.

"If she turned to our side and helped us out, could the cash have come from there?" asked Decker, looking at Brown.

"Depending on the significance of the assistance. But if she were a spy the basic leverage might have been help us or go to prison, not a penthouse."

"But if she wasn't caught but came forward voluntarily?" said Decker. "Maybe she didn't reveal herself as a spy but rather as a citizen with some special knowledge looking to help?"

Brown thought about that. "I don't know how likely that would be."

Bogart said, "The tricky part is how do we organize an investigation along these lines? We have four items here and a dead woman who might or might not have been a spy or a handler or something else."

Decker said, "The first thing we have to do is find out who Anne Berkshire really is. Or was."

"What the hell do you think we've been trying to do, Decker?" exclaimed Milligan.

"But we have more to work with now. If she was Russian, that's something that can be checked out. If she was a handler for a spy within the government, that can be investigated too. We have leads, we just have to run them down."

Bogart said, "If she did help out this country and was paid a substantial sum for it, that is something we should be able to track down."

"But how does that explain Dabney's killing her?" asked Jamison. "We know that Dabney stole secrets, but that was very recently." She looked at Brown. "Do you have anything to show that Dabney and Berkshire were working together?"

Brown hesitated.

"Oh for God's sake, you can at least nod or shake your head," said Jamison in exasperation.

Brown shook her head.

Jamison turned to Decker. "Okay, so what *is* the connection?"

"I don't know," admitted Decker. "But if we find the answer to one, something tells me we'll find the answer to all."

Brown picked up the security badge. "I can check out when these types of badges were used at DIA. We tend to change them on a regular basis, so that will give us some time parameters."

"And she kept that KGB communication for a reason," said Decker.

Brown nodded. "And I'm going to read it from one end to the other. It might provide some clues."

"And the floppy disk?" asked Jamison.

Bogart picked it up. "It's been a while since any of us have seen one of these. We've had the lab go through it. Whatever was on there no longer is. At least nothing that's intelligible."

"Was it Russian?" asked Jamison.

"It was computer ones and twos," replied Bogart. "That made no sense."

Decker picked up the doll.

Milligan said, "You don't expect to get anything from that, surely."

Decker rubbed the doll's hair. "I don't *expect* anything. I just go where things take me."

His phone buzzed. It was a reminder to him of their meeting with Nancy Billings.

Decker stood. "Like right now. Let's go, Alex."

39

NANCY BILLINGS WAS in her late thirties, with light blonde hair, a carefree manner, and a nose ring. When she met them at the Starbucks she was dressed in jeans and a wool sweater. They ordered coffees and sat at a back table.

Decker said, "Just wondering, can you wear nose rings while being a teacher at a Catholic school?"

"No. I just wear it in my off hours. Still pretty strict in parochial school. For teachers and students."

"So what can you tell us about Anne Berkshire?" asked Jamison.

"What do you exactly want to know? I mean, I was stunned to hear what happened to her."

"Did you two talk, interact?"

"We did. She substituted for me a number of times. I was sick some, had to attend some teacher training, and a couple of other times I had to go out of state to help my mom. My dad has dementia."

"I'm sorry to hear that," said Jamison.

"Anne was very good, stuck to the lesson plans, knew her way around the classroom. I never heard any complaints."

"But you *did* interact?" said Decker.

"Yeah. I would meet with her after she taught my classes. She'd fill me in on what had happened, things like that. We also went out for coffee a few times. I think I was the only sort of friend she had. I mean, she never talked about anyone else in her life."

"What *did* you two talk about?"

"Well, I did most of the talking, come to think of it. Anne was quiet. I can't even tell you if she had family living. I mean, she never talked about stuff like that."

"She must have said something."

"The kids. The lessons. The state of education in America."

"What did she think of that?" asked Jamison.

Billings frowned. "She wasn't a big fan, to tell the truth. She thought the kids had it too easy. Had too much stuff."

"Did you know she lived in a million-dollar condo and drove a Mercedes-Benz 600?"

Billings's astonished expression answered for her. "What? I had no idea. I thought she was as poor as me. I mean, she never said."

"What else?"

"My kids would tell me that she was very strict and wouldn't tolerate any horseplay. I mean, that's not a bad thing in a high school. The kids can get out of hand pretty quickly if you let them take advantage. But Anne seemed to have a way about her that commanded respect."

"What would she teach?"

"Math. She had a really good grasp of it. I teach algebra and calculus too. And I think I'm pretty good. That was my degree in college. But I have to admit that Anne was far superior to me in the field. The kids would tell me that she could easily work out problems on the board that she'd never even seen before. And she was never stumped for an answer for any question they might have. In fact, Anne had helped me on some lesson plans and shown me a few shortcuts with some of the formulas. I just assumed that she was a math major too."

Jamison said, "We're not sure. Her résumé said computers, but that may not be true."

"What do you mean may not be true?" asked Billings.

Decker said, "She may not be who she said she was. In fact, it's pretty clear she wasn't."

"I don't understand. Then who was she?"

"That's the $64,000 question," said Decker. "Did she ever speak a foreign language in front of you?"

Billings looked alarmed. "A foreign language? Like what language?"

"Let's leave it at anything other than English."

"No. Although sometimes it seemed that I could detect a little bit of an accent that I couldn't place. My boyfriend was raised in Germany and he has an accent. That's probably why I picked up on it. Are you saying Anne wasn't American?"

"We're not sure," said Jamison.

"Anything you can remember that seemed out of the ordinary?" asked Decker.

Billings looked confused. "Compared to what?"

"Just anything she said that seemed out of character."

Billings drank her coffee and thought about it. "Well, I'm sure it's not important."

"It could be."

"We were sitting in my class one morning. She had come in early to fill me in on a test she had done while I was out. The kids weren't in yet."

"Okay."

"She'd finished, but hadn't gotten up to leave. As a rule,

when Anne was done, she was done. She'd just get up and leave. I mean without saying anything. Not just with me, but with other teachers too. I don't think she meant to be rude, that was just a quirk she had."

"Really?" said Jamison, staring dead at Decker. "Wow, who would have thought?"

Decker ignored her look and said, "But this time she didn't leave?"

"No. She was sitting there just staring off into space. I asked her if anything was the matter. She said no. Then I started telling her about my old boyfriend. I don't know why, but I'd gotten an email from him after not hearing a word from the idiot for two years. I was complaining about him to Anne, but really just talking to myself. I remember saying that I really thought he was the one, you know. The guy I'd walk down the aisle with. Right?"

Decker didn't react to this, but Jamison said, "Yeah, I know exactly what you're talking about."

"So then I said that after four years together I thought I really knew Phil, but turns out I didn't know him at all."

After Billings stopped talking, Decker said, "And then what?"

"Oh, and that's when she said it."

"Said what?"

Billings looked at each of them before answering. "She said that the exact same thing had happened to her."

Decker said, "That she thought she knew someone but turns out she didn't?"

"Yes. And that's when she got up and left, without a word, like usual."

"When was this?" asked Decker sharply.

"Two weeks ago today. I remember because the test was the final one for the quarter."

Billings looked at Decker. "Is that important?" she asked.

When Decker didn't answer, Jamison said, "Yes, it's very important."

Decker got up and walked out without a word.

Billings looked at Jamison and said, "I guess you have one of those on your hands too."

Jamison smiled, stood, and said, "Good with the bad. If we need anything else, we'll be in touch. Thanks."

CHAPTER

40

"She had one like this."

Decker and Jamison were driving to meet Melvin Mars for dinner. Decker was holding the doll they'd found at Berkshire's storage unit.

"Who, your daughter?" asked Jamison, glancing over.

Decker nodded and then put the doll down next to him.

"You don't really talk about your family much," said Jamison cautiously.

"What am I supposed to say?" replied Decker, not looking at her.

"It takes time, Decker. We all process differently. And you process in a way that is totally unique."

"Time doesn't heal my wounds, Alex. For me there is no such thing as time, at least when it comes to memories."

"Don't you have a way of, I don't know, walling things off?"

"If I did, I think I would have tried."

They drove in silence for a few moments.

"What are the odds that two different people, Dabney and Berkshire, would use pretty much the exact same phrase?" asked Decker.

"Who could they be referring to? The same person? Different people? Each other, maybe?"

Decker shook his head. "I don't know. If each other, then they must have *known* each other."

"So apparently she was good at math and had a slight accent. Does that tell us anything?"

"Yeah, that she was good at math and had a slight accent."

Jamison sighed and changed the subject. "So how is it working with Harper Brown?"

Decker shrugged. "She keeps things close to the vest, but I think she wants to solve this case as much as we do. Maybe more since now it's turned into a spy case involving her agency." He paused. "Her father worked at DIA. He's on their Torch Bearers Wall for extraordinary service."

"Huh, maybe that explains things."

"Explains what?"

"Why she's so damn *driven*."

"She's wealthy too. Lives in a big house near Capitol Hill. Her great-grandfather was some fat-cat investor way back. Invested in blue chips long before they were blue chips."

"Wow, just what I wanted to hear."

He glanced at her. "You okay?"

"Sure. Why wouldn't I be? She's a knockout, has this cool career, and she's loaded. Yay! Good for her."

Decker rubbed at his knees, which were crammed against the dashboard. "I have to admit, her BMW has a lot more room than your car."

"Do you want to walk the rest of the way?" Jamison said between gritted teeth.

* * *

When they entered the restaurant they saw that Mars was already seated in the back. He rose and waved to them. They joined him and sat down.

"I've met all the people in the building," said Mars. "Good folks."

"When did you do that?" asked Jamison.

"Yesterday and today. I think you picked a great location, Alex. Thanks."

Mars looked over at Decker, who had said nothing.

"You okay, man?" asked Mars.

When Decker didn't answer, Jamison said, "Case is not going all that well."

Mars nodded and said, "Can't have it good all the time, but you guys will get there."

"We don't always get there, Melvin," said Decker quietly. "The bad guys win too sometimes."

"I got faith in you, Decker. You don't let the bad guys win."

Decker pulled the doll out of his backpack and placed it on the table.

"What is that?" asked Mars, looking puzzled.

"A clue," answered Jamison.

"You're kidding."

"It was used to steal secrets," said Jamison. "It's got a hidden compartment." She picked up the doll and showed him.

"A doll baby, damn," said Mars. "That's going pretty low."

The waitress came and they ordered. She glanced at the doll but said nothing. When the woman walked away, Jamison said, "So how would the exchanges take place, do you think?"

"I'm not sure," admitted Decker. "The doll would need to get from A to B and then back to A."

"It seems sort of James Bond stuff," said Mars. "I mean, don't they just, you know, hack stuff now and steal it electronically?"

"Well, this was back when they didn't do it like that," said Jamison. "They used floppy disks and dolls and, I don't know, microdots. And rolls of film that would fit inside the doll."

Decker took the doll from Jamison. While they ate, he said nothing. He just kept staring at the doll.

* * *

Later that night, after Jamison went to bed, Decker sat at the kitchen table holding the doll. After a few minutes he rose, put on his coat and a ball cap, and headed out. It was drizzling. His walk carried him along the river. He had taken his gun with him because it was just that sort of a neighborhood, especially at night.

He reached the same bench he had when he'd been jogging and sat down.

He liked the night often better than the day. Light tended to intrude on him, even when it wasn't bombarding him with harsh blues in the face of death.

And he could think. And use his memory to try to catch some anomaly, some inconsistency that would point him in the right direction. He closed his eyes, took a deep breath, and listened to the rain falling.

But his thoughts were actually not on the case. He was not thinking about Walter Dabney, or Anne Berkshire, or anything along those lines.

Molly and Cassie.

Daughter and wife.

Dead nearly two years now. And as time passed it would be ten years, then twenty, then thirty, then...

He could imagine the passage of time. He could imagine the lessening of grief, of loss. But he could not imagine that lessening happening to him. All he had to do was reach back into his perfect memory and there it would all be, the discovery of the bodies, in their full hellish glory, with not a single impression or observation subtracted from the equation or diminished by the passage of time.

He opened his eyes and there she was.

"I don't like being followed," he said crossly.

Harper Brown sat down next to him.

"I'm not too keen on *having* to follow you."

"So why do it?"

"Protecting assets, Decker. And DIA considers you a prime one."

"I work for the FBI."

"For now you do. But there's always tomorrow." Before he could respond she said, "What were you thinking about just now?"

"Nothing."

She laughed lightly. "As if."

"Why are you here?"

"I already said."

"They could have sent a flunky to follow me. I see this as a waste of your time. You have bigger fish to fry."

She took something out of her coat pocket. It was a piece of laminated paper. "I finished reading the Russian communication."

"And?"

"And I might have found something."

She handed him the laminated paper. "This is a translation."

Decker read through it. "It says someone named Ahha Seryyzamok was presented with an award for services rendered."

"*Espionage* services," added Brown.

"So who is this Ahha Seryyzamok?"

"I think the answer lies in how the name translates to English."

"How?"

"Ahha is Anna. She'd be called Anna in Russia too. Remember Anna Karenina? But the different alphabet, you know. I didn't translate the name fully because I wanted to keep you in suspense."

He glared at her. "I'm in enough *suspense* as it is."

"Touché."

"And Seryyzamok?"

"It means Greylock."

"Okay, Anna I get, but how does Greylock help?"

"Greylock is a mountain in Massachusetts."

"Still not getting the connection."

"It's the highest mountain...in the Berkshires."

Decker stared down at the paper.

"Anne Berkshire."

41

Bogart said, "We confirmed that the résumé Berkshire submitted to the school was concocted. The database at Virginia Tech was compromised and her background was placed there, her degrees and such. Very professionally done."

"And the fingerprints used to do the background check?" asked Jamison. She and Decker sat next to Milligan at the WFO.

"Someone apparently created a database profile for Berkshire, complete with prints showing no criminal background. And her references looked legit but were also faked."

"All that's not easy to do," said Milligan.

"It might be if you have a foreign government behind you," said Bogart.

Milligan said, "Okay, based on what Brown found in that Russian communication, it seems that Berkshire was a Russian spy going way back. She came to this country perhaps in the eighties and started acting as a handler for some mole, maybe at DIA. Then she surfaced decades later, finally ending up in Reston with a multimillion-dollar condo and luxury car and being a substitute teacher and a hospice volunteer in her spare time."

"And dying at the hands of Walter Dabney, who also recently stole secrets to pay off his son-in-law's gambling debts," finished Jamison.

Bogart said, "But do we really know that it was just recently?"

"What do you mean?" asked Milligan.

"What if Dabney was the mole way back when? Don't forget he worked at the NSA before starting his own company. The stuff that was found in that storage unit didn't say that Berkshire was a handler for a spy at DIA. Despite the DIA visitor's badge the spying could have been at NSA. The timeline works because Dabney was there in the 1980s."

"But we couldn't establish any connection between Dabney and Berkshire," pointed out Milligan.

"Well, if they were spies they would go to great pains to make sure there *were* no connections, or at least no obvious ones. And we've learned from Nancy Billings that Berkshire used the same phrase as Dabney did. 'You think you know someone.' That either shows a connection or it's a hell of a coincidence."

"And remember," said Jamison, "back then I doubt Anne Berkshire was using that name. She and Dabney could have had a connection, but while she was using a different name. Her current name might have been suggested to her by what we saw in that document. Anna Seryyzamok became Anne Berkshire."

Bogart sat back. "So how do we trace a connection between them from the 1980s if we have no idea what her name was back then?"

"We would just have to do it from visual evidence. Show her picture to the folks from back then and see if they recognize her."

"People change a lot over the years," noted Milligan. "I

doubt we'll be able to find anyone who recognizes her. And we don't have a single picture of her from then."

Bogart said, "We can have our technical people reverse the aging process and show what she might have looked like as a younger person."

He paused and looked at Decker. "Amos, you've been unusually quiet. Do you have any thoughts on the matter?"

"Why would she stop spying?"

"What?" said Bogart.

Decker held up the translated KGB communication. "She kept this. She was obviously proud of it. Along with the floppy disk and the doll, tools of her spycraft. She was clearly proud of what she did. So why give it up? We've assumed that she had a change of heart when she started teaching and volunteering. So why keep the stuff that is clearly associated with her past life in espionage?"

Jamison said, "Are you suggesting that she might still have been a spy, right up until she was killed?"

"I'm saying it's possible, because we haven't definitively ruled it out. And we haven't ruled out that Dabney hasn't been spying all these years either."

"Do you have any evidence that he has been?" asked Bogart.

Before Decker could answer, Jamison said, "How about the fact that he was able, in a short period of time, to sell secrets for ten million dollars to enemies of this country in order to pay off his son-in-law's gambling debts? Now, if he was honest and aboveboard, where did he find a buyer for that much money so quickly? One answer is he could have easily if he'd been spying all along and had knowledge of people willing to pay for secrets."

Milligan and Bogart exchanged a glance.

"Damn," said Milligan. "I never thought about it that way."

Decker gazed at Jamison. "*That* was a good insight, Alex."

She smiled and said modestly, "I have one occasionally."

"The devil is in the details, the *small* details," added Bogart. "So do we go back to his days at the NSA and see what we can find out? And then move forward up until the present?"

"I'm not sure I see another path," said Decker.

"We'll need to get some more agents on this," said Milligan. "Because that's a lot of legwork and document review. And the NSA is not known for their cooperation. And on top of that they're definitely not going to be pleased that we're alleging they might have had a spy in their ranks thirty-some years ago."

Jamison said, "How does this reconcile with what Agent Brown told us? She said Walter Dabney stole secrets from DIA and sold them to an enemy of this country. If he were spying all this time, from NSA up until today, are you saying that he was working with Anne Berkshire the whole time? And that the gambling debt spying was just a one-off? They paid him money to save his kid, as a favor for years of service? And if they did so, why kill Berkshire?"

"Like we said before, to silence her if she was indeed his handler," said Milligan. "He was trying to tie up loose ends before he killed himself. Berkshire may not have known that he was terminal with cancer."

Decker stirred. "But if they were working together, why pick a rendezvous spot on a public street next to the Hoover Building? Why make the murder public? He could have killed Berkshire in private. They could have met at some place like her farm cottage. If they were spy and handler, they probably met there regularly anyway. But by murdering her in public he ruined his reputation and brought horrendous attention to his family, who he seemed to genuinely care for. It just doesn't make sense."

"None of it makes sense," added Milligan wearily.

"No, it makes perfect sense to *someone*," said Decker. "We just have to reach that same level of awareness."

"Well, whatever we do, this is not going to be a quick fix," said Bogart. "It might take years to unravel."

"It might," said Decker. "Or it might not."

Bogart said, "I can get the ball rolling on the NSA piece. What are you going to do, Amos?"

"We have yet to figure out Walter Dabney. I'm going to revisit that."

"How?" asked Bogart.

"There's only one way to do it. Talk to his family again."

"But we've already done that," protested Milligan.

"Not with the mind-set that he was a long-term spy."

"You're not going to come out and accuse the man of being a spy to his family, are you?" said Bogart, looking alarmed. "That's not a great recipe to get them to cooperate."

Decker rose. "I think I know how to phrase it."

42

THE HOUSEKEEPER THEY had seen on a previous visit answered the door. She was in her sixties, with gray hair pulled back in a bun. She had on the same garb that Decker had seen her in before. Black slacks, a white smock, and black rubber-soled shoes. Whether she was required to wear this or not he wasn't sure.

"They're not here," she said in reply to Jamison's query about the Dabneys.

"Do you know when they'll be back?" asked Jamison.

"Oh, in about a half hour. They're at the viewing service for Mr. Dabney. The funeral is tomorrow." She shook her head sadly. "My God, what a damn shame. He was such a good man. Can't believe what happened."

"And your name is?" asked Decker.

"Cecilia. Cecilia Randall. But folks just call me Cissy."

"Cissy, do you think we could wait for them?" asked Decker. "It's sort of important."

She looked hesitant but then opened the door farther, allowing them to pass. "I know you're with the FBI, so I guess it's okay. Can I get you a drink or anything?"

Jamison began, "No, we—"

Decker said, "I'd like a cup of coffee if that's not too much trouble."

"No trouble a'tall. They have a Keurig. Just pop in a pod and there you go."

They followed her to the kitchen, where she pulled out a box of pods. "Full strength or decaf?" she said.

"Real coffee, just black."

She busied herself with making the coffee while Decker watched her.

"This is a beautiful kitchen," said Jamison.

"Yes, it is," Cissy said proudly. "Mrs. Dabney's renovated it twice since they've lived here. She's got the eye for stuff like that."

"So you've worked for them a long time?" said Jamison, glancing at Decker.

"Over thirty-five years. I diapered all four of them girls, I can tell you that. All right here in this house."

"Wow," said Jamison. "That's a long time."

"They're a wonderful family."

Decker said, "So Mr. Dabney bought this place while he was still working at the NSA?"

Cissy took a cup out of a cabinet and put it under the Keurig's spout. "Don't know about that. He never talked about work, least with me."

"It's just that I know this area is expensive. I just assumed he bought this place after he started his own company and started making the big bucks."

"Again, I don't know nothing about that. But I do know Mrs. Dabney had some money."

"Oh, she told you that?"

"Not in so many words. But you could tell she came from money. The way she dressed and walked and talked. Mr. Dabney wasn't always such a sharp dresser, and I remember he used to drive a really old car when they first got this place, but then he bought himself this yellow Porsche. Now *that* was a beautiful car."

"Porsche, nice," said Jamison, throwing a glance at Decker. "So the Dabneys have had a nice life. Up until now," she quickly added.

The coffee cup filled, Cissy handed it to Decker before throwing the used pod away in a slide-out trash can. "Well, everybody's got problems, and Mrs. Dabney's no exception."

"So you mean before now?" asked Decker.

"I mean way back." She hesitated and then, in a lower voice, though no one was around, said, "She had two miscarriages and a stillborn baby. Little girl. It was awful."

"Oh my God!" exclaimed Jamison. "Was that before she had her four daughters?"

"Stillborn was. That was before my time, but Mrs. Dabney talked to me about it once. The two miscarriages were in between Ms. Amanda and Ms. Natalie." Cissy wiped up around the Keurig machine with a cloth. "But they have problems too."

"I noted Amanda's arm, and Natalie's toes," said Decker.

"Right, had those since birth. Plus they all got the asthma pretty bad. But they're all smart, and Ms. Amanda and Ms. Natalie have kids."

"And the other girls?"

Her voice dropped lower. "To tell the truth, I've heard Ms. Jules and Ms. Samantha got problems in that department. I mean having babies. Might be why they're not married yet."

Jamison looked around. "Do you think Mrs. Dabney will stay here?"

"Don't know. Have to tell you I'm worried 'bout that.

I've worked here a long time. And they've taken real good care of me. But if she moves in with one of her daughters, she won't need me."

"Well, let's hope it doesn't come to that. She might want to stay."

"Maybe," Cissy said doubtfully. "Now, I've got work to do, so…"

Decker and Jamison thanked her and retreated to the library to wait for the Dabneys to arrive home.

"Wow, I had no idea the Dabneys had been through all that," said Jamison. "Makes it even sadder."

Decker said nothing. He just sat there staring around the room.

Then his eye caught on something. It was a black bag strap sticking out of the drawer of the desk that was situated against one wall of the room.

He walked over, opened the drawer, and pulled out the bag.

"What is that?" asked Jamison.

Decker unzipped the bag and pulled the device out. "A really old video recorder. Uses VHS tapes."

"Anything in it?"

"No, but there's a tape still in the wrapper." He felt around inside the bag and pulled out remnants of a wrapper from another tape. He looked down at the plastic with the 3M logo on it. Next he opened up all the desk drawers and looked through them.

"Anything?" asked Jamison.

"Walter Dabney was a very tidy and organized man. Even the rubber bands are neatly arranged, pencils and pens divided, not a stray scrap of paper." He looked around the library at the books. "We searched this place before and you know what we found?"

"What?"

"That all the books are alphabetized by the last name of the author."

"Organized, like you said."

Decker held up the odd scraps of plastic. "So why not throw this away? There's a wastebasket right next to the desk."

"I don't know."

Decker held up the tape. "And we've seen something shaped like this before."

"We have? Where?"

"In the bag the woman was carrying when she and Dabney were leaving the bank after cleaning out his safe deposit box. You could see the rectangular outline through the bag."

"Wait a minute, you think he used that camera to do a videotape? And that was what was in the safe deposit box?"

"Yeah, I do. And by that time Dabney probably didn't care about being neat and tidy, so the plastic wrapper just got left there."

It was right then that they heard a car drive up. Decker quickly put the camera bag back, looked out the window, and saw the five women get out of an SUV. A few moments later they could hear them coming into the home.

A minute later Ellie Dabney came into the library. "I didn't expect you to be back," she said, her expression weary.

Jules appeared behind her. "What's going on, Mom?"

Decker said, "We just have a few more questions."

"Have you found out anything?" said Jules. "About Dad?"

"We're working on it," said Decker.

Ellie sat down, and a moment later Cissy came in carrying a cup of steaming tea. She handed it to Ellie, glanced surreptitiously at Decker, and then hurried out of the room. Jules sat down next to her mother.

Ellie said absently, "What questions?"

Decker sat down across from her. "Your husband had done well for himself."

"Yes, he had," snapped Jules. "What of it?"

Decker kept his focus on Ellie. "He was at NSA when you got married?"

"That's right. He was there for about a decade, right out of college. He started his business on our wedding anniversary." She smiled weakly. "He said it was good karma, good luck to take the plunge then. The kids were still young. In fact, Natalie was just a toddler."

Jules said, "What does any of this have to do with what happened?"

Decker said, "We're trying to establish certain things in connection with what happened. The first one being is there a connection between your father and the victim."

"I told you that I could think of none," said Ellie.

Decker eyed her closely. "Has Natalie spoken to you?"

"About what?"

"Her husband's gambling debts."

"No, I haven't."

This came from Natalie, who was standing in the doorway, her overcoat still on, and a glass of white wine in her hand.

Ellie looked at her youngest daughter. "Gambling debts, Natalie? What is he talking about?"

Natalie looked sourly at Decker, walked into the room, and flopped down into a chair. She took a swig of her wine and said, "Okay, why the hell not? I guess it's not enough that I had to go and look at my father's dead body today." She sat up, drained her glass, and said, "Corbett had gambling debts. They were huge. The people he owed them to were really bad. They threatened to kill us, and they meant it. I called and asked Daddy for help." She stopped there and looked away.

A stunned Ellie glanced at Decker. "I don't understand."

"Your husband found the money to pay off those debts by stealing classified government secrets and selling them."

Ellie Dabney slowly rose on wobbly legs. "What?"

Jules stood and supported her mother with an arm under her elbow.

"What bullshit is this? Dad stealing secrets? That's crap."

"How else was he going to get ten million dollars?" asked Decker.

Jules paled and shot her sister a glance. "Ten million dollars! Is this true?"

Natalie looked dully at her older sister. "Why in the hell do you think I'm divorcing the prick, because he's no longer good in bed?"

"You asked Dad to come up with ten million dollars!" screamed Jules.

"Who else was I supposed to ask?" her sister screamed right back. "Don't you understand? They were going to kill Corbett, me, and Tasha, okay? My daughter was going to *die*. I had no choice."

The noise of the confrontation brought the two other sisters rushing into the room. Samantha exclaimed, "What the hell is going on?"

"Your bitch of a little sister made our father commit treason to pay the gambling debts of her dickless husband, that's what!" shouted Jules.

The blood drained from Amanda's and Samantha's faces. "W-what?" said Amanda in a quavering voice.

"How could you, Nat!" said Jules, tears now streaming down her cheeks.

"I didn't know he was going to steal government secrets," said Natalie in a hollow voice. "Look, I...I never thought..."

"That's right, you never *thought*," accused Jules. "You never *did* think, except about yourself! And now we know why Dad killed himself. Because he was ashamed of what he did. Of what *you* drove him to do!"

During all this, Ellie had just stood there staring at the floor.

Decker was watching her. He said, "Mrs. Dabney, can we talk privately?" He eyed the sisters. "I think this might be more productive without the histrionics."

"Histrionics," exclaimed Jules. "You sonofabitch! What the hell gives you the right—"

Ellie turned and slapped her daughter across the cheek. "Shut up!"

Jules fell back, holding her cheek and looking stunned.

"But Mom!" began Natalie.

"All of you, not another word," said Ellie. "Leave, just get out, go somewhere, get drunk, I don't care. But just leave this room. Now!"

Looking hurt and offended, the sisters, shooting dark glances at Decker and Jamison, slowly filed out of the room. When the door closed behind them Ellie sank into her chair.

Decker waited a few more moments before saying, "The question becomes, was this a one-off or not."

"What does that even mean?" said Ellie, not looking at him.

"Your husband was able to find a buyer for the secrets relatively fast. If he hadn't committed espionage before, reason would dictate that he wouldn't have been able to do that.

But if he had sold secrets before, then he might have had a ready-made purchaser. You see the logic?"

She slowly nodded. "I see the logic. But I can't believe it applies in this case. My husband was a patriot. He would never betray his country."

"But that's exactly what he *did* do," Decker pointed out.

"Only to save his daughter," she shot back. "That would be the only reason. His family!"

"It's still treason. And we have to find out if he had committed it before."

"I can't believe that he did."

"So you can't help us?" said Decker.

"I knew nothing of his business. I already told you that. If Walt were stealing secrets, I have to imagine that someone at work would have known about it. But they have checks and balances in place for just that reason. He told me that."

Decker shot Jamison a glance. "We should have followed that up before."

Decker and Jamison stood. She said, "We're sorry to be putting you through all of this."

"I didn't think this could possibly get worse." She paused. "Only it just did."

They left her there staring at ... nothing.

Which was maybe all that the woman had left.

43

"So we go back to Dabney and Associates?" asked Jamison.

They climbed into the car. When Decker looked back at the house he saw Natalie at a window staring out at them.

If looks could kill, thought Decker.

He nodded and said, "Yes."

They reached Dabney's office about thirty minutes later. The reception was not one they expected.

The doors to Dabney and Associates were closed and chained shut. The interior of the offices was dark. And two guards in Army uniforms stood out front.

Decker and Jamison walked up to them. Decker held out his FBI creds. The two guards were not impressed.

"Where are the people who work here?" asked Jamison.

Neither guard answered.

"We're investigating this case," said Decker. "And we need to get inside this space."

"That won't be happening, sir," said one of the guards. His hand moved across the butt of his holstered M11 pistol.

"This is a federal investigation," pointed out Jamison.

The guard leveled his gaze on her. "And I've got my orders. Until those orders change, no one goes in. Period."

Jamison was about to say something else when Decker grabbed her arm. "Let's go. We're wasting time here."

They rode the elevator back down to the lobby and ran smack into Faye Thompson. She looked like she'd been crying.

When she saw Decker, her features turned to a scowl. "You bastard!"

"Excuse me?" said Jamison defensively.

Thompson got right in Decker's face. "We were fully cooperating with you. And then you pull this shit?"

"I didn't pull anything," Decker replied calmly. "We just got kicked out too."

"Don't lie to me. This has FBI written all over it."

"In case you hadn't noticed, the FBI doesn't wear Army uniforms."

"You people are all in this together."

"That's not how—"

"Do you realize what you've done?" snapped Thompson, drawing attention from other people passing by in the lobby. "You've ruined us. We're done. Shutting us down like this? We're guilty as charged without ever having due process." She pushed a finger into Decker's chest. "You screwed us over, you prick."

"Actually, he had nothing to do with it," said a voice.

They all turned to stare at Harper Brown. She was dressed in cammies with a sidearm. She walked over to stand directly in front of Thompson. "It wasn't the FBI. It was the DIA. If you have a problem with anything, you can take it up with me."

"You had no right to—"

"We had every right. This is a national security issue. If you want to continue to discuss it, we can do so at DIA HQ."

"Just because one of our partners—"

Brown broke in: "I won't tell you again, Ms. Thompson. If you want to discuss this, it won't be here, in public. You know better than that."

Thompson gazed around at the passersby staring at her. "You're going to hear from our lawyer!" she barked.

"Looking forward to it," said Brown. "Hope you have a good one. You're going to need it."

Thompson seemed about to hurl another comment, but then she turned and stalked off.

Brown turned to Decker and Jamison. "Well, that was pleasant."

Decker eyed her clothing. "Why the military duds?"

"I'm officially wearing my Army hat today."

"So you shut them down?" said Jamison.

"We took all the computers, servers, and records. Our people are currently going through them." She paused and added, "Not to worry. We'll share whatever we find with the Bureau."

"So you decided on a full frontal attack on Dabney's business?" said Decker.

"Let's go up, shall we?"

She led them onto an elevator car and they rode back up to Dabney's floor. When they got off she led them to the entrance, showed her creds to the guards, and they unchained the door and allowed them to pass.

Once inside, Jamison said, "Nice to have the golden key to get in here. Those guys out there wouldn't budge."

Brown said, "Of course they wouldn't budge. They're Army. They have orders. They follow them. There is no room for discussion." She turned to Decker, who was looking around the dark offices.

"So what do you think?" she asked.

"About what?"

"About what we're doing here."

"If I had to guess, I'd say you were trying to flush out a spy by attacking."

She nodded approvingly. "Very good, Decker."

"I didn't say I agreed with the tactic," he added.

"Well, maybe I don't either, but it's been done."

"So it didn't originate with you, then?"

"I follow orders just like those men out there."

"Dabney and Associates has a lot of employees."

"And we're watching all of them. As well as scrubbing their personal financials."

"You really think Dabney was working with someone here to get the money to pay off the gambling debts?"

"I can't discount the possibility."

"Jamison thought it was unlikely that Dabney, if he was always on the legal side, was able to find a buyer for the secrets so fast."

Brown looked at Jamison. "I'm impressed."

"Thanks," said Jamison curtly, though she looked pleased by the other woman's comment.

Brown perched on the receptionist's desk. "You're exactly right. It's *not* that easy to find a buyer from scratch. It's not like you can locate them online or walk down a dark alley and bump into someone engaged in espionage who can find ten million dollars to hand over. More likely than not you'll run right into an undercover operation designed to catch people trying to do just that."

"So that either means Dabney was not as clean as everyone thought, or someone he worked with was dirty."

"The issue is even more complicated than that, Decker. The thing is, it could have been a coworker who helped

Dabney with the sale, sure. Or it could have been someone else."

"Such as?" said Jamison.

Decker answered. "Such as someone on the other side of the equation." He pointed at Brown. "Someone from your side that Dabney was working with."

Brown crossed her arms and nodded, her features turning grave. "The more I think about it, we might have a spy in the ranks of the DIA. I'm not just talking about decades ago. I mean *currently*."

"Wouldn't be the first time," said Decker. "As you pointed out to me previously."

Jamison said, "We thought it might be Dabney who was the spy all these years. From his career at NSA onward."

"But he had to get the secrets from inside the government once he went to the private sector," pointed out Brown. "And there was the old security badge we found in Berkshire's locker. That was from the DIA. And it's very troubling that she had it in her possession."

Jamison said, "But regardless of whether Dabney was in the private sector, he could have gotten those secrets legitimately through his work. The persons he dealt with in the government might not know what he was doing with the information."

"That's true," said Brown. "And I hope that turns out to be the case. But we can't take it as gospel that that is indeed the case."

"So you're investigating your own agency too," said Decker.

"We have to."

"You mentioned the security badge. Did you find out something about it?"

"It was used at DIA back in the late eighties and early nineties."

"No idea who it was issued to?" asked Decker.

"None. Back then it was just laminated plastic with no electronic guts."

"Visitor or permanent?" asked Decker.

"I wish I could tell you."

"Does that mean you don't know or you *can't* tell us?" retorted Jamison.

"I wish I could tell you," repeated Brown.

Jamison looked like she was going to hit her. "Well, you know what they say, be careful what you wish for." Then she turned and walked out of the office.

"She seems to have an attitude problem," noted Brown.

"No, she just doesn't like bullshit. We're on the same page with that."

"Decker, I'm telling you as much as I can. Do you know what it cost me to even have you come to DIA and look at those files?"

"Do you think Anne Berkshire was working with a mole in DIA way back too?"

"It's possible. In fact, with that badge, it's probable that she was."

"But that mole was not Dabney?"

"He was at NSA for part of that time, but then on his own. He did work as a contractor for DIA beginning later in the nineties, so it wasn't his security badge. We can't show that they ever met except for the encounter outside the Hoover Building. And if they had been working together for decades we would have been able to find *something*, Decker."

"So someone else, then?"

"And we're at square one on that."

"But you're obviously hoping to pop something by doing a deep dive on the folks here?"

"It's a long shot, but when you don't have better options, you have to go with something." She paused. "So do you have any leads?"

"Yeah."

"What are they?"

"I wish I could tell you."

Decker turned and left the room.

44

"**W**HY ARE WE here, Decker?"

Jamison was staring down at him as he perched on a couch in Anne Berkshire's million-dollar condo and gazed around.

Decker didn't answer right away.

"I don't like incongruity," he said a few moments later.

"Such as?"

"Such as why buy a condo like this and buy a top-of-the-line Benz if you don't decorate it with your stuff, in the case of the condo, or don't really drive it around, in the case of the Mercedes?"

"So she was eccentric, so what?"

Decker shook his head and stood. "It goes beyond mere eccentricity. She also has a run-down farmhouse and a crappy car that she drives to work and on her rounds as the proverbial Good Samaritan."

"What does that tell you?"

"If you were a spy and had made money, you might buy this condo and that car, but you would enjoy them. Not just have them. Because you would have earned it. Now, if you just *have* them but don't enjoy them, there must be a reason. So in Berkshire's case, what is that reason?"

Jamison thought about this. "I don't know. We speculated she might have felt guilty."

"If she was still spying, she obviously was *not* feeling guilty."

"But there's no evidence that she was still spying. She was a substitute schoolteacher. And look at the stuff in the storage unit. It's old. Floppy disk and an outdated security badge."

"But at her farmhouse we found a *flash drive*. That's not old 1980s technology. And added to that, someone nearly killed me to get it. And why have the old farmhouse with a flash drive hidden in the toilet paper holder if you've long since retired from espionage?"

Jamison opened her mouth to say something but then closed it. "Good point," she finally managed to say. "But if that's the case, then she *must* have been working with Dabney. I mean, otherwise it's quite a coincidence that he commits espionage and ends up gunning down someone who's also a spy."

"Maybe," said Decker doubtfully.

"Decker, it has to be! You don't believe in coincidences, not even small ones. You always say that. So if Berkshire was spying, it had to have been along with Walter Dabney. That would explain why he could find a buyer so fast for the secrets. Berkshire probably arranged it."

"And who tried to kill me at the farmhouse and stole the flash drive? And what was on it?"

"More secrets. Berkshire probably wasn't working alone. She gets killed and her associate goes there to get whatever materials she kept there. You saved them the trouble. They attacked you and found it. That all holds together," Jamison said, a note of triumph in her voice.

Decker went over to stare out the window.

"You forgot to congratulate me on my brilliant theory," said Jamison.

When Decker said nothing, she walked over to him. "You don't think I'm right?"

"Let's put it this way, Alex. I don't know that you're wrong."

"Well, that's something. Do you have an alternative theory?"

"Not right now, no."

Jamison looked around the space. 'What happens to this place? And all her money? They haven't found any family to leave it to."

"Haven't given that any thought."

"How did you leave it with Agent Brown?"

"Vague," said Decker.

"You mean like you're being with me right now?"

"Let's go."

"Where to?"

"To where it all started."

* * *

Decker and Jamison walked the route that Decker had when he'd been unwittingly following Walter Dabney to the man's doom. They passed the guard shack and Decker circled back.

The guard inside was the same man who'd been on duty that morning. He recognized Decker and stepped out of the shack.

"Helluva thing that morning," he said.

"Helluva thing. Glad you were there to back me up."

"No problem. It's my job."

"I'm sure you've already been asked this," began Decker. "But had you seen Dabney before?"

The guard nodded. "A few times. I think the last time was a couple months before. They told me he was going to a meeting that day."

"And Anne Berkshire?"

The man shook his head. "No. Don't remember her. But, man, lots of people pass along here during the course of a day. Faces get jumbled after a while."

"I hear you," said Decker. "Do you remember seeing a clown that day? The person would've been up the street from you, closer to the café where Dabney was waiting."

"Give me a sec."

A truck with "GSA" painted on the sides had turned toward the underground garage entrance and the guard walked over to speak to the driver.

As Decker watched, the driver showed his ID and paperwork and then the guard pulled his walkie-talkie and spoke into it. Another guard came out a few seconds later with a bomb-sniffing dog. Another guard followed with a device that had a mirror used to look under vehicles. The two guards and the dog performed their tasks as the guard Decker had been talking to rejoined him.

The man nodded. "Yeah, I did see the clown. I was thinking it was a little early for Halloween."

"You didn't happen to see where the clown went?"

"No. I keep my eyes roaming around, mostly looking for folks paying the Hoover Building too much attention."

"Is that a problem?" asked Jamison.

"You get crazies for sure. Most are harmless. But it only takes one. And we've had problems."

Decker looked around. "Do you have exterior surveillance cameras?"

The guard stepped closer and his voice dropped. "Dirty little secret is we used to. I mean the cameras are still there and visible, but most aren't operational. One reason we're moving out of this space. Place is falling apart."

"Right," said Decker. "Well, thanks."

They continued on and reached the spot where Dabney had shot Berkshire. Decker stopped and looked down at the pavement.

"Are you seeing blue?' asked Jamison.

He nodded absently, lifted his gaze, and looked around. "If Dabney and Berkshire were working together, why would they meet down here? Dabney had a meeting scheduled with the Bureau. And you wouldn't think he'd want his partner in espionage within a hundred miles of the place."

This comment took Jamison aback as they started walking along. "Okay, I do not have an answer for that," she said.

"And it didn't seem to me that Dabney and Berkshire even knew each other. Forget the point that Dabney apparently needed the clown to signal him that Berkshire was coming. That doesn't necessarily mean that Dabney didn't know what Berkshire looked like. He might have been shown a picture of her, though none was found on his person."

"He might have been given a picture and just memorized her features."

"Right. The clown thing was just about timing, allowing Dabney to intercept Berkshire. But when I saw them together that morning, it did not seem to me that they knew each other."

"And then he shot her?"

"And then he shot her," replied Decker.

"It seems like we take a step forward on this case and then we take two steps back."

"Sometimes it seems that way on *every* case," said Decker.

"But we *are* going to solve this sucker, right?"

Decker didn't answer.

45

MELVIN MARS WAS WAITING out front for them when they got back to their apartment that night.

"Why didn't you just go up, Melvin?" asked Jamison. "You have a key and the passcode."

"It's your place, not mine," said Mars, smiling. "I'm not looking to intrude on your space."

"We haven't had dinner yet. We could go out."

"That sounds great."

They all turned to see Harper Brown striding over from her car.

"I'd been waiting for you to get back too," said Brown. She looked up at Mars. "I didn't know you were doing the same."

"Melvin Mars, this is Agent Harper Brown with the DIA."

Brown looked intrigued. "Melvin Mars, the former football player?"

Mars smiled. "That's not how most people would describe me. Usually it starts with 'You mean Mars, Melvin, that dude on Texas's death row?'"

"And Decker got you off," noted Brown.

"We *all* got him off," said Decker. "Including Melvin. He was there at the very end when we nearly got blown up. And he's already saved my butt up here."

"Impressive," said Brown. "I also read that you got a very sweet payoff from the government."

"No more than he deserved," said Jamison. "In fact, money doesn't come close to compensating him for twenty years of his life."

"I'm not arguing with that. So let's go to dinner and I can get to know your friend better."

"Why?" asked Decker.

"In my off hours I'm actually a very social person, Decker," said Brown.

* * *

They were seated at a table in the middle of a Vietnamese restaurant in D.C. Brown had suggested it.

Decker looked at the menu and said, "I don't recognize one thing on here."

"I can order for you, Decker," said Brown.

Decker dropped his menu. "Sounds good to me. Do they have fries?"

Mars handed her his menu. "I'm in the same boat as Decker, so you can order for me too."

Brown looked at Jamison. "You good, or you want me to do the honors for you too?"

"I love Vietnamese food," replied Jamison in an irritated voice.

When the waitress came, Brown ordered for the three of them, in Vietnamese.

"Impressive," said Mars as the waitress walked off. "I can barely make my way around English."

"Come on, Melvin, you graduated from UT *early* with a business degree," pointed out Jamison.

"Prison doesn't improve one's brainpower. At least not mine. Not after twenty years."

"Did you find anything in the files at Dabney's office?" Decker asked Brown.

She shot Mars a glance. "I doubt he's cleared to hear this."

"Neither are we," pointed out Decker. "You can trust Melvin," he added.

"Okay, no, we found nothing in the files, but we're still looking. We were hoping for a smoking gun but didn't find one. How about you?"

"We haven't found a gun, much less a smoking one. But we have questions, like if Dabney was working with Berkshire, why meet near the Hoover Building? He already had a meeting scheduled that morning. And if she was a spy I doubt she would be attending."

"That's true."

"And as Jamison pointed out, if they weren't working together it's a helluva coincidence to have one spy kill another unrelated spy."

Brown glanced at Jamison. "Another good observation, Jamison. You're showing a real talent for this area."

Jamison didn't respond to this remark.

Decker added, "And if Berkshire wasn't spying anymore, she had a weird retirement. Million-dollar condo and six-figure ride paired with a crappy farmhouse and an old, dented Honda."

"I don't disagree," said Brown. "It's all weird."

"And we still haven't accounted for the person who nearly killed me and stole the flash drive. Berkshire was dead and Dabney was on his deathbed at the time. So there's a third party out there."

"Who wanted that flash drive," observed Brown.

"And I wonder what was on there?" said Decker.

"What else? More stolen secrets," replied Brown.

"You think?" he said.

"What else could it be?"

"If I knew the answer to that I wouldn't be asking the question. But if Dabney and Berkshire were working together, we should be able to find some connection."

"All I can tell you, Decker, is that the first inkling we had that Dabney had gone bad was recently. He's worked on other DIA projects before and we had no problems. And he also had no incentives to steal. The guy was in great shape financially. It was only this gambling debt problem that pushed him over the edge." She glanced at Mars. "You carry this to your grave, okay?"

He put up his hands in mock surrender, smiled, and said, "Hey, I'm on your side, okay? I'm going to forget everything you guys say tonight."

Brown smiled and said, "I knew I liked you." She turned back to Decker. "And Dabney had to routinely take polygraphs to keep his security clearance status up to date. He never failed one."

"So you're convinced that this was just a one-off?"

"Unless you can show me something to the contrary."

Jamison interjected, "But he was able to sell the secrets very quickly."

"I know. You said that before and it's a valid point. But it's a leap of logic to go from that to the conclusion that the guy's been stealing secrets for a long time."

"Well, we'll see if we can get your logic to match up with ours at some point," said Jamison tersely.

The two women did a bit of a stare-down.

Fortunately, their food came right then and they started eating.

Brown eyed Mars. "So how do you spend your time now?"

"Doing a little coaching at the high school level. Basically trying to figure the rest of my life out."

"You two have something in common," said Decker.

"What's that?" asked Mars.

"You're both rich."

When Mars eyed Brown she said, "Nothing to do with me. I inherited. Just luck of birth."

"Yeah, that's just great," Jamison muttered under her breath.

"I don't think of myself as rich," said Mars. "Maybe I would if I had earned the money playing ball."

"You *earned* the money, Melvin," said Decker. "With twenty years of your life."

* * *

After they finished their meal and left the restaurant, Brown walked ahead talking to Mars, while Jamison and Decker were paired up about ten feet behind them.

"Brown has quite the family lineage," said Jamison.

"Well, at least she's not resting on all her dough and spending her time attending galas and soirees and shit like that. She's out there in uniform fighting the good fight."

"Yeah, she's absolutely *perfect*."

Decker glanced at her. "You're sounding jealous again, Alex. It's not a good look on you."

Jamison let out a long breath. "Yeah, I know. But that woman has something about her that just rubs me raw just by looking at her. You ever have anyone like that in your life?"

"Yeah, my fifth-grade teacher, but I got over it."

They watched as something Mars said made Brown laugh out loud. She bumped him lightly with her hip and then tucked her arm through his as they walked along.

Jamison quickly eyed Decker. "Okay, what's *that* about?"

"What's what about?" said Decker, who'd been lost in his own thoughts. He wasn't even looking at the pair up ahead.

Jamison sighed. "Never mind."

46

AFTERWARDS THEY SPLIT UP, with Mars and Brown driving off in their cars and Decker and Jamison going up to their apartment. Decker opened the door to the apartment and they stepped inside.

"Well, that didn't get us anywhere," said Jamison. "Brown obviously really didn't want to share anything that would help us."

When he didn't answer, she said wearily, "You know, Decker, when a person is talking to you they sort of expect a response."

She hung up her coat on a peg by the door and turned around.

And froze.

The man had on a black hoodie tightly closed so she couldn't see his face.

He had a gun that was pointed at Decker's chest.

"Seems we have a visitor," said Decker.

The man jerked his gun upward and Decker and Jamison raised their hands over their heads.

The man tossed a set of cuffs to Jamison. She quickly moved her hands to catch them. The man pointed at Decker.

"He wants you to cuff me."

"I get that. Who are you?"

The man, in response, pulled the hammer back on his gun.

"Just do it, Alex. No more questions."

She cuffed Decker's hands behind his back.

The man came over and inspected them. Then he pushed Decker and Jamison toward the door.

"Where are we going?" asked Jamison.

The man rammed his elbow into Decker's kidney, causing him to collapse against the wall, his features screwed up in pain. Then he hit him across the face with his pistol.

"Okay, okay, no more questions!" cried out Jamison. She tried to help Decker, but the man pushed her back.

Decker finally righted himself and, still listing to one side, moved slowly toward the door. The man opened it and they all passed through.

The man said in a low voice, "We meet anyone along the way, you say nothing. You so much as cough, I'll shoot you both right here. Understand?"

Jamison said quickly, "We understand."

They walked down the stairs and the man held the door open for them. He led them to a black sedan.

"Get in the driver's seat," he said to Jamison.

He put Decker in the passenger seat and then climbed into the rear seat, his gun trained on Decker. He handed Jamison the car keys and then slipped on his seat belt. "Drive. I'll tell you where to go."

They drove off.

The man gave directions and Jamison turned down one street after another.

"Left here," he said.

She turned into an alley and drove to the end. There was no outlet.

Decker peered out the window. The area was blighted and the two buildings on either side of them looked burned out and abandoned.

"Out," said the man to Jamison.

She climbed out of the car.

"Open his door," said the man.

Jamison opened the passenger door and helped Decker out.

The man used his pistol to point to the left. "In there. Through the doorway."

Decker had to duck to avoid hitting his head on the low doorway. Inside it was dark, cold, and clammy.

"We can't see," said Jamison as she moved slowly forward, her hands out in front of her.

A light came on. The man was holding a flashlight in his left hand.

"Down the steps over there."

Decker turned and said, "Look, your beef is with me, not her. She walks, I give you no trouble."

The man shook his head and pointed his gun muzzle in Decker's face. "Down the steps over there."

Decker glanced at Jamison, turned, and led the way down the stairs.

The room below was littered with debris—beer cans, used condoms, and animal feces.

Jamison wrinkled her nose up at the sight of all this. She stepped forward until her path was blocked by a wall. She turned around and looked at the man.

Decker came to stand in front of her, his big body between her and the gunman.

The man shone his light on them, even as Decker turned around and his gaze dipped to Jamison's waist.

He then looked up at her questioningly.

She slowly nodded.

"Turn around," barked the man. "And move away from her."

Decker followed these instructions and stepped to the side, closest to the stair leading up out of the room.

The man set the light down on a pile of boxes so that it was pointing outward and illuminating the room partially. It was then that he opened his hood and slipped it off his head.

Luis Alvarez, the construction supervisor at the building where Tomas Amaya had worked, stared back at them.

"We were wondering where you got to, Señor Alvarez," said Decker. "How's life been on the run?"

Alvarez's face was stone. "You didn't think I was just walking away, did you?"

"You really want to add the murders of two 'federales' to your rap sheet?" said Decker.

"With the greatest of pleasure."

"The FBI is almost here."

"Bullshit."

"I saw our apartment door had been forced when I walked in. I hit the speed dial in my pocket. Special Agent Bogart has been listening to everything we've been saying. And the chip in my phone has led them right here. So you're screwed."

"You're lying."

"Take my phone out and see for yourself. It's been on the whole time."

Alvarez looked nervously at Jamison. "Take his phone out and bring it to me. Now!"

Decker said, "You're wasting precious time, Luis. Chances are good the Bureau guys will just blow your ass away to avoid having to spend money on prosecuting you."

"Bring me the phone!" screamed Alvarez.

Jamison pulled the phone out of Decker's pocket. As she did so she glanced at Decker. He whispered something to her.

She turned, held the phone up, and said, "Here, you sonofabitch." She tossed it toward Alvarez. When he reached a hand up to catch it, Decker gave a roar and bolted toward the stairs.

Alvarez took his eyes off the phone, turned, and leveled his gun at Decker.

A shot rang out.

Decker stumbled and went down.

Alvarez looked over at Jamison. A wisp of smoke was coming off the pistol she held in her hand.

He looked down at the blood coming out of the hole in his chest.

"Y-you, b-bitch!" he screamed.

He pointed his gun at her.

She stumbled back and fell.

The next second Alvarez was lifted off his feet. His small body sailed across the width of the room and he slammed into the brick wall. He slid down the wall, slumped to the floor, sat up for an instant, touched the wound in his chest, and glanced at Decker, who'd blindsided him.

"Y-you, a-assho—"

He slumped over dead before he could finish.

Bogart sat down next to Jamison at her and Decker's apartment. He put a hand on her shoulder.

"You sure you don't need anything?"

Jamison's eyes were closed and tears trickled out. She slowly nodded her head.

Bogart looked up at Decker, who sat at the kitchen table holding an ice pack to his swollen cheek. "You okay?"

"I've got no complaints. Alex saved both our lives."

Milligan was standing next to Decker. "She never shot anyone before," he said quietly. "It's not something you get over quickly."

Decker looked over at Jamison. "She'll be okay. She's tough."

Bogart rose and came over to Decker. "We'll post people outside just in case Alvarez has friends. You sure you guys will be okay?"

Decker nodded. "I'll take it from here."

Bogart and Milligan left, and Decker rose from his chair, crossed the room, and sat down next to Jamison.

"I'm sorry this had to happen, Alex," he began.

She wiped her nose with her sleeve and sat up. "If you hadn't told me what to do, we'd both be dead."

"If *you* hadn't done what you did, we'd both be dead."

She sat back and stared at the ceiling. "I killed someone, Amos."

He looked at her awkwardly. "There's no perfect formula to get over it."

"What did you do when it happened to you for the first time?"

"Honestly?"

She nodded.

"I called Cassie and told her I wouldn't be home that night. I filed my reports, had my interviews with internal affairs, jumped through all the bureaucratic hoops, and then rented a motel room, loaded up with liquor, and got drunk as hell."

"Did it help?"

"No. I woke up with the worst hangover of my life and I still felt shitty about what had happened."

"Thanks for the pep talk," she said in a hollow tone.

"My point is, even with my perfect recall I *did* get over it. Things haunt me, Alex. But I can live with them. And you will too. It just takes time."

She sank her head into her hands. "I'm going to see his face until the day I die."

"No you won't. He made the choice to start it. You just had to finish it. You saved us, Alex."

"I was so scared, Decker."

"So was I."

"But you were a cop. You're used to this stuff."

"You never get used to somebody trying to kill you."

Jamison pulled a tissue from her pocket and rubbed at her eyes. "I'm glad you showed me how to fire that gun."

"Being taught how to fire a weapon isn't that hard. Firing it when you really need to is the hard part. He obviously didn't see you as a threat. He assumed you weren't even armed. Big mistake."

"But after I shot him, I panicked. I couldn't even defend myself."

"So it was my turn to help you out. That's what partners do, Alex. We have each other's back."

"That's the first time you called me that."

"What?"

"Your *partner*." She swiped a strand of hair out of her face. "It has a nice ring to it."

"You need to go grab a hot shower, take a pill, and go to bed, and not think about it anymore for tonight."

"But—"

"You need to turn your brain off. You can start to try to deal with it later. But not now."

He watched her walk off. Right before she closed the bedroom door behind her she turned and said, "Thanks, Amos."

"For what?"

"For...for not being your *normal* self right now." She tacked on a weak smile to this and closed the door. A minute later he heard her shower start up.

Decker rose and stared down at his phone. He'd tried to call Mars a number of times to let him know what had happened, but there'd been no answer.

That wasn't like the man.

He put on his coat, snagged Jamison's car keys, and walked out, locking the door firmly behind him. He passed the FBI agents stationed in the building's lobby.

"Take good care of her, guys," he said as he walked by them.

He knew where Mars was staying. It wasn't that far away.

He wedged himself into Jamison's subcompact, wishing for the moment that he could be a foot shorter and a hundred pounds lighter.

The drive only took about fifteen minutes. There was little traffic at this early hour of the morning.

He pulled into the parking lot of the hotel and grabbed an open space. He was about to get out when a car he recognized pulled up to the front of the building and a man in a uniform got out. It was one of the hotel valets. He turned the keys over to the owner and that person got in the car and drove off.

Decker checked his watch.

It was nearly five in the morning. Decker opted for a change in plan.

He pulled off and started to follow the other car.

Twenty minutes later it veered into an open space at the curb. The door opened and the driver got out.

Decker pulled up, stopped, and rolled down his window.

"You're out early," he said. "Or coming home late."

Harper Brown turned to look at him.

"What are you doing here?"

"You were telling the truth."

"About what?"

"You are quite *social* in your off hours. So how's *Melvin*? Resting comfortably?"

She let out a sigh, leaned against the front fender of her Beemer, and said, "You want to come in for a cup of coffee?"

"I don't know. Do I?"

Decker pulled into a free space two cars down and got out. He joined Brown as she was putting the key in her front door.

"Glad you had a good night," he said.

"Thanks, me too. How about you?"

"Nothing to write home about," said Decker as they went inside.

CHAPTER

48

BROWN FLIPPED ON the lights in her kitchen, put her bag down, and busied herself making coffee.

Decker sat at the table and watched her. She slipped off her jacket, revealing her shoulder holster and pistol.

A couple minutes later she carried two steaming cups over, leaned down, and handed Decker one of them.

That's when she saw his bruised face in the wash of the overhead lights.

"What the hell happened to you?"

"Just a little altercation tonight. Nothing too serious."

"Why do I think you're lying?"

"Whatever happened, it's over and Alex and I are good."

"Jamison! She was involved?"

Decker took a sip of coffee. "Very. So let's move on to Melvin."

She took a drink of her coffee. "You disapprove, of course," said Brown.

"It's really none of my business. But Melvin is my friend and I don't want to see him get hurt either."

"So I'm guessing you think this is all too sudden given we just met tonight?"

"I don't think anything. I don't judge anything. But I

can tell you that Melvin's got a lot of stuff about his life to work out. It's complicated. That can make somebody vulnerable."

She said heatedly, "It's not like I do this all the time, because I don't. It was actually just sex, Decker. That *does* happen, you know, when two people are immediately attracted to each other."

"Just sex for you. Was it just sex for *him*?"

"Maybe it was." She set her cup down and stared at him. "You really do care about him?"

"Why do you sound so surprised by that?"

"Unfairly or not, some view you as this machine without a lot of human touches." When he didn't respond, her features softened. "I don't include myself in that group, Decker. I've seen you being human. You're being human right now with your concerns about Melvin. It's . . . it's nice, actually."

"If you two hit it off, great. He could use someone like you."

"Meaning what?"

"You may have to deceive as part of your job, but I see you as honorable, Agent Brown. Your father got on that wall because he served his country faithfully. I don't see the apple falling far from the tree. And Melvin is a very honorable person. So you two have *that* in common. I would say you both deserve nothing less."

This was obviously not what Brown had been expecting. She took a sip of coffee and looked away. When she turned back her eyes held a shimmer of moisture.

"Let me rephrase what I just said about you being human, Decker. I actually think you're one of the most *human* people I've ever met. And call me Harper, please."

They both sat there in silence for another few seconds until Brown cleared her throat and said, "Why were you at the hotel in the first place?"

"I'd called Melvin a few times and he never answered. I was worried."

"I think he turned his phone off. He was fine when I left him."

"Good to know. Thanks."

She fingered her cup, her gaze pointed at the tabletop. "We did *talk* some. Mostly about you. How amazing he thought you were. How, if not for you, he'd still be in prison."

"That's a stretch."

"Not according to him."

"It was nice of him to say," Decker said quietly, not looking at her either.

"What really happened to your face? I'll find out eventually."

Decker took a few minutes to tell her what had happened. Brown's jaw sank lower with each sentence.

"Is Jamison okay?"

"Not now, but she will be. It's not easy, killing someone. You don't just get over it in a day." He looked over at her. "You know that feeling."

She nodded. "The guy in your parking lot was not my first. And though I know I didn't show it that night, I went home, drank a bottle of wine, and didn't sleep a wink. I kept looking down at my hand and thinking that there was one less person alive that day because of me."

"I figured as much."

She smiled weakly. "I guess I'm not as tough as you thought I was."

"Actually, that makes you *tougher* than I thought you were."

"Every time I think I have you figured out, Mr. Decker, you throw me a curve."

"Not my intention."

"I wonder."

"How did you leave things with Melvin?"

"That I very much wanted to see him again."

"We still have a case to work," he replied.

"I compartmentalize with the best of them. Speaking of the case, any revelations since we were last together?"

"Berkshire was a spy or a spy's handler. Dabney may or may not have been her mole. We have no real record of her past ten years ago. She might not have been in this area all that time, but Dabney has. Same house, same wife, big family."

"So you're saying there's an incongruity if we think Dabney and Berkshire were working together long-term?"

"You tell me. Do the spy and the handler need to be in the same place?"

"Absolutely not. I mentioned Montes before? Her handlers were in Cuba. She'd meet with them sometimes. They'd either come here or she'd go to them. But only periodically."

"So Dabney, who undoubtedly traveled a lot for his business, would have had the means to go to her?"

"Yes. And use the cover of his business to do so."

"And since we have no idea where Berkshire was thirty years ago, we can't trace that. But—"

Brown said, "But we know where she was maybe ten years ago. And we could match that up with Dabney's travel during that same period."

"If she met him in the places where she lived. If not, we might be able to check where she traveled, if she went by train or plane or bus."

"So you're leaning to the conclusion that these two have worked together before."

"Let's put it this way, I can't rule it out," replied Decker.

"But we haven't had any other instances of spying that

we could connect to Dabney, other than the secrets sold to pay off the gambling debts."

"But Dabney didn't just work with DIA. He worked with the FBI, NSA, and at least a half dozen other government agencies."

Brown's features tightened. "If he stole from all of them, it's a big problem."

"I *always* thought this was a big problem," retorted Decker.

"We can start checking out the travel angle to see if we can place these two in the same place at the same time."

"I'll have Bogart's people get on it."

"But Decker, if Dabney and Berkshire were working together all this time, why would he kill her on the street in front of the Hoover Building?"

"Regret? Some friction or falling-out we don't know about?"

"Well, if they were working together, her contacts got him the ten million bucks to pay off his son-in-law's gambling debt and save his daughter's and granddaughter's lives. You'd think he would have been grateful toward her, not homicidal."

"It's funny how the human mind works. It all depends on perspective."

"And the third party you mentioned? The one who almost killed you and stole the flash drive you discovered?"

"They're clearly still out there. They're connected to this at a level I don't understand yet, but that connection is deep. And I have a feeling we're going to have to go face-to-face with them before we solve this thing."

Brown took out her Beretta and laid it on the table. "Well, let's hope they don't get us before we get them," she said.

49

DECKER HAD COME HOME from Brown's to find Jamison still asleep. He caught a few hours of sleep, showered, and changed. By the time he was done, Jamison was up and dressed and sitting at the kitchen table.

"You need some food," said Decker. "And so do I. Let's go."

They drove to a nearby restaurant and ordered breakfast for lunch.

Thirty minutes later Jamison put a last mouthful of scrambled eggs in her mouth while Decker finished his third cup of coffee. He eyed her closely. "How are you really doing?"

"Better actually than I thought I would. Which makes me feel guilty."

"Some people just have it coming, and the guy last night did, Alex. But then I'm biased since you saved my life in the process."

She looked despondently over at him. "Maybe I'm just not cut out for this. I was thinking before that maybe I should just go do something else with my life."

"Maybe you don't need to think about that right now."

"But I do, Decker. I mean, I'm not getting any younger, and I have to make decisions about my life."

"You're a good investigator. Ross would not have brought you on if he didn't think that."

"Come on, Decker, Bogart brought me on because of you."

"Why would he have needed to do that? And you were the one who deduced that Dabney was maybe a longtime spy because of how quickly he found someone to buy his secrets. Even if it turns out not to be the case, I didn't think of that, and neither did Ross or Todd."

"I'm not saying I don't have my moments."

"You have more than moments, Alex. Look, if you want to bag it and go do something else, fine. But don't do it because you think you're not cut out for this, because you are."

She looked at him hopefully. "Do you really think that? You're not just saying that to make me feel better?"

"As you know better than most, that's not how my mind works."

"But I did kill a man," she said, her expression turning dark again. "I'm not sure I could face doing that again."

"This job doesn't call for us to get into shootouts with people. Alvarez wasn't tied to our work at the FBI. So that may very likely be the first and only time you have to draw your weapon."

"Apparently not if I keep hanging around with you."

"You need to get your mind off it. Luckily, we have a very complex case to solve."

"Hey, do you want to call Melvin and have him come with us? He's had some good ideas on this too."

Decker hesitated long enough that she looked at him suspiciously. "What is it?"

"Nothing."

"Come on!"

"It's nothing."

"Decker, you're a shitty liar."

"I just think we need to let Melvin sleep in."

"Why?"

"I don't know. Just a feeling."

"Decker!"

"He had a long night."

"What do you mean by that? He went home the same—" She stopped and stared wide-eyed at him. "Holy shit. Are you not telling me what I think you're not telling me?"

"Alex, I don't even know how to begin to answer that question."

"I'll ask you a simpler one then. Did Melvin sleep with Harper Brown?" Her voice had risen to where people at two other tables stared over at them.

"Why do you think that?"

"Why do I think that? Hello, it couldn't have been more obvious that she wanted him."

"It couldn't?"

"Oh, come on, for a guy who misses nothing, you really have a blind spot sometimes."

Decker looked nervously around before focusing on her. "It's none of our business what they did."

"You need to tell me everything right now."

"Why?"

"Because technically I work for Melvin."

"So?"

"Decker, I swear to God if you don't tell me I'm going to make such a scene right here and now."

Decker sat up. "Okay, okay. Yes, they…spent time together at Melvin's hotel."

"And how do you know this?"

"I went over to Melvin's hotel late last night. Well, it was really early this morning. You were asleep. I'd called him but he didn't answer."

She looked at him incredulously. "Oh, really? And what, you were *worried*?"

"All right, I deserved that."

"And then what?"

"And then I saw Brown come out. I followed her to her house and we...talked."

"You talked about what they did?"

"No. I mean, not really. It was mentioned, but it wasn't like I wanted to hear details," he said, flustered. "They're both consenting adults. They can do what they want."

"They had just met a few hours before!"

"Alex, what do you want me to say?"

"What did Brown *say*?"

"She said, well, that they were mutually attracted to each other. And that it was just...you know, *sex*," he added uncomfortably.

"Does she normally jump into the sack with someone she just met?"

"She says she doesn't."

"And you believed her?"

"I wasn't going to interrogate her about it, for God's sake," he said heatedly.

"She works at DIA. Don't they have rules against this sort of stuff?"

"I don't know. And now I wish I hadn't told you."

"Melvin is your friend. Aren't you worried about him getting hurt?"

"Yeah, I am actually. I told Brown that."

"And what did *Brown* say?"

"That she didn't want to hurt him. That maybe they could have a relationship."

"Oh, please. She's going to dump him."

"You don't know that."

"Yes I do. Do you really see this lasting?"

"So what if it doesn't? Maybe Melvin just wanted sex too."

"Melvin is different."

"Maybe he is. But he's also a grown man who can make those decisions for himself."

"So you're not going to do anything?"

He looked at her in amazement. "What exactly do you want me to do? Tell them they can't see each other because I said so? Christ, Alex. Listen to what you're saying. Next you'll be wanting me to pass notes to him like we're back in middle school."

Jamison slumped back in her chair and stared off. "This is all so wrong."

"Look, I know you have a problem with Agent Brown."

"And I'm surprised you don't since she keeps *lying* to us."

"That's part of her job."

"Oh, great, so now you're defending her? Again!"

"I'm not defending anybody. I'm just stating a fact."

"What do facts have to do with any of this?" she snapped.

An elderly man dressed in a suit and felt cap, who'd been sitting at the table next to theirs, came over on his way out.

"My dear late wife and I used to have arguments just like this. Every marriage has its ups and downs. But don't worry, you two *will* work things out."

He tottered off, leaving Decker and Jamison staring openmouthed at each other.

"Great, now we apparently sound like an old married couple!" exclaimed Jamison in disbelief.

Decker jumped up. "I'll go pay the check."

50

DECKER AND JAMISON said nothing to each other as they drove down the street after leaving the restaurant.

After five minutes, Jamison finally spoke. "I can't read your mind, Decker. Are we going somewhere or am I just driving aimlessly around?"

Decker said, "Sorry, let's head to Berkshire's place. I want to go over it again."

The drive took about forty minutes. The concierge let them into the condo and then returned to the lobby.

Jamison, who had been here before, still looked around in awe. "Wow, I guess espionage does pay."

"Yeah, only ordinarily it doesn't. Not for the people in the trenches."

"Well, she certainly disproved that."

"She's got this big stock and bond portfolio and the fancy car. But for what purpose? Look around at this place. None of this is *her* doing. I confirmed with the building manager that all this furniture, in fact everything in this place, came with the condo when she bought it from the previous owners. Apparently they didn't want to sell it furnished, but she made them an offer they couldn't refuse."

"I wonder why she would do that?"

"Good question, to which I'd dearly love to have the answer."

"Maybe we follow the money," said Jamison.

"What?"

"Where did the money come from to pay for all this?"

"Bogart was looking into that but wasn't finding anything. The records hit a stone wall at a certain point and he hasn't been able to get past that, he said."

"And we're sure the payments to Dabney didn't come from Berkshire?"

"Nothing of consequence has been sold from her portfolio in the last year."

"Okay."

Decker looked thoughtful for a moment. "But there might have been a way."

"How do you mean?"

"What if Berkshire did manage to get that money to Dabney after all?"

"But you said nothing of consequence had been sold in her portfolio."

"But that doesn't mean she couldn't have used her portfolio as *collateral* for the money."

"What, you mean like a loan that you use other property to secure?"

"Exactly."

"But who would loan her that much money?"

"I don't know."

"And she would know if it was going to pay a gambling debt that she would never get it back. That means all of her money would go to pay off the loan."

"But what if she didn't know the money was going to pay a gambling debt. Maybe she thought it was for something else."

"Like what?"

"Like a legitimate business thing. Maybe she thought it was a short-term loan that would be paid back, with interest."

"But we can't even show she knew Walter Dabney. Why would she loan him ten million dollars?"

"She *must* have known him. Or knew someone who knew him. And would vouch for his ability to pay back the loan."

"That seems really out there, Decker. I mean, ten million dollars!"

"But what did Berkshire care about money? Yeah, she has this place and a car she hardly uses. So she wasn't about money. The clothes she had on when she died were from a discount store. Her closet was pretty bare. No jewelry, no expensive handbags. She didn't buy anything to outfit this place. She drove around in a crappy Honda. And she had millions sitting in an account. For what?"

Jamison nodded. "Maybe for opportunities like this one."

Decker cocked his head. "Explain."

"Maybe it wasn't simply a loan, Decker. Maybe Dabney hadn't been spying all that time. But if *Berkshire* was still spying, maybe the money was a way for her to get Walter Dabney under her thumb. They'd know what he did for a living and all the valuable contacts and access to government agencies he'd have. Hell, the 'loan' might have come from Russia for all we know. The point is she might have *known* about the gambling debt. Maybe the Russians were the ones who got Dabney's son-in-law so in debt in the first place. Then Berkshire is there to save the day and Dabney is her mole, bought and paid for."

Decker mulled this over. "So Dabney didn't go and find Berkshire."

"Berkshire found Dabney and helped him so she could blackmail him later into spying for her."

"Only he knew something that she didn't. He knew that he was dying. And he wasn't going to be her mole."

"So he killed her, and then himself. End of story."

"It makes sense, Alex. But we still have to show some connection between Walter Dabney and Berkshire. So far, we've been unable to do that."

"We may never be able to do that," she replied. "They might have hidden it too well. Or used intermediaries."

"Or maybe one intermediary," said Decker.

"You have someone in mind?"

"Maybe the person he confided everything to? The one who had the problem in the first place? And then went with him to Texas to get his death sentence."

"Natalie?"

"Natalie."

"But why would she be involved in that? Her husband was the gambler. She was just trying to get the money to pay off his debts."

Decker didn't say anything. He was staring off.

"Decker, I said—"

"I heard you. I know that's what we've been told. But right now, I don't believe anything I've been told."

"But why not?"

"I've got my reasons. Ten million of them, in fact," he added cryptically.

He pulled out his phone and called the Dabneys' house.

Cecilia Randall, the housekeeper, answered.

Decker asked to speak to Natalie.

"She's on her way to the airport," Randall replied.

"The airport? Why?"

"She's heading back to France. The funeral is over and she said she had to get back."

"What time is her flight?"

"I think they board around five-thirty. She's on Air France."

Decker looked at his watch. "Thanks."

He clicked off and looked at Jamison. "I think she's making a run for it."

CHAPTER

51

NATALIE BONFILS HANDED over her passport and ticket as she prepared to board the Air France flight to Charles de Gaulle Airport. It was an A380, a full-length double-decker airliner that would ferry over five hundred passengers across the Atlantic to the French capital, arriving about seven and a half hours after takeoff given the prevailing tailwinds.

She did not make it onto the jetway to the plane.

Two men in suits held up their Bureau shields and barred her way.

"What is going on?" she demanded.

"This way, please, Ms. Bonfils."

"I'm flying to Paris tonight. My luggage is already on the plane."

"We had it taken off."

"How dare you," she snapped. "Why?"

"This way, please, we don't want to make a scene."

Natalie looked around at other passengers gaping at her. She spun around and walked away from the jetway entrance.

Then she saw Decker and Jamison standing next to Bogart and her face turned ugly.

"What the hell are you doing to me!" she exclaimed.

Bogart came forward. "We need to talk to you. Now."

"I've told you everything I know."

"And I also told you not to leave the area," retorted Bogart.

"I didn't know that still applied, since we *buried* my father."

"One has nothing to do with the other. It applies until I tell you explicitly that it does not apply."

She turned to Decker. "This is your doing, isn't it?"

"We've got a space here where we can talk privately," said Decker.

They led her down an escalator and to a room located across from one of the baggage claims. Milligan and Brown were already there.

"Thanks for the heads-up, Decker," said Brown as they escorted Natalie in.

"Please take a seat, Ms. Bonfils," said Bogart.

Natalie sat, folded her arms over her chest, and stared angrily at each of them. "Should I have a lawyer?" she snapped.

"I don't know," said Bogart. "Do you think you need one?"

"When the FBI pulls you off a plane it makes you think you do, even if you've done nothing wrong."

"We're not arresting you, so we haven't Mirandized you yet. Therefore you're not entitled to a lawyer being present while we question you. But you can call an attorney and you can also refuse to answer our questions."

"Just ask your damn questions. Maybe I can still make my flight."

"That won't be happening," replied Bogart firmly. "But we *will* start asking our questions."

She scowled at him.

Bogart glanced at Decker, who said, "Why the rush to get back to France? I thought you said you were divorcing your husband."

"I am. But my *kid* happens to be there with him. I'm going to get her."

"And bring her back here?" asked Decker.

"I haven't decided that yet. I'm sort of in limbo right now. I might live with my mother, at least temporarily. But what does this have to do with why you pulled me off the damn plane?"

"The gambling debts."

Her features collapsed. "Shit, are you serious? I told you everything I know about them."

"You want to take a minute and think about that answer?"

She tensed and looked around the table. "What is *that* supposed to mean?"

Bogart said, "Based on a hunch from my colleague here"—he indicated Decker—"we spoke with the authorities in France. They've questioned your husband over this matter already, at our request. We asked them to question your husband again immediately. They did so and we have his answers here."

He pulled out an electronic notebook.

Decker said, "So, based on that, do you want to rethink your answer?"

Natalie glanced nervously at the notebook. "Why, what did Corbett say?"

Bogart said, "He told us the truth because he was informed that otherwise he could go to prison and lose custody of his daughter."

Natalie paled but said nothing.

Bogart continued, "He told the French police that the gambling debts weren't actually his. They were *yours*."

"That's bullshit. He's lying! I've never so much as played the lottery."

Bogart hit some keys on the notebook, slid it around, and pushed it over to her.

"That's video feed from a casino in Paris. Hit play."

When she made no move to do so, Decker reached over and hit the requisite key. The screen came to life, showing the floor of a casino.

Bogart pointed to one section. "You, at the baccarat table."

Natalie looked up, her face a dark mass of fury.

Bogart said, "We also have you at two other casinos in Paris, another in Aix-les-Bains, one in Cannes, and two in Nice, over a ten-month period."

Brown looked at Decker and said, "We blew that one. We thought it was Corbett with the problem. Our sources sounded certain."

Bogart said, "He apparently is a much nicer guy than we've been led to believe. He was falling on the sword for his wife and her gambling problems."

"You don't know shit about me," exclaimed Natalie.

Decker leaned forward. "We know enough to put you away for the rest of your life."

Natalie screamed, "For what? It's not illegal to gamble in France."

"No, but it's illegal to be a coconspirator in espionage," interjected Brown.

"I knew nothing about that."

Bogart said, "And I think we can prove otherwise. But once a jury sees what you did, do you really think they're going to be sympathetic to you? They're going to see a spoiled little rich girl who lied about everything and put her own daughter in danger because she couldn't stop rolling the dice. And to get out of this jam she brought her poor, terminally ill father into this whole thing and it cost him everything he had worked his whole life for. And drove him to suicide. You'll be lucky if you don't get the death penalty."

Natalie stared at him wildly for a few seconds and then broke down in tears.

Decker stared at her without a shred of sympathy. "You've done the tear duct dance already," he pointed out. "So don't waste our time. We want answers, and maybe, just maybe, you can cut a deal."

Natalie immediately stopped crying and looked up at him. "What do you want to know?"

"How did you run up ten million in gambling debts so fast?"

"Bad luck."

"No, it wasn't that," said Decker. He pulled the notebook back to him. "We got the Sûreté to check on that too. It struck me as odd that someone like you, without any real money, could find her way into games of chance that would allow you to dig such a hole. You were never a high roller. You never went to the private areas of these casinos where the heavy hitters lose a hundred grand on a single roll. And most casinos would have put the kibosh on your gambling long before you got to ten million. Anyone runs up that much in losses, they already know that person's financials. Casinos are not stupid. They're in business to make money, not lose it. So there are letters of credit on file, methods of guaranteed repayment locked in to cover losses that large. You didn't have any of that, so they'd know you could never pay it back. But I just took it for granted that it was true, because that's what I was told." He shot a sidelong glance at Brown. "But we finally decided to question that conclusion because it made no sense. And conclusions that make no sense are very often wrong."

Decker sat back and looked at Natalie. "The French police haven't gotten back to us yet with the answers to that, but they will. And do you want to know what I think they'll find?"

Natalie said nothing.

"I think they'll find you had gambling debts, all right.

Maybe hundreds of thousands. Enough to sink you. Enough to scare the shit out of you. But not millions."

Brown said, "But Decker, we know that ten million dollars was moved from one account to another."

Decker held up his hand and looked back at Natalie. "And you were approached by someone who was probably watching you the whole time, because of who your father was. And that person made a deal with you. It was your only way out, because I *do* think you'd borrowed money from some bad dudes to pay those gambling debts. And they *would* hurt you and your family if you didn't repay that loan."

Natalie had turned very pale.

Bogart took up the thread. "That person agreed to take care of your debts if you did something in return. You were to contact your father and sell him this story of millions in gambling debts run up by your French hubby, and you and your family's life on the line if it weren't paid. It couldn't be hundreds of thousands, because your father would probably be able to pay that off himself. But not ten million. So what choice does he have? Where else could he get that kind of money so fast? He couldn't sell his house or liquidate his other assets in a day or two. There was really only one way. So that was the bait, and he had no choice but to take it.

"Now, if you want to dispute that and come up with an alternate scenario that makes sense, feel free. We've got no place else to be." Decker folded his arms over his chest, sat back, and stared at her expectantly.

A minute of silence ticked by until Natalie said curtly, "What kind of a deal can I get?"

52

"Boy did I blow that," said Brown.

She, Decker, and Jamison were sitting in a conference room at the WFO.

Bogart, Milligan, and an attorney from the Justice Department were with Natalie in another part of the building going over the preliminary terms of a deal because of her co-operation in the case.

The woman had broken down in sobs when she'd been taken away from Dulles Airport. And even Decker could tell that this time the tears were real.

"We got that scenario totally screwed up. She set her own father up," said Brown. "It never occurred to us. How did you figure that one?"

"Alex here actually made me think it was possible because of something she said about Anne Berkshire getting Walter Dabney under her thumb. Plus, there was no way someone like Natalie would have been allowed to run up millions in gambling debts. They would have cut her off long before."

Brown looked over at Jamison with new respect. "I guess I just assumed that our intel on who was the gambler was true."

Jamison said, "Amos and I have a policy of not believing

anything unless we *know* it to be true. And that's a high bar."
She shot Decker a glance after she said this, but he was lost
in thought.

Brown said, "So Natalie described the guy who approached her. He sounded Russian to her. He made the deal
of paying off her debts. It wasn't like she could really ask her
father. She said she owed about three hundred thousand. He
might have been able to pay that off, but then she'd have to
explain what it was for, and she didn't want to do that. And
she *had* borrowed the money she gambled with from some
not-so-nice people who would have hurt her and her family
if she didn't repay."

Jamison said, "So she sets her own father up."

Brown said, "She says she didn't know anything about
her dad stealing secrets."

"How could she *not* know?" retorted Jamison. "Where
else was he going to get ten million?"

Brown said, "He might have mortgaged their house,
cleaned out his retirement, sold every stock and bond he had.
I wonder how they would have reacted if he had done that
instead of stealing secrets."

Decker interjected, "It was a chance they were willing to
take. And if he did do all that, it would make him susceptible
to selling secrets down the line. He wouldn't have had any
money left for retirement. So either way, they probably win.
It seems that these folks are very patient about how they go
about their work. They think long-term. But they didn't have
to worry about that, because he went for the sale-of-secrets
route first."

"But how do we track down this Russian guy?" asked
Jamison. "He's the only lead we have on this."

Decker said, "We have his description and the name he
gave Natalie, though it wouldn't be his real one. They're

circulating that info to all the agencies here and overseas. Maybe something will pop." He looked at Brown. "You said the money was untraceable?"

"Now that we know it wasn't ten million in gambling debts we're going to take another look at it. But don't hold out too much hope."

"Why not?" asked Jamison.

"First of all, in the digital age, moving money around the world is a lot easier to do and a lot harder to track. And my guess is that whoever struck the deal with Natalie paid off her debts. The ten mill for the secrets that Dabney stole was probably a sham transaction. We know money did change hands, but we lost it in the digital ether. It could have gone out of one account and bounced around the world before going into another account controlled by the same party. The proof to Dabney that the funds made it to where they were supposed to go would be in the form of Natalie and her family being alive and well."

Jamison nodded, obviously disappointed. "That makes sense."

"And if Natalie is telling the truth now, it doesn't seem like she knows anything more that could help us."

"So what sort of deal will she get?" Jamison asked Brown.

She shrugged. "If they believe that she didn't know what her father was going to do, they might be lenient. There's no crime in asking your parents to help pay off your debts. And gambling *was* legal where she did it. If you take the espionage piece out she may be looking at no prison time."

"That hardly seems fair for what she did."

"She lost her father over this," said Brown. "She's going to have to live with that the rest of her life. That might be more punishment than sitting in a prison cell."

Decker said, "But what none of this explains is the core

issue that began this case for us. Why did Dabney kill Berkshire and then himself? They have to be related to what Natalie did. But *how* are they connected? If we don't answer that, we answer nothing. And what the hell is the point of that?"

He got up and walked out.

"The man is ticked off," said Brown.

Jamison settled her gaze on the other woman. "He doesn't like bullshit. He likes to cut right through that to get to the truth." She paused. "How about you?"

"How about me what?"

"Do you like bullshit better than the truth?"

Brown looked at her coolly. "Do I take your aggressive tone to mean that Decker told you what happened between me and Melvin last night? And you're upset about it?"

"He *did* tell me. And I *was* upset about it. But then you're both consenting adults, so there you go. No, I was talking about your 'blowing' it, as you said about the gambling debts. I thought you were supposed to have experience and be this hotshot agent. Decker saved your ass on that one. But what I can tell you is that he will never rely on anything else you say again. Because the man with the perfect memory is never going to forget that a veteran like you made a rookie mistake by assuming something was true when you hadn't bothered to prove that it was actually true. He said your dad was on some honor wall at DIA. Maybe you want to be too. Well, in my humble opinion you'll need to up your game. But then maybe you don't care about that. I'll leave you alone now so you can think about that, if you even want to bother. And tell Melvin I said hello the next time you see him. But if you hurt him in any way, I will kick your ass."

And with those biting remarks, Jamison got up and followed Decker out.

CHAPTER

53

DECKER AND JAMISON drove home in silence. When they got to the apartment she said, "You want me to whip up some dinner? And I don't mean in a microwave. I can do chicken and rice."

He shook his head. "No, thanks. Not really hungry."

"You don't want to get too skinny," she joked, but Decker had already walked down the hall to his room.

He closed the door behind him, sat down on his bed, and picked up the doll. The rain had started back up and the plunks against the window came rhythmically. He stared down at the plastic face with the two large eyes, which looked unblinkingly up at him.

Now every time he looked at this toy he only saw Molly's face. Decker knew this was not healthy, and he also knew he could not stop doing it. At least not right now.

He'd had a daughter, a beautiful little girl who would have grown up into an amazing woman. He had no doubt about that. Only she'd never had the chance. She had gone to her grave not knowing that some offhand remark in her dad's past had set off a catastrophic chain of events eventually leading to her and her mother's deaths.

He stroked the doll's hair with his finger and then laid it

aside. He stretched out on the bed and stared up at the dark ceiling.

It felt like they had been working on this case forever. And yet they had made not a jot of significant progress.

Not a jot.

In many ways, it seemed they had moved *backwards*.

He had been telling the stark truth earlier. Unless they figured out why Walter Dabney had killed Anne Berkshire they were never going to solve this.

And I witnessed the whole damn thing. And I still can't figure it out.

He sat up against the headboard.

Okay, he needed to take this step by step.

Fact: Dabney was duped into stealing secrets to pay off millions in fictional gambling debts.

Fact: By her own admission Natalie had embroiled her father in this scheme.

Speculation: Natalie did not know about the espionage angle.

Fact: Dabney was terminally ill.

Fact: Dabney shot Berkshire.

Fact: Berkshire's past was a mystery and the parts they knew were made up.

Fact: Berkshire had an old cottage and a beat-up car.

Fact: Berkshire had millions of dollars.

Fact: Berkshire had what looked like spy paraphernalia in a storage unit.

Fact: She was a substitute teacher and a volunteer at a hospice.

Fact: She had a flash drive hidden at the cottage.

Fact: Someone had ambushed Decker to get it.

Speculation: The secrets stolen by Dabney had to do with backdoor access into critical national security sensitive platforms.

This last one he had moved into the speculation section because Brown had been the one to provide that information and also because she had lied to him about this question earlier. He did not know it for sure, and Bogart had been unable to verify it because DIA had stonewalled access.

So where did all this get him?

He got off the bed and walked over to the window and peered out.

He closed his eyes and went frame by frame in his memory.

Oftentimes, this allowed him to see something that was off. A red flag where one slice of information did not jibe with another.

Other times it gave him a sense of which direction he should go.

And still other times he came away empty.

As frame after mental frame rolled through he prayed that something, anything, would pop for him. What someone had said or done. An action that was off-kilter. Anything, really.

Come on. Anything.

Come on.

He opened his eyes.

His axiom on Berkshire had been that she did nothing without a good reason. If he was right about that, he had overlooked one-half of the equation.

Shit!

Jamison was startled when Decker came bolting out of his room and shot down the hall like a torpedo. She had just lifted to her mouth a spoonful of cereal that she was eating next to the kitchen sink.

"What the hell?" she exclaimed.

"We have to go."

"Go where?"

"Dominion Hospice."

* * *

The rain had picked up and Jamison's wipers were having a hard time keeping pace. Wedged into the passenger seat like a watermelon in a sock, Decker looked fidgety and upset.

"You want to tell me why we're going to the hospice?" said Jamison.

"Why would she be volunteering there?"

"I don't know. Why would she be substitute teaching at a school?"

"Because her storage unit was right across the street. I think she wanted to be close to that stuff for some reason. And remember her comments to Billings? I think she liked feeling superior to *American* teachers and students. If so, that scratches that one off the list. That leaves the hospice. And if she was still spying, I've crossed altruistic off my list. So why the hospice?"

They arrived at Dominion Hospice. Visiting hours were over, but their credentials gained them access. The director, Sally Palmer, had gone home for the night, but the evening manager, a man named Alvin Jenkins, met with them in his office.

Jenkins was short and flabby, in his late fifties with glasses and a circle of graying hair surrounding a bald pate. In answer to their inquiries he said, "I never met Anne Berkshire, though I had heard the name. I work evenings, and I understand that she would come in during the mornings."

"You have other volunteers?" said Decker.

"Oh yes. Quite a few. Mostly older, retired folks who have the time to come in and visit."

"Do you have a list of them? And one with all of your employees? Nursing staff and admin, everybody."

He turned to his computer and hit some keys. "I can print them out for you, but what is all this about?"

Before Decker could answer, Jamison said, "National security."

Jenkins's jaw dropped, "Oh my goodness, right." He handed them the printed pages.

"I have to go and make my nightly rounds," he said. "Feel free to use my office as long as necessary."

He left, and Decker and Jamison started going over the pages.

"What are we looking for, Decker?"

"Anything that seems out of the ordinary."

"I'm not sure how we can tell that by looking at people's ages and pictures. I mean, what would she be doing here anyway? And we're not even sure if these people were here at the same time she was. I mean, if she wanted to talk to someone they would have to be here, right? And she only visited with a few patients. Maybe we can ask Jenkins if he knows—"

"Prisoner," exclaimed Decker.

He had jumped up and raced out, leaving Jamison sitting holding sheets of paper and looking stunned.

She slumped back in her seat for a few moments before getting up and hustling after him. "I swear to God, one day I'm just going to kill him."

54

DECKER STOOD in the darkened doorway and looked down at the little boy.

Joey Scott was sound asleep in his bed.

The rain continued to pour down outside.

Decker's gaze swept the room, taking it all in. Then he saw what he had come here for.

A moment later Jamison came to stand next to him.

"What are you—"

When Jamison saw Joey she fell silent. She looked up at Decker.

He said in a low voice, "He has leukemia. The really bad kind. He's not going to make it."

Jamison's mouth quivered. "How old?" she said in a crackling voice.

"Ten. His name is Joey."

Jamison's gaze ran along the lines running to his body from the IV stand. The monitor's greenish screen was filled with the boy's weak vitals.

"But why are you here?"

"Because of that."

He walked over and picked the book off the shelf next to the bed. He looked down at the cover.

The Prisoner of Azkaban.

"Hello?"

Decker turned to see Joey staring up at him.

"Hello, Joey."

"You're the Cleveland Brown."

"That's right. Amos Decker."

"What are you doing here?"

Decker looked over his shoulder and said, "I brought my friend Alex to meet you, Joey."

He eyed Jamison, who still stood in the doorway, and inclined his head toward Joey. She slowly came into the room and drew close to the bed.

"Hi, Joey."

"Hi, Alex."

He glanced at Decker's hand. "Did you come to read to me? Is it morning yet?"

"No, it's nighttime. We didn't mean to wake you. I'm sorry."

"That's okay. I wake up sometimes just because."

Decker and Jamison together watched the slender chest rise and fall, as Joey seemed to work to catch his breath.

"Do you need us to get help?" asked Jamison nervously.

Joey shook his head. "No. It happens sometimes. It'll pass."

They waited another minute or so and Joey's breathing became normal.

Decker sat down in the chair next to the bed and held up the book. "Anne was reading this to you?"

"Yeah."

A spear of lightning lit the sky. It was followed by a boom of thunder that made Jamison jump.

"Did she read the first two in the series to you?" Decker asked.

"The first two?"

"Yeah, this one is the third one. There are two books before it and four that come after it. You learn where Harry Potter came from. And how he got to go to Hogwarts and meet his friends. Stuff like that."

Joey looked confused. "No. That was the only one she'd been reading to me."

"And she leaves it here?"

"Well, sometimes. But other times she takes it with her. But then she always brings it back. We don't have too many pages left. I think I can make it to the end." He sucked in a huge breath. "I hope I can anyway."

At this, Jamison looked away, her eyes filling with tears.

Decker looked very tense as he prepared to speak. "Does anyone else come here and read this book to you, Joey?"

Jamison shot him a glance.

"No. Just Anne. Nobody else."

Decker said, "You're sure?"

"Yeah. Just Anne. I think it's her book. Why?"

"We were just wondering, Joey," said Jamison hastily when it didn't appear that Decker was going to answer. "Do you like the story? The Harry Potter series is great. I started reading them when I was in elementary school."

"Yeah, it's good. I like Harry. But Hermione is my favorite."

"Why is that?"

"She likes to read. I do too. I did anyway. Lots of books." He pointed at Decker. "But I played football too, like him, before I got sick. I bet I would have been pretty good."

"I bet you would have been pretty great," said Jamison, trying very hard to keep her voice from cracking.

Decker looked down at the book as though it had somehow failed him.

"Well, thanks, Joey," he said. "Maybe I'll come back and finish reading this book to you."

"And maybe I can come too," said Jamison suddenly, seeming to surprise even herself with the comment.

"That would be good," said Joey. "Thanks. Maybe you can meet Anne."

"Yeah, maybe," said Decker.

"I used to do a lot of volunteer work," said Jamison. "Maybe I can volunteer here. How about that, Joey?"

"Sure," he said, but then his smile faded and all his energy seemed to disappear along with it. He closed his eyes and his breathing deepened a bit.

"This is beyond sad," whispered Jamison. "He's just a little boy. Doesn't he have anybody?"

"No. He was going to be adopted, but the people apparently pulled out when he got sick."

"What bastards!"

"And the world is full of them, Alex."

"What were you hoping to prove with that book?"

"Just trying to make sense out of something. I was pretty sure, but that goes to show that anybody can be wrong."

Decker rose and was about to put the book back when Joey opened his eyes and turned his head to look at him.

"It's funny, though," said Joey.

"What is?" asked Decker quickly.

"I woke up tonight and saw you with the book."

Decker glanced down at the book and then back up at Joey. "Yeah? What's funny about that?"

"Well, I've woken up a couple times I guess during the night, and I saw him with the book too. That was what's funny. I mean, it's not like he reads to me. And then he walked out with it. But when I woke up the next morning it was back on the shelf. Both times."

"Who?" asked Decker, his voice unusually tight. "Who took the book?"

"The guy with the glasses. I think his name is…" He stopped to think for a moment. "You know, like the chipmunk?"

"You mean," began Jamison.

Decker had already turned and rushed out of the room.

"Alvin," finished Jamison before turning and running after Decker.

55

AN IRRITATED DECKER hovered at the front entrance to Dominion Hospice.

Bogart was talking to a police officer in the front parking lot. The man hurried off and Bogart turned and headed over to Decker.

The reality was not a good one.

Alvin Jenkins was nowhere to be found.

He hadn't gone to make rounds. He had apparently fled the premises right after leaving Decker and Jamison in his office.

Decker had called Bogart in immediately. The last several hours had been spent searching the building and finding nothing helpful.

Bogart said, "We have a BOLO out on him. And we have a team at his apartment. Or at least at the address that was in his file."

"I bet the guy had an exit plan that he activated as soon as we came here asking questions. He's probably got a half dozen passports that would pass any scrutiny. Hell, he might be on a private jet, heading back to wherever he came from."

Decker groaned and looked miserable. "I was too slow, Ross. I missed the window."

"I don't fully understand how you even came to suspect this place had anything to do with anything."

"Berkshire would never have wasted time coming here unless it served her purpose." He held up the book. "Your lab guys need to check this book out. There's something in here that was important to both Berkshire and Jenkins. I'm surprised he didn't try to take it before now."

"Will do." Bogart took the book and sealed it in a plastic evidence bag he pulled from his overcoat.

"Harry Potter? What do you think is in here?"

"Maybe a coded message using the words in there somehow."

"So Alvin Jenkins was working with Anne Berkshire. Do you think he was the one who attacked you and stole the flash drive?"

Decker shrugged. "I don't know. I know appearances can be deceiving, but he doesn't look the type to wield a long-range sniper rifle. And he's pretty small and in his fifties. Whoever walloped me? I just think he was a lot younger and a lot bigger. It takes a lot to knock me out."

"So someone else is out there?"

"Well, if it *is* a spy ring they could have a lot of members. Or they could have called in reinforcements from whatever country they're spying for. And since we know Berkshire once worked for the Soviets, that list of possible suspects is pretty short."

"We'll dig into Jenkins's background. He had to undergo some background checks to get a job here, you would think."

Decker just looked out into the darkness, lost in thought.

"Something else bugging you?" asked Bogart.

"The woman was reading a book to a dying kid just as a way to send stolen secrets," said Decker.

Bogart shook his head. "Yeah, I was thinking about that

too." He added, "I always thought I wanted kids. Didn't work out that way. And I'll soon be a divorced man. But I still think about it."

Decker gazed over at him. "You can still marry again. Have kids, Ross."

"I think raising kids is a younger man's game. I'm not far off the big five-oh."

Decker shrugged. "Just saying it's a possibility. But then what do I know? I had a kid. Now I don't."

"You were still a father, Amos. You had a daughter. You would still have a daughter if the world weren't so screwed up."

"Well, I don't and it is. So why wish for something you can't ever have?"

Bogart looked uncomfortable. "Where's Alex?"

"I think she's still sitting with Joey Scott. With all the police activity, I think the patients here got woken up and rattled. She's calming him down."

"So the boy really has nobody?"

"Apparently not. I don't know how much longer he has to live. I guess not long. Sometimes it's enough to make you want to put a gun against your head and pull the trigger." He looked at Bogart. "Just like Walter Dabney did."

"He had choices, Amos. Everybody has choices."

"Yeah, it's just that sometimes all those choices suck."

Bogart said, "I'm going to get this book down to the lab."

Decker curtly nodded and Bogart hurried out into the rain and then into his sedan. Decker watched him drive off. He turned and walked back down the corridor until he reached Joey Scott's room.

Jamison was sitting on the edge of the bed. She looked up when Decker appeared in the doorway.

"He just fell asleep," she whispered, rising off the bed and joining Decker in the doorway.

"Bogart is taking the book to the lab to check it out."

"No sign of Jenkins?"

He shook his head.

Jamison glanced over at the bed where Joey lay sleeping. "Can you imagine anything more heartless than what those people did? Using the cover of a dying little boy to pass along stolen secrets?"

"I've yet to see the limits of people being heartless," replied Decker. "But, yeah, it's pretty damn heartless."

"I can't believe I'm saying this, but maybe Dabney did a good thing by shooting her."

"There would be plenty of people to agree with you. But it still doesn't make it right."

"I know. I'm just venting. What's our next step?" she asked.

"Maybe they can still catch Jenkins. Then he might talk. Or they might find something at his apartment. But if it's anything like where Anne Berkshire lives, it'll turn up zip. Now they *could* find something in the book. That might at least tell us something."

"What about Natalie?"

"She's cutting her deal. And maybe they can get some more info out of her."

"No, I mean does her family know what she did?"

Decker looked taken aback. "I don't think so. Bogart didn't mention talking to them. The Bureau keeps a tight lid on stuff like that."

"I feel sorry for that family. Lost a husband and father. Now a sister might be going to jail too."

"Like Bogart told me earlier, people have choices."

"Do you think Natalie might have told her sisters anything? I mean about what she might have done?"

"I don't know. I'm not sure how close she was to them.

She lived out of the country, after all. She probably didn't see them all that much."

"I wonder why she moved to France in the first place?"

"People do move to other countries."

"I know. But the family seems so close-knit. And the other sisters stayed in the United States."

"So Natalie was an outlier."

"I guess."

Decker glanced sharply at her. "Thank you."

"For what?'

"For reminding me that I need to stop assuming shit that hasn't been proven."

He walked off down the hall.

Jamison started to go, then looked back at Joey. She hurried over to the bed, leaned down, and gave the sleeping boy a light kiss on his forehead.

Then she hurried after Decker.

56

THEY DROVE BACK to the apartment and grabbed some sleep. They woke early, showered, changed clothes, and met in the kitchen. Decker had gotten there first and made coffee for both of them. The rain continued to pour down outside.

Decker sipped his coffee while standing over by the window and looking out.

"Have you heard from Brown?" asked Jamison.

Decker shook his head. "No. Why?"

"Just wondering."

He turned to look at her. "Why, Alex? I know she's not your favorite person."

"She and I had words last night. Okay, I spoke most of the words."

"What did you say?"

"I was brutally candid."

"About what?"

"About everything."

Decker snorted. "Then I'm surprised she didn't shoot you."

"I had a gun too."

Decker walked back over to her. "She's *not* a bad person, Alex."

"But she's not a particularly good one either. And she missed the stuff on Natalie. That was big."

"And you thought back in Burlington that I had murdered my own family."

Jamison's features turned dark. "I never thought that!"

"You *suspected* it."

"I was a journalist back then. I had to cover all the angles."

"So you've never made a mistake?"

"Of course I have. We all have."

"I've made my share, particularly on this case. And I don't see you jumping on my butt."

"Well, you own up to them. And you've done a lot of great stuff too. But I haven't seen her do much."

"Okay, so long as you're keeping score, Brown saved my ass in the parking lot out there. But for her you'd be living alone. And she opened up a lot more about her work than she probably wanted to. When I went to DIA that day it was clear that her colleagues were pissed at what she'd done. And I got the impression that it might even cost her career-wise. But she did it because she wants to find out the truth. So she went to bed with Melvin. So what? The woman probably works hundred-hour weeks and doesn't know what country she's going to be in week-to-week. She has all this money, but she apparently doesn't have anyone in her life. Her parents are dead. She has no siblings. She's probably pretty lonely. Just like Melvin. So they found each other, at least for one night. Good for them."

"Those are all fair points, but I don't see why you feel the need to keep defending her."

"Because men seem to get an easy pass on a lot of things from the ladies. I don't know why, but they just do. It's like women hold other women to a higher standard in some ways."

"Maybe we do," said Jamison. "But women know how other women can be..."

"Cagey? They're doing calculus while men are still adding and subtracting?"

Jamison smiled grimly. "I was going to use another term, but I'm fine with *cagey*."

"The fact is, we need Brown if we're going to get to the bottom of this thing. You don't have to like her, Alex. You just have to be able to work with her."

"After our last meeting, I think that's going to be hard. Maybe more for her than me. I mean, I really laid it on, Decker."

"She might have thicker skin than you think."

"I'll guess we'll find out."

Decker's phone buzzed. He looked at the screen. "Maybe sooner rather than later. She just texted me. Wants to meet."

Jamison put down her coffee cup. "Where?"

In answer he pointed out the window. "She's waiting in the parking lot."

* * *

Decker and Jamison approached the big Beemer a minute later. "Nice wheels," observed Jamison as they drew closer.

"Very nice," said Decker. He glanced at Jamison's ratty sub-compact parked a few spaces away. "And easier on my knees than your ride."

"If you want me to maintain the peace, play nice," Jamison said between clenched teeth. "You take shotgun."

They climbed in and buckled up.

Brown said, "Sorry to drag you out on such short notice."

"Did you hear about last night?"

"Yes. Nice catch. We've put out a global alert on this Alvin Jenkins. But if he made such a blatant run for it after you spooked him, he probably had a prearranged exit plan."

"That's what I told Bogart."

"What do you think might be in the book?" asked Jamison from the backseat.

"It's a bit old-fashioned, but codes in books are actually coming back into style, for one good reason. Printed books can't be hacked. That alone justifies the return to ink and paper. I'm sure the FBI will check it for all the usual techniques."

She put the car in drive and they sped off.

"So where are we going?" asked Decker.

Brown glanced at him before answering. "We have another murder."

"What?" exclaimed Jamison.

"Who?" asked Decker sharply.

"It's connected to the Dabneys."

"Ellie, one of the daughters?" said a stunned Jamison.

"No. It was the housekeeper, Cecilia Randall."

57

THEY WERE NOT at the luxurious home of the Dabneys in tony McLean.

They were in southeast D.C., where eight of the run-down row houses would still not have equaled the square footage of the Dabneys' mansion.

The police were there and the house in question was strung off with yellow tape stretching and pitching in the wind.

"How'd you find out so fast?" asked Decker as he, Brown, and Jamison stared over at the front entrance. Gawkers were out and looking around curiously at all the police activity.

Brown said, "I've got a contact at the metro police. She knew about my interest in the Dabneys. When the call came in and they found out where she worked, my contact called me. I phoned Bogart. He should be here shortly."

A gurney was wheeled out of the front of the house with a body in a black body bag.

"What do they know so far?" asked Jamison. "How was she killed?"

"Metro is keeping a tight lid on this, and they will until the Bureau shows up. DIA doesn't carry as much weight with the locals as the FBI."

"Well, here they come," noted Decker as Bogart's car pulled up and he and Milligan jumped out and hustled over to them.

Brown explained things in a few sentences and Bogart and Milligan headed over to the officer in charge. They watched as the FBI agents flashed their badges and made their pitch. The body language of the officer changed immediately. He pulled a notebook from his pocket and he started talking.

Five minutes later Bogart and Milligan returned to them.

"Okay, small-caliber gunshot to the back of the head," said Bogart. "Looks like a professional hit. She's been dead about six hours, which puts her death at about two in the morning. So far they've found no one who saw or heard anything."

"Forced entry?" asked Decker.

"They're still checking. Nothing so far indicates that, but it's not been confirmed."

"Would she have let the person in?" asked Brown.

"If her death occurred shortly after the person came, who would she let into her house at two a.m.?"

"Someone she knew really well," said Decker.

"This may not even be connected to our case," said Milligan, looking around. "This is not exactly a safe area."

"If it was a break and enter they would have taken things," said Decker. "Anything missing?"

"Nothing obvious, but they're still looking. She might have had enemies. Or the person might have gone to the wrong house."

"Or she was killed because she knew something about our case," said Decker.

"But what could she know?" asked Jamison.

Brown said, "She worked at the Dabneys'. Saw them every day. She might have overheard something. Seen something."

"But why kill her now?" asked Decker. "We've been investigating this case for a while now and nothing happened to the woman. Why now?"

"Meaning something changed?" said Bogart.

"The probabilities lie there, yeah," said Decker. "Do the Dabneys know about this?"

"I doubt it," said Bogart.

"We'll need to tell them. And confirm they all have alibis."

"You think one of the daughters or their mom came over here in the middle of the night and blew out their housekeeper's brains?" said Milligan dubiously.

"I know that one of the daughters got her father implicated in an espionage scheme that ended with his murdering someone who was spying on this country and then killing himself. So I would say nothing is out of the realm of possibility with *that* family."

Milligan didn't look convinced, but he didn't look so dubious anymore either.

Bogart said, "Todd and I will stay here and learn what we can. Why don't you all head over there now and do the interview."

"Works for me," said Decker. "But you think I can poke my head into her house for just a minute?" He followed Milligan and Bogart back over to a pair of homicide detectives who had just appeared in the doorway of the murdered woman's home.

That left Brown and Jamison alone.

The latter looked at the former.

"About our earlier discussion," began Jamison.

Brown looked at her. "You were right about some things and wrong about others. I'll let you figure out which is which."

And that's all she would say.

* * *

"Cissy's dead?"

Ellie looked at the three of them sitting across from her in the library as though they were aliens just landed on earth.

Decker said, "She was murdered. Shot in the head. Looks to be a professional hit. Do you have any information that could help us on that?"

"I can barely process what you're telling me," said Ellie, who looked nearly paralyzed. "I...thought she was here. I just assumed she had come to work, like she always did."

Jules, Amanda, and Samantha were standing beside their mother, still clad in their robes. All of the daughters looked visibly upset. Samantha was quietly crying. Amanda was leaning her head against Jules's shoulder. Only Jules seemed in control of herself. She stared resolutely at Decker.

"Are we in danger?" she said.

Decker looked at her. "It's possible. We can have an agent posted outside the house."

"Let me ask you another question," said Jules. "Where is Natalie?"

"She's in France," said her mother. "She left yesterday."

Jules kept her gaze on Decker. "She's not in France. Corbett texted me last night. She never got on the plane. She called him and said there was a change of plan."

"What change of plan?" exclaimed Ellie. "What is going on? Where is your sister?"

Jules said, "That's what I'm asking them. Because Natalie also told Corbett that she had run into some 'legal trouble' when leaving the country."

Brown spoke up. "I'm with DIA, Defense Intelligence. We were investigating your husband for possible espionage, which turned out to be the case."

"But he was helping out Natalie's stupid husband," said Jules.

"No, unknown to your father, he was helping out *Natalie. She* had the gambling problem, not Corbett. She got your dad involved to solve *her* debt problem."

"That's crap," snapped Jules. "What proof do you have?"

"We have definitive video proof plus your sister's confession. She's already done a deal in exchange for leniency."

Ellie nearly collapsed off her chair. Jules caught her and shouted, "What the hell do you think you're doing telling her stuff like this with no warning?"

"I was just answering *your* question," replied Brown. "But you need to know that the police will be coming here to interview you about Cecilia Randall's death. They'll want to know if you know anything about it."

"What could we possibly know?" demanded Jules.

"They'll also want to know if you have alibis for when she was killed."

"You can't possibly think that we had anything to do with Cissy's death," said Ellie. "She...she was part of our family. She helped raise the girls, for God's sake."

"The police will still ask for alibis," said Decker. "It's standard procedure."

"When was she killed?" asked Jules.

"Early this morning. Say around two or so."

"Well, we were all here asleep," said Jules.

"And each of you can verify that the others were here?" said Brown.

Ellie said, "I went to bed around eleven. I heard Jules and Samantha come upstairs around midnight. I was reading and heard them talking."

"And I opened the door and said good night to Mom," said Jules.

"And I did too," said Samantha. "And Jules and I are sharing a room. We have our own bedrooms, but... I didn't want to be alone. I went to bed around one, but I went back downstairs for my glasses and I checked on Mom. She was sound asleep. And so was Jules when I got back to the room."

"Okay, that accounts for you three," said Brown, turning to Amanda. "And you?"

Amanda abruptly sat down. "I... I went up to bed before anyone else. I wasn't feeling well. I went to sleep and just woke up about an hour ago."

"So you didn't talk to or see anyone else?" Brown looked at the others. "Did any of you check on your sister last night?"

"Oh come on," barked Jules. "Look at her. She's only got one arm. Do you really think she's capable of shooting a gun? And she's seen Cissy, what, maybe a handful of times over the last ten years. Why in the hell would she kill her? Why would any of us, for that matter?"

"We're not saying that you did. We're actually doing you a favor, because when the police come and ask, you'll have ready answers."

Jules seemed taken aback by this and sat next to Amanda and put an arm protectively around her.

Ellie said, "Where is Natalie?"

"She's with the FBI right now."

"Is she... is she going to prison?"

"I have no way of knowing those details," said Brown. "I can tell you that the possible charges against her are very serious. I would not be surprised if she didn't spend some time in prison."

"Oh my God!" gushed Samantha.

Amanda burst into tears. "What the hell is going on? Our whole family is disintegrating right in front of us."

Jules stared over at Brown. "We didn't kill Cissy. We didn't know anything about what Nat may or may not have done. I still don't understand why Daddy killed himself. I...I..." She pulled away from Amanda and put her head in her hands.

In a trembling voice, Ellie said, "Would you mind if we were just left alone for a while? We just need to be...to be together as a family for just a little while."

Decker, Brown, and Jamison stood. Decker said, "We're going to figure this out, Mrs. Dabney. One way or another."

"But that won't bring back Walt, or Cissy. Or change what will happen to Natalie."

"No ma'am, it won't."

They filed out, leaving the crushed Dabney family in the library.

Outside, Brown turned to Decker.

"What do you think?"

"I think something is off, but I don't know what it is."

58

"YOU WANT TO EXPLAIN what you meant?"

Decker had climbed out of Brown's car and headed into the WFO. Jamison had stayed seated. When Decker looked back at her, she waved him on. He glanced at Brown and then walked to the entrance and disappeared inside.

Brown eyed Jamison in the rearview. "I thought I was pretty clear."

"Clear as mud. Right and wrong. You didn't say what about."

"You want to do this now?"

"We can keep putting it off and the resentment will continue to build and maybe we get to a point where nothing the other says will matter."

Brown put the car in park, undid her seat belt, and turned to look at Jamison.

"You were right that I screwed up. But you were wrong that I don't care. I care what Decker thinks about me. And I care about Melvin, even though I haven't known him very long. I got a good vibe from him right away. We talked. A lot. He thinks the world of you and Decker. I would never hurt Melvin, and I know he would never hurt me. He's not that kind of a guy. Believe me, I know the kind that would. I've dated them."

"I have too," conceded Jamison. "Look, I was pretty rough on you, and that wasn't fair."

"I'm used to things not being fair. My father was a good guy and a great soldier. He did wonderful things at DIA. But he wanted a son, not a daughter. But I was all he had. He didn't discourage me from joining the ranks, but it wasn't like he encouraged me either. Maybe he didn't care one way or another. But it still felt like someone had stuck a shiv between my ribs when I told him I'd joined DIA and all he could say was, 'Are you sure you want to do that, because isn't it time you settle down and start a family?' I'd busted my ass to serve at the same agency he had. And that's all he could say?"

"I bet that hurt like hell."

Brown shrugged. "Things are better gender-wise, sure, but they're far from perfect. Most guys I meet, when they find out what I do, they're either scared off or they try to prove they're more of a badass than I am. So that means I don't have many second dates. And at work, it's mostly guys wondering why I'm there taking a slot that a man should have."

"Same with me," said Jamison. "I'm surrounded by guys all day. And then there's Decker."

"*He's* a guy."

"But he's not really a guy. He's . . . well, he's Decker."

Brown smiled and then laughed. "Somehow, I know exactly what you mean. And Melvin is different too. He's special, Alex. He wasn't intimidated by me at all. He . . . well, he's secure enough in his own skin to not be jealous of what I do."

"I agree with you that Melvin is very special. And he deserves someone special. And maybe that someone is you."

Brown looked taken aback by this but said, "Thanks. That means a lot."

"Are we good?" asked Jamison.

"I think we're as good as we're ever going to be." She paused. "I heard what happened. That you saved Decker's life."

Jamison glanced down at her waist, where she carried her gun.

Brown said, "It's not easy, Alex. And it never gets any easier."

"It's changed me, Harper. I'm never going to be the same. I killed someone."

"*You* didn't change. Just a little part of you did. There's a big difference."

"But you can move forward, at some point?"

"You *will* move forward, Alex. I'm not saying it'll be easy, because it won't. But it will happen."

Jamison gave her an appreciative smile, climbed out of the car, and walked into the WFO. Decker was waiting for her just inside the doors. He scrutinized her face. "No bruises, good. Any wounds I can't see?"

"We actually got along very well. I have a whole different opinion of Agent Brown now."

"Well, that's good to know."

"And you came up again."

"How so?"

"We were just appreciating the fact that you were sort of one of the *girls*."

Decker eyed her quizzically for a moment. "I think I'm just going to let that one pass."

They cleared security and rode the elevator up to their floor. Decker had phoned ahead and Bogart met them as they were walking down the hall.

"Got something," he said. He led them into a room off the main hall. Milligan was already there seated at a computer.

Bogart turned off the lights and nodded to Milligan, who hit some keys and a screen affixed to the far wall came to life.

"*Harry Potter and the Prisoner of Azkaban*," said Bogart. "We found some things I don't think J. K. Rowling intended to be in there."

The three sat down and Bogart said, "Dial it up, Todd."

Milligan hit some more keys and a page from the book showed up on the screen.

"I don't see anything," said Jamison.

"Wait a minute."

Milligan hit some more keys and suddenly various letters on the page started to shimmer.

"They're fluorescing," exclaimed Jamison.

"Yes. We had to try a lot of different interactive light sources, but we found one that worked."

"But they're different colors," said Jamison. "The letters are different colors."

"We think we figured that out. If they used this book over a long term, they would have to send separate messages. The different colors are a way for the receiver to know that. The blue you see is one message. The red another. We don't know which is more recent, but we think that's how it works."

"But what does it say?" asked Decker.

"It's not that simple. The letters don't add up to anything that makes sense. Our code breakers are looking at it and we've asked for assistance from both NSA and DIA. It might take a while, but at least we know they were passing coded messages this way."

"Between Berkshire and Jenkins," said Decker.

"Right. She obtained the secrets, encoded them here, and then he used a special light to reveal the letters, copied them down, and decoded it. Then he would send it up the line to whoever he's working for."

"Pretty clever to use a hospice that way," said Decker.

"You mean pretty *cruel*," added Jamison.

Bogart said, "This way Jenkins and Berkshire would never even have to come into contact. They just used the book."

"You think they used this method to communicate the secrets that Dabney stole?" asked Jamison.

"I don't know for certain, but it's a pretty safe bet they did."

"And yet Dabney murdered Berkshire. Why?"

"We do keep coming back to that," agreed Bogart. "Remorse for what he'd done?"

"But we can't show that Dabney and Berkshire actually even met," said Decker.

"Well, they could have met at a secret location. Maybe the old house in the woods?"

Decker said, "So he sells her the secrets. The amount he thinks is ten million, but it's actually a lot less than that. He doesn't even see the money transferred. He knows it went, though, because his daughter and her family are still alive. Then he gets remorse, like you said, and kills Berkshire and then himself. But why out in the open like that? And why would Berkshire have agreed to meet with him near the Hoover Building? That was probably the last place she would want to go. I mean, wouldn't she have maybe smelled a setup?"

"Maybe not," rejoined Bogart. "I mean, he'd just done a deal with the woman. She might have thought he wanted to do another."

"A spy who uses a subterfuge like a book at a hospice so she doesn't even have to meet another spy she's been working with for a long time decides to do a face-to-face with a guy she's maybe done *one* act of espionage with near the headquarters of the American agency tasked with catching spies?" He looked at Bogart. "Really, how much sense does that make?"

"Not much," conceded Bogart. "But it happened."

"No, maybe it didn't," replied Decker.

CHAPTER

59

"Cissy's DEAD?"

Decker stared across at Natalie.

She had been formally charged, had lawyered up, and was being held because she was considered a flight risk. Because of the sensitive nature of the case, the sole court proceeding conducted so far had been done in the judge's chambers.

The woman looked like she had aged ten years since they had stopped her from flying out of Dulles.

Decker nodded. He had asked to meet with Natalie alone. The others were waiting in another room.

"She was executed, actually."

"Why would anyone do that to her? She was our house-keeper."

"Since you were little?"

"Yes. Cissy had worked for my parents since as long as I can remember."

"Well, someone did kill her."

"But why do you think it's connected to our family?"

"I don't know for certain that it is. But I have to check out the possibility. It is a little coincidental, you have to admit."

Natalie nodded. "I guess it is. Do my mom and sisters know?"

"Yes. They all took it hard."

"Mom raised us, but Cissy was always there for us. And Mom loved her. Dad was gone a lot, and I'm not sure what Mom would have done without Cissy."

"I'm sure. You were lucky to have her."

"So why did you want to see me?"

"Have you gotten your deal yet?"

"I think they're still working on it." Her lips trembled. "My lawyer thinks I'll have to do some time in prison." She looked up at Decker. "I won't be able to see my daughter if I'm in prison, right?"

"Have you talked to your husband?"

She nodded and used a handkerchief to blow her nose. "He said he's flying over with Tasha." She rubbed her eyes. "That was all bullshit about him. Corbett's actually a really good guy. All this crap I'm in, it was my fault. I got addicted to gambling and I couldn't stop. He tried to help me, but I was sick, I guess."

"Admitting that is a big first step to getting better."

"Yeah," she said despondently. "I guess my family knows about me?"

"We told them some. They're very worried about you."

"Can I see them at some point?"

"I don't see why not."

"I've really messed up my life, haven't I?"

"You're not the first and you won't be the last." He hunched forward. "But you can help yourself by helping us."

She shot him a glance. "But I've told you everything I know."

"You actually might know some things you don't even know that you know."

"I don't understand. Like what?"

"When the money was sent to pay off your *true* gambling debts, did you call your dad and let him know?"

"Of course I did."

"He thought it was ten million, though, right?"

She nodded. "That's what I told him because that's what they told me to say."

"And they did that because they wanted your dad's only recourse to be selling classified information. That would be the only way he could raise that kind of money in the short term."

"Agent Decker, what if he had just refused to help me? Then what would have happened?"

"They might have had a Plan B to get to your dad."

"And the gambling debts?"

"That would have been bad for you. But they apparently read your dad right. They knew he wouldn't refuse you."

"That makes me feel even shittier. I killed my father. And the only thing he ever did for me was pretty much everything." She put her head down on the table and quietly sobbed.

"Natalie, when you called your dad about the money being paid and your being safe, what did he say?"

She slowly lifted her head. "He said he was so relieved, but that he wanted me to get some help. He said if it came to it he would fly over and bring me home to make sure I got the right help."

"But he never made any mention of how he'd come by the money?"

"No."

"But did you suspect?"

She said slowly, "I didn't know their net worth, but I didn't think they had that sort of cash lying around. Maybe mortgage the house."

"Maybe sell secrets?"

"I won't lie to you. I can't say that it didn't cross my mind. But even though it wasn't ten million dollars, the people I owed the money to *were* going to kill me. That I know for a fact."

"I don't doubt it. I know people who'd slit your throat for an OxyContin pill. Did he say anything else? Other than what he said about thinking you know somebody but really don't?"

She sat back in her chair and wiped her eyes with her sleeves. "I didn't tell you everything. The last time I talked to him was two days before he shot that woman."

Decker leaned forward. "Why didn't you tell us before?"

"I was in shock. I guess I couldn't believe what I'd done to my father. I was terrified everything would come out. And of course it did."

"Did he call you?"

"Yes."

"What did he say?"

"He sounded so...sad. So hopeless, when he was the biggest optimist I'd ever known. I just figured it was the cancer. He knew he wasn't going to be able to beat it. That would depress anyone, right?"

"Right. What else?" prompted Decker.

"He said that whatever happened, I should remember our family as it was. The happy times. When we were all young. Before...before all the crap in life just took over."

"What did you say to that?"

"I tried to cheer him up. I told him I would come and visit him soon. But it was like he wasn't listening to me. He said that when you're looking at the end of your life coming, it was the most clarifying moment he'd ever had."

"Clarifying moment? I wonder what he meant by that?"

"I don't know. I tried asking him. But he just wasn't listening. I thought he was starting maybe to lose it."

"What else?"

Natalie choked back a sob. "It was so stupid. He asked me if I remembered when I was a little girl and we had all gone to Disney World. And I went on one of the rides and I had a really bad asthma attack. I mean really bad. They had to take me to a hospital in an ambulance. Mom was unhinged by it, so she stayed with my sisters while Dad rode in the back with me. He was very comforting because I was so scared. My dad was always so strong, so calm, no matter what."

"What did he say to you about that time?"

"I told him I remembered it really well. I had nightmares about it for a year after. I literally thought I was going to die because I couldn't catch my breath. I had no idea why he was bringing that up now. So when I asked him he said, 'Remember when the going got tough, who was there for you. Remember your old man was right there holding your hand. Always think of me trying to do the right thing, honey. Always. No matter what.'"

"Why do you think he said that?"

"He was dying. I didn't read any more into it other than that. I didn't know he was going to shoot someone two days later and then kill himself. I just thought he wanted me to remember him in a good way. He didn't have to tell me that. I would have done that regardless. I loved my dad."

"But now that you know what he did, does it change how you interpret his words on that call?"

Natalie looked at him curiously through bloodshot eyes. "I...I hadn't really thought about it that way, I guess. Do you think it changes things?"

"I think it might change everything," replied Decker.

CHAPTER

60

Decker sat on the bleachers.

Melvin Mars was right next to him.

They were at a local D.C. high school football field watching the varsity team practice.

"Growing the kids bigger every year," said Mars. "They look like a college team."

Decker nodded.

The sky was overcast and a very fine drizzle had started.

"They're running a pro set," said Decker. "Everybody wants to get to the NFL these days."

"I think a lot of these kids would be okay with just getting a shot at a college education," said Mars.

"You might be right about that."

"So you called me up to watch a high school football team practice?"

"I talked to Harper Brown," said Decker.

"Oh, right. Yeah."

"I went over to your hotel to check on you really early the other morning when you didn't answer your phone."

"And you saw her leaving?"

"Yeah."

"She told me. She also told me about Alex shooting that guy. Damn. How's she doing?"

"She'll be okay." He paused. "So, you and Harper Brown?"

"What do you want me to say? It just happened."

"You don't owe me an explanation, Melvin. You're an adult. You can do what you want."

"It's been a long time for me, Decker."

"You going to see her again?"

"Yeah. I plan to."

"Good for you."

"You mean that?"

"Why go through life alone?"

"Hey, hold on. I'm not popping the question or anything. We're just hanging out. Having some fun."

"Nothing wrong with that."

"What about you?"

"What about me what?"

"You just said it. Why go through life alone?"

"I'm not alone. I've got you, Alex, Bogart, Milligan."

"You know what I mean."

"Hey, didn't you know? Alex and I are like an old married couple. We argue a lot. About you."

When Mars look at him quizzically, Decker said, "Long story. Short answer is, we're both happy for you."

"Thanks."

Both men watched the players for a few minutes.

Mars said, "Their wideout is one fast dude with moves and good hands. You see the post-route stutter he just did before taking it downtown?"

"Reminded me of you. But then you could always just run over someone too, if the moves didn't work."

"Yeah, well, that's ancient history."

"You been thinking about what you want to do?"

"Sure. No answers yet. Just taking it one day at a time. How's your case coming?"

"It's taken a couple of twists, actually."

"Things starting to gel for you yet?"

"Just when they start to, something else comes along and screws it up."

Mars patted Decker on the shoulder. "My money's still on you, bro."

Decker said, "You want to go see someone who likes football?"

"Sure, who?"

"You'll see."

* * *

An hour later they pulled into the parking lot of Dominion Hospice.

"Hospice?" said Mars as they climbed out of the car.

"Come on, Melvin."

Minutes later they were sitting in Joey Scott's room.

Mars stared down at the boy in obvious distress, but Decker said to Joey, "This is my friend Melvin Mars. He was an All-American running back at Texas and was a Heisman Trophy finalist a while back. He never got to play in the NFL, but he would've been a Hall of Famer." He pointed to the picture on Joey's nightstand. "Like your buddy Peyton there."

"Wow," said Joey. He held up his hand for Mars to shake. "Nice to meet you, Mr. Mars."

Mars's hand swallowed the boy's as he gently shook it. "Just call me Melvin," he said, glancing at Decker.

Decker said, "Joey played football too. Would've been a heckuva player."

"Yep, I can see that," said Mars. "I bet you were fast, Joey. You got that build."

Joey nodded. "I was really fast." He coughed and tried to sit up. Mars bent down to help him.

"And I could throw too. I played quarterback in Pop Warner."

"Probably the most important position on the field," said Mars. He pulled up a chair and sat down next to the bed. "I remember one game where we were behind the whole way. We were all discouraged. Pretty sure we were going to lose. Well, our QB comes into the huddle after a timeout and says, 'Okay, guys, we're going to win this game because we're eleven men with one goal. And nobody can stop that. I've got this and I've got your back, so let's do this thing.' And you know what?"

"What?" asked Joey breathlessly.

"We won that game and every one after that, including the Cotton Bowl." He held up one finger. "'Cause one guy believed in us. That was all it took."

Joey smiled as Mars held out his fist for Joey to knuckle smack.

Joey looked over at Decker. "Thanks for bringing Melvin to see me. He's cool."

"Yeah, I think so too," said Decker.

* * *

After they left Joey and were walking back to the car, Mars asked quietly, "So he's got no shot?"

"Apparently not," said Decker.

"Shit, he ain't even had a chance at a life."

"I know," said Decker. "Life sucks. A lot."

Mars looked over at Decker. "I guess we both know that."

"You made his day, Melvin."

"He did the same for me."

"How so?"

"Just makes you think about the future. What I'm going to do. Joey doesn't have that chance. So it makes me not want to screw up with mine. I mean, you only get one shot, right?"

Decker slowly nodded.

They climbed into the car and Mars drove off. "Back to your apartment?" he asked.

"Yeah, Alex is there. You got dinner plans?"

"Yeah, actually I do."

"Brown?"

"Harper."

Decker cracked a smile. "Harper."

"Maybe we could do a double date down the road."

"That requires two couples. And Alex and I are not a couple. I'm more like her big brother. Her *really* big brother."

"I know that. It would just be hanging out."

Mars dropped Decker at the apartment and drove away. Decker watched him go for a bit. He saw Jamison's car in the parking lot, so he knew she was there.

But he didn't go in. Instead, he turned to the east and started walking. Twenty minutes later he was standing outside of Cecilia Randall's row house.

The police and FBI were finishing processing the scene. Decker's creds got him inside. He stood in the small front room and looked around.

An FBI tech closed up her evidence kit and looked over at him. "You were here before, with Special Agent Bogart."

"That's right. What can you tell me?"

"One shot to the back of the head. Instant death. She was found in her bedroom."

"On the bed?"

"No, next to it."

"Did she fall off?"

"No, all forensics point to her being on her knees next to the bed."

"Whoever killed her probably made her do that?"

"That's my thinking. She was in a long shirt and pajama bottoms. The bed had been slept in."

"And I understand no forced entry. All locks work? Windows?"

"All secured. This is not the safest neighborhood. And while she didn't have a security system, she had extra locks on the front and back doors. All the windows had security pins."

"If she was asleep then someone either picked the locks or had a key."

"We checked the door locks. Even the best pick guns will leave some marks behind. We found none."

"So a key, then?"

"Looks to be."

"Anything stolen?"

"She had lots of knickknacks. But there was no jewelry to speak of. No prescription drugs in her medicine cabinet. Her purse was found, and her wallet, credit cards, and cash were still in it."

"So no robbery, then. They just came to kill her."

"I understand this might be connected to a case you're working on?"

"It could be *very* connected."

"Well, good luck. Hope you find who did this."

Me too, thought Decker.

CHAPTER

61

"WE CAN'T FIND HIM. It's like he's vanished off the face of the earth."

Bogart looked immensely frustrated as they sat in his office at the WFO. Decker, Jamison, and Milligan sat across from him.

The FBI special agent's hair was mussed, his tie was crooked, and he had a couple days' worth of beard stubble. These were distinct cracks in the man's normally spit-polished appearance.

"Alvin Jenkins had maybe, at most, a half-hour head start," said Jamison. "We weren't with Joey all that long before Decker figured it out with the book. How could he have disappeared so fast?"

"He must have booked it right after he left you," said Milligan. "We found his car in the parking lot, which means he had assistance. He didn't hoof it on foot. This looks like a well-executed plan already in place. He probably made a call and help arrived."

Bogart added, "We searched his apartment. It was nearby in Herndon. If you think Berkshire's place was barebones, you should have seen Jenkins's digs. There was nothing in the fridge, one set of clothes in the closet, some underwear and toiletries. The furniture was all rented and came with the place. We still tore the place apart and took his toothbrush and other relevant material to run through our databases to try to get a match. Nothing's come back so far. Like Berkshire, I doubt he's on any database."

"But he got to work at the hospice," pointed out Jamison. "They had to do some background checking there."

"Not as much as you might think," replied Milligan. "The pay's not great and they have a hard time finding employees. I think they let things slide on the checking-out phase. But like Berkshire, it could have all been falsified anyway. I can tell you that nothing has come back on this guy yet."

Jamison looked at Bogart. "So we've got *nothing*, then?"

"What we have is a mess," said Bogart.

Decker answered, "We have far more than nothing, even if it is messy right now. If we can just piece it all together." He eyed Bogart. "Someone had a key to Cecilia Randall's home. No forced entry. She was asleep when the killer struck. She didn't let anyone in at that hour."

"The killer could have gotten a key any number of ways."

"Possibly. And we'll need to check them all out."

"You spoke with Natalie," said Milligan. "And she told you the story about the ambulance ride her father recently brought up before everything happened. What do you think that meant?"

"He was trying to tell her something. He couldn't do so directly without implicating her."

"Implicating her?" said Jamison. "How so?"

"He stole secrets to pay her gambling debts, or which he thought were his son-in-law's gambling debts. I doubt he told her how he was acquiring the money. But he knew it was paid, because she was alive. And she told him everything was good on that. But in the course of getting the money to pay off that debt, Dabney ran into Berkshire, somehow, some way. I think in fact that Berkshire was in this from the beginning. I think she knew about the debts—hell, maybe she and her cohorts encouraged Natalie's addiction and thus got her to run up these massive debts, knowing she'd have to turn to her father for help."

"Wait a minute, if that's the case, then Berkshire must have been targeting Dabney for a while. Yet we can show no connection between them."

"Doesn't matter. For argument's sake, let's assume there *was* a connection. Dabney goes to Berkshire with the secrets. He sets his price. She agrees to it, knowing that it won't cost ten million to resolve the debt. The secrets are passed, the money goes out, some of it goes to pay off the debt. Hell, for all we know, whoever Berkshire was working for might have bought out the debt from the original source, so the payee and the payer might well be the same. So money-wise it's a wash for them."

Jamison said, "So if the transaction was successfully completed between them, why would Dabney murder Berkshire?"

"Because while she had the upper hand on him vis-à-vis the truth about the gambling debts, he knew something that she didn't." He paused. "He knew he was dying."

Bogart said, "So he killed her because he knew he would never be tried for the crime? He intended to kill himself instead of letting the cancer kill him?"

"Yes and no."

"Jesus, Decker, this is getting more complicated than an algorithm," exclaimed Milligan.

"I think it's actually quite linear. Yes that he wanted

vengeance because she was a spy that he had sold secrets to and he couldn't live with that. He couldn't get the secrets back, but he could stop her from ever spying on this country again."

Bogart interjected, "Okay, that's the 'yes' part. What's the 'no' part?"

"The 'no' part is how he did it. He lured her somehow to the FBI building and shot her on the spot."

"Why did he do that?"

"He wanted to send a message to someone. A clear message that enough was enough. He wasn't going to do this anymore and they had better back off."

Bogart sat up straight. "Wait, you're saying they were going to make him spy for them again?"

"Of course. Once they had him do it the first time, they had him for good. If he didn't cooperate they would release incriminating information and evidence that would bury him. Berkshire would be long gone by then, so she wouldn't suffer. But Dabney would. And his family."

Bogart nodded. "So he decided to take the bull by the horns and cut off this possibility. Berkshire dead and him dead. And this was made possible because they didn't know he was already dying?"

"Yes. I'd love to know the answer to two questions right now."

"What's that?" asked Bogart.

"What was Dabney trying to communicate to his daughter with the ambulance story, and why didn't he just tell her straight out?"

"And the second question?"

"Who was the damn clown?"

CHAPTER

62

"YOU LOOK MISERABLE," said Jamison.

She was driving and looking over at Decker, who was scrunched in the passenger seat.

"I'm not miserable, just in pain. I'm going to help you buy a new car, Alex. I can't take too much more of this. I think I'm getting blood clots in my legs."

"Remember when you used to take the seat out and just sit in the back?"

"Not really practical since it takes four tools and an hour to do that."

"What kind of car?" she said animatedly.

"I don't care so long as it's at least twice the size of this one, with decent legroom."

The rain was pestering them again, snarling traffic and making gloomy thoughts seem even gloomier. Decker closed his eyes.

"So you said Melvin got to meet Joey Scott?"

Decker opened his eyes and nodded. "When I told him that Melvin nearly won the Heisman and would have been in the Hall of Fame, I thought Joey was going to burst with excitement."

"I'm sure. That makes it even more awful that Berkshire

would have used Joey like that. I mean, it would be heartless with any terminally ill patient, but Joey was the only kid in the whole place. And she sat and read to him just so she could use that book to communicate stolen classified information."

Decker's response to this was extraordinary: "Alex, turn the car around. We're heading to Virginia."

"Virginia? Where?"

"The hospice."

* * *

Sally Palmer was still in her office. She explained that with the disappearance of Alvin Jenkins, she was having to work longer hours until he could be replaced.

"I can't imagine why he ran off like that. And the police won't tell me anything," she said crossly as she sat across from them in her office. "I suppose you can't either," she added.

"You would suppose right," said Decker. "Alvin Jenkins, when did he start working here?"

"Alvin, um, only about two months ago."

"And when did Anne Berkshire start volunteering here?"

Palmer thought about this. "Around the same time, actually."

"And when did Joey Scott come here as a patient?"

For this Palmer had to consult her computer. "That's funny."

"What?" asked Decker sharply.

"Well, Joey came here nine weeks ago. That means all three of them around the same time. What a coincidence."

"I don't think it was a coincidence," said Decker.

Palmer looked at him strangely, but Decker ignored this

and plunged on. "When we first met, you said that Joey was going to be adopted but the couple pulled out when he got sick."

"That's right. Disgusting."

"How did you come by that information?"

"Come by it?"

"Who told you?"

"Oh. It was the caseworker that came with Joey when he was admitted here. She told me. She was as upset by it as I was."

"So the story is that Joey was going to be adopted but then the adoptive parents found out he was terminal and decided against adopting him."

"That's right."

"Do you have Joey's medical file?"

"Yes."

"I know you can't share the details with us, per se. But can you tell us when he was diagnosed with leukemia?"

Palmer looked uncomfortable with this, but consulted her computer. Once more her face displayed amazement. "I don't understand. This doesn't make any sense. I'm surprised I didn't put two and two together before."

"About what?" said Jamison.

Decker answered, "Anyone with cancer is going to go through treatment, especially a child who could conceivably have his whole life ahead of him. With Joey's form of leukemia he probably had been diagnosed years ago, had the whole spectrum of treatments until it was determined that nothing else could be done. Then he came here. So the couple that wanted to 'adopt' Joey would have known all of this long ago. They would have had no reason to 'unadopt' him."

Palmer said emphatically, "That's right. That's exactly right."

Decker looked around. "This is a nice hospice. A private hospice. How can an orphan like Joey afford this place?"

"Oh, well, the couple I was talking about, they had *some* goodness in them. They've been paying the bills here for Joey."

"So they're paying the hospice bills of a kid they 'un-adopted' and never come to visit," said Jamison. "How does that make sense?"

Decker said, "It doesn't at one level. But it does at an-other. How did Joey end up coming to *this* place?" he asked Palmer.

"It was the couple. They paid the bills and so they got to pick the place."

"So Berkshire and Jenkins both started coming here *af-ter* Joey was here."

"Yes, that's right. Shortly thereafter, but Joey was here first."

"And Berkshire asked to read to Joey?"

"Yes."

"How did she know he was even here?"

This puzzled Palmer. "I'm not sure. I do remember her coming in and asking if we had any children. She said she wanted to bolster their spirits."

"I'm sure. And the only young child you had at the time was Joey?"

"Why, yes. It's unusual for a little boy or girl to be in a hospice. But it does happen, unfortunately."

"Right," said Decker.

"As I said, I thought their paying his bills made up a little for them abandoning Joey."

"Yeah, well, you can stop thinking that."

"What?" said a startled Palmer.

"Do you have their name and address?'

"That's confidential."

"And I'm afraid I'm going to have to insist."

"Why?"

"Because they've been using your hospice to pass stolen classified information to enemies of this country. If that doesn't work for you, we can always get a warrant and surround this place with a SWAT team. Your call."

CHAPTER

63

UPPER MASSACHUSETTS AVENUE on the way to Maryland. It was the land of foreign embassies and enormous and vintage private residences. Old money and new dollars uneasily commingled here. Unless one had a net worth in excess of nine figures, one did not get to live in this area.

And it was a neighborhood unaccustomed to having a police presence unless it involved a visiting foreign dignitary and a motorcade with flags on the fenders.

"Okay, Decker, I hope to hell you're right about this," said Bogart nervously.

He, Milligan, and Jamison were seated in a parked car across the street from a 1930s Tudor-style mansion fronted by iron gates and a high stone wall.

Decker said, "I hope I am too."

"Let's do this."

They got out and approached the house. Bogart spoke into a walkie-talkie. "Everybody in place. All points covered?"

The response came and he nodded.

"Okay," he said.

They reached the gates and Bogart punched the button on the call box. There was a screechy sound but no voice came on. He hit it again, with the same result.

"FBI, please open the gates."

Again there was no response.

"This is the FBI. Please open the gates or we will be forced to open them by force."

Nothing.

"Nobody home?" wondered Bogart. He looked around and pulled out the walkie-talkie again. "Breacher up."

A minute later a truck roared up and two men in SWAT gear climbed out. They unloaded a hydraulic-powered ram set up on a wheeled platform.

"Hit it," said Bogart.

They powered up the ram, set it against the gate, locked the wheels down, and one of the men hit a button on a remote he held. The piston-powered punch shot forward and smacked the gates squarely in the middle. They broke open.

"Hit it," said Bogart into his walkie-talkie.

A SWAT team poured out of the truck and dashed up the long drive. On the other sides of the property other FBI agents scaled the wall and charged toward the mansion.

Bogart, Milligan, Decker, and Jamison followed closely behind the SWAT team. They reached the front doors, where the lead agent pounded on the wood and announced the FBI's presence. There was no answer.

"Take it down," ordered Bogart.

The portable ram was brought up and it slammed against the doors, bursting them open. The agents poured through.

It was an enormous house with lots of places to hide. But they didn't have to look very hard.

The library was a beautiful room, book-lined with a marble mantel topping a mammoth blackened fireplace. An ornate writing desk was set in the middle, a high-backed leather chair situated at the kneehole. There was a black leather sofa against one wall and two wing chairs on the other side of a wood and wrought iron metal coffee table that had probably set the owners back five figures.

Not that they cared anymore.

The man was in one of the chairs. The woman was sprawled across the couch. They each bore the blackened tag of a bullet entry smack in the middle of their foreheads.

"Alfred and Julia Gorski," said Bogart.

"They're taking care of loose ends," opined Milligan.

Bogart said, "We need to search this place from top to bottom."

"I'll call in the tag-and-bag team," said Milligan. He pulled out his phone and moved over to a far corner of the room.

Bogart looked at Decker. "So they used this dying kid as a means to pass classified material?"

Decker nodded. "They knew Joey was dying. That's why they picked him to 'adopt.' They never had any intention of doing that. They brought him to Dominion Hospice. And that's why Berkshire started going there. It was a perfect cover to pass the secrets. I mean, who would have suspected? We discovered that Jenkins got the job as the night manager when the woman who'd originally held the position didn't show up for work. I wonder when they'll find her body?"

"Damn. This thing just keeps expanding," exclaimed Bogart, rubbing the back of his neck.

"So does the universe," replied Decker.

A voice said, "But the good news is we're dismantling their spy operation by default. They've now lost four operatives and counting."

They turned to see Harper Brown standing in the doorway.

She came forward and looked down at the couple.

"You know them?" said Bogart.

"I know *of* them. The Gorskis host charity balls, cut ribbons on hospital wings, throw great parties, one of which the head of my agency has attended."

"What's their background?" asked Bogart.

"They were immigrants. From Poland. Built a huge import-export company."

"I guess we know what they were importing and exporting now," said Jamison.

"I'm surprised if they're so prominent that they didn't get negative publicity for what they did with Joey," said Bogart. "I mean not adopting him."

Brown said, "That's why you have PR people. And they were paying for his stay at hospice. No one's going to ding them after that, if anyone really even knew about it. They've funded construction of a new at-risk youth facility in Southeast. No one's going to hold one kid against them, as awful as that sounds."

"I wonder how the PR folks will spin their being spies," snapped Jamison.

Bogart said to Brown, "How did you end up here?"

Brown looked at Jamison. "Alex called me and told me. I appreciate the heads-up."

"You're welcome," said Jamison as Decker gave her a curious glance.

"Do you have any idea who the Gorskis could have been working for?" said Bogart.

"Obvious suspects are the Russians, of course. But you can't rule out the Chinese, the North Koreans, or some of the players in the Middle East."

Jamison said, "Would Middle Eastern terrorists use people like the Gorskis? You wouldn't think they would trust them."

"Lots of people who look like you and me have been radicalized," replied Brown. "The same for North Korea and the Chinese. And sometimes it comes down to money."

"Well, if the Gorskis have been this rich for decades and have been spying this whole time, we might be able to rule out the Middle East," said Decker. "That didn't come into play really until after 9/11."

"You'd be surprised," said Brown.

"Were the Gorskis in a position to actually steal the secrets?" asked Bogart. "Or were they bankrolling those who did?"

"The latter. Neither of the Gorskis could have come into contact with places where the secrets are actually located. But they also moved in high circles and they came into contact with people who do have those secrets. Some at the highest levels. I'm talking politicians, military, bureaucrats, executive leadership of defense contractors. They've all probably been in this house at some point."

"That's a lot of very high-level possibilities," said Bogart.

"Just calling it like I see it, Agent Bogart."

"So we think the secrets that Walter Dabney stole moved through this network?"

"I wouldn't be surprised to find that the Gorskis paid off Natalie's gambling debts in exchange for the classified information. It might have gone from Dabney directly to Berkshire. She then passed it along to Jenkins and he on up the chain." She looked at Bogart. "My people have broken the code in the Harry Potter book."

"And?"

"There were at least nine months of classified info on there in various colors that fluoresce. As we suspected that included a back door into three highly sensitive DIA databases. That was what we believed Dabney stole. Our undercover ops overseas have been severely compromised. We've already lost five assets on the ground because of it."

"But Dabney wasn't stealing secrets nine months ago,"

pointed out Bogart. "His came later when Natalie got into trouble with the gambling."

"He's obviously not the only spy they were working with," said Brown.

"But surely he wouldn't have had that information simply because he was a contractor to DIA," said Jamison. "That sounds more like something you guys would keep internally."

"It absolutely was. But Dabney used his relationship with key people there to ferret out the entry passcodes for that data. We figured all this out after the fact, of course, but by then the damage was already done."

"What assets?" asked Decker. "That might narrow down who's behind this."

"Syria and Libya."

"Does that help us take some players out of the equation?" said Decker.

"Thirty years ago, it might have, but Russia is so heavily invested in the Middle East's geopolitical equation that they *could* be behind it. Putin is ruthless and he has firmly in mind a plan to make Mother Russia a global player once more. And to do that he needs influence everywhere, particularly in the desert. And we can't rule out China either, because they have similar goals. All you need is to see what they're doing in the South China Sea to understand that. And both countries are beefing up their military capabilities. And then you have Un in North Korea as a wild card who's determined to build a nuke that can reach the West Coast."

"Sounds like Doomsday is coming sooner rather than later," said Jamison in a resigned voice.

"Unless we can knock out spy operations like this, I wouldn't make any retirement plans," said Brown. "They might prove unnecessary," she added ominously.

64

D ECKER WAS SITTING on the couch with his eyes closed and his head tilted down.

Jamison had just walked out of the bathroom dressed in a long shirt with gym shorts. She was brushing her teeth with one hand and carrying a small plastic bag of trash with the other. She padded barefoot down the hall, glanced at Decker, shrugged, and dropped the plastic bag into a large trash receptacle located on one side of the kitchen island.

That's when the knock came at the door.

Jamison looked around and observed that Decker did not appear to have heard the knock.

She tried to speak and watery toothpaste dribbled out of her mouth. She caught it in one hand and hurried over to the sink. She rinsed out her mouth.

The knock came again.

"Decker, can you get the door?"

He didn't budge and his eyes didn't open.

"I'll take that as a no!" exclaimed Jamison. She used a paper towel to wipe off her mouth and hurried over to the door. She looked through the peephole and her eyes widened.

"Yes?" she said through the door.

Four men stood outside, all dressed in suits. One of them held up his open cred pack to the peephole.

"Holy shit," Jamison muttered.

She opened the door and stepped back.

The four men didn't move. The one in the lead looked her up and down, and then glanced over at Decker, who still sat on the couch.

"Amos Decker?" he said.

"Yes," said Jamison. "I mean, that's us. I...I mean..." Flustered, she drew a quick breath, composed herself, and said, "I'm Alex Jamison. And *he's* Amos Decker."

"I'm Special Agent Nathan Deel, with the United States Secret Service. Mr. Decker, you need to come with us."

"When?" asked Jamison.

"Now."

"Why?" she asked.

"Now."

Decker opened his eyes and looked over at them. "You better go change, Alex."

"The invitation did *not* include your friend," said Deel sharply.

"Then I'm not going," said Decker. He closed his eyes and settled back on the couch.

Deel glanced at one of his men and then at Jamison. "Our orders are for him only."

"Decker," said Jamison. "It's the Secret Service, for Christ's sake."

"Unless they have a warrant for my arrest, I don't go unless you go. And if you guys want to try to carry me out of here, be advised that I'm a big load."

Deel frowned, took out his phone, and stepped down the hall.

A minute went by before he rejoined them. Deel let out

a long breath, glanced at Jamison, and nodded curtly. "Okay, you're in."

She stared at him openmouthed for a long moment and then said, "Can you give me like ten minutes to change?"

"Make it *like* five. We have *people* waiting."

She raced off down the hall into her bedroom and slammed the door behind her.

Deel stepped into the apartment, looked over at Decker, and took in his rumpled clothes and general dishevelment. "Do you need to change clothes and clean up too?"

Decker stood, towering over the man. "There wouldn't be much point."

"Why?" snapped Deel.

"Because all of my clothes look just like these."

Surprisingly, Deel cracked a smile. "I was told you walked to the beat of a different drummer. It's actually refreshing."

* * *

"Oh my freaking God," exclaimed Jamison.

She had changed into slacks, a short-waisted jacket, and a white blouse with black boots. She'd done her hair up in the back and secured it there with a barrette. She and Decker were in the very back row of a big-ass GMC Yukon with tinted windows.

She was staring up at the White House.

"God doesn't live there," said Decker. "The president does."

"I can't believe this is happening."

"I've been there before, actually."

She gaped. "The White House? How? When?"

"The year the Buckeyes won the national championship.

We had a booster who was rolling in money and had connections to the administration back then. He got us in. Met the President. Got the photo op. Pretty cool. I was only twenty."

"You never told me that."

"I guess not."

"Where's the photo?"

"It got lost over the years."

"You took a picture with the *President* and you lost it?"

"Well, yeah," he said indifferently.

She shook her head. "Why am I not surprised?"

They pulled through a side gate and the Yukon stopped at a doorway. The agents escorted them into the White House and down a hallway to a small room. Inside the room were Bogart and Brown.

"Moving in exalted circles tonight," said Bogart with a smile tacked on.

"How exalted?" Jamison wanted to know.

"National Security Council," replied Brown. "Not the full Council, but enough."

Bogart said, "I didn't expect to see you tonight, Alex. It wasn't my call to leave you out of things, but I got overruled."

"Decker told them he wouldn't come unless I came too."

Bogart grinned. "Can't say I'm surprised. You guys are a team, after all."

A broad smile broke over Jamison's face.

Nathan Deel returned and said briskly, "Let's go."

They were led through several long passageways until they arrived at a set of doors. Deel opened the doors and ushered them inside, before closing the doors behind them.

The conference table was long and rectangular. There were TV screens on the wall, all dark and silent.

Six people were seated around the table.

Jamison recognized the Secretaries of State, Defense,

and Homeland Security. Then her gaze alighted on a woman she did not know but would later learn was the National Security Advisor or NSA. There was a broad-shouldered gent in a naval full dress uniform—the Chairman of the Joint Chiefs. And finally, at the head of the table, was the President of the United States.

Jamison took a deep breath and tried to calm her nerves.

In her ear Bogart whispered, "His being here tells you how serious this is."

The President asked them to sit. They all immediately did so.

The President looked at Bogart. "Agent Bogart, I'm due to give out an award shortly to the FBI for a successful joint mission that saved a great many lives."

"Yes sir, I'm aware of that."

"Well, if your team can help us with this, I think another award will be in order." The President turned to the woman. "Gail, you want to start this off?"

"Thank you, Mr. President," said Gail Charles, the NSA.

She nodded at the visitors and said, "The Council has been briefed on the matter at hand and we want to ask some follow-up questions as well as impart some additional information that might be relevant to your investigation."

Bogart lifted his hand. "Ms. Charles, just so we're crystal clear, while Agent Brown and I are cleared for any such discussion, Agents Decker and Jamison may not be."

Charles said, "We are aware of the pending security clearances, and we feel comfortable proceeding under the current scenario."

"Understood. Thank you."

Charles continued in a businesslike tone, "The latest development regarding the Gorskis? Has any information come to light after the search of their home?"

Bogart said, "We are still searching, but we have found nothing that would tie them into a spy ring. I think it doubtful that we will, in fact."

"But you're still confident that they are involved somehow in espionage?"

"We are very confident. They provided financial assistance to a young boy at a hospice in Reston. A book being read to this young boy by Anne Berkshire, who we are certain is a spy, contained coded classified information stolen from various agencies. In addition, on my way here tonight, I was informed that we traced a financial wire going from a Gorski corporate account to an account in Switzerland. From there the money went to Estonia and then disappeared en route to what we believe is an account in France. This, we think, was the payoff for the gambling debt that caused Walter Dabney to steal classified secrets."

The President cleared his throat and said, "So you think it's the Russians behind this?"

Bogart said, "Sir, let's just say that while we're considering all possible players, our investigations are pointing toward Russia being involved."

"Well, considering the hacking they've been doing to us, I guess we shouldn't be surprised. They're showing their muscle in the skies, on the seas, and in the cyber world."

Brown said, "As Admiral Howard here has been told, sir, the information most recently stolen from us has compromised our undercover operations overseas. As of two hours ago, we have now lost ten operatives. And while it may very well be Russia behind this, we can't rule out the possibility that Russia is partnering with certain regional powers in the Middle East to carry this out. The majority of our lost operatives were in Syria, Libya, and Yemen. While Russia has strategic interests in that sector, so do several countries in the Middle East, Iran and Saudi Arabia included among them."

Charles said, "We are well aware that Moscow is aligning itself with certain regional powers, and I'm not simply talking about obvious ones like Assad. The loss of those operatives is unfortunate and can't be allowed to stand without a response."

Admiral Howard interjected, "Knowing definitively who is involved in this would allow us to craft a *precise* response. No more and no less than is called for."

The President eyed Howard before focusing on Decker. "Agent Decker. I spent part of this afternoon being debriefed on you."

"I hope it wasn't wasted time," said Decker.

Bogart gave a sharp intake of breath, but the President smiled. "On the contrary, it was very informative and interesting. We're fortunate to have someone with your *abilities* working on our side."

"I just try to get to the truth."

"Well, you picked a challenging city in which to do that."

"Yes sir."

"Do you have theories on how we might get to that truth?"

Decker looked down for a few moments.

Bogart glanced at him, seemingly afraid that Decker was not going to respond. Just as he was about to speak, Decker stirred.

"Most or all the facts we need to solve this, I think we have. We just have to put them in the right order. The key questions for me are, why did Walter Dabney kill Anne Berkshire, and why in front of the FBI building? Next, who assisted him that day dressed as a clown? How did Walter Dabney, who Agent Brown does not believe ever stole classified information before now, come to hook up with a longtime spy like Anne Berkshire in the first place? There had to be a catalyst. Last, what was in Dabney's safe deposit box that he was forced to remove shortly before his death?"

"All good questions and to which I hope you speedily find the correct answers," said the President. He looked at his NSA. "And now we need to provide you some information which may prove germane to your investigation, and perhaps lend it even more urgency. It's why we called you here tonight, in fact."

All eyes were fixed on Charles. She took out an electronic notebook and scrolled through some digital pages.

"This just came in, which prompted our meeting tonight. The Joint Chiefs have been briefed, as has the full Council." She paused to read down the lines on the page and continued, "As you probably know, the secrets stolen by Mr. Dabney may have allowed enemies of this country to hack into some of our more secure databases. That was worrisome enough. Now our colleagues over at Fort Meade have picked up chatter suggesting strongly that an attack on this country is imminent. We don't know what shape or form the attack will take, but the quarters we're receiving this from—though they have no idea we're listening in—have been very reliable in the past."

"No idea as to the target?" asked Brown quickly.

"Based on further analysis just completed, we believe that the target may be symbolic somehow. The world has become a very different place in a fairly short time. We have a new Cold War starting up at the same time we have hot spots erupting all over the Middle East. Fascist movements are taking root in some of the governments of allies of ours and much of the world is a tinderbox. So we can't rule out any possibility, quite frankly. And if an attack does come and we identify its source, we will have no choice but to respond accordingly. And that could set in motion a chain of events that could have global repercussions of the most negative kind."

Admiral Howard cleared his throat and said, "The military agrees with that assessment."

"As does the State Department," added the Secretary of State.

The head of Homeland Security nodded in agreement.

Decker voiced the obvious question. "You called us here tonight because you evidently believe your concerns are connected to our case. Why is that?"

Charles glanced at the President, who nodded.

She turned to Decker and said, "Because the chatter we intercepted was all *Arabic*, except for one word."

"What word?"

"It was a name, rather."

"What name?" asked Bogart.

"Dabney."

CHAPTER

65

"I've got to call my mom," said Jamison when they got back to their apartment.

"Why?" asked Decker.

"Do you really have to ask?" she said incredulously. "I just met the *President*."

"That meeting was classified, Alex. You can't talk about it to anyone. You can't even acknowledge it ever happened."

Jamison looked doubtfully at her phone. "Maybe I could tell a little white lie and say we just ran into each other?"

"You just *ran* into the President of the United States? Where? At the gas station? Or a Starbucks?"

She put her phone down. "I guess you're right."

Decker took off his jacket and hung it up on a peg by the door. "Dabney," he said.

"I know. That's really weird. To hear all these words in Arabic and then to hear that name? Freaky."

Decker sat down on the couch and put his feet up on the coffee table.

Jamison perched on the arm of the couch. "I wonder if Melvin and Harper have gone on a second date yet?"

"Yeah, I'm surprised she didn't bring it up in the Situation Room at the White House. The President was probably wondering too."

She cuffed him on the shoulder. "You know what I mean."

"I just don't like to get caught up in other people's lives like that."

"But getting caught up in other people's lives is a really big part of *most* people's lives, Decker."

"Not mine."

She sighed. "The meeting tonight puts things in a whole new perspective. I mean, if an attack on this country is planned, we need to solve this thing really soon."

Decker closed his eyes.

She stared at him in disbelief. "Are you going to zone out on me? If so, I'll just go to my room and go to sleep."

"Okay. Good night."

She pushed his legs out of the way, sat down next to him, and said, "Damn it, Decker, will you please talk to me?"

He looked at her, clearly annoyed. "What do you want me to say, Alex?"

"Our country is going to be attacked. What are we going to do to stop it?"

"I'm thinking about it. I *am* working on it. But I'm not a magician."

"But everyone thinks you are, me included. The things you can do. It's amazing. You never fail."

"I actually fail lots of times. And I'm not a damn machine. So if you're worried about the sky falling, don't look to me to fix it."

He abruptly stood, grabbed his jacket, and headed out.

"Decker, wait, I didn't—"

But he had already slammed the door behind him.

He trotted down the stairs and out into the coolness of

the night. And he started walking, each exhaled breath re-
leasing tiny clouds into the sky.

He was angry and he didn't want to be. He knew that
Jamison was actually complimenting him, voicing her complete confidence in his abilities. But he *was* feeling the
pressure of preventing an attack. Even in his altered state
where he didn't "get" normal social cues, he clearly understood what was at stake.

This was a long way from being a PI in a rust belt town
back in Ohio, hustling for clients in all the wrong places.

*Not that long ago I was living in a cardboard box. And
now I'm supposed to be the savior of the country? How effed
up is that?*

He shoved his hands into his pockets, pointed his head
down, and kept walking.

He reached the river and stood and looked out over the
expanse of water.

It mirrored his thoughts: dark, murky, deep.

He had to get traction on this case. Something to hang
on to. There were so many moving parts, and just when he
thought he had something, it fell apart, or was overtaken by
a new development.

Was that intentional? *Are they trying to keep us reactive?*

He shut his eyes and let the frames roll through. It occurred to Decker that this process was like how the old-time
animators would do their job, drawing slightly different ver-
sions of a character on multiple pieces of paper that you
would then flip through to show motion.

Well, he was hoping for some motion of the forward variety.

He decided to begin at the beginning.

One more time.

And something had just occurred to him.

It had to do with real estate.

He made the phone call, and on the third ring Faye Thompson, Walter Dabney's partner, picked up.

"What is it?" she said when Decker identified himself.

"I was just wondering about something."

"Look, I'm up to my ass in lawyers and federal investigators. I don't have time—"

"If you cooperate it will look better for you," interjected Decker.

He heard her sigh and then she said, "What do you want to know?"

"When you joined the firm it was doing well?"

"Yes. Very well."

"How about when Dabney first started out? Was he in the same office space you're in now?"

"Of course not. It was only him way back when. So he didn't need that much space. And he couldn't have afforded it anyway."

"Because he was building up his business."

"Yes. It takes a lot of work and hard times to build something like Walter did. He started out on a shoestring and slowly built from there. He maxed out his credit cards more than once, I heard. But he was hugely successful in the end."

"So money was tight?"

"Well, if you have plenty of cash why would you max out your credit cards?" she said snidely.

"Right. I understand that he had a yellow Porsche when he still worked at NSA?"

"I know nothing about that. Are we done here?" she added.

"I had one more question about his house—"

But Thompson had already hung up on him.

Next, Decker used his phone not to make a call but to

order an Uber. Jamison had set an account up on his phone a few weeks ago. Five minutes later he was heading to Virginia.

It seemed chillier on this side of the Potomac as the car pulled up the stately drive. The car stopped in front of the house and Decker got out.

His knock was answered by Samantha. She looked like she had been crying.

"What do you want?" she said in an unfriendly tone.

"Is your mother here?"

"She's in bed. Can't you leave us alone?"

"I wish I could," said Decker. "But I can't. Can I come in?"

"Why?"

"Please?"

She stepped to the side and allowed him to pass. She closed the door and stared up at him. "Well?"

"So you all have lived here since you were little?"

"Yes."

"In this house?"

"Yes!"

Jules came out of another room and saw Decker. "What are you doing here?" she demanded.

"Just asking a few questions."

"What does our living in this house when we were little have to do with a damn thing?" said Samantha.

"I'm not sure at this point. So your parents have lived here for what, thirty-five years?"

Jules said, "About that, I guess. I'm thirty-seven and it's the only place I remember."

"I saw some family photo albums in the library. Do you mind if I look through them?"

"Why?" said Jules.

"Because this case has taken on a heightened sense of

urgency. We have reason to believe that unless we solve it, something bad is going to happen in this country."

Jules and Samantha exchanged glances. Jules said, "You're bullshitting us."

Decker stared back at her. "I really wish I were."

She looked taken aback by his words. "Look, if you want to pore through old photo albums, knock yourself out."

Leaving Samantha in the hall, Jules led him to the library, pulled the albums off the shelf, and set them down on the coffee table. When she started to leave, Decker said, "Do you mind sitting here with me to answer questions I might have?"

Jules sighed resignedly but sat next to him as he picked up the first one.

The albums were arranged chronologically, so Decker was able to get where he wanted to go relatively quickly.

"These are your grandparents?" he said, pointing to several old photos.

Jules nodded and pointed. "My dad's mom and dad. They're dead now. They were from Princeton, New Jersey. We used to go and visit them. He was a professor of political science there."

"Impressive. They look like they were pretty well-off."

"No. They lived in a house provided by the university. I know my dad helped them out financially when they got older."

He pointed to another photo. "And these folks."

"My mom's parents. They lived in Oregon."

"Did you visit them out there?"

"No. I never knew them. They had a small farm. They died in a mudslide when my mom was little. It swept the entire property away, the house, barn, everything. Her parents' bodies were never found. She was at school or she would have been killed too. After that she went to an orphanage. Then came east when she was an adult."

"How did your parents meet?"

Jules's features softened. "It was sort of romantic, actually. My dad was working in Maryland, right out of college. My mom worked as a waitress at a café near there. She was putting herself through college. Some of the people at Dad's work would go there for breakfast and lunch. She would wait on him and they struck up a friendship. Mom was a knockout back then and I'm pretty sure she had plenty of suitors. When she got off work one night he was waiting in the parking lot with flowers and tickets to a play at the National Theater. Needless to say, they hit it off. The rest is history."

"Very nice. So your mom didn't come from money?"

"From money? No, not that I know of. Why?"

"Just something somebody said. It's not important."

He closed the album.

"Anything else?" asked Jules.

"Have you heard from Natalie?"

Jules nodded. "She sounded okay. She said she was so sorry for everything."

"And what did you say to that?"

Jules shrugged. "I hate what she did. I mean, it totally destroyed our family. But she's still my sister."

"I get that. Family is family."

He rose.

She said, "Have you found who killed Cissy?"

"Not yet. Still working on it."

"I don't understand any of this, I really don't."

"Well, you wouldn't be alone on that."

Decker left the house, then turned around to look at its exterior.

He should have seen this before, he knew. He had two possible conclusions. Now he just had to see which one was right.

66

"EIGHT HUNDRED and forty-nine thousand dollars," said Milligan. "They closed on the property a little over thirty-five years ago. Tax tables show it's worth probably four times that now, and even more on the open market. Wish I had that kind of asset in my retirement future."

Decker looked over his shoulder. They were in Milligan's office at the WFO.

Decker had returned home the previous night and apologized to Jamison for walking out. She had, in turn, apologized to him for her comments.

"We're all under a lot of pressure," she'd said. "But you probably more than anybody else. I didn't mean to add to your burden."

And they had left it at that.

Decker looked at the computer screen and said, "Thirty-five years ago. Couple years after Jules was born."

"Right."

"And Dabney was still working at the NSA?"

"Right. He'd been there about four years by then, started right out of college. He left to start his own firm six years later."

"Do we know what his salary was at NSA?"

"Ballpark, yes, and to jump to answering your obvious next question, it could not have supported the purchase of that house. So at age twenty-six he bought a mansion. Definitely should have been a red flag for someone."

"Do we know if they paid cash or took on debt?"

"That's the rub. The documents I found showed that they put four hundred thousand down and financed the rest. His wife had a job back then too. She worked at a real estate firm as a Realtor."

"Could her income have covered it?"

"Not all of it, no. Not even combined with his. But where did the four-hundred-thousand-dollar down payment come from? You would think the NSA would have asked the same question."

"Maybe they did, and it was satisfactorily answered," replied Decker.

"Maybe," said Milligan. "And we can try to ask them, but my experience is you don't get fast answers from those guys, if you get answers at all. Bogart's been trying to get them to respond to questions about Dabney, and so far all he's gotten back is silence." He looked at Decker. "What made you think about all this?"

"Big, expensive house purchased by a young couple without a lot of money. Pretty basic."

"I guess we should have seen that too. But it's all perspective, I suppose. Dabney was super-successful over the years and his house just sort of fit the picture of that success. I didn't think about the timing of the purchase all those years ago."

"Cecilia Randall also told me that Dabney bought a yellow Porsche around the same time as they closed on the house. And she said that she thought Mrs. Dabney came from money, the way she dressed and conducted herself. Now,

Jules did tell me that Ellie's parents were killed in a mudslide and she was sent to an orphanage. Maybe she got compensation from that. But if that were the case, why would you be working as a waitress to put yourself through college?"

"You wouldn't," replied Milligan.

"So if we can find out the source of the money maybe we can figure out what happened all these years later."

"You think they're connected?"

"I think they have to be."

"Dabney was at NSA. He certainly would have had access to classified material. And then he starts his own firm. I know we were speculating that he only recently committed espionage to help Natalie. But do you think he might have been spying all these years?"

"Hard to say. He might have worked with Berkshire over three decades ago and then quit spying for some reason. And somehow turned back to her all these years later to sell the secrets and get the payoff to help his daughter. That might solve the question of why we could show no connection between them. We didn't look back three decades."

"I think you might be on the right track, Decker."

"On the other hand, Dabney couldn't have killed Cecilia Randall. He was already dead."

"We don't know for sure that her murder is connected. It might just be a random killing."

Decker shook his head. "I don't think so."

"If he has been a spy all this time, it's not going to be easy for his family to learn this, not after everything else they've been through."

"Nothing about this case has been easy," replied Decker.

He left Milligan and walked down the hall to an office he was sharing with Jamison. He filled her in on his discussion with Milligan.

"That theory does fill in some holes," she said.

"But it doesn't get us any closer to who's behind this. Or where they might be planning to strike. And that's what we really need to find out."

"I spoke with Bogart a few minutes ago. They found nothing helpful at the Gorskis' home."

Decker sat down across from her and stared at the ceiling.

"But you're not satisfied with your own theory?"

"Why do you say that?" he asked.

"Because I *know* you. I can tell."

He turned his head to look at her. "Okay, you're right. I'm *not* satisfied."

"What would make you satisfied?"

"Something that makes total sense, not piecemeal."

"You might not get that."

"I'm coming around to that possibility." He put his size fourteens up on the desk and leaned back in his chair.

"Heard from Harper Brown?" asked Jamison.

"Not a word."

"She and Melvin saw each other again."

"How do you know that?"

"I talked to Melvin just now. They went to lunch, well, a picnic really at Roosevelt Island. He said they had a great time."

"I'm glad she can find time for pleasure while working a case involving the fate of the country."

"Everybody needs to take a break now and then," said Jamison.

"So now *you're* defending her," said Decker with a snort.

"Hey, I'm a progressive. We're always moving forward, not backward."

Decker stood. "Well, I'm looking to make some progress too, so I better get to it."

"Where are you going?"

"Not sure, but I'll let you know how it turns out."

"Hey, Decker?"

He turned back. "What?"

"Why did you stick up for me with the Secret Service and insist I go to the meeting at the White House too?"

"I'm surprised you have to ask."

"What do you mean?"

"That's what I meant when I said I had your back, Alex."

He turned and walked out.

67

"Ever think you're looking at a case ass-backwards?"

Harper Brown stared across the width of the café table at Decker. "In this case, how so?"

He had called her on the way out of the WFO and they had arranged to meet here.

"Dabney kills Berkshire and then himself. The case starts from there and we proceed linearly."

"Right, but there are back stories we have to check out too. And we have been. This didn't start with him killing her."

"Granted, that was the *result*. But as we've been checking out the histories, it seems that we've been focusing mainly on Dabney."

"Well, we can't find out jack shit on Berkshire, except that she was definitely a spy. We have nothing else to go on."

In response, Decker pulled the doll out of the backpack he'd brought and set it on the table between them.

"We have this."

She stared at it momentarily before looking up at him in disbelief. "This? A doll? We already know it was probably used to transfer stolen secrets in the hidden compartment. But so what?"

"Why a doll?"

"Why not?"

"Let's play this out logically. You steal secrets, put them in the doll, and carry it to another person, presumably Berkshire."

"Right."

"So, again, why a doll?"

"Why not? It's innocuous, most people wouldn't give it a second look."

"Well, they might if a *guy* was carrying it around. It's too large to put in your pocket. And a bag might be searched."

"So you're saying the other person was probably a woman?"

"Either a woman, or maybe a man with a little girl."

"Wait, do you mean Walter Dabney?"

"It's possible. The doll might have belonged to one of his daughters. The Bureau determined that this doll was manufactured about thirty years ago. So the Dabney girls are the right age for that. And like you said, it's innocuous. Who would suspect a little girl with a doll of transporting secrets? And these people seem to like using kids as cover. Look at Joey Scott and the book."

Brown looked thoughtful. "That's true. So do we ask the daughters directly about the doll?"

"Yes, we do."

* * *

"Where did you get that?" asked a stunned Jules.

Decker and Brown were seated in the living room with Jules, her mother, and her two sisters.

Ellie exclaimed, "Jules, isn't that your doll, Missy?"

Jules took it from Decker and held it.

"You're sure it's yours?" said Brown.

In response Jules sniffed the hair and then looked at the doll's left foot.

"See the red dots on the shoe? I spilled paint on it when I was little. It wouldn't come out. And I recognize the smell of her hair. Where did you get it?"

"During the course of the investigation," answered Decker, taking the doll back. "When do you remember having it last?"

Jules sat back. "I...I don't know. I didn't take it to college." Her cheeks reddened. "I actually wanted to but changed my mind. I didn't think to check on it since I got here."

"So the doll stayed here, in the house?" said Brown.

Ellie said, "We've kept the girls' bedrooms exactly as they left them for when they come back. They all had dolls. I thought they were all still there. Cissy keeps—" Her voice broke off. "Cissy *kept* every room neat and organized."

"Can we see them?" asked Decker.

Jules led them up to the bedrooms. After she left them, Decker and Brown found three dolls with the same secret compartments behind the batteries.

"Shit," said Brown. "This was spy central, apparently. Four daughters and four dolls with secret compartments."

"This *confirms* that Walter Dabney must've known Berkshire. They were working together."

"And that explains how they afforded a place like this all those years ago."

Decker looked at her. "So you thought of that too?"

"I have my moments of epiphany," she said modestly.

"Let's check the Dabneys' bedroom."

It was far larger than the daughters' spaces, with an attached sitting room and a fireplace. They searched the bedroom, then the two large closets; Ellie's was a spacious walk-in. Decker next looked in the en suite bathroom and went through the drawers and the medicine cabinet where there were a number of prescription bottles. These included heart meds and cholesterol-lowering drugs, and an asthma inhaler.

Sucks getting old, thought Decker.

He closed the door of the medicine cabinet and rejoined Brown in the bedroom.

"No dolls," she said.

They went back downstairs carrying all the dolls and reentered the room where the Dabney women were still sitting. Jules was holding her old doll.

"What are you doing with those?" asked Samantha, indicating the dolls.

"We need to take them with us," said Brown.

"Why?" asked Samantha.

"They're evidence."

Samantha was about to say something, but she glanced at Jules and sat back.

Decker sat across from Jules. "I want to show you this photo again and see if you recognize the woman." He held up Berkshire's photo.

"I told you I didn't recognize her," said Jules.

Decker passed the photo around to the others. Ellie and the others shook their heads as they looked at the picture of Berkshire.

"Imagine her with darker hair, fewer lines on the face?" prompted Decker.

They studied the photo for a few moments. Jules shook her head. "I really don't know this person." She looked at her sister and mother. They all, too, shook their heads.

Ellie said, "What does all this mean? With the dolls and all? I don't understand."

"We don't either, if it's any consolation," said Brown.

"Are you... saying that Walt was involved in something having to do with these dolls? How does that make any sense? They were the girls' toys, not his. I never remember him walking around with a doll. It's absurd."

"Right now, we're not saying anything," replied Brown. "We're still in the collecting stage."

They left the house with the dolls and walked to Brown's car.

Decker turned around and looked at the house. "You know the game kids play, 'You're getting warmer, warmer'?"

"Yeah."

"Well, every time I leave this place I think I'm getting colder."

As they drove off, Brown said, "Melvin and I are having dinner tonight. You and Alex want to join us?"

"After your wonderful picnic?"

Brown actually blushed at this comment. "It *was* wonderful. He brought me flowers."

He glanced at her. "You sure you want the company?"

"We're working our butts off, the fate of the country in the balance. I think a few hours of distraction might actually be good for all of us."

"Okay," said Decker.

CHAPTER

68

THE DINNER HAD BEEN GOOD and the conversation light and humor-filled. It had been a nice respite from the investigation, allowing them to recharge their batteries. Now the four of them had driven over to Brown's home near Capitol Hill.

Jamison stared goggled-eyed at the luxurious interior. "Harper, this place is beautiful."

Brown handed Jamison a glass of wine and said, "Most of it was my grandmother's doing. She had the eye. But I've put in some of my own things too. A few paintings, that sculpture over there, and some rugs. And a special feature or two," she added offhandedly. "It's comfortable and cozy."

"Yes, it really is."

Decker and Mars were on the other side of the room. In lieu of wine the pair were each cradling a bottle of Dos Equis.

"Fun time tonight," said Mars. He was dressed in jeans and a dark green turtleneck that seemed barely able to contain his chiseled physique.

"Always like hanging with you, Melvin."

He looked over and caught Brown eyeing Mars. She smiled appreciatively and turned back to Jamison.

"And you obviously have a fan in Ms. Brown."

Mars took a swig of beer and grinned like a schoolboy. "She's fun. Lady's been everywhere, done everything. I've been nowhere and done nothing." He looked around. "And she comes from money but doesn't act like it. That's cool in my book. And she's quite an athlete! I mean, she's built like one, but she's got the goods too, 'cause you never know, right? We went for a run early this morning."

"Before your picnic?" said Decker.

Mars's smile broadened. "I know. But we like hanging out together. Anyway, she had no problem keeping up with me. Hell, I think she might have been going easy on me."

"And she's kind to children and loves puppies. Quite the catch."

Mars's smile broadened. "I know, I know. I'm just rambling here, being kind of goofy. And I know we don't really know each other all that well, but we just kind of clicked, you know?"

"I know, Melvin. And I'm really happy for you."

Decker glanced at his watch. It was late, after midnight.

"I'm going to finish this beer and then call it a ni—"

The lights went out, sending them into darkness.

"What the hell?" exclaimed Mars.

"Did a circuit breaker trip or did a transformer blow outside?" said Decker.

He felt someone pass him and a few moments later Brown said, "Other homes on the street have power. It must be—"

She stopped, turned, and ran back over to them. She grabbed Decker and Mars by the arm. "Move it. Now! Jamison, to the right and down the hall."

"What's—" began Mars, but she had tugged on his hand and pulled them out of the room.

A few seconds later the front and back doors burst open and masked men poured in. They had short-barreled MP5s and night-vision goggles, and they opened fire as they swarmed through the house.

As Brown and the others sprinted down the hall, Decker, who was bringing up the rear, turned and emptied half his mag.

Bullets whizzed past him, exploding a lamp, ripping chunks of plaster off the wall, shredding paintings, and causing bursts of fabric and filling to erupt from furniture.

Decker emptied the rest of his ammo and Jamison opened fire too as they fled down the hall.

Brown kicked open a door at the end of the hall and pushed them all through it. She slammed the door shut and turned the lock.

"Over here, quick!"

Bullets thudded into the door but none burst through.

Decker glanced at her.

"Steel-lined," she hissed back.

Brown took out her phone, hit a key, and a section of the wall swiftly opened. Behind it was a metal door. This opened on whisper-quiet hydraulics.

"Get inside, now!" she urged. "Hurry!"

They hustled into the revealed room and Brown hit another key on her phone. The door closed and the section of wall slid back into place.

A light came on in the room and Decker and the others looked around. There was a TV screen on one wall. It obviously had feed from just outside the door, because they could all see the room they had just been in.

As they watched, the door to the room burst open and the armed men moved inside.

Decker said, "We need to call the cops."

"My security system automatically did that when I activated the door to the safe room."

"So that's what this is?" said Jamison, gazing around. "A safe room?"

"Steel-wrapped, soundproof, bombproof, bulletproof, with its own air supply, independent power source, and enough food and water for a week. Plus a portable potty."

"Is this room your doing?" said Jamison.

"It's one of the 'special features' I mentioned."

"You need a safe room?" asked Decker.

"Given what's happened just now, apparently so. And, Decker, you're bleeding." She pointed to his face.

He rubbed at the spot. "Something must have hit me there. It wasn't a bullet. Maybe some debris stripped off by the gunfire."

"I wasn't that lucky."

They turned to see Mars holding his bloody forearm. "Think it's just a graze, but boy does it burn like a bitch."

Brown grabbed a first aid kit from a cubby on the wall and began, with Jamison's assistance, to treat Mars's arm.

As Decker watched on the screen, the men searched the room.

"Cops are on their way," said Decker. He could hear the siren sound from the audio feed tied to the TV.

Frustrated at not finding them, the masked men sprayed the walls with gunfire. Yet none of it could penetrate the shelter they were in. Then the men turned and dashed from the room as the sirens drew ever closer.

Four minutes later they all emerged from the safe room in time to meet the cops peering cautiously into the room. Brown pulled her creds and did the explaining.

The cops looked slowly around at the devastation. One of them said, "Somebody really doesn't like you, lady."

"Well, that's why you have homeowner's insurance," quipped Brown.

After the police finished their search and took down particulars, they left, leaving the four to stare anxiously at each other.

"That was close," said Mars. "How did you even know they were coming, Harper?"

"When I looked outside I saw the red dots on their night-vision goggles lined up with the middle of their foreheads. That's because they were wearing an older-generation device. Our agencies have phased them out for obvious reasons. Way too big of a target."

"Well, thank God for safe rooms," voiced Jamison.

"I wonder what the hell they wanted?" said Mars. "Other than to kill us."

"They must have been following us," said Brown. "And cut the power before making their attack."

"I wonder," said Decker thoughtfully.

"You wonder about what?" asked Brown.

But Decker never answered her.

CHAPTER

69

It was raining once more.

It was actually bucketing down outside, accompanied by bold streaks of lightning followed by guttural punches of thunder.

Oblivious to the inclemency, Decker sat in a chair staring at his laptop in the kitchen of their apartment.

There were two FBI agents in a car outside the building as there were at Harper Brown's home. Mars had stayed over at her place.

Bogart and Milligan had come to the scene of the attack. Forensics had found nothing but a mountain of shell casings tossed out by the MP5s and an open power box the attackers had broken into to cut off the lights to Brown's home. Neighbors had heard the gunfire, and two had seen the men jump into a waiting SUV, but the license plate had been blacked out. With nothing more to do, Decker and Jamison had come back here, leaving Mars and Brown to pick through the pieces of the attack.

Decker had been sitting here for over an hour now. Jamison had long since gone to bed. He touched the spot on his face where a piece of debris had impacted. Brown had cleaned up the cut for him and bandaged it.

He refocused on the computer screen. He'd been staring at one page now in particular for about twenty minutes.

He closed his eyes and thought things through. When he reopened his eyes he checked his watch.

It was nearly seven in the morning. He'd not been to sleep yet but strangely felt quite energized. He made a phone call and the woman answered. A minute of conversation later, he snagged Jamison's keys off the hook, waved to the FBI agents in their car, hustled across the parking lot—getting drenched in the process—and climbed into her car.

He drove to the Hoover Building and, by prearrangement, met the ME, Lynne Wainwright, in the autopsy room.

She was dressed in scrubs and her eyeglasses hung at the end of a chain across the front of her chest. She yawned and said, "It was a bitch getting in this morning. D.C. drivers and rain do not mix well."

"Right."

"So what's up?"

"Had some questions. Wanted to do it face to face"

"That I figured."

She led him over to a desk in the corner and they both sat down. "Fire away," she said.

"Let me give you some medical symptoms and maybe you can give me a root cause."

"Okay."

"Birth defects in children. Toes missing off a foot and a deformed arm."

"Okay. There could be lots of reasons for that."

"I'm not finished. Add to that asthma in all the kids?"

"That narrows things down a little, but not enough, Decker. Where are you going with this?"

"Let me add to that some medications."

He had written them down from memory and handed over the slip of paper.

Wainwright ran her eye down the list.

She pointed with her finger. "That one's for a liver condition. This one for kidney disease. The Lipitor is for high cholesterol. Because of the TV commercials, most people know that. Zoloft is for depression, and that one is to increase bone density."

Decker nodded. "Anything in Dabney's postmortem results that struck you?"

"Not really. We got the blood work and tox screens back. As I told you before, he was on painkillers but he had no other drugs in his system, in case you were wondering whether he was high on something when he did what he did."

"None of the prescription bottles were under his name. They were all under his wife's."

"He was actually in decent shape, except for the brain tumor, of course. Absent that, he was probably good for at least another twenty years."

"Luck of the draw."

"*Bad* luck," amended Wainwright.

"Yeah," he said absently, staring off.

She said, "What are you thinking?"

"I'm just wondering why such a healthy-looking family has so many physical and medical issues."

"Well, the asthma can be inherited."

"One of the daughters said it was her mother that had it, not the father."

"Right. Dabney's lungs, nasal passages, and esophagus were clear. I didn't detect any irritability of the lining in any of those places that would indicate any sort of asthma or other pulmonary issue."

"So that leaves his wife and all her meds."

"Look, this country is overly medicated, from kids to se-
niors. My mother took twenty-four pills a day for the last
three years of her life, and she had friends who took even
more. And it seems that every other kid today is on Ritalin
or something like that. It's ridiculous but it's also true."

"I get that," said Decker. "But it's still bugging me. And
I don't have an abundance of leads on this."

"So you might be grasping at straws?"

"I might be. But I'd prefer to think that I'm closing in on
finding the needle in the haystack."

DECKER'S KNEES WERE ACHING. Partly from the rain. Partly from old football injuries.

And partly from the fact that they were crammed up against the dashboard of Jamison's clown car, with the steering wheel basically resting in his crotch.

I really have to get my own damn ride.

The windshield wipers slung the rain off and more immediately replaced it. With each rotation of the wipers, Decker's mind seemed to swivel as well.

His thoughts had centered on something that might be valuable.

Cecilia Randall had spoken to them.

Shortly thereafter, Cecilia Randall was murdered.

They had spoken to the Dabneys. Shortly thereafter, they had almost been murdered.

Was it cause and effect? If so, how?

He cast his mind back to their discussions with the housekeeper.

She had thought that Ellie Dabney had come from money. Turns out she hadn't. So how did that explain the house purchase and Walter Dabney buying a Porsche while still working at the NSA as a low-level grunt? That could be explained by Dabney spying. Ellie Dabney had myriad health issues, miscarriages among them. Three of the daughters were tall and athletic-looking but were hampered by breathing problems. Natalie was missing toes, Amanda part of an arm. The Dabneys were wonderful people, Randall had told them, none better in her mind.

And then someone had put a bullet in her head.

Then he and Brown had talked to the Dabneys about the doll.

They had found the other dolls with the same hidden compartments.

They had left there, gone to dinner, come back to Brown's, and very nearly been massacred by a team of killers with submachine guns.

Again, cause and effect? And in both instances the cause perhaps had been conversations at the Dabney house.

Is the place bugged?

Maybe by whoever had ambushed Decker at Berkshire's old house in the woods? And was the same force behind the hit team last night?

And then there were the dolls. How exactly did they come into play? As Ellie had said in defense of her husband, Walter Dabney had not walked around with dolls. He presumably hadn't carried any to his office, stuffed them with secrets, and then handed them off to a third party, only to retrieve them so they could be returned to his daughters. That hardly made sense. A man walking around with dolls would have been noticed. You couldn't exactly walk into the NSA carrying a doll.

But maybe he didn't have to. Maybe that exchange was on the *other* end.

Decker suddenly whipped the wheel around and pointed his car in a new direction.

He parked across the street from Cecilia Randall's home. The police had gone, but the door to her place was partially open. He got out of the car, hustled across the street as the rain pelted him, and knocked on the door.

No one answered. He took out his gun, edged the door open, and peered inside.

"FBI. Anybody here?"

Again, there was no answer. But he heard the creak of floorboards and looked up.

Someone was upstairs.

He quietly made his way up the stairs and took a quick look around. There were only two rooms up here. And only one had a light on.

He scuttled over to that door and was about to put his hand on the knob when it turned.

He stepped back, his gun aimed at the door.

The woman screamed when she saw him and dropped the box she was holding. "Oh my God, what do you want!" she yelled. "Please don't hurt me."

Decker dug into his pocket and pulled out his credentials. "I'm with the FBI. I'm not going to hurt you."

The woman staggered sideways and gripped the doorjamb. "Oh, sweet Jesus, you nearly scared me to death."

Decker put his gun away and studied her.

She was black, thin, and around forty, with short graying hair.

"Who are you?" asked Decker.

"I'm Rhonda Kaine."

"What are you doing here?"

"This is my mother's house."

"Cecilia Randall was your mother?"

"Yes."

"I'm sorry for your loss."

She looked down at the box. "I just came by to pick up some things. Don't know what I'm going to do with this place. Sell it, I guess."

"Do you live in the area?"

"Baltimore, so not that far." She gazed up at him with a stern expression. "You people find out who did this?"

"Not yet. But since you're here, do you mind if I ask you some questions?"

"The police have already talked to me."

"My questions might be different."

"Look, as far as I know, Momma had no enemies. Nobody who'd want to hurt her. She worked hard, went to church, she raised me, and she was a good person. I think somebody came here to rob her. I've been begging her to get out of this neighborhood. This is the house where I grew up. The neighborhood was okay back then, but not now. There're dudes around here who'll kill you for a quarter."

"I don't disagree, but I don't think that's what happened to her."

"Why not?"

"You just said your mother worked hard for a living. She worked for the Dabneys, correct?"

"That's right. For well over thirty years."

"So you must have known them too."

"I did. When I was little I would go over there with her."

"So you knew the daughters?"

"I'd play with them. I was a little older. Sometimes, I'd watch Jules or Samantha. When Natalie was a baby I'd change her diaper and feed her."

"Nice of you to do that."

"Oh, they paid me. They insisted on that. Mr. and Mrs. Dabney were very kind, Mrs. Dabney especially. I saw a lot more of her. Mr. Dabney was always working or traveling.

Momma and I would be long gone before he got home from the office."

"Do you know where Mr. Dabney traveled to?"

"Why?"

"We're looking into his death as well."

"I heard he killed himself."

"He did. But we still have to figure out why."

"Oh, well, I'm not really sure where he went. I think a lot of places in this country, different states. One time I was helping Momma put his luggage away after he came back from a trip and the airline baggage sticker was still on it."

"Do you remember the initials of the airport on it?"

"No. But I do remember it wasn't an American airline. I just can't remember which one it was. But I remember Momma telling me that he traveled a lot overseas too."

"How did she know that?"

Kaine smiled. "When she was little, Samantha got ahold of her daddy's passport and hid it in the kitchen. They were looking all over for it. Momma found it in the sugar bin. She had to open it up to clean off the pages and get all the grains of sugar off it. And she said it was full up with stamps and stuff from all the countries he'd been to."

"Did your mother ever tell you anything out of the ordinary about the Dabneys?"

"Out of the ordinary?" Kaine gave him a penetrating look. "Where is all this going?"

"To the truth, I hope."

"The Dabneys are good people."

"I'm sure they are, but Mr. Dabney *did* murder someone."

Kaine's expression changed to one of bewilderment and then sadness. "I still can't believe he did it. He would have been the last person in the world I would have thought was capable of that. And him killing himself? And leaving Mrs. Dabney? They were so much in love. They were the perfect couple."

"Well, looks can be deceiving."

Decker glanced down at the box. "What's in there?"

Kaine smiled. "This was my old bedroom. It was just Momma and me. I had a brother, but he died when he was a baby, and my daddy passed when I was four."

"I'm sorry."

"She kept some of my stuff. I've got two daughters, so I thought they might want it, but they're getting a little old for some of it."

"You mean toys?"

"Yeah."

She stepped back and opened the door more fully. Decker saw a neatly made bed, a white chest of drawers, and two tall shelves packed with items.

"These days if you can't hook up to the Internet kids don't want it. Dr. Seuss books, Easy-Bake Oven, puzzles. And even dolls. Now it has to be that American Girl thing. Do you know how much those cost? Mine were way cheaper and just fine. All you had to do was use your imagination."

Decker was only half listening. On one shelf he was staring at a series of dolls all lined up in a row.

"Are those your old dolls?"

"Yes."

"Did you know that they're exactly like the ones the Dabney daughters have?"

"Are they? Well, I guess that makes sense."

"Why?"

"Because the Dabneys bought them for me."

71

"THEY ALL HAVE the same secret compartments," said Milligan.

Decker was standing next to him while Bogart sat in his desk chair. Jamison and Brown were seated across from Bogart.

Jamison said, "So Cecilia Randall's daughter's dolls were identical to those of the four Dabney girls and they all had places to hide stolen information?"

Decker nodded and picked up two of the dolls. "This is Missy, which was Jules Dabney's doll. This doll belonged to Randall's daughter, Rhonda. Care to try to tell them apart?"

They all drew forward and looked at the two dolls.

"There's even paint on the same shoe," said Brown.

Decker said, "Smell the hair of each."

Brown and Jamison did so. Jamison said, "They smell the same."

"Exactly. Jules identified her doll by the paint and the smell. My daughter used to do the same thing with the smell test. Lots of little kids do. Whoever was behind this was good at sweating the details."

Brown said, "So does that mean Randall was also part of the spy ring? Hell, she must have been."

"Not necessarily," said Decker. "Her participation might have been unwitting."

"How could it be?" scoffed Brown.

"After she told me about the dolls, I had a long discussion with Rhonda Kaine. She went on to tell me that she went with her mother to the Dabneys' every day when she was too young for school. After she became school-age, Randall would go and pick her up from the local school. Apparently the Dabneys arranged for her to attend a school near their house. Randall would bring her back to the Dabneys' and she would stay there and play or do her homework until it was time to go home. When she got older she helped with the kids and did some babysitting. She even helped her mother with tasks around the house. This was all after school as well, but she was there most days."

"But as she got older surely she didn't carry a doll around with her," said Jamison.

"No. She didn't. But for years she did. And she couldn't tell me for certain whether the dolls were ever switched. I couldn't really get into it with her without revealing confidential elements of the investigation, so I didn't go there."

"Okay, but let's say the dolls were used to convey stolen information," said Brown. "How do you see it playing out? How did they do it?"

"Walter Dabney brings secrets home from work. I don't know how he got them out of NSA, but we know that people in the past have succeeded in doing that. Once he started his own business, taking secrets home would be much easier. Next, he has to get them to his buyer or handler. He puts them in one of the dolls. When Rhonda Kaine comes with her doll it gets switched out somehow. Rhonda takes her doll home. She told me that when she was little she would take her doll to school sometimes, or else her mom would bring it with her to work so she could play with it when she got to the Dabneys'. And when I asked her about it, she said that she would rotate her dolls out, play with one one day and another the next. So they wouldn't get lonely."

"And then what would happen?" asked Brown. "If Cecilia Randall isn't in on it?"

"When Randall went to work someone could come into their house, take the information from the doll, and leave. She had no security system. It would have been easy enough."

"That could work," observed Bogart.

"That way Dabney never has to come into contact with the other person. Cecilia Randall was the go-between and would never have even known it. And it wasn't like they were doing the doll thing every day. Dabney might have had a system in place that would somehow alert the other party when something would be in the doll."

"And when the kids got older and the dolls stayed on the shelf, Dabney probably turned to another technique," said Bogart. "Like Berkshire and her use of the book."

Brown said, "So this guy has been spying and selling out this country for well over thirty years?"

"Looks to be," said Bogart.

"You would have thought he would have been caught at some point," noted Milligan. "I mean, other spies, even ones who got away with it for years, were eventually found out."

"We know about them *because* they got caught," pointed out Decker. "There could be lots of spies out there who were never caught."

Brown nodded. "So Dabney's weak spot was his daughter. He thought she was in danger and maybe he moved faster than he wanted to. Or else he had stopped spying and was rusty. Either way, he seeks out an old contact to do the deal to help Natalie. But we caught on to it this time. But too late to stop him from selling the secrets and then killing Berkshire and then himself."

"Well, another factor that was different was that Dabney knew he was dying," said Bogart.

"We've already speculated that maybe by killing Berkshire and then himself, he was trying to make amends for all the wrong he'd done over the years," added Jamison.

Bogart looked over at Decker. "What do you think about that?"

Decker didn't answer right away. When he did his tone was distant, as though he wasn't even speaking to them.

"It all makes sense, but I'm not convinced it's what happened."

"But why not?" asked Brown. "Why don't you think it's the right theory?"

"It leaves too many questions unanswered—principally, who ambushed me and took the flash drive? And who killed Cecilia Randall? Because I think it may be the same people who set up Walter Dabney to steal the secrets to rescue his daughter."

"Well, it could be the spy ring that had worked with Dabney in the past," said Brown. "Let's say he stole secrets for years but then retired. They weren't happy about that, but if they went after him he could retaliate and blow their cover. But then Natalie gets in trouble gambling and they see a way to manipulate him into spying again. If he believed she owed ten million dollars he would know that the secrets he would have to sell would be major ones. And they were. He provided a back door into our secure databases."

"And you're sure about that?" asked Decker.

"What? Yes."

"How can you be?"

"Because we traced the stolen information to Dabney. He had access. His passcodes were on various entry points, entry points that he knew because of the work he did with DIA."

"It couldn't have been someone else at his firm?"

"There was also a biorhythmic security threshold, Decker. It was Dabney, plain and simple. It was a complicated electronic trail, which is why we didn't get to him before he accomplished what he set out to do."

"So the recipients of this information have had the back-door access for a while now?"

"Yes."

"And they could have learned certain secrets already?"

"Undoubtedly they did."

"Any in particular of special importance?"

"They're all important!"

"Granted, but anything really important come to mind?"

"I already told you that it included overseas assets. And as I said, a number have already been killed."

"Anything else?"

She sighed and thought about the question. "It wasn't all having to do with DIA, actually. There was information involving other agencies—NSA, CIA, internal reports from the Joint Chiefs, DEA, even the FBI."

"Having to do with what?"

"Having to do with things you're not cleared for, but in the spirit of cooperation, I can tell you they had to do with joint agency ops in the Middle East, the hardening of several facilities, the strategies to be employed with ISIL, intel from the war in Syria, and Russia's intentions toward the Baltic states and NATO's responses thereto. Quite the assortment, actually."

"And they could be acting on any of these," said Decker.

"Because you said the chatter mentioned Dabney and that a threat was imminent?"

"Exactly. It's a lot of ground to cover. *Too* much, in fact."

Bogart said, "But we were told at the White House that the attack would be here, in the United States."

"And I'm not saying that intel is wrong," said Brown. "I just have no way to confirm it."

"Berkshire was not Middle Eastern," said Decker. "And yet the chatter was all in Arabic."

Brown said, "Well, the Russians could be working with factions in the Middle East. Look how involved they are in Syria right now. They want to be a regional power, and then build on that to become a superpower again. If we get distracted by an attack on our country to become even more isolated, it allows for a vacuum that Moscow could fill over there."

"I could see that strategy working," said Decker.

"Any recent chatter?" asked Bogart.

Brown shrugged. "We haven't heard the name Dabney used again, but we've learned from NSA that the same source where the chatter originated is increasing in frequency. In our experience that means things are building to a head. When that chatter ceases it means the attack is about to take place. At least that's been the case in the past."

"So when they go silent, that means the bomb is about to go off?" said Decker.

"Yes."

"Then let's pray for chatter."

CHAPTER

72

Decker was running. Only not in real life.

In a dream.

He wore the uniform of the Cleveland Browns. His twenty-two-year-old self was sprinting down the field on opening day of a new NFL season. He had made the team as a rookie walk-on due to his special teams ability, which largely meant running with abandon and throwing your body at other similarly sized young men with a recklessness bordering on insanity.

Then out of nowhere had come the hit. The blindside plastering that had lifted him off his feet, knocked his helmet from his head, and tossed him down three feet away, unconscious and, though no one knew it at the time, dying.

And when he awoke in the hospital the Amos Decker who had once inhabited his body was no more.

He had been replaced with pretty much a complete stranger. As different from the original Amos Decker—emotionally and mentally—as it was possible to be.

With this last fragment of the dream ricocheting through his brain like a fired round, Decker opened his eyes and sat up, breathing hard, sweat bubbling on his face though the room was cool.

He stared across the darkness of his room. Outside he could hear car traffic, and a few moments later the throaty roar of a plane doing its climb out after lifting off from National Airport. Some rain drizzled at his window.

Still, he stared across the room, his thoughts remaining on that football field. On the person he used to be. As precisely perfect as his memory was now, he couldn't wrap it around the young man from twenty years ago.

I can remember who I was, just not with any real accuracy. How ironic is that?

He turned and looked at the doll resting on his nightstand. The one like Molly used to have. Only this one had probably been used for espionage.

He lay back down and in his mind started parceling things.

He had many strings in hand, but none that seemed paramount or more capable of leading to an answer than its neighbor. He could sense that all they were doing was running in circles, never proactive, never ahead of the curve.

He was a detective and a good one. He had solved lots of cases over the years, but few as inscrutable as this one. He had told Brown that maybe they were looking at this the wrong way round, even if she hadn't understood exactly what that meant.

Maybe I don't either.

Everything seemed to come back to Walter Dabney. That was partly by default. They had been able to thoroughly dig into his past, whereas they had had far less to go on when it came to Berkshire.

By far his biggest asset was his memory, so he turned to it once more.

His eyes closed and the frames flipped past.

There was something that someone had said. He wasn't

sure it was even related. For some reason it seemed an outlier comment, but perhaps with a secondary meaning that
would shed light on something.

The frames slowed and his brow furrowed.

It was almost like the reels of a slot machine clacking
away and then slowing as the cycle neared its end, showing
you to be either a loser or a winner, if the images all lined up
perfectly.

*Come on. Line up for me. Make me a winner. I could use
it.*

Surprisingly, the image of Melvin Mars came into his
head. They had been talking about something at Harper
Brown's house right before they had been attacked.

The clacking sound diminished; the frames continued to
slow.

Mars had said something about Brown. It had sounded
perfectly innocuous when he had said it. It had flowed very
naturally from the conversation they had been having. It
wasn't related to the case at all.

One...two...three.

The clacking slowed down more. The whirring images
too, so that Decker could start to see a firm image taking
shape.

Mars had been telling Decker how impressed he'd been
with Brown. How well traveled she was, but how she put on
no airs even with all the wealth she possessed. Mars had said
he had admired that. He liked hanging with her.

She was fun and cool and she made him feel good.

But, no, it was not that. It was something else.

It was like he was holding a piece of flypaper, and bits
of confetti, representing the facts of the case, were swirling
in the air. If he could just get them to drop down and stick to
the flypaper, things might start making sense.

More clacking and more spinning images.

Five...six...seven...eight.

Jackpot.

The single word burst into his head, jumping out in the same way the highlighted ones in the Harry Potter book had leapt from the page.

He sat up so fast he became a little dizzy.

Athlete.

73

DECKER WALKED OUT of the FBI morgue after having talked to Lynne Wainwright again. He had had new questions and she had given him helpful answers.

He went to the WFO, sat at a computer, and started searching. The information started to flood in, and the pieces started dropping into place at an increasing pace. It was like the dam had opened and the water was flowing freely.

Finally.

He found terms he had never encountered before, including several he couldn't come close to pronouncing. He looked at pictures of people from decades ago.

So many of them.

Disgraced now.

Diseased now.

In pain. Dying before their time.

It had all been monstrous. And the world had largely looked the other way.

But it had obviously given others opportunities. And they had seized them.

And he had also remembered something else.

A picture where a picture should never have been.

He should have seen it before, but he hadn't. It had seemed unimportant, when he should have realized that there was no such thing as something unimportant in an investigation.

He got up, walked out, and headed to Bogart's office.

The FBI agent was there with Milligan and Jamison. They told him that Agent Brown was on her way.

Decker said, "Tell her to meet us at the Dabneys'."

"Why?" asked Bogart. "What's there that we need to go back?"

"Pretty much everything."

* * *

Thirty minutes later they pulled up in front of the impressive mansion. Brown's BMW was already parked near the front door. She got out as they headed to the house.

"What's up?" asked Brown. "Why are we here?"

Milligan pointed at Decker. "Because of him."

Jules answered the door. Decker said, "We need to speak to your mother."

"She's not here."

"Where is she?"

"If you must know, she's at my father's grave."

"Where is that?" asked Decker.

"Can't you just leave her alone?"

"Where is it?" Decker asked again.

Jules hesitated and then told him.

"One more thing," said Decker. "I need to look at one of the photo albums you showed me earlier."

* * *

They pulled into the cemetery through a set of open wrought iron gates. Brown had left her car at the Dabneys' home and ridden over with them.

"I hate cemeteries," said Jamison. "Buried in the dirt and eventually people stop coming to see you. No thank you. I'm being cremated."

"I think you've got a while to think about that," noted Bogart.

He steered the car down a side road using the directions Jules had given them.

A Jaguar convertible was parked at the curb. As they pulled up, they saw Ellie Dabney sitting on a stone bench in front of her husband's freshly dug grave. The tombstone was not up yet.

As they all got out of the car, Brown said, "Decker, are you going to tell us what's going on?"

"You're going to hear *everything* in about two minutes," he replied. He led them up a path until they reached Ellie.

She looked up at them with unfriendly eyes. "Jules called me to say you were headed here. I don't mean to be rude, but I'm visiting my husband. I would appreciate some privacy."

"I can understand that," said Decker. "Unfortunately, this can't wait."

He sat down on the bench next to her as the others encircled them.

From his pocket Decker took out a photo and held it out to Ellie.

"My parents," she said. "Where did you get it?"

"They died in a mudslide?"

"Yes, it was horrible."

"And everything was washed away? The house, the barn, them? Their bodies were never found. That's what Jules told us."

"If I hadn't been at school I would have died too."

"So you lost everything? Your family? All your possessions?"

"Yes! I had nothing left except the clothes on my back. I had no family left. I was sent to an orphanage."

Decker nodded. "So where did this photo come from, then?"

Ellie started to say something but then stopped. She cleared her throat and said, "Fortunately, I had it with me. I carried it with me always."

Decker nodded. "I thought you might say that."

"Because it's the truth."

"I spoke this morning with a medical examiner from the FBI. Fortuitously, she had an uncle who worked as a team physician for the U.S. Olympic Team back in the seventies. He told her about what went on back then, with other countries. And she educated me about it this morning."

Ellie said nothing.

Decker said, "Stasi, fourteen twenty-five? Ring a bell?"

Ellie's eyes widened, but it was barely noticeable.

But Decker noticed.

"What?" she said sharply. "What is that?"

"You already know, but for the benefit of the others it's the name of the East German program that built up a powerhouse Olympic team by giving anabolic steroids to mostly unwitting athletes. Translated into English it means State Plan Fourteen point Two-Five."

"East Germany? What has that got to do with me? I was born in Oregon."

"Oral Turinabol was the steroid of choice for the East Germans. It has another name that, frankly, I can't even begin to spell, much less pronounce. It was a real turbocharger for athletic performance, but without some of the worst side effects. Still, it *did* have side effects. You remember the East German female swimmers from the seventies? They had facial hair, deep voices, and huge muscles. One American swimmer complained about it quite vocally, but everyone put her down as a sore loser. Turns out she was absolutely right, but the Germans still won all the gold."

"An interesting history lesson," said Ellie slowly. "But what the hell does it have to do with me? I'm not East German and I was certainly never in the Olympics."

"But my guess is you *were* in the national athletic youth program they had over there. You were being groomed for the Olympics. From an early age, probably. You have the perfect athletic shape. Tall, lean, muscled. Over the years you were given Oral Turinabol or something like it, along with all the other hopefuls. They wanted to build something akin to Hitler's perfect Aryan race. But even with that kind of chemical help, it's a tight funnel on the road to the top in any sport. I know that better than most with my football career. Only the best of the best get to go, and they'd know by the time you were in your early teens."

Ellie looked at Bogart. "Is he insane?"

Bogart said nothing.

Decker continued, "But you had other value to them. You couldn't cut it as an athlete, but maybe as something else."

"This is ridiculous."

"You were taught English until you could speak it fluently with no accent. You were given a history, which you learned as if it was your own. Rural Oregon. Decades ago. A mudslide. An orphanage. No family. You came east to start a new life. Who could disprove any of that? You became a waitress at a place near, where else? The NSA. You would meet lots of people from there because everyone has to eat. You targeted the young Walter Dabney and he fell for beautiful Eleanor hook, line, and sinker. You married soon after. He brought work home and you stole it. He left the NSA and started his own firm and you hit the jackpot. Now he was doing work not just with the NSA, but with multiple agencies.

Back in those days they had safeguards in place, but nothing like today. I can only imagine what was in his briefcase each night when he walked in the door. We always thought your husband was the spy, but it was actually *you*."

Ellie stood and screamed, "How dare you insult me with all these lies right in front of my husband's grave!"

Decker glanced up at her. "The problem was how to get this treasure trove of intel out to where it needed to go. But you weren't working alone. You had a handler." He paused. "Anne Berkshire."

Bogart exclaimed, "*She* was working with Berkshire? And not her husband?"

"Neither of us was working with anyone," said Ellie shrilly.

"When your kids were little and you had Cecilia Randall working for you, the answer became clear. The dolls. You'd ship the information out using the dolls. I don't know if Randall knew what was in those dolls. Maybe she did and maybe she didn't. I speculated that she might have been innocent, but maybe not. I mean, you've kept her on all this time even though your kids have long since moved on. Randall's daughter said you took great care of them. I wonder what an inspection of Randall's finances will show? And what will yours show? How did you buy your house all those years ago when your husband was still working at the NSA? The expensive Porsche? Did you tell him you had gotten a big settlement from the mudslide? An inheritance from some distant relative?"

Ellie started to walk off, but Bogart put a hand on her arm. "You're not going anywhere, Mrs. Dabney."

She ripped her arm free and said, "Are you arresting me? If not, I'm leaving and calling my lawyer and he's going to sue all of you!"

"We're *detaining* you, which we have every right to do," said Bogart firmly.

She glared at him and then folded her arms over her chest and gazed off into the distance.

Decker said, "After the dolls became useless because the kids grew up, I guess you could have gotten rid of them, but you were perhaps afraid that someone might find the hidden compartments. Better just to keep them."

"Just because you say something does not make it true."

"When did you realize that the anabolic steroids were responsible for the stillbirth and the miscarriages? And your health problems? And your daughters' health issues and birth defects? I understand that Jules and Samantha have had trouble in that department."

"I had no control over that. It was…it was genetics. It was natural."

"There was nothing *natural* about it. It was chemical-based. I wondered how such fit-looking people could all have such bad health. So I decided to trace the source back. And I did. To you."

She slowly turned to look at him.

"It must have been a shock when all the stories came out about Stasi, about Oral Turinabol. It causes both liver and kidney disease, bone density loss, high cholesterol and asthma, all conditions which you have and for which you're currently taking medications."

Ellie pursed her lips but still said nothing.

"And it also causes miscarriages, and birth defects, like the ones your daughters have. And you're also on Zoloft, for depression. I can see how you might be depressed."

"How did you know about the stillbirth and my miscarriages?" she said quietly.

"I think you know the answer to that," replied Decker.

When she didn't reply, he said, "Cissy Randall. She told me. She told me about the girls' issues too. And then you found out she had. And she had to be taken care of because you had no way of knowing what else she might say."

"You think I killed Cissy! I was in bed asleep."

"Your daughter checked on you at one. Randall was killed between two and three. At that late hour it gave you plenty of time to go there, kill her, and get back. There were no signs of forced entry. Randall had a key to your house. What are the odds that you had a key to hers? If we search your house thoroughly I think we'll find it."

Ellie turned and looked at her husband's grave.

Decker rose and stood beside her. "You knew Anne Berkshire when her name was Anna Seryyzamok. She was your handler, until you did something, I think, that no one expected you to do." He paused as she glanced over at him. "You stopped spying."

"I am not a damn spy!"

Decker ignored her. "You quit. But Berkshire still was working with other spies in the area. This is D.C. after all. If you're going to spy, this is the place. We found out about her recent use of Dominion Hospice and her work with the Gorskis and Alvin Jenkins. But you quit on her. And she wasn't happy about it. But she couldn't expose you without you exposing her. She made a comment to a teacher at the school where she volunteered. 'You think you know someone, when you really don't.' I think she was talking about you."

Ellie simply shook her head but remained silent.

Decker said, "And everything was fine for a very long time, and then along comes Natalie and her gambling problems. And that cratered everything."

"I knew nothing about that."

"You knew *everything* about that. Your husband would have never kept that from you. You were too close. I don't believe then that he had any idea you had been a spy. He loved you, unconditionally. Everyone said he was a great guy, which ordinarily makes me suspicious. But as it turned out, he *was* a great guy. What you didn't know was that Berkshire had never forgiven you for what you did, abandoning the cause, and was on the lookout for any way to get back at you, or better yet, get you back in the fold. And Natalie was her opportunity. Ten million bucks or your child and her family get slaughtered by the Russians. And you knew how cruel the Russians could be. Natalie told him and he told you. You were well-off, but where could your husband get ten million dollars in a matter of days? He must have been frantic. But you knew there was a way. And that meant you had to tell the man you loved that you had been stealing his secrets all that time and sending them to the Soviets." He stopped and stared at her. "How did he take that, Mrs. Dabney? How did he take that betrayal by his wife of decades, by the mother of his children? How devastated was he? I can tell you that *he* also told Natalie that he thought he knew someone, but he really didn't. Like Berkshire, he was talking about *you*, his own wife, the love of his life."

Tears now were spilling down Ellie's cheeks. She shook her head but said nothing as a cold wind whipped through the cemetery. She started gasping for breath, pulled an inhaler from her pocket, and took three quick puffs on it.

They all stood there watching her as the chill wind pummeled them.

74

JAMISON FINALLY DREW CLOSER to Ellie, handed the woman a tissue she had pulled from her jacket pocket, and then stepped back. Ellie used it to dab at her eyes.

Decker said, "So I'm thinking you contacted Berkshire through an old communication channel. You told her of your dilemma and she told you what it would take to get ten million dollars from her organization. You told your husband and he made it happen. And Natalie was saved.

"But then something happened, didn't it? Natalie spilled the beans that the debt had *not* been ten million. She had been forced to say that by Berkshire's people to make you panic and resort to espionage. Berkshire was probably monitoring your family for any weakness to use against you. And she found the mother lode in Natalie. And she was just waiting for you to contact her. But now you realized Berkshire had deceived you. And you told your husband. And, reeling at the guilt of having betrayed his country, and knowing that he would never have to stand trial for it, he decided to murder Berkshire. With *your* help."

Ellie put her inhaler back in her pocket and walked over and sat back down on the bench.

"Mrs. Dabney, I'm not here to judge you. My job is to find out the truth. That's it."

Bogart added, "If you cooperate, it will definitely be better for you."

Brown said, "We're convinced that something is in the works, Mrs. Dabney. Some attack. If you help us out on that, your future will look a lot brighter than if you don't cooperate."

"And telling us the truth would be a good start," said Decker.

A long minute passed.

When she spoke, Ellie's voice was husky but firm. And her tone was resigned.

"God, I'm just tired. So tired of all of it." She paused. "Walt told me about his cancer. He would never have kept that from me. Even after he found out about... what I had done. Although he had Natalie go with him to Houston to confirm the diagnosis instead of me." She paused and looked over at the grave. "It wasn't Walt's idea to kill Anna. It was mine. *I* wanted to do it." She slowly shook her head, her eyes closed for a moment. "But Walt, gallant to the last, insisted that he would do it. Like you said, he would never stand trial for the crime."

"You were the one dressed as the clown," said Decker. "You were the signal to your husband."

Ellie wiped her eyes with the tissue. "I had parked my car in a garage near the FBI building. I went in there, changed out of the costume, got in my car, and drove home. I knew what Walt was going to do. I cried all the way. It was like I was in some sort of nightmare. My mind was numb."

Bogart said, "Before he killed Berkshire, we saw a woman on a video with your husband removing items from his safe deposit box."

"I don't know for sure, but I assume it was one of Anna's people. You don't know this, but they tried to recruit Walt after he stole the secrets to pay for Natalie's debts. Anna always played the long game. Getting back at me was a secondary goal. Getting Walt as part of her spy ring would have been a great coup for her. They met with him, told him some things. Walt would never have done that. But Walt was a brilliant man. He and Anna were evenly matched there. He played along because he had his own plan. He later videotaped himself naming names and talking about the secrets he stole so your government would be warned to bring down Anna's spy ring. But they somehow found out about his plan and took the evidence."

"Did he name you as part of the spy ring?" asked Bogart.

"No. He wanted me to be spared from that."

"A very understanding man," snapped Brown. "Considering how cruelly you had used him all those years."

Ellie looked up at her. "You have spies working for you, do you not?"

"Yes."

"Do they infiltrate places and pretend to be something they're not?"

"That happens," admitted Brown.

"And you believe they are doing important work on behalf of their country?"

"Of course. They're incredibly dedicated and brave."

"So in your eyes spies are only incredibly dedicated and brave when they're working for the Americans?"

Brown flinched but said nothing.

Decker said, "So with that video evidence gone and your husband's plan ruined, is *that* when you two decided to kill Berkshire instead?"

She nodded. "After my athletic hopes ended back in East

Germany, I was recruited by the MfS. The East German Ministry for State Security," she added when they looked confused. "They worked closely with Moscow and the KGB. They had formed a joint intelligence program that would deliver agents into the United States, not as foreigners but with the background to make them appear to be *citizens*. It was thought that in this way we would have more paths to success. I was put in the most intense training for years. It was also during that time that I met Anna, who was also in the same joint program, but on the KGB side. She was brilliant and cunning and dedicated to the cause of the Soviets. I was the spy and she was my handler. We never became friends. That was not the desired relationship. We became something much stronger. We were operatives whose lives would be forfeited the instant we were discovered. That bond is very strong, nearly unbreakable."

"I can see that," said Brown, drawing a quick glance from the others.

Ellie continued. "I was indoctrinated. I won't say brainwashed, because I was proud to serve my country. And I did so, faithfully, for years. The money for the car and the house? I told Walt it was from a trust fund set up for me by the logging company that was at fault for the mudslide that killed my 'parents.' I told him it had been earning interest and dividends all that time until it was worth hundreds of thousands of dollars."

Decker said, "Okay. Although I'm surprised he didn't want to save it and put it into the business he was probably planning on starting even back then."

She smiled wistfully. "That was our little compromise. He got the car of his dreams and I got the house of mine. I had passed by our home often in the past when it was owned by others. I always loved it. Back in my country I lived in a one-bedroom flat. To have such a house, well, it seemed impossible. But for me, it could be possible."

"I can see that."

She turned to Decker. "And then something happened."

"You found out about the anabolic steroids?" he said. "And what they had done to you and your children?"

She waved this off dismissively. "No. I had long since learned of that. Yes, I was devastated by the stillbirth and the miscarriages. And by how my girls suffered. But there was nothing I could do about that. But I could do something about what I came to this country to do. I could stop spying."

"And what was the catalyst for that?" asked Bogart.

She smiled, the expression on her face both tragic and wistful. "I realized that I loved my family more than I loved my country," she said simply. "And each day that went by I was terrified that they would find out who I really was. So...I stopped doing it. I turned my back on my country. And you're right, Anna was livid. But I didn't care. She threatened to expose me. But I had taken steps to protect myself. I had information, evidence that would have crippled her operation. So we reached a détente. And that was how things stood." She let out a long breath. "Until Anna outwitted me by using Natalie."

She stood and walked over to Dabney's grave. "Even after Anna was gone, her circle was still in place. And they contacted me; like Walt, they wanted me to spy once more. Even with Walt dead, they had positions for me that would help them. I didn't answer them. I thought if I said no, they would kill all of us. But they've been watching us. And you kept coming back. I also believed they bugged my house. They must have heard things."

"Like when we found the dolls?" said Decker.

She nodded.

Brown interjected, "They wasted no time on that one. They hit us the same night."

"How did Anna end up with Jules's doll?" asked Decker. "Did she have it all this time or was it more recent?"

"She demanded it from me in return for helping with Natalie. I guess she considered it a symbolic victory considering how we had used them for our spying."

Decker looked at her. "It's funny," he said.

"What is?" Ellie demanded.

"Jules told me she believed you were incapable of keeping secrets from the family. She was obviously wrong about that. Did Cecilia Randall knowingly help you with the dolls and the spying?"

"No, she knew nothing about it."

"Did you kill her?" asked Decker.

She shook her head. "I could never do that. But her house key, which we kept in the kitchen, went missing. I can only think that Anna's people heard something that she said that distressed them. And they killed her."

"I think you might be right about that," said Decker. "She told us about your coming from money. And your family's health issues. They were probably worried she might say something else that would make us suspicious."

Bogart walked over to Ellie and said, "Eleanor Dabney, I'm arresting you on the charge of espionage against the United States." He read off her Miranda rights as Milligan handcuffed the woman.

No more tears passed down her face as this was being done.

She looked once more over at her husband's grave. "I'm sorry, Walt. For everything."

Before Bogart and Milligan led her away, Decker said, "Mrs. Dabney, I have another question."

"What is it?" she said wearily.

"Why did your husband shoot Berkshire in front of the FBI building? Was that your choice or his?"

"I had arranged to meet with Anna that day. Only she didn't know that she instead would be running into Walt. But to answer your question, it was Walt's idea to meet her there. The actual meeting place I had given Anna was to be around the corner at a café. But Walt told me that after I signaled him he was going to confront Anna in front of the FBI building and shoot her there."

"And then kill himself?" said Decker.

She nodded, looking down at the ground.

"You're an amazing actress," said Jamison. "When you were at your husband's bedside at the hospital I never would have guessed that any of it was an act."

In a quavering voice Ellie said, "I had just lost the only man I'd ever loved. My tears were very real, I can assure you."

There was an awkward moment before Decker said, "But why in front of the FBI building?"

"Walt said he wanted to scare the bastards really badly. And killing Anna there would send a powerful message, he told me. I just wanted to see that woman dead."

"So he said nothing to you that would indicate why?"

She shook her head and then let out a low sob. "Maybe he didn't trust me anymore. And who could blame him?"

She was led away by Bogart and Milligan.

But Decker didn't follow.

He walked over and stood next to the grave. Jamison and Brown sat down on the bench and watched him.

Brown whispered. "What do you think he's thinking?"

"The Lord only knows," replied Jamison. "I've never, ever been able to get inside that mind of his."

At the grave Decker looked down at the freshly turned earth. "I'm sorry, Mr. Dabney. You deserved better. A lot better."

CHAPTER

75

"Do the daughters know?" asked Jamison.

She was looking across at Decker in their office at the WFO.

He nodded. "They were stunned, to put it mildly. It's like they've been hit with one tsunami after another. They won't be able to see her for a while, but Bogart has informed them of everything. They're getting her a lawyer. She's going to need a really good one."

"She helped us. She told us a lot."

Decker looked over at her. "She's in her sixties. And in addition to the espionage, she conspired to kill Berkshire. So even with favorable treatment it's doubtful she's coming out of prison alive."

"I know. But talk about being caught between a rock and a hard place."

"She *chose* to become a spy."

"Oh, come on, it was the Soviet Union. Do you really think she had a choice? They would have shot her or sent her to Siberia if she'd refused."

"It doesn't matter, Alex. The law doesn't make exceptions for that. They searched the house and found multiple surveillance devices. That's how they knew what was going on. They were all wireless and could be picked up by some-one sitting in a car a quarter mile away."

She slumped back in her chair and fiddled with a pen taken from a holder on her desk. "What did you mean when you were asking her why Dabney had chosen the FBI build-ing to shoot Berkshire?"

"Because I wanted to know if she had the answer."

"Well, I know that. But why do you think that's impor-tant?"

"Because it's inexplicable."

"Right. And you don't like inexplicable?"

"Like Anne Berkshire, everything we know about Walter Dabney shows that he's a person who does nothing without a good reason. He was smart, accomplished, methodical, fo-cused. It's not easy to build the sort of business he did. You remember he had put together a video and other evidence to try to nail these bastards? He wanted to beat them at their own game. He'd worked in the intelligence field his entire adult life. He knew how much damage these people could do with what he had given them. He wanted to try to make it right before he died. And I don't think that plan simply in-cluded blowing Berkshire's head off."

"But Mrs. Dabney answered you. He said he wanted to send a message to those people."

"I know that is what she *said* he told her."

"Are you saying you don't believe her? What reason would she have to lie to us now?"

"I don't know. And we're almost out of time."

"What do you mean?"

"Brown texted me. The chatter has gone silent. The prep is done. They're ready to execute the plan."

"Oh shit."

"Oh shit," he repeated.

* * *

Decker set the beer down and wiped his mouth.

Mars mirrored this move next to him at the bar they were in. As he put his beer down, he winced.

"How's the arm?" asked Decker.

"Hurts a lot less than when you hit me on that screen pass back in college."

"You're just trying to cheer me up. That was the only time I tackled you all game."

"Still a good hit."

"Yeah. You hit me so hard about fifteen times that I stayed in bed for three days because I couldn't feel any part of my body."

Decker refocused on his beer, but his attention was obviously far away.

"Things not going so good?" asked Mars.

"I wish I could tell you, but you're not cleared for it. Hell, I'm probably not cleared for it either."

"*Nothing* you can tell me?"

"You could say we only half finished the job. And the most important half is still out there."

"Alex was a little more forthcoming. She said there was big shit maybe going down soon, only you guys didn't know what."

"That sums it up pretty well, actually."

Mars took another sip of beer. "Anything I can do?"

"You got a miracle in your pocket?"

"Not last time I looked."

"Then, no, I don't think there's anything you can do."

"That bad, huh?"

"That bad. You seen Harper since the shootout at her house?"

"No."

"How come?"

"I think she wants to cool things, at least for now."

Decker looked surprised. "Why? I thought she liked you."

Mars sighed. "She does. Maybe too much."

"I'm not following."

"I think she's afraid I'll get hurt if I keep hanging around her."

"Well, the same could be said for me."

"Hell, I need to hang out with *somebody*, Decker."

"I won't stop you."

Mars looked at him quizzically. "How come?"

"Because I don't *like* you as much as Brown does. For obvious reasons."

Mars grinned and lightly punched him on the arm. "Asshole!"

Decker's phone buzzed. It was Jamison. Well, it was her number, but it wasn't Jamison.

"Mr. Decker?"

"Who is this?" said Decker sharply.

The voice said, "Irrelevant to the matter at hand. What is relevant is that Ms. Jamison is a guest of ours."

Decker stood. "Where's Alex? What do you want?"

"Excellent question. The answer to that would be you."

"I want to talk to Alex. Now!"

Mars had put his beer down and was standing next to Decker looking concerned.

A moment later Jamison came on the phone. Her voice was shaky.

"It's me, Amos."

"Where are you?"

"I don't know. I was getting out of my car when—"

There was a scuffle and the man's voice came on again.

"She's alive, for now. You're a very intelligent man, so you know what I'm going to ask you next."

"Where?"

"Not quite that easy, since we don't want your mates at the FBI to join the party."

"How, then?"

"We understand that you have a good memory."

"What of it?"

"I'm going to talk fast. Don't forget a thing. Your friend won't appreciate it."

The man spoke for about a minute.

Decker clicked off and looked at Mars. "I gotta go."

"So do I."

"See you later."

"No, I mean I'm going with you."

"That's not going to happen, Melvin."

"Then your ass ain't leaving this bar, Decker."

"Melvin, I—"

"I heard what you said on the phone. Alex is in trouble. So it's either we both go or neither one of us is going."

"Do you remember the last time we went somewhere to meet somebody?"

"Considering we almost got blown to shit, yeah, I remember."

"Well, these people have no incentive to let any of us live."

"Never doubted it."

"And you're still in?"

"Like you got to ask. Lead the way, dude."

CHAPTER

76

THE INSTRUCTIONS Decker had been given were complicated, which didn't surprise him.

First, a bus that carried him west. Next, a rental car in his name waiting for him at an airport.

Then he drove according to the directions he'd been given.

He passed rolling hills and flat expanses. The trees bent under blustery winds, which grew stronger the farther he went. It was colder and the sky had swiftly changed from clear to foreboding. He looked behind to see if there were any headlights back there.

He was armed but knew that would be useless once he reached his destination. They held all the cards since they had Jamison.

He slowed as he came to the junction he'd been looking for.

He pulled off the road. A van was waiting there. It blinked its lights. He got out and the side door of the van slid open.

A man crouched there aiming a gun at him. He had on no mask, so Decker could clearly see his features.

Well, that wasn't good. They obviously weren't worried that he was going to live to tell anyone anything.

The man flicked his gun at Decker and he walked over to the van. His legs were stiff from the long drive and he tripped over his feet, hitting the dirt right next to the van. The man didn't move to help him. Decker gripped the side of the van as leverage to hoist his bulk back up, while the man kept his gun trained on him all the way.

"Not very light on your feet, are you?" said the man snidely.

"I guess not," said Decker, a bit out of breath.

Two other men climbed out of the back of the van. They searched him thoroughly, even using an electronic wand, but found only his gun and no tracking devices.

His hands were bound with zip ties and he was pushed roughly into the van. The door was closed and the van pulled onto the road and sped off.

The men said nothing and Decker was not inclined to conversation. The van had no windows, so he couldn't see where they were going. Not that it mattered.

I just want to see Alex, alive.

They drove for about a half hour and finally the van pulled to a stop. The door opened and Decker was hustled out. He looked around and saw that they were in front of a dilapidated house with a waist-high falling-down wooden fence surrounding it. When he looked around he saw no other structure. The place looked to be in the middle of nowhere. All he could see in any direction was darkness.

There were lights on in the house, but they were low. Decker doubted the electricity was on in this place. It looked abandoned.

His captors marched him up to the sagging front porch. The door opened and he was led in.

When the door closed behind him and his eyes adjusted to the light, Decker could see that he had been right.

Battery-operated lanterns were situated in several different places, giving the place a low glow, like pockets of lightning bugs were flitting around. The room smelled of mildew and decay.

As soon as he saw her he couldn't take his gaze off her.

Alex was seated on a couch whose stuffing guts were spilling out through holes in the cushions. She had on a gag but her eyes were staring back at Decker.

He finally drew his gaze from her and looked around.

Five other men and one woman were standing around in the small room.

Even without the wig Decker recognized the woman as the one in the bank video with Walter Dabney. He was surprised to see that two of the men looked Middle Eastern.

The woman moved forward and appraised Decker. "You are stubborn," she said, her accent pronounced.

Decker held her gaze. "You're much younger than Anna. Are you her protégée? Since she's dead I guess you can move up now."

Her features turned ugly. "She should never have died."

"We all have to die one day," said Decker.

The woman glanced at Jamison and then back at him. "And so this is your day."

"Killing us won't stop the investigation. The FBI is a pretty big organization. This will just make them try harder."

The woman smiled at this. "No one knows what the future will bring." She paused. "But I think I can predict your and your friend's future."

"I can see why you might think that."

"I am surprised you came so willingly to your death."

"Alex is my friend. She has my back, I have hers."

"Then this is good. So you can die together. You and your *friend*."

"Maybe one day, but I don't think today."

"You have no control over that."

"That's true."

"Then you speak nonsense."

"Believe what you want to."

The woman's features turned suspicious. She said something to one of the men in another language that Decker didn't recognize. The man answered her and looked toward the window. He motioned for two of the men to check outside.

The woman looked back at Decker. "You are either very stupid or very brave."

"Right now, I'm not sure I'm either, actually."

The woman pulled a gun from her pocket and placed it against Decker's forehead. The door to the house opened as the men came back inside, shaking their heads and gesticulating with their hands.

The woman smiled at Decker. "No, let us go with very *stupid*, shall we?"

There were two windows in the room in addition to the door. All three were blown inward and mini explosions rained over them, the smoke dense and acrid. The woman holding the gun screamed as she dropped it and fell to her knees.

Jamison slid sideways off the couch. The other men toppled to the floor.

Decker could see something at one of the windows, but only for an instant before his eyes closed and he too fell heavily to the floor.

CHAPTER

77

"FLASH-BANGS REALLY SUCK, ROSS."

Decker was sitting up in a chair still looking woozy.

Bogart patted him on the shoulder. "Sorry, it was the best we could do. And I'd think you'd agree, it's better than being dead."

They were at an FBI field office fifty miles from the place where the kidnappers had taken Jamison. Melvin Mars was on the other side of him. He said, "I think it was a good thing you didn't rely on me to get you out of that jam, Decker."

Decker rubbed his ears and said, "It was enough that you were willing to walk the plank with me. But you're right, I figured we'd need the big guns."

Bogart said, "You did the right thing calling us in, Decker. We put the plan together pretty quickly. It was crazy and risky as hell."

"But it worked."

Bogart held up a small device. "You did a good job planting it."

"I tripped over my own big feet and fell next to the van. I used that opportunity to stick it under the side step. Luckily, I was able to do it before they searched me. If I hadn't been able to do that?"

"You and Alex would be dead."

"They never saw you coming," said Decker.

Bogart smiled. "Hey, Decker, we *are* the FBI."

"How's Alex?"

"Still resting. They banged her around some when they kidnapped her. And sedated her. But no permanent damage."

"You're sure about that?" said Decker quickly.

"I'm sure, Decker. She'll be fine."

"And the others? Did they bug the Dabneys' house? Did they kill Cecilia Randall?"

"We haven't gotten a word out of any of them, and I don't think we will, actually. They're a tough bunch."

"So we're back to square one, then?" said Decker.

"Well, it is a plus that we just captured a bunch of foreign operatives."

"I think they were speaking Russian."

Bogart nodded. "We think so too. If nothing else, it'll give us some leverage with Moscow."

"But some of them were Middle Eastern, Ross. And the chatter was in Arabic. You think the Russians have teamed up with jihadists?"

"I've found in this job that anything is possible."

"But we still don't know where the strike is coming from," pointed out Decker.

"No. But if we let it be known that we have their agents, then they might just call off whatever they're thinking about doing."

"We can't count on that," said Decker.

"We absolutely can't."

Mars said, "So what the hell do we do?"

"Figure out what they're planning to do and stop it," said Decker.

Milligan came into the room and sat down next to Bogart.

"Okay, the State Department has been on the horn to their counterparts in Moscow. They are disavowing all knowledge of any of this."

"That's no surprise," said Bogart.

"None at all."

"But this is a surprise."

They looked up to see Brown stride into the room. She had caught a ride on the FBI jet with Bogart, Mars, and Milligan.

"What is?" asked Bogart.

"Folks at DIA just got off a secure communication with Moscow. It seems the Russians have also received similar threats through chatter."

"Similar threats?" said Milligan. "And you believe them?"

"We never believe anyone a hundred percent, but our folks think they're actually being straight with us. They know that relations are delicate right now between Washington and Moscow. They have regional aspirations for sure, but it's not like they want to be drawn into a direct confrontation with us. That would only end badly for them. Their Achilles' heel is their economy. It's nearly all fossil-fuel-based, and the world's supply far exceeds demand. Because of that Russia's economy is in free fall. They already have sanctions on them for the shit they pulled in Ukraine and Crimea. Another round of sanctions and you might be talking revolution over there."

"So what does that mean for our situation?" asked Bogart.

"Because of all that, they were more forthcoming than they otherwise would be. They told us some things that jibed with things we'd previously discovered." She paused and drew an anxious breath. "Bottom line, it might be a worst-case scenario."

"How so?" asked Milligan.

"We might be looking at a rogue third party. Berkshire's spy ring might have gone mercenary. If so, the traditional restraints that would keep Russia in check are not going to apply. We're totally in uncharted territory now."

"Shit," muttered Bogart.

Milligan added, "Maybe someone's trying to start something between Russia and us. Two superpowers going at it, it might leave an opening for another organization to gain an advantage somewhere."

"And there are certainly enough mercenary players out there where they could recruit talent," opined Bogart. "And that would explain the presence of the Middle Easterners and the chatter in Arabic."

Decker said, "So Berkshire might not have been working for her country any longer."

"Maybe she hasn't for a while," said Bogart.

Decker said, "That might explain the million-dollar condo and the expensive car. Rogues get paid in cash, not medals. She might have gotten tired of simply serving her country."

Mars looked at each of them before his gaze settled on Decker. "So you guys are really gonna have to solve this thing. And fast!"

Decker groaned and rubbed his head. "It would help if it didn't feel like Big Ben was pounding in my brain."

"Like you said, man, flash-bangs suck," said Mars.

78

"Y OU SURE YOU'RE OKAY?"

Decker was sitting next to Jamison on her bed back at their apartment.

"I'm good, Decker, just tired. They roughed me up some before they drugged me. I don't know what they used, but it kicked the crap out of me."

"I'm sorry this happened."

"It's not your fault, Decker. You're the reason why I'm back here and not dead."

She suddenly sat up in bed and hugged him.

Decker looked surprised by this, but finally patted Jamison on the back.

She released him and said, "Bogart told me how things stand. This rogue organization. We don't know what they're targeting."

"No, we don't. And whatever it is will happen soon."

"Even though you captured some of their people?"

"We can't assume it won't happen. By default rogues are unpredictable."

"What are you going to do?"

Decker gazed over her shoulder out the window where it was raining again.

"I'm going to go for a walk."

* * *

His hood up, Decker trudged along in the rain. He didn't know why he liked bad weather.

Well, maybe he did.

On the day he'd found his family dead it had been gloriously beautiful, not a cloud in the sky, a gentle breeze, the sun shining like a beacon. And he'd come home that night to find the two people he loved most in the world murdered.

I'll take the gloom.

He reached the river and paralleled it on his walk. The windswept water was churning up whitecaps and seagulls were doing barrel rolls in the air.

He found the same bench and sat down, oblivious to the rain pelting him and soaking his pants and shoes.

Decker would never admit this to anyone, maybe not even to himself. He was terrified that there would come a day when he closed his eyes and flipped through his extraordinary memory and the only thing that came out would be…nothing.

For that reason he was now avoiding even doing it. This wasn't some secret weapon, like waving a magic wand that would produce exactly the answer you needed. Much of Decker's success in the past he could put down to simple, basic investigative legwork. Asking questions, looking at evidence, pondering how it all fit together, and finding in a quagmire of fact and fiction a lead that might take you where you needed to go.

He had a lot to ponder this time. Maybe too much. But he had found out a lot too.

They had uncovered and busted up the spy ring's use of Dominion Hospice.

They had discovered that it was Eleanor Dabney and Anne Berkshire who had worked together all that time as spies.

They had found the truth behind Natalie's "gambling debts" and with it the impetus for Walter Dabney to do what he had done.

They knew why he had killed Anne Berkshire.

And that his wife had, dressed as a clown, served as the signal that Berkshire was on her way.

They had most likely found out what had happened to Cecilia Randall and the secret behind the dolls.

They had, thankfully, rescued Jamison and captured members of the spy operation. Maybe they would eventually get some answers from those people.

Yes, all those were good, positive things.

But what they really had not determined was *why* Walter Dabney had chosen to shoot Anne Berkshire dead outside the Hoover Building. Despite what Ellie had told them about her husband wanting to send a message, Decker wasn't convinced.

Then, just as the word *athlete* had popped into his head previously, another word did too.

Literal.

He jumped up and raced back to the apartment, changed into dry clothes, and checked on Jamison. She was sleeping soundly, and he grabbed her keys and went to her car, pointing it in the direction of where all this had happened.

Along the way he called Mars and then stopped to pick him up. As it turned out, Harper Brown was with him, so

Decker left his car at the hotel where Mars was staying and they drove together to the place where it had all started for Decker.

"What's in your head, Decker?" asked Brown.

"Too many things."

"Come on, you need to give me more than that."

"I told you before that I thought Walter Dabney was being quite literal when he did something?"

"Yeah, I remember that."

"Well, I think he was being quite literal when he killed Berkshire where he did."

Brown exchanged a curious glance with Mars. "I'm not following," she said to Decker.

Only Decker wasn't listening.

Traffic was a bear. Sirens were screeching all over and they caught sight of a motorcade thundering through cleared lanes.

Brown turned away from Decker and said to Mars, "I hate it when we have visiting dignitaries. Screws traffic royally."

"We never worried about that in West Texas," said Mars. "If you got behind another car on the road *that* was a traffic jam."

Brown rolled her eyes at this comment and said, "Funny."

The traffic got so bad that they finally parked in a garage and hoofed it the rest of the way. The rain had let up some, but it was still a nasty, gloomy day.

Her jacket hood up against the drizzle, Brown said, "Okay, here we are near the Hoover Building. Now what?"

Decker was walking along slowly, covering the same route he'd taken on the morning that Dabney had shot Berkshire. He had done this so many times before that he had no idea what he thought he could possibly discover now.

Possibly nothing.

Probably nothing.

But he had come here for a particular reason. He had thought of it when he'd been sitting on the bench by the river. It wasn't because his memory had served him particularly well. This was based on something far more simple—an educated hunch. He'd long relied on them when he'd been a detective back in Ohio.

Now, this was where having perfect recall might really come in handy. He looked at everything in front of him, both sides of the street. Up, down, left, right.

While he was doing that Brown was saying to Mars, "This is one interesting town. You might enjoy living here."

He eyed her. "Is that an invitation?"

"I make no commitments," she said coyly. "And expect none in return. But I do enjoy your company."

"Thought you wanted to cool it after what happened at your house. Then you showed up out of the blue."

"Well, after some serious deliberation I thought it might be safer if I were there to protect you."

He laughed. "Okay, I have to admit that's the first time I've heard *that* from a woman."

"Well, maybe you haven't been hanging out with the right women," she shot back.

"I think you definitely have a point there."

Left, right, up, down. People, places, things.

Decker closed his eyes and flipped back to that day, every frame, everything he'd seen.

Okay, got it.

Now he superimposed the template he'd just taken in over the scene as it existed on the day Dabney had shot Berkshire.

He immediately noted that some things were different.

The burrito food truck was gone.

The guard was not in the shack.

The construction going on in the building across the street had ceased.

But, like the last time he'd been here, the manhole cover was replaced and the work site was gone.

He looked up at the Hoover Building—squat, ugly, crumbling.

Toilets that didn't work.

Fire alarms out of order.

Nets to catch falling chunks of concrete.

And surveillance cameras that didn't work...

He started running.

Brown called after him, "Decker!"

Mars said, "Hey, Amos!"

They ran after him, easily catching up. Decker turned the corner and came to a stop on the street paralleling the one they'd been on.

"What is that?" he asked as Brown stopped beside him, breathing a little bit hard.

"What is what?"

He pointed to the street. "That!"

"Jesus, what do you think it is: It's a motorcade."

"Whose?"

"I don't know whose." She studied it more closely and then looked around at the tops of buildings. "Okay, judging by the motorcade's length and the firepower with it, and the countersnipers on those rooftops, and all the suits with ear comms, I'd say VP on up. Maybe POTUS."

"So *he's* at the Hoover Building today?"

"He *does* go there from time to time."

Mars snapped his fingers. "Hey, I was watching TV in the hotel gym this morning when I was working out. And that's when I saw it."

"Saw what?" snapped Decker.

"The President was coming here today to give out some award. It had to do with something we did with the Brits and the Germans. The prime minister and that lady's who's the head of Germany are there too."

Brown said, "The President mentioned that when we met him at the White House. He was giving out an award for some sort of joint mission that saved lots of lives. Bogart knew about it."

The blood slowly drained from Decker's face. "And the British Prime Minister and the German Chancellor are in there."

Brown looked at him curiously. "Decker, what is it?"

He turned to her. "Walter Dabney knew something, only I don't think he knew exact details. Ellie Dabney said he was trying to send the terrorists a powerful message, she thought, to back off. She was right about him sending a message but *wrong* about the recipient. He was trying to give *us* a message."

"A message about what?"

"A message with no words."

"You're making no—"

"A message with no words. He told us by his actions."

"His actions?"

He looked at her. "He committed an act of *violence at the Hoover Building!*"

Brown slowly turned and glanced at the standing motorcade, then at the Hoover Building, and finally back at Decker.

And then the blood drained from her face too.

"Oh my God."

79

DECKER RUSHED BACK around to the other side of the building. He noted the empty guard shack again. With the President's visit, the guard was probably inside helping with security, he thought.

Brown and Mars once more caught up to him.

She said, "Decker, what are we going to do? Do you think they're going to somehow try to assassinate the President and the two other leaders? Do you think the shooters are already in the building?"

"Call Bogart, tell him what we suspect. Melvin, come with me."

They rushed off as Brown made the call.

Decker ran over to the street and looked down at the manhole cover. And then he looked over at the Hoover Building.

"The day Dabney shot Berkshire there were men working at this manhole."

"What were they doing?"

"I don't know." He closed his eyes and thought back to that day. "There was no utility truck that I could see."

Mars looked more closely at the manhole cover. "It says Washington Gas."

"Can you open it?"

Mars bent down and gripped the top of the cover. "Decker, it's been sealed, look."

Brown had come up to them. "The Secret Service seals all the manhole covers the motorcade will pass over." She paused and looked confused. "But the motorcade is on the other block. So I don't think they came down this way."

"Did you reach Bogart?" asked Decker.

She nodded but looked sick to her stomach. "Decker, he's in the Hoover Building at the ceremony."

"Dammit. Did you tell him they need to evacuate the building?"

"I told him what you *suspected*, but Decker, he can't stop the ceremony and evacuate the building based on that. He said to call him back if we come up with something else."

"What, like when the President's dead!" snapped Decker.

In a calming voice Mars said, "Decker, what else do you remember from that day?"

Decker focused on him. "I remember a utility truck going into the FBI building. And the guard told me that most of the exterior surveillance cameras are out of order."

"Anything else?"

Decker glanced sharply at the building across from the Hoover.

"There were workmen carrying materials into that building."

He led them over to it and they tried to peer through the windows, but they were taped over with thick paper on the inside. Decker tried the door. It was locked. He stepped back and looked up. "I don't think there's anyone in this building."

"It's being renovated," said Brown, pointing at a sign on one of the windows.

"Then you think people would be here working, wouldn't you?"

She looked confused. "Do you think there's a sniper's nest in there? But the motorcade is on the next street over. They'd have no shot from here."

Decker said, "Call the gas company and find out if they had a team out here working on any lines under that manhole on the day Berkshire was killed."

"That might take some time."

"Just do it!" snapped Decker.

Decker pulled his phone and called Bogart. The FBI agent answered and, speaking in a low voice, said, "Decker, I already told Brown, I *can't* evacuate. The ceremony just started. But—"

Decker interrupted: "What was the meeting about that Dabney was supposed to attend at the FBI when he shot Berkshire?"

"What?"

"The meeting! What was it for?"

"Why does it matter? He obviously never intended to be there."

"But he picked *that* day to kill Berkshire, Ross, so just tell me!" snapped Decker.

"Okay, okay. Dabney's firm was consulting on some renovation work here. As you know, a new building is a long way off so they have to do work on myriad systems here—security, electrical, and other infrastructure—"

Decker clicked off.

He glanced around and then hustled to an alley and turned down it.

Mars and Brown, her phone to her ear, ran after him.

Decker reached an exterior door to the building. He tried the knob but it was locked.

Brown and Mars reached him and she said, "Decker, what the hell is going on?"

"Ellie Dabney said Berkshire's spy ring wanted her husband to work for them."

"But he refused."

"I think he was smarter than that. He did that video, right? I think he met with them, pretended to be interested, and felt them out for what they were interested in. And what they were interested in was his work with the FBI on renovating their building. That was the meeting he was going to when he shot Berkshire. That was his second message to us, after the *location* of the attack."

"You mean the President is the target?" said Mars.

Decker didn't answer.

"But why not just tell us directly *before* he shot Berkshire?" said Brown.

"Probably because he didn't know their exact plan. And they found out about the video and removed it, which probably told him that they were watching his every move, monitoring his every communication. They probably threatened him and his family: He does anything else to thwart them, they're all dead. This was probably the only way he could see to do it."

"But why didn't they kill him after they found out what he did with the video?" asked Brown.

"Because that might have drawn suspicion to him at a time when they couldn't afford it. They probably decided it was smarter to keep a close watch on him and then strike if he showed any signs of trying to go around them again. They didn't know the Dabneys were planning to kill Berkshire."

He looked at Mars. "Want to pretend that door is a blocking sled?"

Mars smiled and nodded. "I feel like I wanna hit something."

They backed up and charged forward. Nearly six hundred pounds of flesh and bone hit the door at speed.

And the door lost.

They fell to the floor on top of it but were quickly on their feet. Brown hurried in after them. Decker raced forward with the two on his heels.

The interior of the building was a shell, with cables and electrical lines dangling from the ceiling, a set of scaffolding set up in one corner, some buckets with mops in them, and a few hand tools and power saws on workbenches. And a couple of sets of working lights.

The only thing missing was anyone actually working.

"Where are the workers?" said Mars.

"Maybe because the President is here?" said Brown doubtfully.

Decker said, "This all looks staged, in case anyone bothered to look."

"Wait a minute, what are you saying?" said Brown.

"The woman who kidnapped Alex? I told her that even if she killed us, the FBI was a big organization and would keep after her. She said, *No one knows what the future will bring.*"

"You're not saying?" gasped Brown.

"The target isn't *just* the President and the two other leaders. They're just the bonus. They told us the target might be symbolic? Well, the Hoover Building is pretty symbolic."

"There are over eleven thousand people in that building," Brown exclaimed.

"This way!" Decker barked. He was pointing to a set of stairs leading down. As they raced down the steps he said, "Anything from the gas company?"

"You won't be surprised to learn that they put me on hold. I'm currently listening to the Bee Gees."

They raced down two flights until they reached the basement. This too was an open shell. They looked around until Mars said, "Over here."

They joined him at the spot.

They were staring at a huge spool of cable against one wall. It was taller than Decker.

"What would this be doing down here?" asked Brown.

Decker peered through the opening in the middle of the spool where ordinarily a forklift's tines would be inserted to lift it. "I can't see through." He stuck his arm in and felt around. "It's been filled with something. It feels like concrete."

"Why would they have done that?" asked Brown.

Decker tried to look behind it, but the spool was set right against the wall. "One reason would be to completely cover up whatever might be behind it," he replied. He looked at Mars. "Ready?"

He and Mars put their shoulders against one side of the spool, squatted down, and started pushing. The spool was immensely heavy, but the two men were enormously strong and, at least in their youths, accustomed to pushing large objects around. They strained and their feet slipped against the floor, and they swore and sweated and their veins bulged, but inch by inch the spool rolled.

Finally, a hole in the wall was revealed. It had been punched right through the concrete.

Decker peered into the dark tunnel that stretched ahead.

"Anybody got a flashlight?"

Brown held up her phone and clicked on its light. Then she pulled her gun. Decker did the same.

She led the way.

Mars looked at Decker. "You got any idea what's going on here, Decker?"

Decker glanced at him, his expression probably as serious as Mars had ever seen on the man.

"The end of the chatter, Melvin. And maybe the end of everything else along with it."

80

THEY WORKED THEIR way down the tunnel, finally coming to a junction where they saw a single beam of light from far above them.

Brown pointed her phone light that way. "It's the underside of the manhole," she hissed. "The light is coming from the grab hole in the plate."

"Which means we're under the street," said Decker. "Way under the street."

"This must be what that manhole work was about," said Brown. "They were somehow connecting up from the building we were in to this utility tunnel." They hurried along and finally came to another junction. There was rubble and dirt piled up.

"They also broke through here," said Decker. "This appears to be where the utility tunnel originally ended."

They passed through the hole and into another tunnel.

"How did all this happen right under the street and no one notice?" said Mars.

"It's not right under the street," replied Brown. "We've been angling down this whole time. My guess is we're over thirty feet down and there's tons of dirt above us. Natural soundproofing."

They kept walking.

"So where the hell are we now?" asked Mars, looking nervously around.

Decker glanced at Brown. She looked ominously back at him. She said, "I think we're under the Hoover Building."

They kept moving forward until they reached another hole punched in the wall. Only this one bled off to the *side* of the tunnel they were in.

They cautiously entered a large space. They moved forward and rounded a corner. Another hole had been broken through the wall here. As they drew closer to it all three immediately began to cough and wheeze.

"What the hell is that?" gasped Mars.

"It's gas," said Decker, who pulled his jacket over his nose and mouth.

He crouched and passed through the hole and into another room. There were enormous blackened concrete columns, a low ceiling, and a pile of rubble in the center of the room.

His mouth and nose still covered, Decker looked down at the hole next to the pile of rubble. An exposed pipe was lying in the trench. It looked to him like a long, venomous serpent.

Brown and Mars, their mouths and noses covered as well, joined him and stared down at the pipe. There was a hissing sound coming from the trench.

"The pipe's been compromised," Brown said hoarsely. "That's where the gas is coming from."

"Shouldn't they have sensors or alarms for this?" said Decker.

Brown pointed to the ceiling where several white-domed devices were attached. "They do, both. But I bet they've been bypassed somehow."

"What's that thing?" said Mars, pointing to the right.

Brown and Decker looked there. And both of them froze.

It was a cylindrical metal device with wires coming out of the top. It looked like an oxygen tank that a scuba diver would use. It was attached to the pipe.

Brown immediately said, "It's a bomb."

"And it's got a timer," said Decker.

The flashing digital clock was counting down. There were four minutes to go.

"It looks too small to do too much damage," said Mars. "Especially all the way down here."

Brown shook her head and coughed. "The bomb's only the trigger. This place is full of gas. That's where the explosive punch is going to come from." She looked over at the columns. "And I'm betting those are load-bearing. The bomb goes off, the gas ignites, and those columns are going to go."

Decker added, "And the entire Hoover Building and everyone in it are going to come down. It's like how they implode buildings scheduled for demolition."

"Let's just take the bomb and get it out of here, then," said Mars.

He reached for it, but Brown grabbed his hand. "No. Do you see those blue wires? They're accelerators. You take it off the pipe the countdown clock goes to zero. And boom."

"How do you know that?"

"She was a bomb specialist in the Army," answered Decker.

Brown said, "Decker, you've got to call Bogart and tell him to get the President out of here and then evacuate this place. Now. Don't make the call from in here. I have no idea if something in the phone might either set off the gas or accelerate the countdown. And you probably can't get reception here anyway."

"But—"

"Decker, move your ass. This is what I did for a living. Go! It's the President, for God's sake."

"Okay, but—"

"Just go!"

'I'm staying with you," said Mars. "I can help."

"You can do jack shit. Now go with Decker. I'll be along when I'm done."

"But Harper—"

She screamed, "Dammit, Melvin, I've got three minutes to do this. Get out of here!"

Decker grabbed Mars's arm and pulled him away.

They reached the hole and went through it. Mars looked back at Brown, coughing and wheezing, her jacket over her nose and mouth, as she squatted over the bomb.

Then he and Decker raced down the tunnel. When they were far enough away from the gas he got a signal and called Bogart.

All Bogart said was, "Got it."

Decker looked at his watch.

Mars did too. "Two damn minutes," he said, staring at Decker. "I got to go back, Decker. I got to go help her."

"Me too."

They ran back down the tunnel. When they got close the gas was now so thick that they clutched their heads and staggered. Mars hit the wall, and Decker nearly sank to his knees, his head pounding.

"Come on!" screamed Mars, righting himself.

They stumbled down the tunnel, reached the hole, and fell through it. Both men were violently sick to their stomachs.

"Harper!" called out Mars.

He had dropped his phone and couldn't see in the darkness.

Far above, Decker thought he heard rumblings.

They were evacuating the building, his muddled mind realized.

He and Mars got up and staggered forward, but they were now both disoriented as the gas overwhelmed their brains and their lungs.

"We've got to find her, fast!" said Decker. "Before we pass out."

"Over there," Mars managed to say.

They crawled forward.

The pile of rubble was still there.

But there was no sign of Brown.

Gasping, Mars reached the hole first. Decker joined him a second later. They both stared down at the burning red numbers on the detonator.

They were not moving.

They were stuck at four seconds.

Two wires had been pulled free from the device.

"Where's Harper?" gasped Mars.

Decker, his jacket pulled over his mouth and nose, looked groggily around. Harper Brown had fallen into the tunnel two feet from the bomb, her body wedged between the pipe and the wall. Decker reached down, grabbed her arm, and pulled. Mars saw what he was doing, jumped across the hole, and helped him. With their combined strength, they quickly pulled her up. Mars slung her over his shoulder.

They stumbled to the hole in the wall and then picked up speed, racing along and occasionally bouncing off the walls of the tunnel. When they were far enough away to where they couldn't smell the gas, they stopped and Mars set Brown down. They sucked in air, their heads clearing. Brown's eyes were closed. She was turning blue. And there was something else.

"Decker, she's not breathing!" screamed Mars. He dropped to the floor of the tunnel and started performing CPR, pumping her chest.

"Help me, Decker, help me!"

Decker dropped down next to him and started breathing into Brown's mouth after pinching closed her nose.

"Come on, come on, breathe," pleaded Mars. "Please, Harper, please. Don't go. Don't leave."

He kept pumping.

And Decker kept breathing.

And despite all that, Harper Brown remained still.

81

DECKER WAS IN a suit and tie. His hair was cut and neatly parted at the side. And plastered down with lots of hair gel.

Melvin Mars was next to him, dressed as formally as his friend. Behind them was Jamison, in a black dress and matching stockings.

Decker checked his watch. "It's time."

They walked down the hall to an auditorium. It was full, and Bogart and Milligan were already there in the front row.

Bogart looked up and caught their eye. He indicated the empty seats next to them.

On the raised dais was a podium with a microphone. Behind that was the United States flag on one side and the flag of the DIA on the other. On the wall behind was the DIA seal.

Decker stared at the seal and his mind went back to the first time he'd seen it and how Brown had described it to him. The black represented the unknown, while the flames and eagle represented knowledge and intelligence.

And didn't those seem in short supply these days?

Yet they had broken through the unknown, hadn't they?

But everything came with a price.

The director of the DIA appeared from the left side of the stage and approached the podium. He brought the ceremony to order and gave a few introductory remarks. Then he turned it over to a man who came out from stage right.

Everyone in attendance instantly rose to his or her feet.

Those in uniform saluted.

The President of the United States walked to the lectern. He had no teleprompter and he carried no notes. He adjusted the mike and looked out over the audience.

"Though exactly what happened at the Hoover Building has been largely kept classified for obvious reasons, we are here today to honor a patriot who acted with great heroism, without regard for her personal safety, and whose unselfish acts saved a great many people. As you know, this award is ordinarily given out by the Office of the Director of National Intelligence. However, since I number myself among those that she saved, I owe our recipient a great personal debt. One which I'm afraid I will never be able to repay. As some of you already know, her name will today be added to the DIA's Torch Bearers Wall, not far from her father's."

In the front row Mars put a hand over his eyes and bowed his head. Decker put a supportive hand on his shoulder.

The president continued, "Thus it is with tremendous honor and the greatest respect that I present to Major Harper C. Brown the highest honor the National Intelligence community can bestow, the National Intelligence Cross for valor and heroism above and beyond the call of duty."

As one the crowd rose to its feet as Harper Brown, in her full dress uniform, appeared from backstage and wheeled herself out to the podium. From the chair, she crisply saluted the President. He returned the salute, presented the award, draping it around her neck, and then shook her hand.

They both turned to the audience as the President said, "Major Harper Brown, your National Intelligence Cross award recipient."

Everyone in the room cheered, with Melvin Mars perhaps the loudest of all.

Brown looked over the crowd, waved, and smiled even as the tears rolled down her cheeks. Then her gaze searched for and found Decker.

She smiled and her eyes crinkled.

He smiled and gave her a salute.

Then she spotted Mars next to him.

She winked.

He grinned.

When she looked away, Decker said, "The doctors think she'll be back to full strength pretty soon."

"Thank God for that."

"Why were you crying before, Melvin?"

"Damn, Decker, we almost lost her. The EMTs told us she'd probably died. But that we brought her back. It was that close."

"I know. But she's alive, Melvin. Keep focusing on that."

He looked over at Jamison, who was still clapping and grinning. He caught her eye and she said, "She looks great, doesn't she?"

"Never better," said Decker, grinning.

"And you don't look bad in a suit and tie," added Bogart.

Milligan nodded appreciatively. "In fact, you're starting to look like a real FBI agent, Decker. Maybe we need to start holding you to a dress code."

Decker's smile faded and he stopped clapping.

* * *

Decker, Mars, and Jamison got out of the car in front of Dominion Hospice. Mars was holding a box.

Jamison said, "We're going to Harper's for dinner tomorrow night, don't forget."

"Already bought the wine," said Mars. "And she lost the wheelchair for good. They said she had some temporary weakness because of what happened with the gas. But she's all fine now."

"And does that mean you're moving to the area permanently?" asked Jamison coyly.

"Already got a contract down on a house that, what do you know, is only a couple blocks from her. We can go running together."

Jamison said, "Hey, I'm in on that."

"Cool, Alex."

Mars looked at Decker. "How about you?"

"How about me what?" he groused.

"You want to run with us?"

"Only if you're chasing a criminal."

As they walked to the front doors Jamison said, "Hey, Decker, couple of questions."

He looked at her.

"So I get that Dabney's work at the FBI gave the bad guys the idea for attacking the FBI. But what was the information exactly?"

"He was working on the building's infrastructure. To do that he had been given highly classified information about the building's support structure and that gas line running under it. Plus info on the maze of tunnels under the street and the Hoover Building. That's what Berkshire's people really wanted. Bogart found out that they had already leased the building across the street, probably for surveillance purposes on the FBI. But now, with what Dabney had given them, they were able to draw up a new plan and worked around the clock to link up with the utility tunnel and take it under the Hoover Building and then sabotage the gas line. They also found out when the President and other world leaders would be there. They wanted to take them all out—kill eleven thousand people and cripple America's premier crimefighting agency."

She nodded, taking this in. "Okay, remember when Walter Dabney told Natalie about the story from Disney World? His riding in the ambulance?"

"Yeah, what about it?"

"Why did he tell her that?"

"Because he's only human."

She looked confused. "What?"

"Dabney knew at that point about his wife's spying. But he was too honorable to tell his kids. He didn't want them to hate her. But he also knew he was going to shoot Berkshire and kill himself, so he couldn't resist telling his daughter a story that had him being the one who was there for her, and not her mother."

They entered the building and started down the hall.

"Any word on what will happen to Mrs. Dabney and her daughter?" asked Mars.

"Even though she voluntarily stopped spying, Ellie Dabney is going to do some serious prison time. Natalie might get off with some sort of probation. They can't prove she knew anything about the actual espionage."

They checked in at the front desk and were led back to Joey Scott's room. The little boy was lying in the bed with his eyes closed.

Their escort, a nurse, gently roused him. When he opened his eyes, she told him about his visitors, then turned and left.

The three of them drew closer to the bed.

"Hey, Joey," said Mars.

Joey smiled weakly and lifted his hand in a wave before it dropped back to the bed.

"Got something for you."

He opened the box and pulled out a football. He held it in front of the boy and said, "Look who signed it for you."

Joey looked at the writing on the ball and his eyes grew large.

"*To my friend Joey, Peyton Manning,*" read Joey.

Decker added, "And he sent a signed picture too." He held up the framed photo so Joey could see it. "I'm going to put it on your nightstand. You can look at it whenever you want."

They all drew up chairs and sat next to the bed. Mars placed the ball next to Joey. The little boy put his hand on the pigskin and rubbed the spot where Manning had signed.

Jamison whispered to Mars, "How did you score that?"

"Friend of a friend who works at the NFL. They told me that when Manning heard about Joey he wanted to fly out here and meet him. I think he's actually going to do that."

"Wow," said Jamison. She took a book from her bag and opened it to a certain page. "Joey, I'm going to finish reading *The Prisoner of Azkaban* to you, okay? The last part is so exciting!"

He smiled. "Okay."

While Jamison started to read, Decker put his hands on the bed rail and stared down at Joey. Every once in a while, Joey would look up at them and smile.

And Decker found himself each time smiling back.

He had lost Molly at about the same age Joey was now.

And he knew that Joey didn't have much longer to live. It hadn't been that long since Decker had first met the boy, and Joey already seemed much weaker. Decker could see his body shutting down little by little.

But for now, Decker saw no blue at all. He just saw a boy smiling while holding a football signed by a hero of his.

Decker's life was complicated, his future probably even more so. But for right now he forgot about having a perfect memory, or the horrific way by which he'd acquired it. He stopped thinking for at least a little while about the family he had lost.

He glanced at the two people next to him, who were his friends. Two people who, despite his many shortcomings, would always be his friends.

Then he looked back down at Joey. The boy's eyes were closed, but his hand remained firmly attached to the precious football.

Decker reached out a big hand and gently stroked Joey's head. As he did so he felt his eyes moisten.

But for now, right this instant, things were okay.

* * *

Decker had taken to thinking of this now as "his" bench. The skies were growing darker and the wind was picking up. The river flowed in front of him and in the swift currents he could see his own thoughts hurtling along. He put his hands in the pockets of his jacket and closed his eyes.

Yet this time he was not engaging his prodigious memory. No perfect recall was required for what he wanted to think about. For a man who didn't like change, there was a great deal of it heading his way. A new job at the FBI. Being a "landlord" with Jamison. Mars moving here. Harper Brown becoming a fixture in his life through her relationship with Mars. He didn't even know if Jamison wanted to continue working at the FBI. She might leave and do something else. For all he knew Mars and Brown might get married and move away. Bogart and Milligan might get transferred.

And then it would just be him.

Amos Decker from Small-town Ohio, transplanted to this very strange land known as Washington, D.C.

Alone.

Again.

He rubbed his eyes and put his hand back in his pocket. The good moment sitting with Joey Scott had been a welcome one, but it was now over. Though he could never equate what he was going through with the terminal illness that the little boy was enduring, Decker knew that his future was crowded with uncertainty. His damaged mind could change at any time. He could morph into yet another person as unrecognizable as the one he was now, eroding even further the person he used to be. The sheer force of his memories could end up destroying him. He could be living in a cardboard box again. He could be...alone, with nothing and no one. As the anxiety he was feeling built, he closed his eyes and took several deep breaths.

Just keep it together, Decker. Just keep it together.

"You look like you could use this."

He opened his eyes and saw Jamison standing there. She had two cups of takeout coffee. She handed one to him and sat down on the bench.

"How'd you know where I was?" he asked, rubbing his eyes again and not looking at her.

"I have my little sources," she said, smiling and then taking a sip of her coffee. "It's pretty here."

"Is it?" asked Decker.

She glanced at him. "You look like you have a lot on your mind."

"Just the usual."

"There is nothing *usual* about you."

He drank his coffee and said, "So Melvin moving here? Him and Brown a couple? What about you?"

"What about me what?"

Trying to keep his voice nonchalant and failing miserably, Decker said, "You going to stick with the FBI?"

"Are you?"

"I don't have anything else in my life, Alex."

"I think you have a lot more in your life than you think."

"So you'll stay?"

"If you do, I do."

He looked at her strangely. "That simple?"

She nodded.

"Why?" he asked.

"I'm surprised you have to ask, Decker."

"What do you mean?"

"That's what I meant when I said I had *your* back."

She tapped her coffee cup against his, sat back, and closed her eyes.

Decker watched her for a few moments and then turned to look at the river.

This time he kept his eyes wide open.

ACKNOWLEDGMENTS

To Michelle, the #1 in my life.

To Michael Pietsch, for always piloting the ship with a deft touch.

To Lindsey Rose, Andy Dodds, Karen Torres, Anthony Goff, Bob Castillo, Michele McGonigle, Andrew Duncan, Christopher Murphy, Dave Epstein, Tracy Dowd, Brian McLendon, Matthew Ballast, Lukas Fauset, Deb Futter, Beth deGuzman, Thomas Louie, Oscar Stern, Michele Karas, Stephanie Sirabian, Brigid Pearson, Flamur Tonuzi, Blanca Aulet, Joseph Benincase, Tiffany Sanchez, Ali Cutrone, Mary Urban, Barbara Slavin, Anne Twomey, Sean Ford, Rachel Hairston, and everyone at Grand Central Publishing, for going the extra mile for me.

To Aaron and Arleen Priest, Lucy Childs Baker, Lisa Erbach Vance, Mitch Hoffman (and thanks for another fine editing job), Frances Jalet-Miller, John Richmond, and Matt Belford, for being great friends and advocates.

To Anthony Forbes Watson, Jeremy Trevathan, Trisha Jackson, Katie James, Alex Saunders, Sara Lloyd, Amy Lines, Stuart Dwyer, Geoff Duffield, Jonathan Atkins, Anna Bond, Sarah Willcox, Leanne Williams, Sarah McLean, Charlotte Williams, and Neil Lang at Pan Macmillan, for continuing to lift me to stellar heights overseas.

To Praveen Naidoo and his team at Pan Macmillan in Australia, for a fantastic job.

To Caspian Dennis and Sandy Violette, for being so wonderful.

To Kyf Brewer and Orlagh Cassidy, for your terrific audio performances.

To Steven Maat and the entire Bruna team, for doing a great job.

To Roland Ottewell, for a terrific copyediting job.

And to Kristen White and Michelle Butler, for keeping Columbus Rose sailing straight and true.

ABOUT THE AUTHOR

David Baldacci is a global #1 bestselling author. His books are published in over 45 languages, with more than 110 million copies in print, and have been adapted for both feature film and television. David Baldacci is also the cofounder, along with his wife, of the Wish You Well Foundation, a nonprofit organization dedicated to supporting literacy efforts across America. Still a resident of his native Virginia, he invites you to visit him at DavidBaldacci.com and his foundation at WishYouWellFoundation.org.

Lethal government assassin Will Robie returns in David Baldacci's explosive new thriller...

Will Robie comes home from a mission overseas to discover that his boss—codenamed Blue Man—has vanished. His last known location was in remote Colorado, and there have been no other sightings or communications since. But there is violence brewing in this small mountain town, and Robie and his sometime-partner Jessica Reel will be lucky if they make it out alive, with or without Blue Man...

Look for *END GAME*

Coming in November 2017

A preview follows.

CHAPTER

I

THIS EXACT MOMENT in time would be the absolute safest that Will Robie would be for the next twenty-four hours.

The undercarriage of multiple reinforced wheels touched down, grabbed the tarmac, and the thrust reversers engaged. The world's largest commercial airliner taxied to a stop at the gate. Four doors, both forward and aft, on the upper and lower cabins opened. The passengers trooped down the jetways and into Terminal Five at Heathrow Airport.

The English skies were slicked with fat, darkened clouds and the rain was falling.

Robie, wearing a navy blue two-piece tailored suit and fitted white collared shirt, was among hundreds of passengers deplaning the British Airways superjumbo A380 just landed from Washington, D.C.

The flight had become bumpy midway over the Atlantic. However, Robie hadn't noticed. With his flat business-class seat, he'd slept pretty much the whole way.

He cleared customs through the non-E.U. citizen section, informing the border officer that he was there solely on business of an academic nature. He had carried on his single small bag and thus had no reason afterward to go to baggage claim. Everything he would need was already in London.

It was seven-thirty a.m. local time.

Robie took a multicolored taxi into the city, a journey that, with traffic and the rainy weather, took well over an hour. He was dropped off at an address near Marylebone Road. It wasn't a hotel, but a nondescript private row house near Marylebone's juncture with Baker Street. Robie punched in a code on the electronic box set next to the front door and the fortified portal unlocked. He walked in, locked the door behind him, and took the stairs two at a time.

He changed his clothes, his two-piece suit and dress shirt exchanged for more casual wear. He popped open a wall safe in the closet and took out the flash drive. His agency used cloud computing, only it didn't fully trust that it couldn't be hacked, since these days it seemed anything could be hacked. He pulled out his laptop and inserted the drive in the USB port. He tapped some keys and up on the screen appeared the only reason he had come to London.

It was a read-only document, and it was not remotely business of an academic nature.

He absorbed the information on the screen. It ended with a note from his superior, Blue Man, real name Roger Walton. The epithet "Blue Man" came from his exalted position at their agency. The note was brief and to the point, just like Blue Man always was.

I won't wish you luck, because it's never really about luck. You can do this for one simple reason: You're Will Robie.

Robie understood that in those few words was a volume's worth of meaning.

I am Will Robie and I've been through hell and back. This is just another day at the office.

He next performed an NSA-level wipe of the flash drive, tantamount to smashing it flat with a brick and then setting it afire. The ones and zeroes were permanently gone, now existing only in his memory.

He stretched out on the bed and stared up at the ceiling.

Mississippi seemed a long time ago.

His father seemed a long time ago.

Everything seemed a long time ago.

He was back in harness and glad for it, because all the other elements of his life sucked.

Don't bullshit yourself. This is *your life.*

Like the NSA cleanse on the flash drive, he erased these thoughts from his head and closed his eyes. Despite his rest on the plane, he needed sleep. He would not be getting any tonight. He set his internal clock to wake him six hours later.

He rose in the afternoon and checked the sky. Still cloudy, but no more rain. Since this was London, the little island in the middle of big water with no buffer against any punishing weather system heading its way, that could change at any moment.

He went out, ate a late lunch at a pub, and walked. His relentless gait carried him past many buildings and hundreds of people walking along in what he knew was blissful ignorance of what was coming. Then again, full knowledge might have started a panic. And they couldn't have that, could they?

Instead, they had sent Will Robie.

He returned to his row house, made some calls on a secure line that bounced off one particular bird in the sky, and was told that everything was a go for the moment. He knew that could always change.

Like a false start in the hundred-meter dash. Cocked and locked and fired and then called off. It could be unsettling.

Robie sat by the window for two hours, like a sentry

on watch, missing nothing. This place was heavily, though discreetly, fortified and monitored 24/7 by eyes on another continent. Still, his stone cold rule was to rely on himself and no one else. He was the one who would die if everything went to shit. The "eyes on the other continent" might simply get a memo on how to fix the cock-up in the future.

A little too late to do him any good.

Darkness came as the globe spun on its axis and another part of the world got to see the light.

He checked his phone. The solitary bird in the sky told him that his mission was still a go.

Big Ben chimed midnight. It was a soothing, familiar melody to most Brits. To Robie it was like the sound of a time card being punched.

He donned a customized lightweight one-piece waterproof black motorcycle suit and left by the back door. He opened the locked door of a garage in the mews, climbed astride a black Ducati XDiavel parked there, and key-started it. The big engine bled noise and power through its stacked twin oval-exit pipes. He slipped on his helmet, popped the kickstand, gunned the throttle, and blew out of the garage riding a power plant that displaced over twelve hundred ccs at a max rpm of 9500. Its Bosch fuel injection system was a full ride-by-wire package.

For most, this was simply an expensive toy that, fully racked out, would set you back about twenty grand.

Tonight it was simply Robie's ride to work.

He headed northwest.

The bike's Pirelli Diablo tires gripped the asphalt firmly and threw up rainwater as he flashed through nearly empty streets. A bit later his destination was up ahead. Well, it was the *first* of his destinations tonight. He thundered into an alley and then quickly slowed.

He cut the power to the bike, hopped off, and used a tool hidden behind a dustbin to lift the manhole cover located there. This was destination number one. He used the metal rungs to clamber down about a hundred feet.

He kept his helmet on for one reason only.

He hit a switch at the back of the helmet and it became the latest-generation panoramic night-vision optics, the same platform used by American combat pilots. It enhanced the visuals in the darkened utility tunnel to such a degree that it was almost as if he was on the surface of the sun, only without the heat. Researchers were now working on contact lenses utilizing a thin layer of graphene between glass that could take the place of the current bulky devices, but the percentage of light pickup was not yet where it needed to be to make the innovation viable.

So for now Robie wore a helmet to see in the dark.

To outsiders this all would no doubt seem very much like a James Bond film, but for Robie it was all standard operating procedure to enable him to do what he did.

High tech to kill.

And it wasn't like the other side came to the battle with six-shooters and World War II–era optics.

He looked at his watch. He was one minute ahead of schedule. He slowed his pace. Early in his line of work was never a good thing.

He was forty-one years old, about six-one, a buck eighty, and physically ripped because his job required it. His endurance levels and pain tolerances were off the chart, again, because they had to be. He had been selected for this line of work with the basic requirements already in place: He had a body, he had a mind, he feared basically nothing, and he apparently had not a single nerve in his body.

And then over the years they had ground into him a

whole other being, still possessing the basics plus a hell of a lot more.

Some days it was hard for Robie to see where the machine ended and the human began. If the human was in fact still there. In Mississippi it had shown itself. Now? It had receded.

Perhaps forever.

His face was lean and his eyes both deep-set and alert. His hair was always cut short because he had no time to bother with it. He had old wounds and scars over his torso and limbs; each told a story he would rather forget.

As he walked along he moved his right arm in a slow circle motion. All surgically repaired; scar tissue removed, tendons and ligaments all *tidied up,* as the Brits would say. It was ninety-nine percent of what it used to be, the docs had assured him. That was really good. But really good rarely cut it in Robie's world.

They rebuilt me. But am I as good as I was? Or am I a slightly lesser version?

He would find out tonight if the missing one percent made the key difference between him walking away from this, or remaining behind as a corpse.

Destination number two was just up ahead.

If the Ducati had gotten him to this point, what was coming up would get him back.

Alive.

He used a key to unlock a door set in the wall of the tunnel he was in.

Inside, he gunned up.

H&K UMP45 chambered in .45 ACP with a customized thirty-round box mag. He checked all working parts of the weapon and then slung it over his shoulder. He slipped two extra mags into long pockets on his one-piece designed for just this purpose.

He figured if he couldn't do the job with ninety rounds he didn't deserve to come back. Yet just in case there were twin M11s chambered in ten mil with laser sights built under the barrel. Where the dot hit so did the bullet.

He slipped the gun belt around his waist. Both pistols rode on the left side so he could pull with his dominant right hand, though if it came to it, he could kill ambidextrously quite efficiently.

A German-made KM2000 combat knife in its holder was attached to his belt.

Two M84 stun grenades were cradled in pockets on the rear of his belt.

Robie closed the door behind him and walked on.

Destination number three was a quarter mile away.

In a fairly short time, Will Robie would know if he would get to see another sunrise or not.

CHAPTER

2

Oxford Circus.

It was currently the busiest station on the London Underground, having overtaken both Waterloo and King's Cross the previous year in a back-and-forth battle for the statistical title. It was in an upscale part of London with pricey and fashionable Regent and Bond Streets resting above it. The Underground carried nearly three billion passengers total per year, and nearly a hundred million of them came through the Oxford Circus station annually.

The Underground had suffered a terrorist attack on July 7, 2005, when Islamist extremists had blown themselves up on three separate train cars. A fourth had detonated on a London bus. In all, fifty-two victims were killed.

The explosive devices used that infamous day were powerful, but not nearly so powerful as what was currently being planned.

A cobalt bomb was at the center of this. One had never been detonated before. Also known as a salted bomb, it was a thermonuclear device designed to maximize the radiation fallout, leaving a large area contaminated for a hundred or more years.

Fortunately, it was a very difficult thing to accomplish.

Unfortunately, it was not impossible.

Even more unfortunately, one was now in London.

The mic in Robie's helmet relayed information to him as he walked along.

His final destination was just up ahead.

As he walked along he spun a suppressor onto the barrel of the UMP, and then did the same for the twin M11s.

Stealth was called for tonight.

He reholstered the military-grade pistols and touched his chest. What was underneath there might end up saving his life tonight. He had the same protection on both thighs. Right below these shields were his femoral arteries, twin pipelines of massive blood flow. If those got pierced, he was a dead man. The bleedout from a punctured femoral was almost never survivable.

Four people had given their lives in order for the intel leading up to the mission tonight to make its way to the Americans, who had then shared it with the Brits. They were close allies and had been pretty much ever since the English redcoats burned down the American White House. Yet this mission had drawn them even closer. According to the intel, the planned London op was merely a dress rehearsal for what would come later, in the United States.

Just like a manufacturer did in trying to commercialize a new product, terrorists needed to work the kinks out too.

The kink was why Robie was now ascending a hundred feet to the surface.

Where he would be coming out would not be another alley. It would be a basement.

Of the four people to die in this operation so far, the third had sacrificed her life to maneuver the target to stay in this building. Situated on the outskirts of London on a lonely street of few residences, the structure had been used during

World War II as a safe house and operations center for senior government personnel. An escape tunnel and bomb shelter had been paramount, and so they had been added. Over the last seven decades a tile floor had been put over the basement concrete and the trapdoor covered.

And forgotten.

It was no longer covered. And it sure as hell was no longer forgotten.

London was an ancient city, and no one truly knew or understood all the passages and tunnels and labyrinths that lay underneath it, or how they all connected. A series of tunnels beneath that basement eventually intersected with a concrete pipeline that, with some minimal wall piercing, would allow one eventually to reach an equipment storage room under Oxford Circus station. In that room the cobalt bomb was to be planted and detonated at the busiest hour of the day for the station. In all, it was estimated that over two million persons would be affected by the blast..

And the high-priced, densely populated area would be uninhabitable for a century or two at least.

Some dress rehearsal, thought Robie.

He didn't want to see a far larger encore on American soil.

The terror cell he was targeting tonight planned to use the tunnel to their advantage.

Robie planned to use it first, and to their supreme disadvantage.

The reasons why an army of police and special forces were not descending on this cell instead of one man were complicated but, distilled to bare essentials, easily understood.

Panic.

When an army moved, it could not be kept a secret.

But when one man moved, a secret could be maintained.

And to avoid revealing what had been planned to the world and causing just such a panic as the terrorists no doubt would have rejoiced over, Robie had been sent in to have a shot at taking them down. Alone.

However, nothing was being left to chance. There *was* a hidden army surrounding the home. If Robie failed, the army wouldn't.

Of course, then it would no longer be a secret. And London and the rest of the world would be reeling from this for God knew how long. It would not be as bad as if the cobalt bomb had actually exploded, but in the warped way terrorism worked, a defeat could be turned into victory simply by scaring the shit out of the civilized world and forcing people to live in constant fear.

There were two homes on either side of the target. The residents in them had been prevented from returning home that night. Thus Robie had a bit of breathing room to operate and still keep the mission out of the morning broadcasts.

Hence the trio of suppressors on his gun barrels.

He finished climbing the rungs to the trapdoor. Though the people inside had no idea their mission had been compromised, they had taken standard protection procedures. The trapdoor was securely locked and also alarmed. But using three different tools provided him, Robie ensured that it no longer was locked or alarmed.

He received one more communication in his headset.

"Vee-one."

It was the same warning given pilots on takeoff. Vee-one meant there was no going back.

Robie acknowledged that command and then turned his comm pack off. From now, until he was either dead or his opponents were, there would be nothing more said. It wasn't like he'd have the time to chat.

His helmet was fitted with a wireless camera so that his handlers could see everything that he could. They would either watch Robie win, or see the bullets that would kill him.

And all from a safe distance.

An M11 in his right hand, he eased open the trapdoor and looked around.

Nothing.

He climbed up and quietly set the trapdoor back into place. The basement was what one would expect in a crappy old house in a tattered neighborhood—moldy and dirty.

But there was one element of interest. In a far corner was a metal box about six feet in length. He slipped over there, squatted down, pulled an instrument from his belt, and ran it over the box. He looked at the readout meter.

Cobalt bomb confirmed. It wasn't armed yet. They wouldn't do so until they moved it to Oxford Circus.

And Robie also knew that he would keep himself between them and the bomb at all times.

He holstered his M11 and readied his UMP.

He rose and moved to the wooden stairs. The fourth riser up squeaked. Thus he went from the third to the fifth.

There were currently seventeen people inside this place in addition to him.

His goal was to kill sixteen of them.

The fire selector on his UMP was set to two-shot burst. One shot was enough to kill any man if placed properly, but Robie had left no room for chance. Two shots would guarantee the kill beyond doubt.

The basement door was partially open.

He peered through it into the kitchen.

Two men sat at a table drinking what looked to be cups of coffee. The smell permeating through to the doorway confirmed this. The men were pulling a late night. They needed a stimulant. Well, he would provide something far stronger than coffee.

He looked at his watch through his panoramic goggles.

The second hand was just sweeping to twelve.

Four...three...two...

On cue, the lights in the house went out as the power was cut.

Through his helmet Robie saw the two men clear as day jerk forward and then stand.

And then he watched them fall from suppressed bursts delivered to their chests.

Two down, fourteen to go.

Robie was through the kitchen in three seconds and then hit the hallway. His finger nudged the shot selector to full auto.

He did so because darkness tended to make people congregate closer together.

Sure enough, coming down the narrow hall were three men, all with guns.

They opened fire. With pistols.

Robie pulled the UMP's trigger and two seconds and twenty-six rounds of concentrated fire later there were three more dead men on the floor of this humble abode. The UMP's ejector sent the spent casings tumbling to the floor, where they sounded like metal pearls from a broken necklace.

Five down, eleven to go.

He ejected the mag, slapped in a fresh one, and turned and rolled to his right as more gunfire came at him.

He counted two heads through his goggles.

He emptied half his UMP mag at them.

Seven down, nine to go.

Two more men appeared at the head of the stairs and fired down at Robie.

He could see that they had on NVGs as well, so his tactical advantage had lessened.

He pulled a stun grenade, released the pin, and threw it up the stairs at the same time he looked away.

The blinding flash of light did not blind him, nor did the concussive sound paralyze him since his helmet cushioned him from this effect.

The two men at the top of the stairs could not claim the same.

One tumbled down and landed at the bottom of the stairs.

One slash across the neck from his KM2000 severed two critical arteries, and Robie added another body to his bag tonight.

Eight down, an equal number to go.

The other man slowly rose at the top of the stairs, but was obviously concussed. He fell back down and lay unconscious. That was the only thing that saved his life.

That and two men attacking Robie from his right and left flanks.

The M11s came out, one in each hand. Robie simultaneously aimed an M11 at each attacker and then trigger-pulled ten shots from each gun, sweeping up and down from chest to thigh, the arc of fire evenly spaced over the relevant radius. It was a kill-zone field of fire delivered with max efficiency.

Jacketed rounds tore through flesh. These sounds were followed by two thumps, as corpses hit carpet.

Ten down, six to go.

Since the cat was definitely out of the bag, he sprayed the stairwell using the rest of his second mag on the UMP. He then raced up the steps.

A bullet fired from above struck him in the abdomen.

The liquid armor vest he wore hardened within a millisecond, catching the round and wringing out virtually all of its kinetic energy by displacing it along the breadth of the vest. The armor then lost its rigidity and became flexible once more.

Robie had no idea who had invented this stuff, but if he survived tonight, he would buy the person a drink if he ever met them.

His second stun grenade flushed out the shooter and Robie shot him once in the knee with an M11 to incapacitate, then performed the kill shot to the head on the upper stairwell.

Eleven down, five to go.

He reached the upper hall, reholstered the M11s, and reloaded the UMP with his final mag, just as a body launched from a dark corner and blindsided him. They tumbled back down the stairs. His attacker had a gutting knife and he managed to strike Robie in the thigh. Robie's liquid armor once more seized up and the knife didn't even penetrate to the skin.

Robie's right hand clamped down on the wrist with the knife. He torqued himself around so that he was on top when they slammed into the floor at the bottom of the stairs. The man beneath him was stunned by the impact, but only for a second.

That was still a second too long for survival.

Robie had pulled an M11 and blown a contact wound into the man's left temple at the same time he used the man's own knife to slit his throat. Arterial spray danced across his visor.

He hoped the handlers back in their safe space were enjoying the show.

It wasn't nearly as much fun on his end.

Twelve down, four to go.

He rose, turned, and rolled out of the way as a volley of machine-gun fire blew down the stairs, ripping off part of the handrail, shredding the wall, and exploding a slew of the risers.

With his night vision Robie could see from where it was coming.

Instead of trying to attack back up the stairs, he moved to his left, where the upper part of the stairway was partially covered by the wall rising from the lower floor.

He pointed the UMP at a forty-five-degree angle up and five clicks to the left. He pressed the trigger and fired half his mag. The ACP rounds blasted through the cheap drywall. Robie counted to three and watched as the shooter's body rolled down the stairs and landed at the bottom on top of the gent who'd had his brain blown out courtesy of Robie.

Robie made sure the shooter was dead with an M11 round dotting the man's forehead.

Thirteen dead, one concussed and unconscious, so three to go.

And those three were upstairs.

Now it became a pure tactical game. They had the high ground and Robie the low. In order to attack, he would have to move through a funnel where they could concentrate their fire, and he couldn't count on the liquid armor to see him through.

What Robie wanted was the high ground, and as he looked to his left, he saw a way to take it.

He popped open the window, climbed out, and found handholds in the uneven brick surface. On past missions he'd scaled what appeared to be sheer rock walls, so this was not a stretch for him.

The window was just above. The floor plan of the house told him exactly where this opening would take him. He spent three seconds calculating—his allotted time to think at any interval during a mission such as this.

Holding on to the windowsill with one hand, he jimmied the window with his knife. He did a controlled tumble through the opening and rolled up to a defensive position. His climb outside had given him the tactical advantage. He went into full offensive mode.

Robie charged into the upstairs hall and saw one man peering cautiously down the stairs, unaware that his rear flank was fully exposed.

His life ended with a pair of M11 rounds in his back.

Fourteen down, two to go.

The next man came out of another bedroom with the exact same weapon that Robie held.

It was UMP versus UMP.

But not really. It wasn't just the hardware. A gun was a gun. The same models worked pretty much exactly the same.

What really mattered was the software.

And the shooter was always the software.

Robie threw himself through a doorway as the muzzle of the opposing UMP swung up at him.

He transferred his UMP fully to his right hand, making sure by touch that his selector was still on full auto. The only part of him exposed was his gun and the lower part of his arm. He used the doorjamb as his fulcrum, because the recoil kick on a UMP was not always kind if the collapsible stock was not firmly against one's shoulder. That might foul the shot, and Robie didn't have the time for that.

The UMPs fired at the same time.

The man's UMP managed to take a chunk of polymer off Robie's weapon.

Robie's UMP managed to blow the head off the man.

Robie dropped the UMP, his ammo exhausted.

Fifteen down, one to go.

But what a one it would turn out to be.

The young woman stepped out of a room and into the upstairs hall.

In her hand was not a weapon, at least not a conventional one.

Clenched in her fingers was a dead man's—or in this case a dead *woman's*—trigger wired to the vest around her torso. Strapped there were six packs of Semtex wired together. More than enough to collapse the house and kill her and Robie, and maybe crack the belly of the cobalt bomb in the basement and radiate the neighborhood until the twenty-second century.

He understood at once. She was the designated failsafe.

She smiled at him.

He didn't return it.

The KM2000 flashed through the air. It severed the wire from the trigger to the suicide vest before coming to stick in the wall.

The woman looked down at the useless trigger, then back up at Robie. She screamed at him even as her hand went to the vest.

Robie did not wait for her to detonate another way. He shot her in the head and she fell to the floor wrapped in her bombs.

Sixteen down.

None to go.

Time clock punched.

Sunrise coming.

Ninety-nine percent was apparently good enough.

CHAPTER

3

THE CLEANUP WAS quick and efficient. To keep things as secret as possible, they made use of the same tunnel that Robie had. The house was going to be razed in the next week and the debris buried forever. The tunnel was being permanently plugged. Any complaints about the sounds of explosions or gunfire that night would be referred to the appropriate agency, with instructions to bury it as deeply as the remains of the house.

The concussed survivor was revived and would be interrogated until he gave up every secret he would ever have. Then he would disappear into the permanent shadows with no ability to harm anyone again.

The cobalt bomb was removed and disarmed and would be reverse-engineered to see how the terror cell had done it. Neither the Brits nor the Americans were under the illusion that a terrorist cell group alone had had the wherewithal to pull this off. This operation smacked of a serious institutional backer. Whether it was the Russians or the Iranians or even the Chinese—who were making grand noises about wanting to play in the international warfare big leagues—they would trace this op back to its source.

Then the diplomats would have their shot at deescalating this sucker.

If the statesmen failed, it would be the generals' turn.

And no one wanted that scenario.

Robie had received accolades from all professional quarters for his work that night. When the British tactical team had entered the house, Robie had taken off his helmet and was calmly sitting on the couch in the living room.

The team took its time viewing all the carnage, including the suicide bomber, and being calmly filled in by Robie on how he had disarmed her with only a second to spare and no margin of error. "Bloody hell"'s resonated from all corners of the house as the cleanup team saw the man's handiwork.

One armored assaulter had sat down next to Robie and asked him if he needed anything, politely addressing Robie as "sir."

Robie had shaken his head and said, "I'm good."

"Actually, sir, you're far better than good. In fact, you're the best I've ever seen, mate."

Robie appreciated the sentiment, but he had exited the house with no positive feelings, despite having defeated a maniacal attempt to throw the world off its proper axis.

He was now wheels up on a private ride back to the United States.

He rubbed his gut and then his thigh where the rounds and the knife had struck, respectively.

Either one would have disabled him. And then he would have been fresh meat to kill. Just another corpse on the floor.

And that made a person think.

Robie closed his eyes and tried to sleep. But while slumber had come easily on the flight over, it was not so easy on the way back. He had killed sixteen people the previous night. And nearly been killed himself about a half dozen times.

It was all in a day's work for him, on one level.

On another level, part of him couldn't process it.

It wasn't like an endorphin high after winning a Super Bowl or World Series, chiefly because nobody died in those events. However, it *was* clearly a contest, of sorts. There *were* winners and losers in Robie's world, only the losers left the field of battle in body bags, not with second-place trophies.

He opened his eyes and his thoughts reached back to Mississippi.

The reunion with his father. A reunion from hell. But the ending was what mattered. And it had ended better than it had begun.

And he and Jessica Reel had been together. Battered, but together.

Now nearly six months had passed and Robie hadn't seen Reel in all that time. He had called, emailed, and texted. Nothing. She was still working for the agency, that he knew, but he had no idea where. He had asked. And received not a single answer.

After what happened in Cantrell, Reel—then in a wheelchair because of injuries sustained during their time there—had told Robie that they would always have each other. That they might fall, but together they were unbeatable.

That had been the only thing keeping him going through his own rehabilitation.

Yet when he'd been released from rehab and was working his way back into shape, Jessica Reel had not been there. No calls. No emails. No texts. Nothing.

So much for together being unbeatable.

They'd obviously been meaningless words.

He slipped something from his pocket.

It was a drawing of two stick figures with a heart between them.

It had been drawn by his half brother, Tyler Robie. Robie

hadn't known he even had a sibling until he had gone back to Cantrell. The little boy had some developmental issues, but he indisputably possessed a huge heart. Robie intended to visit him and his father at some point. He just didn't know exactly when that might happen.

And right now his head was wrapped up with Jessica Reel.

Or the lack thereof in his life.

He landed back in D.C. and went immediately to his apartment, a nondescript space in an unremarkable building near Dupont Circle.

Robie had nothing of a personal nature in his apartment.

But that was about to change.

He took out the stick-figure drawing, inserted it into a picture frame, and placed it on the nightstand in his bedroom.

And that's when he saw it.

The envelope on his bed.

There was no writing on it.

It had not been there when he had left for London.

Robie's first instincts were defensive. He slipped the gun from its holster and held it at the ready.

He gripped the envelope with his free hand and shook the letter out.

It was one page folded over.

He recognized the handwriting. The words were few, but still managed to cut through him like the KM2000 had sliced neck arteries back in London.

It's complicated. I'm sorry. JR

Robie put his gun away and folded the letter back over and placed it in his pocket.

He walked over to the window.

It was dark now and the rain had started.

This was a perfect time for Robie to take a walk. He

didn't like crowds. And right now he was in no mood for sunny and fair weather.

He made his way along his favorite route, which led him invariably to Memorial Bridge. Arlington Cemetery was across the bridge and the Lincoln Memorial was behind him. He stood by the rampart and looked down at the waters of the Potomac.

It was flowing far more freely than his thoughts.

What exactly did she mean by "it's complicated"? They both knew everything about their lives was complicated. So what had changed between Mississippi and the note being left on his bed?

He looked around.

The last time he had been here, Blue Man had appeared out of the darkness and given him some much-needed advice. Robie could always count on Blue Man. He always told him not what he wanted to hear, but what he needed to hear.

As if on cue a figure appeared out of the darkness.

Only it wasn't Blue Man.

The gun came out and was pointed at the approaching figure.

The person stopped.

"They told me you might be here."

"Who are you?" asked Robie.

The person drew close enough so that the lights on the bridge illuminated them.

It was a woman.

But it was not Jessica Reel.

"I know you," said Robie, peering at her.

She nodded. "I work with Blue Man."

Robie looked around. "Where is he? Why did he send you?"

"He didn't. I mean, he *couldn't*."

"Why not?"

"Because Blue Man has disappeared."

CHAPTER

4

S<small>AND.</small>

And not from a fun day at the beach.

It was in your mouth, your lungs, and your nose.

And possibly your dreams.

Gritty, omnipresent, there was no way to avoid it.

Jessica Reel was using a tactical scout sniper periscope to safely get eyes on those she would later try to kill.

Iraq looked like Iraq had ten years ago, at least to her. Buildings were in ruins, people were dying violently, armies massed and attacked. Terrorists counterattacked, deploying an array of weapons either stolen or bought from countries around the world.

Everything was for shit here, although the politicians tried to put positive spins on it all. Or blame others for when the spin no longer worked.

Right now, the fighting was divided neatly into urban and desert.

Reel wasn't sure which she preferred. Urban was more complicated and potentially more lethal. One wrong step and a hidden IED would take you away from life in a millisecond. Or someone you thought was an ally would confront you with a C4 suicide pack strapped around his waist. Or a kid hiding a gun under his shirt would walk up to you asking for candy, and you would have a millisecond to decide whether to kill him or not.

In the desert there was nothing between you and them except sand. And killing from long range could come at any moment. Reel knew this for a fact, being a major source of her country's long-range kills during this tour of duty.

She lowered the periscope and made some notes in her log, or DOPE, book, as snipers called it. In it she had made references and notes on every shot she had fired during this deployment. All the hits and the rare misses.

She learned the most from the misses.

She was part of a fifteen-person team that had only two snipers. She was also the only female in the group. They didn't care that she could run three miles in under eighteen minutes or that she could do twenty or more dead-hang pull-ups or perform two hundred crunches in four minutes. That was what the Marines required at their sniper school. Years ago Reel had passed every test there and been the first female candidate to complete the course successfully.

They only cared whether she could do her job, which meant pulling the trigger and eliminating someone on the other team whose only goal was to kill Reel and her team.

Still, there had been some grumbling about her from some of the men, mostly the younger ones. Younger ones these days were those barely freed from their teens. After the first two days, when Reel had laid down nine out of nine targets, the grumblings had mysteriously vanished. And she was suddenly one of the guys.

Every member of the team was only about one thing: the mission.

The second unspoken goal, but of no less importance to all of them, was survival. None of them wanted to die in the desert. All of them wanted to get back home—Reel included, though she really had no home to go back to.

And a sniper who could consistently kill people trying to kill you was a valuable friend indeed.

Tikrit, Ramadi, Falluja, and finally Mosul had been taken back from the enemy. Although like putting Humpty Dumpty back together again, it was proving nearly impossible to make the situation right. The terrorists had had a long time to inflict maximum destruction on these cities and the people living there. Most of the places were simply uninhabitable because basic things like water and sewage lines were no long operating and electrical power was spotty at best. And added to that, the cities were still filled with hidden explosives and other death traps.

But rebuilding was not Reel's job. Her mission was to kill as many of the enemy as she could.

Her group consisted of Americans, Brits, French, Australians, and two Iraqi force members who still looked at her with unfriendly eyes, even though she could outshoot and outwork both of them. And maybe that was why they looked at her the way they did, other than her being a woman, which in this part of the world was disqualifying for most occupations, and certainly one that required wielding a gun.

The boom of mortar fire and RPGs constantly filled the air along with gunfire and IEDs sending the unwary or the unlucky to early graves. Overhead, called-in airstrikes happened with great frequency, with the U.S. providing most of the muscle in the sky.

Reel had been here nearly six months, the only member of the team to volunteer for this duty. She was not in the military; she was from a civilian agency that performed military support, and thus she could be somewhere else in the world if she so desired.

Reel did not so desire.

She sniped during the day for the most part unless there was a particular mission on. At night, she was still on duty, but would alternate with her partner. Each sometimes acted as spotter for the other, and sometimes, due to the dictates of combat, they went solo.

She knew one thing clearly: She was the single most lethal person on this battlefield, able to precisely and consistently kill at over twelve hundred meters. The other side knew this as well. Thus the bull's-eye on her was a large one. And if she were ever captured?

Well, in addition to being an American and a woman, snipers historically were not known for receiving a kind reception from their captors.

If she were about to be captured, Reel had long since decided to eat a round instead.

The time came and she readied her rifle.

Years ago her head had been turned into a ballistic computer, analyzing on paper the key physical forces on a bullet fired long-range: altitude, temperature, humidity, and wind, particularly wind two-thirds of the way to the target. But now, with long-range sniper systems, these calculations were done faster and more accurately by machine than a human ever could. Automation was hitting even the ranks of the elite snipers, not just working Joes on assembly lines in Detroit. Thus devices like a ballistic computer, projected reticle display, digital compass, meteorological and incline and cant sensors traveled everywhere she did. She had ballistic software downloaded on her iPhone. It was all fed into her optics, which had cost twice as much as her gun.

As the old saying among long-range shooters went: Buy once, cry once.

Now covered with a ghillie suit the color of sand, she lay prone and went to work.

The key attribute for any sniper was patience. You worked in a bubble of focus, staying sharp and alert despite exhaustion. And you didn't move. She wore a diaper in case she had to pee.

She'd already zeroed her weapon at the range she would be shooting. Her computer had allowed her to laze her target, and a ballistic solution crosshair had been spit out.

When holding her weapon, Reel never *gripped* anything. She never performed any movement that required muscular exertion. Because muscular exertion caused the limbs to do something no sniper could tolerate: It caused the limbs to shake, however imperceptibly. It was called the "death grip" in sniping circles, because if you missed because you shook, that meant the other side got a chance to take you out. It was a chess match, only with killing rounds for game pieces.

Thus her left forearm ran straight and true along her weapon's stock. If you angled your arm right or left, you used muscle to hold the gun. But with vertical on vertical it meant gravity was doing the job for you. Her toes were pointed out, the sides of her feet flat to the sand, like she was performing some fancy yoga stretch. She could and had held such a position for hours, because no strength was required.

Her main sniper rifle was based on the tried-and-true Remington 700 platform with some customization. Her spare was a Barrett M82. For this tour of duty she had switched over her ammo from the legendary .338 Lapua Magnum rounds to the 6.5 Creedmore rounds. Her rifle barrel held a right-hand twist, which meant the bullet coming out of it would cheat a bit in that direction, a phenomenon known as spindrift, which she had accounted for. And she was shooting over such a long distance that the earth's rotation also came into play; it was known as the Coriolis effect. If you didn't compensate for it, the earth's constant movement would rotate your target right out of the kill zone. A millimeter error of calculation on this end would result in the shot being a foot off on the other end.

Ballistics confirmed, her spotter satisfied, all data dialed into her optics, she was ready to execute.

Her finger went to the trigger. She would pull with the soft part of the finger midway between the tip and the first joint. This was the area of the finger that moved the least sideways.

She slowly squeezed the trigger on the down breath right at the point where she no longer needed to exhale or to start inhaling again. This respiratory phase was the stillest your lungs would be without duress or discomfort, and that meant it was the most calmly immobile your body would be. When you inhaled, the muzzle dropped; when you exhaled, the muzzle rose. But the sweet spot was on the exhale breath, and in-between a heartbeat; that's what every good sniper strived for.

Reel kept a smooth, consistent trigger pull pressure all the way through the shot and then led the trigger back to its forward position.

The bullet blasted out of her barrel and was immediately subject to the rules of drag, and also of gravity, meaning it began to fall back to earth. The Creedmore round covered thirty percent of its max flight in a heartbeat. Two-thirds of the way to the target, drag was minimized and gravity became the biggest obstacle to a clean shot.

And that was why Reel had fired at a steep angle that would equate to the target being a giant in height. But by the time it got to the end of its flight path, the bullet would impact the target at a lowly fifty-four inches off the ground, meaning directly into the brain of the five-foot, ten-inch man seated at a rough wooden table on the other end.

Before the ISIL field commander who had caused her

side endless grief even fell dead, Reel's scope had come directly back to her such that after recoil she saw the same image through her optics. If this had been on the range for practice she would have received top marks.

Since it was combat for real, someone's life had just ended.

Her shot had covered nearly fifteen hundred meters, or a little under a mile. A superior distance, it still would not have put her in the top ten of longest kill shots. The current number ten on that list was a Marine sniper who had done the deed from over sixteen hundred meters. Number one on that list was a Brit who had killed two Taliban soldiers from nearly twenty-five hundred meters with a single bullet.

Now things got interesting.

There were few events that got the adrenaline going faster than knowing that a sniper was in town. Seconds after the dead man slumped forward on the tabletop, his comrades were running and ducking and throwing themselves behind whatever they could find that would stop their fate from being the same as that of their commander.

And with her spotter constantly feeding her data and Reel inputting that information into her optics, she kept firing.

Six trigger pulls later her Creedmore rounds had found five fleshy entry points. The only one that didn't impacted the rifle barrel of the target that he had moved to the front of his chest *after* Reel had already fired. The round glanced off the barrel and buried itself in the sand.

That was the major problem with sniping at this distance. The targets had to be stationary. If they moved after you fired, the round would miss, because it would take the bullet two or three seconds to get there. And Reel couldn't just keep shooting rapidly. She had to acquire targets and then fire at them without ever placing them in the crosshairs because of the bullet's drop factor. Shots aimed over five stories high were her bailiwick for the most part.

At a hundred yards away she could mow down the other side because she would have targets, running or stationary, in her sights, and at that distance external factors like gravity and drag, wind and humidity had minimal effect on the shot. The supersonic bullet merely powered through it all to arrive at the body in the crosshairs.

Yet being only a hundred yards away from an enemy carried another set of complications. Reel and her team would be subject to a variety of counterattacks and the threat of being physically overrun. Right now she had her spotter and four other soldiers with her. The target they were attacking held a hundred ISIL fighters and an assortment of hand-me-down armored vehicles in which they could counterattack.

Being nearly a mile away gave Reel and her team a lot more latitude. And time for "exfiltration," which was a fancy military term for getting the hell out of Dodge.

Her work finished for now, she filled out her DOPE log and put away her weapon. They drove back to their base, only to be told that they would be heading out that night to support a SEAL team attack on a compound where it was rumored the number two man in ISIL would be, along with three hostages, one of whom was a U.S. Marine captured two weeks prior.

Reel and her team attended the briefing, she grabbed some shuteye, and then they geared up and moved out.

Just another night in the neighborhood.

Only it wouldn't be like any other night for Jessica Reel, ever.

5

SEAL TEAMS DID everything in the fast lane.

The stealth chopper came low and fast over a rise in the sand, its engine and prop wash as quiet as the best and brightest of American engineering could make them.

Ten SEALs fast-roped down to the interior of the compound.

Moving as one unit they hit the sole entrance of the building and disappeared inside.

A football field in length away, Reel, her spotter, and other team members watched the proceedings closely.

Reel lay prone behind her sniper rifle. Her optics held on the interior of the courtyard, which could be seen through an opening that had once held a gate.

Four of the other team members had optics on the target zone. They were also commed together and following over their headsets what was happening inside the compound.

A minute later the all-clear was given. The mission was a bust. There was no one inside.

As quickly as they had come, the SEALs departed. The stealth chopper disappeared over a sandy ridge and was gone.

Reel and her team were packing their gear and about to board two Humvees when explosive rounds hit both vehicles. Second explosions came when the hardened fuel tanks punctured and the gas vapor inside combusted.

The twin explosions cremated the driver and the grunt riding next to him in one vehicle and the driver in the second Humvee. The concussive blast ripped limbs off another team member and he bled out seconds later.

Reel and her spotter rolled to the left and sighted their weapons in the direction from where the rounds had come.

Another explosive hit behind them, sending three more team members to the hereafter, in pieces.

"We're fucked," screamed the spotter as incoming fire poured in from *behind* them as well. "This was a setup!"

Reel already knew this. She spun her weapon around and crab-walked over so it was pointed to their rear flank.

That's when she saw what was coming.

Into her headset she said, "Get air support in here. Now!"

There were three lightly armored Toyota pickup trucks and maybe twenty-five fighters in total on them. Another dozen armed men were hustling behind the cover of the trucks. Mounted in the beds of the Toyotas were .50 cal machine guns.

Fifty calibers didn't wound when they hit you; they pretty much vaporized whatever they struck.

Reel looked behind her as another mortar round struck. Two more of her team were blown away, their helmets spinning through the air before coming to rest as a mangled composite a hundred feet away.

And one of them was their communications person.

Reel turned to her spotter. "Use your phone. Call in our coordinates. And we need some—"

The fifty cals opened up and the decibel-shattering barrage canceled out whatever else Reel was going to say.

Two rounds hit her spotter and Reel was instantly covered in blood, brains, and guts. The spotter's right arm flew through the sky in a long arc before plummeting back to the sand.

Now, with bare seconds having passed, there was just Reel and one other man left alive, a Brit named Hugh Barkley.

Reel waited until the .50s ceased firing to reload, and then she sighted through her optics.

Three quick trigger pulls and the ISIL member manning each machine gun toppled off the backs of the trucks.

Reel had bullets and she had enemies, and she set out to merge the two forevermore.

Three men tried to take the place of the machine gunners. And three men caught Creedmore rounds in their heads for the trouble.

Then the ISIL force wised up and the trucks went into evasive maneuvers, with the lead truck providing cover for the other two.

Reel grabbed her spotter's weapon, and without taking her eyes off the targets, her fingers snagged the ordnance she wanted to deploy next. She fed the rounds into the spare rifle, took aim, and fired.

The incendiary round found its mark and pierced the gas tank of the lead truck. The round ignited and so did the vapor in the tank.

The concussive force lifted the Toyota pickup straight off the ground, like a rocket taking off. Then gravity took over and the truck flipped and came to rest on top of the second truck, crushing it.

Reel sent another incendiary round into the second truck and then into the third. The gas vapor detonated and also caused the .50 cal ammo stacked on the truck beds to explode, turning the night sky as bright as day. Bodies and weapons and pieces of Toyotas hurtled across the sand, some landing as far as a half-mile away.

When the smoke cleared Reel could not see one living person in front of her. Just wreckage, flaming objects, and burned corpses.

She had not a second longer to dwell on this, because firing came from behind her and she saw Barkley strafing the ground in front of him with rounds from his MP5.

Reel sprinted that way, planted her weapon on the sand, slid into firing position, and sighted through her scope and fired. And kept firing.

But bullets were coming at them far faster. And then launched grenades landed and started exploding all around them.

Barkley moved to his left, which was a mistake. The heavy round sliced right through his body armor and blew out his back. He moaned once, gurgled twice, and fell facedown in the sand.

Now it was only Reel left.

She sighted through her scope, looking for targets, when it emerged out of the smoke and dust.

"Shit!"

It was an *American* M1117 armored personnel carrier. A bunch of APCs had been captured by ISIL from the Iraqi army. It weighed 30,000 pounds, and could cruise at 40 mph. It had a grenade launcher and a .50 cal machine gun in addition to a second machine gun, all mounted on the rotating turret. That's what had been firing at them. That's what had rained grenades on them, and a round from the .50 had just killed Barkley.

Reel grabbed the other rifle she always brought to battle, the Barrett M82. It was already chambered with the most powerful ordnance Reel had to combat the armored rhino coming for her. She would only use it if everything had gone to shit.

Now seemed the perfect time.

The round she was about to fire was technically known as the Raufoss Mk211, developed by a manufacturer in Scandinavia. It was often referred to in military circles as "multipurpose," or simply the "Raufoss round." It was so devastating that, under the Geneva Convention, it was not supposed to be used against humans.

And the "humans" she would be aiming at were encased in a metal monster. She didn't try to change locations. If she got up and ran, they would simply mow her down with the .50 cal like they had Barkley. She didn't move a muscle. They might assume she was already dead.

Reel aimed her weapon, centered her breathing, and her finger slipped to the trigger. The M1117 had good armor, but armor needed to be maintained. And she had spotted some missing plates on the front underbelly of the vehicle, probably from a previous run-in with an IED when the APC was still working for America.

Yet Reel didn't aim there. Her muzzle was pointed at the front window of the APC. The glass was bulletproof, but the Raufoss's tungsten core could punch a hole in eight inches of concrete at four hundred meters or an inch of steel at two thousand yards. Well, she was a hell of a lot closer than that. And glass, even bulletproof glass, was not steel or concrete.

"Do it, baby, do it," she murmured as she slowly pulled the trigger.

The round blew right through the glass, probably killing one of the crew on contact. And she followed that up with two more rounds where the missing armored plates had been.

Its ability to pierce armor was not the reason she'd selected the Raufoss. Like the rounds she'd used to take out the Toyotas, the Raufoss had an incendiary component. But the Raufoss also had a high-explosive charge built in. It could take out aircraft, choppers, and ships.

And, as it turned out, APCs.

The trio of explosives detonated and the ammo and the fuel in the APCs ignited a millisecond later.

Reel had to look away and bury herself in the sand to escape from being blinded by the flash. Debris, flaming objects, and body parts rained down all around.

She sprinted away and threw herself under one of the destroyed and still smoldering Humvees as large objects struck it and the ground all around.

After a minute things stopped falling and it grew quiet.

Another minute passed and Reel dragged herself out from under the Humvee.

She looked around at her destroyed team.

She looked at the body parts of her attackers.

She looked at all the burning vehicles.

She was still sitting there when a chopper flew over and swept a light over the area.

When the SEALs fast-roped down to her she didn't acknowledge them, though she did let them attach a harness to her. The winch was engaged and she was swept into the air and hauled aboard the chopper.

A minute later they were heading back to base, and to safety.

Jessica Reel didn't say a word all the way.

END GAME

Coming in November 2017
Preorder now!